DEATH SENDS A MESSAGE

A THEA KOZAK MYSTERY
BOOK 11

KATE FLORA

ePublishingWorks!
love what you read.

DEATH SENDS A MESSAGE

ALSO BY KATE FLORA

The Thea Kozak Mystery Series

Chosen for Death

Death in a Funhouse Mirror

Death at the Wheel

An Educated Death

Death in Paradise

Liberty or Death

Stalking Death

Death Warmed Over

Schooled in Death

Death Comes Knocking

Death Sends a Message

———

The Joe Burgess Mystery Series

Playing God

The Angel of Knowlton Park

Redemption

And Grant You Peace

Led Astray

A Child Shall Lead Them

A World of Deceit

Book and cover design by eBook Prep
www.ebookprep.com

October 2022
ISBN: 978-1-64457-202-3

ePublishing Works!
644 Shrewsbury Commons Ave
Ste 249
Shrewsbury PA 17361
United States of America

www.epublishingworks.com
Phone: 866-846-5123

ONE

It was a clear and sunny early September day, the kind that usually makes me feel good to be alive. MOC was tucked up in a baby wrap, small and warm against my chest, sound asleep. I'd been told that a baby who slept was a good baby, which MOC was, but just as the little creature had been in utero, MOC was nocturnal. Don't wake a sleeping baby might be good advice, but I longed to wake the child and remind him that it was daytime. There was a brand new world to be studied and discovered. Days were for being awake and nights for sleeping. But no. Mason Lemieux wanted to sleep and despite being only a bit over a week old, he was proving to be as willful as both his parents.

I was searching through a discombobulated bin of clearance baby things, trying to find a summer hat small enough to fit a tiny head. In all my hasty and interrupted prep for this kid's birth—bad guys with guns in my kitchen will do that—I'd forgotten to get one and I'd been scolded for my negligence by an elderly lady who thought I was committing child abuse. I hate shopping. Trying to find a summer hat at the end of the season was impossible. I kept striking out. This was my third store and my temper was as worn as the meager supply of summer goods I was perusing.

At last, almost at the bottom of the bin, I found it, a small yellow number embroidered with a tipsy-looking duck. The duck matched my mood perfectly. Sleep-deprived new mothers can feel tipsy without going near alcohol. No more Thea the Great and Terrible for me. I was now a Thea who had no idea what she was doing.

Hat purchased, I headed back out into the late summer sunshine.

On my way into the store, I'd passed another new mother—at least I assumed she was a new mother since the infant in her expensive carriage was tiny. So tiny it looked like a doll in the enormous carriage. She was sitting on a bench outside the shop eating an ice cream cone.

The sight had inspired me. I planned to stop at the ice cream stand before I got back in the car. Black raspberry with chocolate chunks. I could almost taste it. Almost feel the sticky warm-cold as it dripped toward the edge of my hand and I caught it with my tongue. Even in the midst of my anticipatory delight, I realized that my choice might be risky. I didn't yet know how MOC reacted to chocolate.

When I came out of the air-conditioned shop into the bright sun, the woman, well, a girl, really—she didn't look a day over eighteen—was standing beside the carriage, waving her arms, screaming like I have never heard anyone scream in the real world. Believe me, I've been in plenty of hairy situations where people screamed, and she was definitely the champ.

She was small and skinny, with pale arms and legs that had somehow missed the summer sun. No substance to her except what I took for nursing mother breasts and a tiny post-delivery belly, something I'd recently acquired myself. Her nearly waist-length hair was thick and blonde and wavy. Magazine cover hair. Model hair. Hair that required time and money to create such a carefree look. She wore a blue striped sundress that came no more than halfway down her thighs. Not quite long enough to cover some purple bruises on her legs. Her high, elaborately strappy sandals were in a matching blue. Her lips shone with gloss. She wore more eye makeup than I've worn in the last ten years. The noise she was making was so loud it blurred whatever she was screaming about.

For a moment, I thought it was theater. Some street thing staged to grab tourists' attention. With a short season to make a living, Maine businesses did a lot to attract customers. But her panicked expression said no.

I didn't want her screams to wake my sleeping baby. Jerked abruptly to wakefulness, Mason would add his own screams to the situation. Sleep with a newborn was a rare enough thing that I cherished these quiet moments when I could enjoy his small, soft body without also having to deal with misery and unhappiness. Without pacing the floor in a darkened room. Still, I was concerned. She was a new mother like me and something had set her off. I waited for someone to stop, to approach her and ask her what was wrong. There were plenty of people about who could have helped her besides me. People not encumbered with a newborn of their own.

Plenty of people around who evidently didn't give a damn. They flowed around the screaming girl and her huge baby carriage like she was a rock in a stream. Averting their eyes or pumping up conversation, as though volume proved its importance and excused a failure to offer help to someone in trouble. I wanted to go home, hand Master Mason Lemeiux off to his doting father, and put my feet up. But no one was helping when obviously someone needed to help.

I just didn't want that helper to be me. I have done my share. More than my share. As Thea the Human Tow Truck, I have stopped too many times to help, and far too often it has embroiled me in situations I would have preferred to avoid. Whatever was up with this girl, I didn't want it to become my problem.

Help her, dammit! I thought as I stood and watched the scene like it was something in a movie. The beautiful damsel in distress. The expensive carriage that was empty. The drama. The fear she was projecting. The absolutely hateful, shameful way people were ignoring her.

Damn them all! How could they not help?

If anyone had been with me, anyone who knows me, they would

have said "Thea, don't!" and dragged me away. But except for MOC, I was alone and while my kid might be good at using noise to manipulate me, he hadn't learned to say "don't" yet. Or to hear it, as his nocturnal wailings proved.

I should explain MOC. Andre and I were the atypical couple who didn't want to know our baby's sex. We had three possible names—Mason, Oliver, or Claudine—so before our baby was born, we called it MOC. I was still getting used to saying Mason.

Folding a protective arm around Mason, I took a step closer. Near enough to see into that elaborate carriage. Near enough to see something that would make any mother scream. The carriage that had held a small, sleeping infant when I went into the store—a boy, if all that blue was a true indicator—was empty and the screaming girl wasn't holding a baby.

All she was holding was a forgotten ice cream cone. A melting cone that was dripping chocolate over her hand and up her arm. Staining her pretty blue and white frock with chocolate.

I grabbed a breath, gave the rest of the world another minute to find its compassion, and when no one stepped up, I walked over to the girl.

"Tell me what's happened," I said. "And let's get you some help."

TWO

S he turned on me, eyes wide with fear. "He's going to kill me. I've gone and lost his precious baby and when he finds out, he's going to kill me."

"Try to calm down," I said, "and tell me what's going on. Do you think your baby has been taken? Do you want me to call the police?"

She'd stopped screaming, at least. Now she looked at me with blue eyes the color of the sky above us and said, "Obviously my baby has been taken. Do you see him anywhere?"

What a contrast between her looks and her speech. She looked like a hapless, helpless beauty whose child was missing. Her screams suggested terror and trauma, yet her reaction to my question sounded like a cynical townie. Still, however coarse and cynical her response, she had said that someone, some "he" to whom the baby evidently belonged, was going to kill her. Even if I wanted to walk away, and I sure did, I couldn't ignore that. I am, by nature and profession, a fixer.

"The missing baby," I said, trying not to get annoyed with her too quickly, "is he yours?"

She swung her beautiful hair and said, in a tone that said "Duh?" even if she didn't, "Of course he's my baby."

"Then you need the police."

She didn't respond.

I tried to prompt her. "Do you have any idea who might have taken him?"

Again, I got no reply. She just stood there staring into the empty carriage like she was paralyzed.

Beyond her, I saw a police car crawling slowly down the street, eyeing the summer crowds.

"I'm getting you some help." I moved toward the street, waving my arms to flag it down. The girl needed help. That was what cops were there for. And I needed to get Mason home. He needed to be fed and changed and I needed to sit down. Or lie down. If we were here much longer, I'd need to be changed as well. Nursing was a lot more complicated and messy than anyone had ever suggested. As a strong and fit woman in my mid-thirties, I was astonished by how much childbirth had taken out of me.

The car stopped and a cop got out, strolling over to us as though this wasn't a serious situation. As though he had all the time in the world. I suppressed the word "Jerk" that leapt to my lips and reminded myself that my only job here was to hand the frantic girl off to him and get myself gone.

When he was close enough, I pointed to the girl and said, "She says that someone has stolen her baby."

That galvanized him. He motioned for his partner in the car to park and join him, and strode toward the girl.

My cue to exit, stage right. Except that as he began to speak to the girl, she looked over at me, pure panic on her face, and motioned for me to join them. People in distress are my weakness. I knew I had to reform if I was going to be a good mother to Mason. At this point, he was a tiny, helpless person who didn't need his mother larking off to help others.

I shook my head and started walking away. I got about ten feet before the other cop stopped me. "Not so fast, Ma'am," he said.

"Yes, so fast," I said. I shifted MOC, uh, Mason, who was beginning to fuss, to my shoulder and patted his warm little back. "Got to get this little guy home and feed him. Babies do not have patience."

He stayed blocking my path, perhaps not aware that brand new mothers did not have much patience either.

I lowered the baby to the crook of my arm so I could use my other hand to fish in my purse. Got out my card and handed it to him. "If you need me for anything, here's my contact information. But right now, I am taking my newborn home where he belongs. Go and help that poor girl. She's the one with the crisis."

Not waiting for his permission—I've had enough experience with cops, both good and bad to know that hesitation was a mistake—I stepped around him and walked to my car, where I stowed Mason in his approved car seat, fastened the zillion approved straps, and shut the door. The cop lingered there on the sidewalk, staring at me like he still might stop me from leaving. I didn't wait for him to make up his mind. Instead, I got in, fired up the Jeep, and drove away.

True, I felt like a bit of a rat, leaving that poor girl by herself to deal with her awful situation. Hopefully, the tough girl I'd had a glimpse of could handle it. The thing was that Andre and I had both vowed to reform our workaholic ways in the interest of our newly expanded family. This was my first test, and I didn't want to fail it. In the rearview mirror, I could only see the dark fuzz on the top of Mason's head. I knew having babies ride backward was safer, as was the use of these complicated car seats, but I wished I could look back and see his beautiful dark eyes. Andre's eyes. Especially right now, when someone else's baby was missing.

Mason was a lucky little guy. Andre had wonderful eyes, a rich, warm brown. His son would carry that forward and in fifteen years or so, teenage girls would be swooning at his feet. Okay. Now that was not a very feminist thought. I could hope that Andre and I would set good examples and our son would kindly set those swooning girls back on their feet and become their friend.

The drive home was about twenty minutes. Well, twenty minutes when the old Thea was driving. Maybe it would pass but for now, I drove like an old lady. Or someone who had six cartons of eggs balanced on the back seat. Luckily, my way wasn't impeded by a hay wagon or an ancient driver who braked for every hill and curve, or someone on their cell phone whose speed slowed and lurched along with their conversation. In thirty minutes, by which time Mason was letting his displeasure be known in no uncertain terms, I was home.

Andre must have been watching at the window, because he had the door open and was releasing the little captive from his seat before I'd shut off the engine.

"What took you so long?" he asked.

Though I resented his implication that I'd dawdled, I knew he was just as anxious and new at this as I was, and gave him a pass.

"Had to go to three stores before I could find a hat," I said. "And then there was a screaming girl whose baby had been kidnapped."

"And you stopped to help?"

"And I paused to ascertain what the problem was, then flagged down a passing policeman and left him to handle it."

I watched his face and knew he was thinking about what a struggle it must have been for me to walk away, just as it would have been for him. You can't be a Maine state police detective and walk away from a distressed mother and a potential kidnapping easily.

"Second cop tried to stop me from leaving, so I gave him my card and left before he could stop me."

"Good for you," Andre said, and then we both had a moment when we looked at our brown-eyed son, so tiny in his father's big arms, and thought about how challenging it was going to be to walk away from other people's problems. And how important it was to do just that.

"Good for you," he repeated. "Let's get this little guy inside. He's wet and hungry and doesn't look happy with either of us."

"I expect that will be a continuing problem," I said, following them inside.

"You sit," Andre said. "I'll change him and then you can feed him."

I sat, very grateful to be off my feet. I could have closed my eyes and gone to sleep, but first Mason needed to eat. Still, I was slipping off to dreamland when my husband returned, handed me the baby, and said, "We've got company coming tomorrow."

I closed my eyes as the baby latched on and asked the all-important question. "Friend or foe?"

"Friend."

That meant not my mother and not my brother or his awful wife. A week after her second grandchild was born, my mother still hadn't appeared and I was torn. My relationship with my mother is fraught at the best of times, so avoiding her company is good for my blood pressure. But it meant my dad also hadn't been to see the baby, and that bothered me. I've spent—or wasted—way too much time trying to please my impossible mother and to get my father to admit that sometimes she is extremely unfair. Tried and failed. But I was always close to my father and I was sorry he wouldn't make the effort to meet Mason even if my mother would not.

So my parents weren't coming and neither was my brother. I considered other possibilities. Andre's family had already trooped through, inspected the baby, and the baby's room, and me, and seemed to think that I wasn't going to be terribly bad at mothering. They'd even brought useful presents and shared some helpful advice. My business partner, Suzanne, and office mates had indicated a desire to meet Mason, but said that they'd wait for an invitation. Suzanne, who had two little ones, remembered what those early postpartum days were like, and the others would take their cues from her.

I smiled at my husband. I thought I knew who was coming. My analysis of potential visitors led me to conclude that we would be seeing Mason's godparents, Dominic and Rosie Florio, who had shown up a month earlier, bringing enough food to feed an army. They had come to insist on their right to be MOC's godparents when he was born. They were going to be perfect godparents.

"Oh good." Still smiling, I gave myself up to feeding my son.

Our perfect family moment probably lasted no more than twenty minutes before there was a knock at the door, and Andre admitted a police officer.

"Thea Kozak?" the man asked.

I nodded.

"We need to talk to you about a kidnapped baby."

"Hold on," Andre said, stepping between the eager officer and me. Andre is about six-one, broad and strong. Only a fool messes with that.

My hero, I thought. Too bad Andre couldn't pitch a fellow public safety officer out on his ear.

THREE

The officer was tall and gangly, with an unfortunate buzz cut
that made him look like he'd been scalped and made his ears
look oversized and vulnerable. He was pressed and shined and obviously took himself and the job very seriously. He also appeared to
have no idea whom he was visiting, as he tried to step around Andre
with a brusque, "Excuse me, Sir. I need to..."

Andre gave him one of those cold cop looks. "As you can see,
my wife is feeding the baby right now," he said. "Let's give her a few
minutes and then I'm sure she'll be happy to answer whatever questions you've got."

"It's important," the foolish fellow said.

"So is feeding a hungry newborn," Andre said.

The guy tried to step around Andre again, which would have
made me question his judgment if it wasn't already in question.

I tried to stay calm. Control my breathing. Mason might only
have been a little more than a week in the world, but he and I had
lived together for nine months before that, and I knew him. He was
very sensitive to my moods and if he thought I was anxious, he'd get
anxious. I'd already put the little fellow through a lot even before he
was born and it had taught me that Mason did not like conflict.

Before birth, he'd been an acrobat. Now that he was here, he was using those muscles to flail his tiny limbs and scream. Neither Andre nor I needed that right now. We had enough adjustments to make.

"I'm going to take him upstairs and see if he'll nap," I said, getting up.

"Ma'am, please don't go anywhere," the officer said.

Like what? I was a suspect? A person of interest? Like he thought I'd somehow been involved in what had happened to that poor girl's baby? Maybe he thought I'd stolen the baby and was now nursing it in my kitchen? How did he suppose I would have pulled that off? Well, never mind. In the past, I've been pretty clear about taking care of myself and not being "the little woman" who needed to be rescued by the big, strong guy, but right now, I was happy to let Andre handle the constabulary while I tended to our child.

"You want to talk to me undisturbed, you'll let me settle the baby," I said, as I stood and walked out of the room. Maybe I growled it. Protective maternal instincts are pretty hard-wired. I also growled at anyone who followed too close to my car, and a man who'd leaned in to admire Mason in his stroller had jumped ten feet when I snapped at him to back off. This was a new side of me that I was discovering and it was a trip and a surprise.

"Ma'am. Wait. Don't leave. I need to ask you some questions."

Andre, still being surprisingly mild-mannered for him, said, "Relax. She'll be back as soon as she settles the baby."

"Sir, I need..."

"You got kids?" Andre asked.

"No, sir."

"Well, you'll learn. You don't mess with a new mother. It's like getting between a lioness and her cubs."

"Sir," the guy protested. "This is an urgent police matter. I need to warn—"

"What's your name, son?" Andre asked, cutting him off. There probably wasn't much more than a decade between them, but Andre was tough and seasoned and wore command presence like he'd been born with it. He used the word "son" deliberately.

The guy gave up a name. Jeremy Bartlett. And his department.

Freeport. Which gave Andre the opening to say, "Detective Sergeant Andre Lemieux. Maine State Police."

After which there was silence and I gave up listening from the stairs, carried a squirmy, fussy Mason into his room, and closed the door. "We are going to finish lunch and then you are going to take a nice nap," I told him.

We settled into the wonderful grayish green upholstered rocking chair I'd found, and my little son slurped and gurgled his way through the rest of lunch, then settled on my shoulder making sweet baby noises. Babies, I was learning, are not quiet. At last, as we rocked and I rubbed his little back, he stilled and I carefully put him in his crib.

I turned on the baby monitor and headed downstairs.

Andre and Jeremy Bartlett were at the table having coffee. Iced coffee, given that it was early September and still summer, and Andre had put out a plate of cookies.

I poured myself a glass of iced tea, sat down, and snagged a cookie. "So what's up?" I asked Bartlett. "What did you want to ask me?"

"For starters," he said, "can you walk me through what you witnessed this morning with respect to Addison Faraday and her child?"

So her name was Addison Faraday? Addison was a good name for her. Modern. Not very girly. Though she was very girly. I reminded myself that you can't know much about your child's path when they're born.

"I went to Freeport to buy Mason a hat."

He looked puzzled, so I added, "Mason is our baby. I was heading into my third store when I saw a young woman, small, with long blonde hair, standing next to a baby carriage. She was wearing a short blue striped dress and strappy wedge sandals. A lot of makeup. Her legs were bruised. As I passed, I glanced into the carriage and saw a very small baby wrapped in a blue blanket. The girl was sitting down on a bench beside the carriage and was eating an ice cream cone. She appeared to be alone. I remember thinking that maybe when I was done in the store, if I found what I was looking for, I might get a cone, too. I went into the store and was in there for maybe ten or twelve minutes. When I came out, she was screaming."

I paused, running through my memories to see if there was anything else to tell him. "She was clearly in distress, although it was hard to tell what she was upset about. I waited for someone to step up and help her. There were plenty of people around. But no one did, so I went to her and looked into the carriage. It was empty. I asked if I could help her, and she said something like 'he's going to kill me. I've lost his precious baby.' I asked her some more questions but she wasn't responsive. She seemed almost hostile, especially when I suggested she needed to get the police involved. But it seemed to me that she needed some official help if her baby had indeed been kidnapped, so I flagged down a police car, gave the officers my card in case there was a way I could be helpful, and left them to deal with the situation."

His expression said he was just beginning and would have a lot of questions, so I quickly added, "That's all I can tell you. It all happened in a couple minutes. The girl and I didn't talk much."

"Walk me through it again," he said.

I was getting as fussy as my baby. The advice for new mothers is when baby naps, mommy naps, and this fellow was interfering with my nap.

"If you have questions, ask them," I said.

"Walk—" he began.

"Do you have questions?" Andre asked. He growled, too. We were sleep deprived and still dazed from the new adventure we were embarking on.

Young Jeremy Bartlett held his ground. "I'd like her to go through it again."

I sighed. I was losing patience with the fellow, and what was worse, being in throes of hormones, I was afraid I was going to burst into tears. "I've told you everything I know. If you can think of something that might help, the best way to get at it is with a question."

I was getting the impression he didn't like me very much, which was fine, since I didn't like him either. I try, whenever possible, to cooperate with the police. My husband is a police officer and I know how hard their job is. But when they get pushy or when they try to bully me, my desire to cooperate dissipates like morning mist. Mine was almost entirely dissipated. I gave Andre a "do something" look and he nodded.

"Officer Bartlett," he said. "We very much value cooperating with the police, as you can imagine. Right now, my wife has just given birth and she's exhausted. If you have questions, she'll try to answer them, if there's anything she can add. Otherwise, you should pursue your investigation in other venues. You've learned everything there is to learn here."

Bartlett imitated my sigh.

I didn't know whether he'd come here thinking I'd snatched the baby, or whether he thought I was a friend of the girl's and could offer some insight into her situation. Neither was true. I waited to see what he would do next.

"How well do you know Addison Faraday?" he asked.

Had he not listened to a word I said? Nothing pushes my buttons like someone to whom I've given a thorough explanation who refuses to listen and starts asking inane questions. As a busy professional, I've learned to value my time. As a new mom, I was doing the same. Still, cooperation might get him out of here sooner, so I said, "I don't know anyone named Addison Faraday. If that's the name of the girl I described, the one I tried to help by summoning the police, it's news to me."

"What about her significant other, James Milton Faraday?"

Significant other? Was that the current term? I thought it was partner. Either way, all I could say was, "Never heard of him."

"You and Ms. Faraday didn't meet in a birthing class?"

Had she told them that, I wondered? And if so, why? Why pretend we had a relationship? I shook my head. "No. We didn't."

"She says that you did."

My patience was like a kite string running rapidly through my fingers. "I'm not responsible for what people say about me, Officer. I have no idea why she'd tell you something like that. I can assure you, however, that we did not meet prior to this morning, and I wouldn't even consider that those events constituted a meeting. I tried to help a young girl in distress. That is all. Obviously, it was a big mistake."

I was thinking that as a society, we get incensed when bystanders don't help someone in trouble. I was getting a lesson here in why they didn't.

He looked like he didn't believe me, so I added, "If you need corroboration, I'm sure the hospital can provide you with a list of the women who *were* in my birthing class."

But now Andre's curiosity was piqued. He said, "What else did Addison Faraday tell you, with respect to my wife?"

Bartlett looked uncomfortable as he shifted from one foot to the other. One thing to bully the poor woman, quite another to find himself questioned by a state police detective sergeant.

"She... she said that she and your wife were friends who'd met in their birthing class and they had agreed to meet this morning to show off their babies. That they both got ice cream and while they were talking, someone snatched her baby. She said she was worried that somehow your wife was in on the kidnapping since the meeting had been her idea, and—"

"My God!" I interrupted. "That's a pretty detailed story for someone to spin who's supposedly hysterical about the disappearance of her child. And she spun it fast, too, since you got here only about forty minutes after I got home." Admittedly I had driven slowly. But not so slowly there had been much time for her to spin her tale.

Andre was shaking his head. "Quite the little liar, isn't she? We don't know anyone named Faraday, not Addison and not her husband, boyfriend, or significant other. There was no one by that name in the birthing class. My wife made no plans to meet anyone today. She only went out to do a quick errand to find a hat for the baby. She was there because she bought a hat. The rest of the story is bullshit."

He gave it a beat, then said, "You can check if you want, but Thea and I are done. No more questions and no more of the BS story the woman who called herself Addison Faraday spun. Did you check that her name really was Addison Faraday?"

We both waited for Bartlett's answer, which was only a shake of his head. "That's what I was told. I mean, I was there. I heard her story, but I didn't check her ID. I assume the first officers on the scene did."

Andre and I exchanged looks. Bartlett wasn't looking at a long and successful career if he went around assuming essential facts instead of checking them. Trust, then verify was the name of the game, as good cops always want more than one source of information. Good cops and Thea Kozak, who is sometimes mistaken for a cop herself. For all Bartlett knew, the woman, or girl, who called herself Addison Faraday might have been a kidnapper herself. Stole a baby and then the real mother stole it back.

Except I'd seen the signs of someone who'd recently given birth, but maybe something had happened to her baby and she'd helped herself to someone else's. Women did that. But Bartlett didn't seem to know much about childbirth or childbearing. He wouldn't necessarily have noticed her body. Uh. Well, he was a guy, and she was pretty and blonde, with amazing, tossable hair, so he'd probably noticed that. But he might have missed the little pot belly. He'd probably noticed the breasts, but not how out of proportion they were to the rest of her, nor how they didn't fit into her dress.

I reminded myself that implants could produce that effect as well. By then, I was tired of imagining possible scenarios. Honestly, I didn't care. I just wanted Bartlett gone. I was sick of this. Tired of playing the new mother card, which didn't seem to register with Bartlett anyway, and very tired of people who lied, especially at my expense. It shouldn't be wrong to offer to help someone in distress, but maybe those other people, the ones who'd just walked on and ignored her, were right. Maybe they'd just turned cynical earlier. I was ready to embrace cynicism, though. I've given enough help to people, the honest and the liars, over the years, and paid a high price for doing so.

I was about to toss the annoying fellow out when Andre, who is a very good reader of people, did it for me.

"Sorry we couldn't be more help," he said, using his body to herd the officer toward the door. "I'll be interested to hear what you learn about this young woman. What her situation is. Appreciate it if you'd give us an update when you can."

He produced a card from his wallet and handed it to Bartlett, then walked him to the door. Bartlett's weedy height didn't stand up to Andre's scarily fit body. Right now Andre was wearing a "don't mess with me, son," face. To his credit, Bartlett finally read the room and let himself be ushered out.

When the door closed behind him, Andre said, "Mommy naps when baby naps. I'm going to see what I can find out about Addison or James Milton Faraday."

Through my yawn, I said, "And you'll fill me in?"

"And I'll fill you in, but we are not getting involved in this, okay?"

Normally, I resent people who tell me what to do. Not today. As had been the case when Bartlett came through the door, I was thrilled to let Andre take charge.

I went into our lovely living room and lay down on the sofa, pulling a soft blanket over myself. In about four seconds, I was asleep.

FOUR

W e were having dinner—leftover grilled chicken and veggies
from our garden—when Andre's phone rang. He checked
the number and looked at me. "Looks like it's Bartlett."

We were trying to keep people—and work—out of our little
bubble. Andre was on paternity leave, but if taking this call could
clear things up and ensure no further visits from the police, that
would be good. "Take it, then. Maybe we'll learn what this crazy
business is about."

He answered with his usual brusque, "Lemieux," and waited.

I watched his face while he listened but there was nothing to see.
When he wants, he has a perfectly impassive cop's face. Not the face
I'd seen in the delivery room when the nurse plopped our baby into
his arms and he'd positively glowed as he looked down at the swaddled mite and said, "Hello, Mason." Until that moment, we'd call
the little creature MOC. Now our challenge was to remember to
call our son Mason instead, disproving all the people who'd told us
we'd be calling our baby MOC forever. Anyway, that wasn't the look
my husband was wearing right now, so I'd have to wait.

He said, "Thanks for the update," and put the phone down.

"The plot thickens," he said, with a grin acknowledging he

never talked like that. I figured he was quoting Bartlett—the cop, not the collection of familiar quotations. In Andre's world, unraveling the plot was the name of the game. If anything, it was thinning, not thickening.

"Seems they got in touch with James Milton Faraday," he said, "whom I gather is kind of a five-hundred-pound canary in Freeport. Lotta money, likes to throw his weight around. And guess what?"

"He doesn't have a wife or girlfriend named Addison or a newborn baby?"

"He has an ex-girlfriend named Addison Shirley. Local girl. Pretty. Has a reputation as a gold digger."

He paused. "I didn't know they still used that term. Seems kind of outdated to me. Anyway, according to Bartlett, Faraday told him they've been broken up for at least eight months. That she moved on to another guy. He said he knows nothing about a baby."

I nodded, feeling very sorry for a baby that seemed to be a pawn in some kind of game his mother was playing. But if—I was letting my speculation run rampant here—she was playing some kind of game, who had taken the baby? If she was a gold digger—might we say, opportunist?—could it be that this other man in the picture, the one she left Faraday for, thought the baby was his? Perhaps she'd deliberately let him think the baby was his? Was Faraday even telling the truth about the timing or their relationship or his ignorance about the baby?

Obviously, I've spent too much time around cops. I was cautious and skeptical and like them, wanted to know more before I was satisfied. Except right now, I didn't want to know more. I wanted to wind back the clock and erase that screaming girl and her tiny baby from my mind. I had enough going on in my own life. Plus I'd made a vow to myself and Andre that if somebody in trouble needed my help, they'd have to find a new rescuer. I kept telling myself I was done being the human tow truck.

So far, I wasn't doing very well.

Still, I asked, "What about that stuff she said, about how now that she'd lost his child, he was going to kill her. The "he" was never named. Do you think she's playing two guys off against each other, making each of them think he's the father? And did someone really take the baby or was that just part of some game she was playing. Maybe she had an accomplice who took the baby so she could make her big scene?"

Andre shrugged. "I have no idea, and it sounds like Bartlett and his department don't either. Did she seem genuinely upset or like she was faking it?"

"I really couldn't tell. It happened so fast. But other people ignored her while I stopped to help. Were they seeing something I wasn't? Was I drawn in because of Mason?"

He shrugged again. "I trust your judgment, Thea." He looked down at his plate, surprised to find it was empty. "Here's the twist: the girl has disappeared."

"Disappeared? As in what? She gave them an address and she's not there?"

"Bartlett says she told them she was staying at a local B&B. When they went to talk with her further, after they'd spoken with Faraday and gotten his denials, the owner of the place said she wasn't staying there and they'd never heard of her."

We *were* letting ourselves get drawn in. "We said we weren't going to do this," I reminded him.

He nodded. Shrugged. "Guess we'll have to try harder." He smiled. "Habits are hard to break."

I looked at my empty plate, like him, disappointed that there wasn't more dinner. I've never had one of those ladylike, Scarlett O'Hara appetites. Like my husband, I'm not a small person. Andre and I both like to eat. It's true that I often get wrapped up in my work and forget to eat, but right now, I didn't have any work, and I was definitely eating for two. Tiny as he was, Mason was a greedy little pig.

Andre didn't miss my look. He's a detective, after all, and a very good one. He smiled. "Good news. Your friend from the library dropped off a blueberry pie," he said.

There are so many reasons I love my husband. This was definitely one of them.

"I would love some blueberry pie. I would love a great big piece of pie with vanilla ice cream."

"Coming right up." He paused. "Sure you don't want chocolate ice cream?"

I shook my head. I do prefer chocolate ice cream on blueberry pie but I didn't yet know how Mason felt about chocolate. Or about so many things. I was taking it slowly.

"You know," I said, as he got up to fix us each a big slice of pie, "she must be staying somewhere local, unless she drives some honking big SUV, because she had one of those baby carriages I think of as belonging to British royalty and coming with a starched and uniformed nanny. It's not the kind of thing you pop out of your trunk and unfold. You practically need a butler just to get it set up and it doesn't exactly lend itself to a hotel room or a B&B. At least, it's something that would be noticed if she went out strolling with it. And she'd have to be close to where I saw her. No one walks for miles with a behemoth like that on Maine's crowded summer sidewalks. Especially not in the shoes she was wearing."

I thought about it more, and said, "In retrospect, it felt staged. At least she wanted to be seen. And with that equipage, she could hardly be missed." I tried to imagine her pushing that perambulator through the crowded Freeport streets. It didn't make much sense to me.

We would never want a carriage like that. We had a jogging stroller, a hand-me-down from my partner Suzanne's husband Paul. It folded up neatly and compactly, but neither of us was ready to take it for a test run. Not with the remnants of Maine summer traffic still clogging up the roads. It's way too easy for some lookie-loo to be admiring a farmer's twelve-foot sunflowers or those giant hay bales that look like a field full of marshmallows and run down a poor pedestrian. For now, Mason's outings would be only in safe places and strapped tightly to my body or Andre's. I wasn't even comfortable having him in the car. If looks could kill, many of the other drivers who'd been around me today would be dead.

What is it about safe following distances, something we learned about in driver's ed, that people can't remember? Andre and I had often joked about mounting a harpoon on my Jeep that could be launched at miscreants. I was ready to give it serious consideration.

Thinking back to my brief encounter with the girl now identified as Addison Shirley, I wondered how she could be so immersed in an ice cream cone she didn't notice someone abducting her baby. Exhaustion? which I could relate to. Or the warmth of the summer sun? Was I sure there had been a baby and not just a bundle of blue blankets? No. I was observant. Trained by an experienced detective. I had seen a baby in that carriage. I was too attuned to babies right now to have imagined it or gotten it wrong. How could she not have been vigilant about her baby?

Speaking of imagining, whatever visions I'd had of finishing dinner undisturbed were just my imagination. I'd only taken my first bite of pie when Mason woke up. The baby monitor on the table spat out a few little warm-up cries and then our son began to sing. One thing was certain—we didn't have to worry about the kid's lungs. When Mason Lemieux wanted attention, he was not shy about demanding it.

"I'll get him," Andre said. "You eat your pie."

He left eagerly, practically racing up the stairs. He had wanted this baby as much, or more, than I, and couldn't get enough of the little guy. He was very willing to get up in the night and change a diaper before bringing the baby to me. It was wonderful, and sadly, it wouldn't last. Not because his interest would flag. The Maine Department of Public Safety would soon be needing his services again, and our blissful little domestic trio would be no more. Crime doesn't stop because the investigator wants to be on paternity leave. Andre had insisted, but cop world is a macho world, and letting a homicide investigation languish because a daddy wanted to bond with his baby was not in the cards.

"Enjoy it while you can," Suzanne had said, and she was right. We might be in marriages of equals with demanding professional careers, but until the world found a way to let fathers nurse their babies, more of the infant care would continue to fall to mothers.

Okay. Truth? I was just as besotted as Andre. From the moment in the hospital when they'd handed me the tiny bundle that was Mason and I'd looked down into his wise brown eyes, I'd been his.

As I ate my pie, my mind drifted back to Addison Faraday, uh, Shirley, or whatever the girl was really named. I was angry with this girl I'd only briefly met because now she was occupying real estate in my mind that I didn't want her to have. This time was too precious. Soon enough, I'd have to find a nanny and get back to work myself. It was the beginning of the school year at private schools, and our business was all about private school issues. EDGE Consulting, the firm Suzanne and I ran, did everything from writing emergency campus response plans and school honor codes to helping schools attract their desired applicant pool.

In the week since Mason's debut, I'd already fielded at least a dozen calls. It's a sad fact of life that work doesn't go away just because a business partner gives birth. Our staff would do their best, but I was the troubleshooter. I was Jane Wayne, the woman in the white hat called in when there was a campus crisis. Sooner or later—and sooner was a better bet—I'd be called in on something that would require my actual presence.

I ate the last delicious bite—pie must be healthy with all that fruit, right?—and sighed. I'd found Suzanne's wonderful, competent nanny while working at a client school. Maybe life would deliver another one as good to my doorstep, but I doubted it. Just not yet, please, if the universe *was* sending one. Mason and I were still busy bonding and nothing was supposed to interrupt that.

Given the way my life has gone so far, it wouldn't be far-fetched to imagine Addison Shirley turning up on my doorstep and asking for help, even though I hadn't given her my name or my card. I had only said my name was Thea and asked if I could help. I'd just given my card to the cops so that I could escape. But what if they'd gotten careless? What if they'd shared my information with her? Maybe because they believed we had some connection? I could imagine Bartlett or another careless cop asking how she knew Thea Kozak, if she and Thea Kozak were friends, if Thea Kozak was somehow involved in her baby's disappearance? Yeah. That could have happened.

I looked across the room at the kitchen door. We'd gotten into the country custom of leaving it unlocked. Now I wondered: should I lock it or was I just being a nervous new mom?

Why not? We'd had more than our share of unwanted company, and this was a worse time than ever to be disturbed or invaded. Plus if Addison Faraday, or Shirley, was as unbalanced as my observation and our meager facts suggested, she might assume my momentary offer of help was open-ended and show up. I didn't want her in my house—unbalanced people bring such bad vibes—and it was such a country thing to have unlocked doors and for people to just walk in.

Not long ago, a pregnant woman had appeared on my doorstep and dragged Andre and me into a world of trouble. Helping her had been scary and dangerous. Going forward, hard as it was not to help, that incident had sworn me off getting involved in other people's troubles except where they arose through my work. Over the years, there had been plenty of that. Besides, right now even that wasn't supposed to happen. I wasn't working. I was on maternity leave. I'd taken on extra loads when Suzanne was on both her maternity leaves. I expected the same.

I looked around my lovely kitchen, one of the few rooms that were finished when we bought the house. The tall cupboards. Blue countertops. The small pile of colorful produce on the counter—cucumbers, tomatoes, fresh onions, eggplant, and summer squash—waiting to be eaten. It was so peaceful and domestic. I wanted to keep it that way. I crossed the room and locked the door, then went into the living room and I settled in my favorite chair. A big, soft blue wing chair that was perfect for nursing. I closed my eyes and listened to Andre, upstairs, talking to Mason while he did diaper duty. Sleep had almost claimed me when he appeared beside my chair and handed me the baby. All swaddled like that, Mason looked like a tiny brown-eyed bundle.

"Little beast is very hungry," Andre said.

"Takes after his dad."

"And his mom. You need anything?"

"Nope. Perfectly content. I've had pie."

He took a seat across the room while I fumbled my blouse aside and Mason latched on. He started sucking like there was no tomor-row, and Andre made a curious humming sound while he watched. Among the baby gifts I'd been showered with was something called a nursing cover. It might be useful going forward but I certainly didn't need it in the privacy of my own home.

"This is amazing," he said.

Which it was.

I put Mason on my shoulder and patted his warm little back. "I'm worried," I said.

Andre leaned forward, suddenly alert. He can go from relaxed to alert faster than anyone I know. It's part of the job. Cop world can be a dangerous place. "About Mason?"

"No. No, he's fine. About that girl. Woman. Whatever. About this not being over, despite what we told Bartlett about my only contact being that brief stop to offer help. I'm worried that when they questioned her, they told her my name. You know, as in using it and then asking if she knew me. Especially after the lies she's told. It's probably just new mother paranoia, but I'm worried that she'll show up here."

I took a breath and tried to calm down. Reminding myself again that an anxious mother is not good for nursing babies. I was normally tough as nails, but I'd never been responsible for a small, helpless life before. "I locked the door."

"Your office is easy to find," he said, trying to reassure me. "This place? Not so much. We haven't been here long enough to be in a lot of databases." He smiled. "And if she does find us? I'm here, and she won't get past me."

The image made me smile. Andre is tall with rock-hard abs and serious shoulders. Handsome in a fierce way. He has an intimidating cop's stare and short dark hair and absolutely looks like someone you wouldn't want to mess with. Addison Shirley was a tiny wisp of a girl who barely topped five feet.

"That is comforting."

"I'll make some calls," he said. "See if there's more to be learned about the girl. And about Faraday." He tilted his head thoughtfully. "And about the other guy she was seeing. If there is such a guy. If, as you say, she's kind of a knockout, she won't have gone unobserved. And if Faraday has a reputation, we should be able to learn what that is pretty easily. Beyond five-hundred-pound canary, I mean."

Andre got up. "I'll do that now," he said, then left the room.

I was still unsettled and didn't like him gone.

I looked down at Mason, so small and helpless. In the space of a week, I'd gone from Thea the Great and Terrible, the tough gal, the fixer, the one people turned to when there was trouble, to a woman who didn't like her husband out of her sight. How quickly life changed. Taking care of Mason would never go away, I knew, but I hoped this helplessness would eventually fade, and like with the flu, I'd recover soon.

Mason nursed. I tried to relax. In the other room, I could hear Andre on the phone. Outside, a perfect September day was fading quickly, the way days did at summer's end, the world outside deepening into shadow. I had no reason to be anxious and yet, as I looked out into the yard, I couldn't shake the feeling that someone was out there watching, or would be, and that soon someone would knock on the door bringing chaos and trouble into our lives.

FIVE

When Andre returned from his phone call, he looked troubled. "Talked to a friend on the Freeport police force. A captain. Seems that these days, Faraday styles himself as a respectable businessman. Got himself a restaurant, a building with a block of stores, and a lot of other real estate around town. Golfer. Chamber of Commerce. Very involved in civic affairs. But he wasn't always such an upstanding citizen. There's suspicion that he got his money from drugs. Never been charged, and it seems no one dares to come forward who knows anything. People who cross him have an unfortunate tendency to die or disappear."

For Andre, this was information. For me? Concern. "You're not making me feel more secure," I said.

"I don't suppose 'knowledge is power' is comforting," he said. "Or forewarned is forearmed?"

I shook my head. "I don't want to be warned or armed. I want to be left alone to bond with Mason." But I wasn't the wishful thinking type, so I asked, "Is there any way Faraday could become interested in us?"

Andre looked regretful. "I hope not. But the captain says that Officer Bartlett has kind of a big mouth and not a lot of discretion."

My instinctive distrust of the guy was confirmed. "What about the girl? Addison Shirley?" I asked. "Is she also known to them?"

"He didn't know the name, but says he'll ask around. He did say that Faraday's romantic life has been more than a little turbulent."

"He give any specifics?" I asked, wondering why I wanted to know this when it wouldn't make me feel better.

"Faraday may have a talent for making money but with respect to his love life, he's attracted to bright and shiny objects. Man's been married twice and there have been allegations of domestic violence," he said, hesitating. "My contact says the women always recant. Nothing sticks."

"The big canary problem," I said.

Mason wailed.

"Your son doesn't like the tenor of this conversation," I said.

Andre grinned. "Guess we're going to have to learn to have our serious conversations out of his hearing. We don't want to upset him."

"Given what his parents do, that's going to be hard. We'll have to get used to asking the nanny to take him out of the room like the royals do. Or one of those Hollywood couples."

"Nanny? What nanny?" Andre said. "Do we have one of those?"

"We do not. Maybe you can arrest one and bring her home?"

"Not your best suggestion," he said, holding out his hands for the baby. He tucked Mason up on his shoulder, his big hand spread across the little back. "Son," he said, "did you know that your mama is already scheming to hand you off to some stranger?"

"I am not scheming." I said it lightly but felt I was on the verge of tears. Those damned hormones. "Just being practical. Who knows how soon your boss is going to want you back?"

"Need me back," he corrected. "They know I'm on leave. They won't call me in except as a last resort."

My tired brain started doing a riff on the idea of a "last resort." Definitely not a place I'd want to stay. It had such a final sound. I switched to thinking about how soon I might be called in myself. We were a small operation, but campus crisis was my specialty. As the fall semester got underway, trouble would start. I could handle some of it by phone or video conference, but sometimes I had to be there in person to whack some sense into a headmaster or a board of trustees or even walk an anxious staff through a complicated PR situation. I was good at it, but it was exhausting and emotionally draining.

Was I too young to retire? Yes. I was. Besides, we needed the income to finish our house, pay our mortgage, and now start saving for college.

"Is it too early to go to bed?" I asked.

He tucked Mason into the crook of his arm and checked his watch. "Oh, it's very late," he said. "Almost eight-thirty."

I hadn't slept more than a few hours at a time since Mason's debut so that sounded plenty late to me.

The phone rang. Andre answered, then held it out to me, mouthing, "It's your mother."

After more than a week, and not seeing her grandson yet, she was finally calling? My brother Michael had beaten me to the punch in the grandchild department, so he wasn't her first. Even so, after the zillion times she'd asked me if I was pregnant yet, she should have visited or at least planned a visit. But even before I said, "Hello," I knew what she was going to say.

"It's been a week," she said, "and I haven't seen my grandson yet. When are you and Andre coming to visit? Your father is dying to see him."

I refrained from saying, "But you aren't?" because sarcasm was wasted on her.

"We're not traveling that far with him yet," I said, "but you and Dad are most welcome to come and visit. Your grandson is totally adorable, with the biggest, brownest eyes you've ever seen, and he has such a sweet nature." I didn't add, except during the night, because she wouldn't care, or would likely launch into a description of what a difficult baby I had been. Or she might have compared a restless Mason to my useless older brother. She remembered him as being absolute perfection. I remembered him as being such a jerk that I'd had to step up to the responsible oldest child's role.

"We're awfully busy," she said. "You know that I'm taking care of Michael's boy one day a week to give Sonia a break."

My sister-in-law Sonia was the perfect match for my brother. They were both self-centered, self-indulgent, and unbearable, characteristics my mother had missed or maybe admired.

Because I sometimes can't help being provocative—she drives me to it—I said, "Maybe Dad wants to come by himself, if you're too busy."

"Your father has to work," she said. "He has an important job."

As if I didn't know that my father had a job? She was implying, I supposed, that my work wasn't important. But it was late and I was tired and didn't want to get into it with her, especially since I already knew I could never win. I'd spent the better part of thirty years trying to please her. When I finally stopped, it was like the magic of not knocking my head against the wall. It felt so good. After years of biting my tongue and trying to avoid conflict, I've gotten much better at not letting my mother's indifference and criticism get to me. Most of the time.

The phone buzzed to tell me there was another call. It could go to voice mail and if it was important, they'd leave a message. If it was the Maine Department of Public Safety looking for my husband, they could go to hell. Or call him on his cell phone.

I said, "Well, we're around this weekend if you want to come and see Mason. You don't even have to call. Just show up." I yawned into the phone, not even having to fake it. "Sorry. I'm pretty tired. You know how it is when you have a newborn. Talk to you soon."

She was starting to say something, likely a complaint about how I was being difficult, which I'd heard too many times already, when I disconnected. There are probably people who think I should be nicer to my mother, but believe me, I've tried. There is no way to please her.

I was sorry, though, that my father wasn't planning to come and meet his new grandson. On his own, he'd be an excellent grandfather. He'd find Mason adorable, much cuter, I was sure, than my nephew, Michael's baby. But I am prejudiced. I'm supposed to be.

I put down the phone and sighed. "She's too busy to visit," I told Andre. "She wants us, or me, to bring the baby to her."

"No way," he said, which echoed my feelings exactly. "He's not ready to spend that much time in the car. They want to see him, they know where to find us."

He didn't say what I knew he was thinking—that my mother was being her usual pain-in-the-ass self. My mother disapproved of Andre. She wanted me to marry someone with a "respectable career" and not some Maine cop. For that matter, she wanted *me* to have a different career, either a realtor or a banker, not that she has any idea what I do. She just wanted me to have an important-sounding job so she can boast about it to her friends.

"There was a call while she and I were talking," I told him. "I suppose we should check voice mail."

Before I could, his phone rang and he answered. He listened, handed me the baby, and left the room.

It was bound to be bad if he couldn't talk about it in front of me. Unless it was more information about Faraday or Addison Shirley and he was just leaving to give Mason a tranquil atmosphere. The lad needed a tranquil atmosphere. In utero, he'd been nocturnal, a kickboxer or an acrobat and seemed to be carrying on those antics, and that schedule, now that he'd been born. He liked to kick and flail his little limbs about, vocalizing as he did so. It wasn't crying, it was just noise, but it was far from peaceful. Somehow, during his development, he'd failed to get the memo that babies are supposed to sleep and eat and poop and not much else.

If I were to mention that to my mother, she'd probably tell me it was what I deserved for being such a fussy baby myself. But Mason wasn't fussy. He was just rehearsing for his career in the circus. If she didn't like my job and Andre's, how would my mother handle having a grandson who was an acrobat?

I sat down and put him on my knees, facing me, so I could look into his expressive face. He looked so alert and wise and like he was taking it all in and assessing what he was seeing. "You are magical," I said. "Just wait until you meet Dom and Rosie Florio. Your godparents. You guys are going to love each other."

I'd met Dominic Florio when my college roommate's mother was murdered and I went to give her support. Florio was the lead detective on the case who quickly decided that I was going to be a useful person to help him understand the victim and her family. We started out as adversaries and became good friends, and now he and his wife, Rosie, are like a second set of parents. A more supportive and kinder set.

Not long ago, they'd driven to Maine, where we now lived, from Massachusetts, to see our new house and to check up on me and ensure that I was taking care of myself. I have a bad habit of not eating, and of getting myself into situations where my concern is taking care of others. The Florios figured I needed to be reminded to take care of myself and the soon-to-be-born MOC. They were barely through the door before they announced their intention to be our baby's godparents. Andre and I were thrilled. Now they were coming to meet their godson, and if past history was any guide, they would arrive with enough food to keep me and Andre fed at least until Thanksgiving.

I couldn't wait for them to meet Mason. Their eagerness helped soften my disappointment at my parents' indifference. My mother's "we'll see him if you're willing to drive your newborn a couple hours in summer traffic," might be expected but that didn't mean it wasn't painful.

I know. I should get over it. Expecting a different result was what? The definition of something. Mason looked up at me with his wise eyes and I said, "Do you know what it's the definition of?"

Evidently, he didn't want to talk about my mother, because he spit up and started to cry.

"Sorry, kiddo," I said. "Your mama is being insensitive."

I was soothing the savage beast, or was it the savage breast—my brain wasn't what it had been—when Andre returned.

We are both practiced in reading body language, and right now, his said he had bad news and didn't want to talk about it. This man, who could be perfectly sanguine while up to his eyeballs in crime scene gore, was now stuck in the doorway, rocking from foot to foot and looking anywhere but at me.

Watching, my mind started racing, filling in the blanks of what he wasn't saying. Something bad had happened, that much was clear. But how bad? Was it the girl? Faraday? Oh God! Was it the baby? Suddenly I felt like I couldn't breathe.

"Just spit it out," I said. "It can't be worse than what I'm imagining."

Still, he rocked, unwilling to speak. And this was a man who'd notified dozens of people about the worst of bad news. It was part of his job. "It's... uh..."

Mason, who was already an incredible barometer of bad news and parental tension, began to wail in earnest. Oh, man. Given our respective careers, we were in for it. I put him on my shoulder and rubbed his back, murmuring soothing sounds.

Andre waited, as though getting the baby calm would make his news easier. As though he didn't realize that the moment his words were out, our barometer baby would begin to wail again. Being a new parent was already stressful enough. Why hadn't anyone told us we needed to create a world of perfect calm?

When Mason was calm, Andre sat in the chair across from me and said, "Bad news."

I politely refrained from saying "Duh," since he was trying. This was hard for him. He didn't want to burst the bubble of our little trio any more than I did.

I waited.

"That was my friend in Freeport. The captain. They've just found a body."

Oh God! No! I waited some more. Whatever was coming was bad news. Would it be Addison Shirley, leaving that poor newborn motherless? Or Faraday? I didn't want to know and needed to know.

"In a car," Andre continued. "A Tesla. Parked on a dirt road near some land that's being cleared for construction."

I thought I knew what "in a Tesla" and "construction" were leading to. Faraday was a well-to-do developer.

"The car belongs to Faraday," he said, in a way that told me a "but" was coming.

I waited for it, pushing away visions from other scenes. Andre wasn't the only one who had a lot of bad images stuck in his head.

When the "but" came, it was a complete surprise. "But the body in the car belongs to Faraday's estranged wife, Lucia Faraday."

Now I was totally confused.

SIX

"I thought you told me Faraday had been divorced twice," I said. "Is this wife number three, or were he and number two merely estranged?" As though estranged wasn't serious enough. As though estrangement didn't often lead to one partner killing the other. Usually a man unable to allow a woman to leave him. But it also went the other way. I could think of a lot of reasons why someone might kill a wife, especially if the killer wanted to become a wife herself.

Then, before he had a chance to answer, I asked, "How was she killed?"

"Shot once. In the head."

Which led to a whole bunch of new questions. I'd been involved in enough situations involving dead bodies that I'd become almost cop-like in my thinking. But I suppressed them. I didn't really need to know. This wasn't my problem. This wasn't either of our problems. Was it? But then why had his department called him?

I looked over at Andre, shifting nervously in his chair. Why was he nervous? Of course, I already knew why.

I said, "No. They are not calling you in on this. Absolutely not. You are not the only competent detective in Maine, and you are on leave. We've only had a week to get used to our child. Do not tell me they've somehow decided that only you can handle this situation. Or that a week is considered sufficient time to adjust to a newborn."

Not that I was naïve or anything. We live in a culture that doesn't build in space or support for families. Not to welcome babies, care for children, or allow for the care of elderly parents. Someone is born, someone dies. Get on and get over it. There's work to be done.

What a cynic I've become. Or was I a realist?

He didn't say anything, though the ghost of a smile hovered around his mouth. I knew what that was about, too. I'd just told him he couldn't officially tell me that he'd been called in on the case, so he wasn't telling me that. But he knew I could read him well, just as he could read me. We really didn't need words to communicate a lot of the time.

Mason made a snuffling sound and wiggled himself into my neck. I liked to do the same to Andre. It was my safe place. I guess the kid took after me in that respect at least. I looked over at my husband. The smile was gone and he looked sad and angry, confirming my suspicions. He didn't like this any more than I did.

I said, "No. Seriously, no. They can't call you in. Can they?" which was dumb because of course they could and we both knew it. If men gave birth, things would change in a hurry.

"But it's only been a week!" I repeated it because I had nothing else left.

I'm sure I sounded as whiny as I felt, and I am not the whining type. I'm the buck up and get on with it type. Right now, though, I was sleepless and sore and terrified of being left alone with this tiny person.

He started a litany that began with two people are on vacation, one is sick, and two are away at a seminar. Then the litany stopped because I didn't need to hear it. It wasn't helpful or comforting to either of us.

"Cover your ears," I told Mason, even though the poor little fellow couldn't do that, and then said some words I rarely utter aloud, ending with "You can't leave because I cannot do this alone."

"Maybe it will be straightforward," he offered. He wasn't referring to parenting.

"Right. Sure. Maybe the killer left a note on the dashboard or something. Or the gun with fingerprints all over it."

He looked away, staring out the window at nothing but darkness. We both were too aware of what can lurk in darkness. After a long silence, he said, "There was an infant car seat in the car. And a diaper bag."

It felt like my heart skipped a beat. "But no baby?"

"But no baby."

So things were more complicated than just a homicide, as if there was any "just" about a person being killed. There was presumably an infant missing. Maybe kidnapped twice, if it was Addison Shirley's baby. Had she done this to get her child back? I didn't know enough to speculate, and really, I didn't want to, but I couldn't help it.

It was night and I, as brave as a barrel full of bears, was afraid of being left alone. What if something happened and I needed Andre? What if Mason got sick? Babies are so small and fragile it's hard not to worry about everything.

"You're the most competent woman I know," he said. "You'll be fine. I probably won't be gone for long. I'll just get things underway and then I'll come home."

As though we hadn't been together for years and gone through a lot of crimes, both together and apart. I knew how he could disappear into the night and not be seen or heard from for days if that was what the job required. I looked at him and he knew what I was thinking.

"I'll call you. Often. And if you call, I promise I'll answer."

Great to hear but we both knew there was an implied "if I can" behind those words.

Some damned hormonal tears were leaking from my eyes, even though I was trying to be brave. He looked like he was ready to cry as well. We'd had so few days to settle into our happy little threesome and already it was being busted apart. A taste of how our lives would really be.

"When are Dom and Rosie coming?" I asked.

"Tomorrow."

"Morning? Afternoon?"

He hesitated. He hates to give me bad news. Finally, he said, "Afternoon, I think. You want me to call and tell them to come sooner?"

I shook my head. If the past was any guide, Rosie would still be cooking in the morning. There would always be one more dish she had to make, one more delicious dessert she was sure we needed. Her food was ambrosia. How do you tell a kitchen angel that she needs to stop cooking and get in the car? No. I'd have to be a grownup about this, even if I felt like a bereft child. Mason was the child, I reminded myself. If I hadn't already been an adult, his arrival made me one. You can't be focused on yourself when another life depends on you. Besides, I needed to send Andre off to his crime scene with a clear mind. The victim deserved that.

"You'll call when you can?"

He nodded.

"You'll be very, very careful?"

He already had one foot out the door, torn between his need to be gone and his need to be here. "I'll be careful."

"We will be fine," I lied.

"You *will* be fine," he agreed. "But dammit! I don't—" He stopped. He's belonged to the police longer than he's belonged to me. That was how we met—when he was investigating my sister Carrie's murder. When he and I were both investigating Carrie's murder after my parents refused to get involved.

He shrugged. No sense in saying it. We both knew how he felt. How we both felt. We were slaves of duty. It was one of the things that had brought us together.

My husband crossed the room, suddenly, and took Mason from me. Kissed the soft little head and then nuzzled it with his chin. "He changes things," he said.

Then he handed Mason back, grabbed his gear, and left.

SEVEN

After his taillights had disappeared down the driveway, I went upstairs, put Mason in his bassinet, and got ready for bed myself. I lay down, knowing I should try to sleep while Mason did, but sleep wouldn't come. I'm a professional problem solver by trade, and I've puzzled my way through mysterious situations too many times.

Even if I couldn't turn off my brain, rest mattered, so I didn't get up. I just lay there with my eyes closed and went back over my two brief encounters with the girl who called herself Addison Faraday. The first wasn't really an encounter, it was more of an observation, when outside the shop I'd envied her happy absorption in her ice cream cone. Second, when I'd come out to find her screaming and distressed while surrounded by indifferent people.

What had happened in those intervening minutes while I was searching for a hat to protect Mason's small, soft head from the late summer sun? Had she done something that caused people to ignore her? Had there been some kind of confrontation? Had her baby cried and she'd ignored him? Or was I just looking for reasons for people to be so callous?

Andre and I like to play a game designed to tune-up my observation skills where I look at something briefly and then describe it to him. I hadn't had my focus on the scene this morning. I'd been on a mission to find a hat. Perhaps I'd still noticed things, though, thanks to Detective Sergeant Andre Lemieux's training.

Lying there with my eyes closed, I let my mind go back to this morning as I approached the shop that sold children's clothes. It was a cheerful yellow building with lavish flowerboxes beneath large display windows and then those benches on each side of the door. The flowerboxes and benches had been painted aqua, as was the shop door. I'd come from down the street so the store was on my left, and the girl who called herself Addison Faraday was standing beside the nearer bench. The carriage had been parked at an angle beside her, partially obstructing traffic on the sidewalk, like a rock in the flow of a river.

The carriage had been angled away from her, I realized, so that she was behind the—what was it called? The hood? The bonnet?— so she couldn't see into the carriage. That was how I was able to see the baby and note the blue blankets as I passed, because it was angled toward me and toward the street and not the way you'd expect a cautious mom to park it, so that she could see in and watch her infant.

Funny how that hadn't struck me at the time. I could barely take my eyes off Mason. But I had noticed what she was wearing. Her carefully styled hair and the impractical shoes that gave her height but weren't good for walking on crowded sidewalks. How exhausted she looked despite her careful makeup. I'd noticed how the tiny summer dress clung to her full breasts and the little belly that pregnancy had left. I'd noticed the ice cream cone—black raspberry— and envied her. Thought about getting one for myself if my errand was successful. Eating for two made me constantly hungry.

What else had I noticed? Had I seen anyone who looked suspicious?

Like rewinding a film, I backed up my recall until I was farther away and considered what I'd seen. A family where everyone— mother, father, and three blond children—looked alike. Three older women in red, white, and blue who were clutching shopping bags and eagerly talking over each other. An elderly man on a bench smoking a cigarette with such relish, he might have been next going before a firing squad.

A younger man. Well-dressed, looking like a businessman who'd stepped out to grab a sandwich. Khaki pants. Blue checked shirt. A belt with whales. Boat shoes with no visible socks. Sunglasses. Carefully gelled hair. Had there been anything concerning about him? Nothing beyond the way he'd stared at Addison Faraday and bumped into a fire hydrant. A thirty-something woman in denim cutoffs had smirked as she passed.

Was that all?

There were cars parked on both sides of the street and yes, there had been a man in a car who seemed to be watching Addison Faraday. Addison Shirley. Since she wasn't married to Faraday, I decided I should use her correct name. Could I remember anything about him?

Sometimes I wished Andre had never taught me this game. Especially at a time like this, when I wanted to put the whole thing out of my mind and sleep and instead was forcing my tired brain to recall all these little details. Had I noticed the make of the car? Alas, no. It was too generic. Just another dusty silver, smallish SUV. If he was a Mainer, it was probably a Subaru.

What about the man? It had been dim in the car, hard to see through the sunlight on the windshield. I had an impression of large, dark hair and sunglasses, and maybe wearing something khaki, like a uniform shirt. Short sleeves, because the hand that gripped the steering wheel led to a bare arm and a large, important-looking watch. He'd been wearing a ring with a stone in it. Beyond that? I had nothing.

Okay. I could share that much non-information with Andre the next time he appeared, just in case it was relevant. Now I had to move on to what I'd seen when I came out of the store.

Except that would have to wait, because Mason, the world's worst sleeper, was already awake and beginning to fuss.

I thought of all the times when I was tired and frustrated, especially with some of my more difficult clients. Wouldn't it have been great if I could have just started fussing and they would all stop being so difficult?

A girl can dream. Someday soon I would have to go back to work. Given the childish behavior of some of those clients, I just might try it.

I got up, pulled on my robe because the nights were already getting chilly, and picked up the baby. Those big brown eyes stared up at me. I'd read that most babies have blue eyes at first and change to other colors as the melanin develops. Mason didn't seem to have gotten the memo. I figured that was okay. It was great that when Andre looked at his son, he saw his own eyes looking back. Good for bonding and all that. And comforting to me.

Since Mason seemed happiest when he was close to my body, I put on a baby wrap and settled him there. He quieted at once, which was good since it was too soon for him to be hungry. Although if he's inherited his father's appetite, he'll always be hungry, even if he is too young for steak and chocolate cake. For now, he wasn't even getting chocolate cake secondhand. Much as I longed for the pleasure and comfort of chocolate right now, I wasn't taking chances with his little stomach.

I grabbed my phone off the nightstand, first checking for a text from Andre, who might not call if he didn't want to disturb the baby. Nothing from Andre, but a text I'd missed earlier from my partner, Suzanne. Normally, texts from Suzanne, even though she's a dear friend as well as business partner, announce some urgent work that needs to be done. This one was different. It was potentially good news—she had found a woman who was interested in a job as a nanny and she wanted to know if we'd like her to contact us.

That could send me into a happy dance. We'd need a nanny soon enough. But I just didn't even want to think about leaving Mason. Not yet. Still, wisdom said to follow up. Nannies didn't grow on trees.

I checked the time—only a bit after ten—and sent her a reply saying to please share my contact information with the woman.

Then I went downstairs to make some tea. I could go through some of the stacks of material from work that had been piling up.

At first, I tried to put Mason in his baby seat, but he wasn't having it, so back into the sling he went. No sooner had I bent over my work, though, than my mind returned to the scene this morning, and what I'd noticed when I came out of the store with Mason's hat.

Before I'd focused on Addison Faraday, I'd almost bumped into a woman carrying a basket who was hurrying away. I closed my eyes and tried to recall the scene. Had I noticed anything about her or had I been too distracted by the screams?

Actually, I hadn't almost bumped into the woman. She'd almost bumped into me, or more particularly into Mason, tucked away in his sling. I'm in protective mother mode these days, and I'm sure I glared at her and growled, because I remembered being surprised that she hadn't turned or slowed or said excuse me or done any of the usual things people do when they bump into someone. I wasn't sure whether I—we—had been bumped by the woman herself or by the rather large lidded wicker basket she was carrying. It seemed like an odd thing to be carrying on a crowded street.

Had I noticed the woman or just the basket?

I breathed slowly in and out and let my mind wander back to the scene. Andre says that most witnesses could tell a lot more if they could relax and remember, but that talking to the police is stressful and so they don't. But there was a baby involved here, a helpless one, and I had no idea whether he was taken because he was coveted or because someone wanted him out of the way.

That question distracted me from my recall and made me wonder what James Milton Faraday's wife, Lucia, was doing with an infant seat in her car. Andre hadn't mentioned that Faraday and his wife had a child. Did they? Was it possible Lucia Faraday was the woman who'd bumped me on the street?

Before I spun myself some elaborate scenario where Lucia Faraday was somehow involved in a scheme involving Addison Shirley's baby, I opened my laptop and started searching for Lucia Faraday. If he was a big deal in Maine, there ought to be photos of him with his wife, right? For all I knew, she was a big deal in her own right. Had been. My questions were mere speculation. For all I knew, she was—had been—a bitch from hell who had enemies of her own.

God, I was so sick of people being killed. I didn't even want the thought in this room with Mason, who was just beginning his life. Unfortunate fellow to be stuck with parents like me and Andre.

I shook off the thought and started searching. There were plenty of shots of Faraday, pictures that revealed him to be a vain and handsome man who was quite a fashion plate. Was "fashion plate" outdated? No doubt "clothes horse" was. What was a more contemporary term? The one that fit was dandy. It went with pocket squares. Why did I even care? Because I'd put in a decade of report writing and liked to be precise? After pages of Faraday and his exploits, each one showing him perfectly coiffed and immaculately dressed, I finally came to a picture of him with his wife. The picture knocked me back in my chair like I'd been struck.

She was wearing a gauzy, aqua summer dress, her curly, shoulder-length blond hair slightly wind-blown. Tall and slender. Attractive in a patrician way that looked neither warm nor welcoming. She was standing beside a picnic table decked out with way too much pottery and fabric for a simple picnic. She was holding a basket identical to the one I'd seen her carrying this morning.

Holy whatnot, Batman! I reached for the phone, then pulled my hand back. It could wait. Andre was busy processing a crime scene right now. Fast on the heels of that thought came another: what if she had had Addison's baby in that basket? I picked up the phone and dialed. I went straight to voicemail. So much for Andre's reassurance that he'd pick up if I called.

Why had I thought things would be different? Hoped, really, not thought. I'd always known I was sharing my husband with his work.

Swiping the back of my hand at my tears—new mother hormones—I put down the phone without leaving a message and went back to scrolling through the pictures. Why, I couldn't say. Maybe simply because it gave me something to do besides sitting here weeping. I've never been a sad sack or indulged in self-pity and I didn't want to start now.

There were more photos of her as I went along, and in all of them she looked like her stylist had just stepped out of the picture after carefully arranging her dress, hair, and scarf but she was displeased anyway. In the photos of her with her husband, there was always a space between them and they weren't looking at each other. There was much more to this story, I was sure. I reminded myself that I wasn't a detective. Andre was. I was a consultant to independent schools, and for the present, I wasn't even that.

The stack of papers on the desk in my little cubbyhole office said otherwise. Maybe that was why I was sitting in the kitchen instead. Of course here in the kitchen, there was a different problem: the refrigerator. It seemed like Mason wasn't the only one who was always hungry these days. I was trying to eat only the best and healthiest foods, but there are few people in the world who crave carrots when there is cake to be had, or pie or muffins or banana bread. All the delicious things people drop off when a baby is born.

True, there had been some veggies as well. It was late summer in Maine and people with gardens were still trying to foist off their excess produce on others. A ripe tomato, however delicious, is no match for a triple crème cheese. But maybe eaten together?

To fix a snack, I'd have to get up and disturb Mason, who was sleeping quietly in his little sling. So, no snack. I went back to scrolling through photos of the Faradays. After a while, I found I was looking at pictures of Faraday and a different woman, a woman the captions identified as his wife Rebecca. Unlike her successor, Rebecca Faraday looked like a person I might like to know. She was a dark-haired beauty with dark eyes, full lips, and serious curves, but she didn't dress to show them off. She dressed like a hippy, with billowy linen shirts open over tank tops and long flowing skirts, her hair in a thick braid over her shoulder. Her smile looked genuine, the kind that reached the eyes as well as the lips.

There was one photo of her arriving at a gala with Faraday in a clinging black dress and jewels that showed she "cleaned up good," as the expression went. I scrolled back through and could see that in the earlier photos, she and Faraday were close, his arm around her waist, her face turned up toward his. As time went on, they literally grew apart.

Why would a man trade an exotic beauty for a cold, handsome wasp? If the rumors of his early life of crime and drug dealing were true, maybe he was trying to buy himself some class? What had Andre said? The man had a reputation for domestic violence? So maybe the space between Faraday and his wives came from his behavior?

Where did Addison Shirley come in? Was Lucia as cold as she looked and he was seeking some warmth? Did he periodically try to trade in for a younger model? The second Mrs. Faraday didn't look like she would be easily dumped. She looked like she'd hold out for a generous divorce settlement. Could that be why she was killed?

How old was Faraday, anyway? He looked to be in his forties, with decorative touches of gray at his temples and attractive crinkles at the corners of his eyes, but he could be older, early to mid-fifties. Guys were getting work done these days, too, and he looked like the type.

Ha! By the time Mason was done with me, I'd need some work done, too. I could imagine wanting something that erased the weariness from my face and the stretchmarks from the rest of me. But right now, it was more appealing to imagine going into a treatment room, lying down on the soft, heated table, being covered with fluffy blankets, and left to sleep for as long as I wanted. Someone might say that I'd only been a mom for a week and why was I complaining so much, but I'd carried the acrobat for nine months, and for some of those, he'd been kicking the dickens out of me.

Was this be careful what you wish for? I'd take more than being kicked for the joy of this little guy's company.

I was about to return to my recall of this morning's events and see if I'd noticed anything else when my phone rang. I had the ringtone turned way down and it was so soft I almost didn't hear it. At my quiet "Hello?" Andre said, "You called me. Is everything okay?"

"Mason and I are fine. I called because I remembered something about this morning, something that I thought you ought to know sooner rather than later."

Now that neither of us was dying, he was instantly professional. He said, "Which is?"

"As I came out of the store this morning, before I focused on Addison Shirley having hysterics, a woman bumped into me. She was coming from Shirley's direction and carrying a covered wicker basket, a rather large basket. She didn't pause or say she was sorry, as most people would, but hurried away. Then she looked back a few times as though she was afraid she was being followed. That was odd enough, but the reason I mention it is that the woman with the basket was Lucia Faraday. I know because I looked her up online. It was definitely her. Now you say she had an infant's car seat in the Tesla. Do the Faradays have a baby? Because if not, I wonder if she had Addison's missing baby in that basket."

EIGHT

Andre was silent for a minute. Then he said, "Good thinking. I'll look into it. But why are you up? Shouldn't you be trying to get some sleep?"

"Our son had other ideas."

Then we were both silent, still kind of amazed at terms like "our son." I swear the kid knows when we're talking about him, because he stirred and began to fuss.

"Guess you've got to go," Andre said.

"Soon," I agreed. "This is just his warmup act. So, how are things on your end?"

"Aside from a deputy who almost screwed up the crime scene by adjusting the body—he said she looked uncomfortable—it's fine. Shouldn't take much longer."

"You take his head off?"

"Kinda."

"I'll leave a light on for you."

"Story of our marriage," he said. "Thanks. I'd do the same for you."

I knew I had to let him go. He had important work to do. But I wanted to hold on to him a little longer, so I said, "Suzanne says she may have a potential nanny for us."

"I wish we didn't need one," he said.

"Me, too. But we're realists. Eventually, we will. It takes two salaries to support this house, and now we're going to be saving for college."

"They say it's a fast eighteen years," he said.

"And they say that the first year is about ten years long."

He murmured his agreement. "Sorry I didn't answer. I was in the midst of removing that deputy's head and I didn't want to lose momentum, or cred, by taking a call from my wife."

"Tough guy," I said. "You gotta preserve your image."

"As a hardass? You bet. Let people think you're soft and they get careless." He switched topics. "You didn't leave a message."

"It wasn't critical. I figured when you got home was soon enough. Except, if there *is* a missing baby, looking into the possibility that your victim might have had him is important. I'm awfully worried about him."

"We all are." A pause. His "see you soon" was almost drowned out by Mason's wails.

As was my final question, "I don't suppose you found a picnic basket in the car?"

But he was gone.

By the time Mason was changed and fed again, I was so sleepy I could have dropped off leaning against the changing table. I put him in his bassinet, took off my robe, and climbed into bed. The task of reviewing this morning's events was unfinished, but I was finished. I wasn't used to waiting so long to review what I'd seen. Still, if the memories were there, they could wait.

I woke a miraculous three hours later to Mason's warm-up act, the little fusses that would soon lead to full on hue and cry. Before I could get my eyes fully open, I heard footsteps and Andre crossed the room and picked him up. His deep voice rumbled as he carried the baby to the changing table. I loved that rumble, being snuggled up against him when he talked. Would Mason feel the same? Maybe. Those whimpers had quieted.

How on earth did single mothers do this?

I propped myself up against the pillows and waited for my guys to return. One of them would certainly be hungry. Probably both of them.

When Andre came back, he handed me the baby, then lay down on his side of the bed. "Little bugger doesn't want us to sleep, that's for sure," he said.

"You just got home?"

"Just."

I hesitated to ask but I needed to know. "Was there a basket?"

"Not that we found. We'll do a wider search of the area in the morning. But there was a car seat. We can check for DNA, though that's not helpful unless we've got someone to match it to."

"There's Faraday," I said.

"And I've got to go and see him in the morning. He wasn't at home and didn't answer any of the numbers we've got for him, so we've got people looking for him. But will he be forthcoming with his DNA?"

DNA wasn't my department. "You think loose-lipped Bartlett tipped him off that the state police would want to talk to him?"

Andre shrugged. "It's possible, although I've got my buddy in the department keeping an eye on him. Can't keep an eye when he's away from work, though. For that, we have to rely on a stern warning."

"Which doesn't always work. When Freeport PD interviewed Faraday, did they ask about a child?"

"It was pretty cursory and they took Faraday's word for the fact that he and Addison Shirley were long over and he knew nothing about any child she might have had."

"I wonder if Mrs. Faraday felt the same way? I wonder if she had issues with her husband having a child with another woman. Or if she wanted the child for herself? Or if she wanted the child out of the picture?"

"If the child is Faraday's. We have a lot of questions and very few answers," he said. "But you definitely saw a baby in that carriage, right?"

"Right."

"An actual baby, not just a bundle of blankets?"

"Who trained me in being observant, Detective Lemieux?" I probably didn't entirely keep the edge out of my voice.

Mason had latched on with a vengeance and was making happy baby sounds.

Instead of answering, Andre said, "Good thing Dom and Rosie are coming tomorrow. I'll likely be up to my ears in this thing."

"First twenty-four and all that?"

"And all that. I'm trying to put my resentment aside so I can give the case what it deserves, but I am not happy about it."

"That makes two of us. Unless it's three. So now we've got two missing people. Faraday and Addison Shirley. Three, including the baby."

I figured this was a good time to fill him in on what I'd recalled. "So I was doing that thing you taught me, about recalling as much as I could about what I'd seen this morning. That's when I remembered the woman with the basket. How brusque she was. How rude."

I tried to recall what I'd noticed about her. "She was wearing a red polo shirt, white capris, and navy shoes. A red, white, and blue headband. Is that what she was wearing when... uh... when she was found in the car?"

He shook his head.

So she must have gone home and changed. But where was home? "If she and her husband were separated, do you know where she was living?"

"He was the one who moved out. At least, that's what we've been told. Another thing to follow up. Supposedly he's living on a boat, or in a cottage with a boat moored right off it. That's one of the numbers we called—the cottage landline. Nada."

"I remembered some other things, too, if you'd like to hear them."

"I'm listening," he said.

He looked tired. It had been quite a week, and quite a month before that. I should shut up and let him get some sleep.

Mind reader that he was, he said, "It's okay. It's important. I'm listening. And you're good at this."

"Taught by the best."

I told him about how Addison Shirley had parked the carriage. How odd it seemed that she'd point her baby toward the passing crowds of strangers instead of parking it so she could watch her baby. I told him about how indifferent she'd seemed, all her attention on enjoying an ice cream cone and none on her child. I told him about the man in the car who was watching her. Or watching the baby. What he was wearing, the fancy watch, the ring.

I considered, and said, "I haven't had time to get to the rest of it. See what I could recall about what happened next."

He pushed himself farther up on his pillows and said, "You want to do that now?"

"I don't want to do it at all. I don't want any of this interfering with our first weeks with Mason. I just want to sit and watch his expressive face and admire his tiny fingers and toes."

"I know. But if you noticed anything that might help us with this investigation? Or to find the missing girl and her baby?"

"Then I am a slave of duty."

I focused back on those moments after I was bumped by the woman with the basket. What else had I seen? Obviously, I'd seen the woman I learned was Addison Shirley screaming for help, saying that her baby had been taken. The ice cream cone was forgotten and she'd gotten up off the bench, but the carriage was still angled away from her and she was standing by the closed end. Which was weird.

I told Andre that and focused again. Was she holding something? Yes. A small bit of blue that might have been a baby blanket. What about the people around her? In the moment, I'd been struck by the fact that no one seemed to be paying much attention to her. No one was stopping to help. When I offered to help, how had she seemed? On reflection, I realized that despite her apparent distress, her makeup was flawless. If something had happened to Mason, my face would have been red and tear-streaked and I would have been on my phone to the police even as I corralled passersby and asked them for help.

How had she responded to my offer of help? Not with a request to call the police. Not with a request to help her look for the baby. Her concern, I realized, had been for herself. She'd lost the baby and now he—whoever he was—was going to kill her. Again, I found myself wondering if she'd been playing two men, making both think they were the father of the baby. Had both men wanted the baby? Had either one? A friend who'd worked for the state enforcing child support told me that too often, the guys just walked away, never mind what that meant for the child.

But she hadn't been killed, had she? The person who was killed was Faraday's wife.

It was all very strange.

I told Andre about her bruises, livid and purple on her arms and legs. "I wonder if the cops took photos when they interviewed her? Did they ask about the bruises?"

I wished I'd been present when the police interviewed her. I might have learned a whole lot more. For that matter, I wondered what the interview with Faraday had been like. Had they taken his denials at face value or had they been skeptical?

I shared my rambling thoughts with Andre as I had them. He didn't need coherence. He'd trained me to be observant, so he ought to know what to do with what I'd observed.

"It all happened so fast," I told him, "and I just wanted to get out of there before I got caught up in a police investigation. I barely got away as it was."

Did that make me seem unfeeling? I wasn't. I also hadn't been prepared to spend however much time the cops took to get around to asking me questions while Mason had a meltdown, and nursing in public was still not on my to-do list.

I closed my eyes and forced my thoughts back to those moments on the street. Had I noticed anyone else? Anyone who was paying attention, as opposed to all the people doing their best to ignore her?

The man from the car. He'd gotten out of the car and was

standing with his back to a storefront, about twenty feet away. He'd tried to appear casual but his eyes had been locked on her. When I stopped to help, he didn't move, but when I grabbed the police officer and sent him her way, the man had turned suddenly and walked away.

What could I add that I hadn't seen when he was in the car? His dark hair was curly and graying and in need of cutting. He was tall, probably six four or five, lean, and his pants were a uniform khaki brown like his shirt. No facial hair. Sunglasses. When he hurried away, he walked with the suggestion of a limp, like someone with an old injury. Had he been holding something or was it just that his arms were folded in front of his body? I didn't know.

Not Faraday, for sure.

I shifted Mason to my shoulder. "And that is that," I said. "Now the well of observations is dry. I'm going to finish feeding this greedy pig and then I'm going to sleep."

"You did good," my husband said.

I settled Mason in his bed and got into mine.

Beside me, Andre's soft breathing told me he was asleep.

A blissful three hours later, we were all dragged awake by the ringing of his phone. If I could time travel, I would do major harm to Alexander Graham Bell.

NINE

My partner Suzanne told me that in the early days with an infant, to keep from feeling like a failure, it is important to celebrate small accomplishments. She and I are used to knocking off great stacks of work every day while managing our staff, juggling phones, and keeping our often frantic clients happy. As I tossed an armload of tiny clothes, blankets, and burp cloths into the washer, I wondered: was it possible to consider doing laundry an accomplishment?

Suzanne said everything counted. And to be gentle with myself, which was easier said than done. Outside our unfinished house, the world went on as usual. Inside, nothing would ever be the same.

"Get over yourself, Thea," I said aloud. "Just suck it up."

From the doorway, Andre laughed. "What is talking to yourself a sign of?" he asked. My handsome husband looked almost as tired as I felt.

"Mental illness. Dementia. Or New Mother Syndrome," I suggested, resisting the temptation to throw something damp and smelly at him. I resisted because he had Mason on his shoulder, even though Mason was a prime source of the damp and smelly.

"Cheer up," Andre said. "I've made you breakfast."

Andre had many virtues but making breakfast wasn't among them. The cynic in me said, "What? A bowl of cereal?"

"And toast. And fruit. And quiche. Did I mention coffee?"

"Okay. You are my hero. Who was on the phone?"

"Update," he said. "Still no sign of Faraday or Addison Shirley."

"They needed to call at six in the morning to tell you that?"

"No. It was to tell me the autopsy is scheduled for ten this morning." He turned to go, then called back, "Come along or your coffee will get cold."

Why there are microwaves, right? But I couldn't do more laundry until this load was finished, so I followed him to the kitchen. Cereal, toast and jam, a bowl of berries, and coffee. No wonder he was the man of my dreams.

I'd taken one sip of coffee and poured milk on the cereal when there was a knock at the door. Peering in through the window was my second-favorite Maine state police detective, Roland Proffit. I am so specific because Dominic Florio is my second favorite cop in the entire world. But Roland has saved my bacon more than once, and he is great company. He always has a story to tell. A lot of them are moose stories—he collects those—but also other tales of life in Maine, often involving those folks Mainers call "people from away."

Andre went to answer the door with Mason attached to his shoulder and Roland entered, laughing.

"That's quite the accessory you've got there, Lemieux," he said.

"One of a kind," Andre said. "You want coffee?"

"Coffee's great. You got any food?"

"Oh, we've been the recipient of our neighbor's largesse for sure. You want quiche or a blueberry muffin?"

Roland, who is over six feet four and always hungry, said, "Yes. To both." Then he turned to me. "I'm so sorry this mess is dragging your husband away, Thea." Then he dropped his eyes. He might be sorry but he was as big a slave of duty as Andre was.

Andre handed Mason to me so he could fix Roland some food. Roland sat down across from me and gave me a cop's scrutiny.

"How are you doing?" he asked. He's seen me at my worst, so he has a baseline.

"It's an adventure. How are you doing?"

"Oh. I have met the girl of my dreams."

He was such a joker I didn't know whether to believe him. I studied his face, looking for signs he was kidding. Instead, I saw a blush. "You're serious," I said. "Tell me about her."

"She's a cop," he said.

Which made sense. "State or local?"

Andre put the quiche in the microwave to heat. The crust would be soggy but it was fast.

"Local. Portland."

Roland would have told me more, but his phone rang. He said, "Excuse me," and walked away, phone to his ear. Being considerate of Mason, I figured. Kind of him, since the kid was snoozing quietly on my shoulder. Good thing cereal can be eaten with one hand. The fruit was going to be harder. Berries like to bounce around. Putting a positive light on it, I supposed I could consider chasing them around the floor as a form of exercise.

There was murmuring, and then Roland was back. "They're starting the wider search soon," he said. "Any luck finding Faraday?"

Andre shook his head. "I think we need to go rattle a few people. Showing up is always better. You should come with me. The two of us will scare the crap out of people."

Two big tough guys with scary looks on their faces? Yes, they would.

"And the girl?" Roland said.

"Nothing. Except the landlady who said the girl wasn't there and hadn't been staying there. I think she merits a second look. I went over the local's interview with the girl. She said she walked there. That fits, because Thea says that the carriage is too big to fit easily into a car, at least a small car. It would take some serious wrestling. So she was likely staying somewhere nearby. Maybe she still is. We should also talk to the kids at the ice cream stand."

He took out the quiche and set it down before Roland. Not a

slice of quiche. A full quarter, as befitted a man of Roland's size. In moments, there was nothing left but some crumbs, and he made the blueberry muffin vanish as quickly.

"Much as I enjoy the image of the two of us scaring the pants off people," Roland said, "I think we should split up. One of us looks for the girl, the other for Faraday." He gave it a beat, then added, "Lotta people don't look that great without pants."

Andre agreed with the sentiment and the plan.

"But what about the baby?" I said. "Somewhere in all this there's an innocent infant who had no hand in this."

"We've found no record of an Addison Shirley or Addison Faraday giving birth," Andre said.

"I saw a baby," I insisted. "Maybe it was a home birth?"

"We believe you," Andre reassured me. "We also believe Faraday and Shirley are our best leads to finding him."

"Either of you have a theory about why Lucia Faraday had a baby seat in her car? Do the Faradays have a baby?" I considered. "Was that her car? Or was it his car? Is there a car registered to Lucia Faraday? Is there a car registered to Addison Shirley? Addison Faraday?"

Roland looked at Andre. "What have you been teaching her?"

Andre laughed. "Don't look at me. Her work requires a fair amount of detective work and interview skills. And she's a natural."

"Against my will," I said. "People have started asking me if I'm a cop."

Roland sighed. "You wouldn't want to admit to that. Not the way things are these days. People used to trust cops. It was an honorable profession. Now?" He shrugged. "Better say you're a private detective. TV has made that a cool job."

"She'd need a license," Andre said.

"Guys. Stop it. Just stop it."

I didn't add that some of the people who thought I was a cop were very scary and dangerous. I waved my free hand airily and said, "Go find witnesses. Catch bad guys. Locate missing persons and leave me and Mason in peace. And Roland?"

Proffit, halfway out of his chair, waited for what I had to say.

"Look after him, please."

"Will do." Roland stood, and he and Andre headed for the door.

With the door open and one foot out into the world, Andre turned. "I expect to come back and learn you've solved it all while we were out. Call me if anyone turns up on the doorstep."

If I hadn't been holding the baby, I would have thrown something at him. The kind of trouble that turns up on my doorstep is no joking matter. I graciously refrained from asking whether he'd answer if I called. Not going there. Not today.

"Won't matter who turns up. I am not answering the door, except for Dom and Rosie."

"That's my girl," he said, using 'girl' because he knows it pushes my buttons. Just like "little woman" or "the wife" or anything that treats me like I'm not an equal partner.

"Go," I said, and he went.

Mason's stirrings told me he was awake, so I settled him on my knees and looked down into his adorable face. I know I'm not alone in being able to watch my child for hours. "What shall we do today for fun and excitement?" I asked.

He didn't answer, but a sensation of wetness told me what our first activity would be. "It's a good thing you're cute," I told him as I carried him to the changing table.

While we were thus engaged, my phone buzzed in my pocket. I ignored it. If it was important, they would leave a message.

A while later, when he was settled again and I'd started a second load of laundry, I remembered to check it. A voicemail from Suzanne. She got straight to the point. "Sorry to disturb you. I know you're on leave, but we've got a problem school, and since you wrote their crisis management plan, they really want to talk to you."

Right. Like she or Lisa or Bobby couldn't handle it? Heck, probably Magda, Suzanne's gloomy Hungarian secretary could handle it. But keeping the clients happy paid our bills, so I called her back.

"Sorry, Thea. I'm so sorry. I don't even know if this is in our wheelhouse, and neither does the client."

She hesitated, which told me it was serious and complicated. Of course, I'd already known that, since she wouldn't have bothered me otherwise. "That is, it didn't exactly happen at the school. Uh... it's a smallish school. Northwest of Boston. One of their claims to fame, along with small class size, personal attention, yada yada." She paused. "Excuse me, I should avoid clichés, right? One of their recruitment attractions is that they have a great sports program. They've been holding a pre-school program for the football team, getting the new players oriented and building team spirit, that sort of thing. Anyway, so those guys were on campus doing their thing, and at the same time, there was a similar orientation for the girls' soccer team."

There was another silence, but I knew where this was going even before she said, "One of the boys was local, and his parents hosted a cookout for the football team, and the guys invited the girls, and there was drinking, and—"

"And one of the boys got one of the girls drunk and took advantage of her?" I said.

"Three of the boys," she said. "Kind of a Brett Kavanaugh thing? There wasn't rape, but there was definitely an assault, and the girl is traumatized, her family is out for blood, and her father is politically connected. One of the boy's families also has influence or something, and it's—"

"If I were Andre, I'd call it a clusterfuck, but since we're genteel, I'll say a royal mess."

"Exactly."

"What do they want us to do?"

She sighed. "Make it all go away."

"We can't do that."

"Then help them handle it."

"Do we need to add a sexual assault plan, and consent education, to our suggested list of offerings?"

She sighed again. "Probably. But for right now, they need advice about how to proceed, and they want it from you."

I looked around my lovely kitchen, such a nice change from our last apartment, and felt the warmth of my sleeping child against my shoulder. In other times, I'd probably get off the phone, call the client, and then get on a plane or in my car. In my experience, people listened better when I was in the room. I was *not* getting on a plane. Or in my car. "You told them I was on maternity leave?"

"Of course I did. But it's an emergency, and like many of our clients, they believe their emergency trumps our personal lives."

"Give me a contact number," I said. "Who is it, anyway? Head of School or Head of the Board of Trustees?"

"Head of School."

"Have the trustees been notified?"

"It was one quick phone call asking for help, Thea," she said, sounding annoyed.

Not half as annoyed as I was. But I kept that to myself, never mind that I'd picked up the slack twice for her maternity leaves without dropping something like this in her lap. Crisis management is my specialty. Things blow up and they call me. I'm the girl in the white hat who rides into town and sets things straight. Sometimes.

Despite the brain-addling hormones, I was already running lists and organizing what I'd say when I made the phone call.

"Are you still there?" she asked.

"I'm still here."

"You going to call them?"

"I'm going to call them."

"Then call me back and let me know how it goes."

"You could just call them yourself, you know."

"And I will if you absolutely refuse, but you're better at it. I'm charm and light. I'm little fitted Chanel suits, understated jewelry, and let's work together for the good of the school. You're the tall, no nonsense woman who gets them to snap to attention and listen up because this is serious type."

"I am not a type. You know, it would be great if we had Lindsay to work on this. Her insights would be so valuable." Lindsay Livermore had been our summer intern and she was fantastic. She'd just left to go back to school. One more semester to finish and she'd be a full-time employee at EDGE. We could hardly wait.

Suzanne laughed. A nervous, I'm a little worried about what you'll say next kind of laugh. "I'm afraid this can't wait until next semester. So you'll do it?"

"I'll talk to them. I'll give my best advice. But I am not getting in a car. The roads are full of cars and meeting rooms are full of people and people carry germs."

"Those protective maternal instincts are a bitch, aren't they?" she said. "Sorry. I've got another call. Good luck."

And I was again alone in my kitchen with a sleeping infant and head full of strategy. Why wouldn't people just leave me alone?

TEN

"Because you are a slave of duty, and your partner knows it," said a little voice in my head. I hated that the voice was right. I've been responding to independent—read private—school emergencies for so many years I'm like the fireman when the alarm goes off. I just fly down that pole and jump on the truck. I've got a reputation in the business as the person to call when things get tough, and I'm enough of a grownup to know that the world of business, any business, doesn't care about people's private lives. Also that if one expert isn't available, the client will find another. I'm the best, but I'm not the only one.

"Don't you worry, kiddo," I told Mason, who was starting to fuss, "Your mama isn't leaving you any time soon. I'm not just mama, you know, I'm breakfast, lunch, dinner, and snacks."

He stared at me with those serious dark eyes, like he was closely attending to what I was saying. He stretched his little arms, opened his hands like small pink starfish, and kicked a few times, just to show me he remembered how to do it. As if I could so quickly forget what the little pugilist had been up to before he was born. Pugilist? Or was that kickboxer?

I put him in his seat and wound up a mobile for him to watch. It

70

played "Fly Me To The Moon," which seemed like an odd tune for an infant, but he liked it. The music was tinny, or chirpy, not like the mellow voices of famous singers, but maybe research has shown babies responded to that. I perched the seat on my desk while I made some notes and then picked up the phone.

I was calling someone named Barron Thompson at the Stonegate Academy. We'd done a crisis management plan for them, and an honor code, but it had all been arranged remotely. I hadn't been on the campus and didn't have a sense of the people in charge, beyond their being far-sighted enough to want these plans in place.

After I was passed along by his secretary, no doubt as busy as a one-armed juggler today if word of the assault had gotten out; Thompson answered. He had a deep, reassuring voice. I'm kind of a reader of voices, having spent so much time on the phone with clients, and what I was hearing was forced calm and in charge with jittery undertones of anxiety.

He had called us, but I already had a checklist of questions from other schools' situations to run, so I asked him if it was okay if I took him through it.

"Ms. Kozak, that would be perfect," he said. "We're not quite at sea here, but it is a serious situation."

"Before we start with my list, can you give me an overview of your situation? Suzanne told me what she could, but it helps to have insight into the parties involved. Oh, and has your Board of Trustees been informed?"

"They're informed. They're meeting this afternoon, which is one reason we wanted to touch base with you. I'd like to be able to go into that meeting with a management strategy. Our board chairman is new, and it would help him to have some guidance."

"I'll do my best," I said. I was watching Mason, who was screwing up his face and looking like he was about to cry. Dammit! Andre should be here so he could take a turn with the baby, and I could do some work.

Nothing I could do about that now.

"The girl is a freshman," he said. "New to the school. New to the team. A local girl, a day student, not a boarder."

"And the boys? Suzanne did say that three were allegedly involved?"

"That's what the girl says. And two of the other girls who were at the party. Oh. Sorry. Her name is Ma'Kayla Watson." He spelled it for me. "Not that it makes any difference, but she's Black. Well, mixed race."

"And the boys?"

"Two seniors and a junior. Two white, one Black."

"Their names?" I asked, pen poised.

"Randall Martinelli. The party was at his house. Aaron Short. Devon James."

"The other two. Local or boarders?"

"Boarders."

"And the girls? Local or boarders?"

"Ma'Kayla is local. The other two are boarders."

My pen poised, I asked, "The names of the other two girls?"

Silence. I wondered whether he had to look it up. Or didn't know, which would be a pretty big omission on his part. I heard papers rustle. He cleared his throat and said, "Sadie Kim and Jess Hawthorne."

"What does Ma'Kayla say happened?"

He cleared his throat. Talking about sexual assault is hard for most people. In my experience, usually harder for men. "Uh. The boys are back on campus early because there is pre-season conditioning for the football team. The girls are back for the same reason. For soccer, I mean. I guess that Randy's parents wanted to give a cookout for the team, a kind of welcome back and spirit-building event. The boys suggested that the girls' soccer team be invited. Mainly because... uh well, Randy is dating Shari Prescott, who is captain of the girls' team. Ma'Kayla says that her mother phoned Randy's mother in advance to be sure that adults would be present."

"And were they?"

There was another silence while he decided how to respond. "Uh... they were there in the early part of the evening. I mean, present and available. Then, according to Ma'Kayla and two of her teammates, Jess Hawthorne and Sadie Kim, they disappeared. The girls don't know whether they were somewhere in the house or whether they left. All they can say is that after a while there were no parents visible at the party."

"Go on."

"Ma'Kayla says that while they were eating, one of the boys, she thinks it was Aaron, brought her a Coke. It was already open, but she didn't think anything was concerning about that. She drank it, and a little while later, she began to feel odd and spacy. She couldn't find her purse, which had her phone, or she would have called her parents. Instead, she asked Jess to help her find the purse. Jess couldn't find it, either, so they used Jess's phone to call Ma'Kayla's mother to come and get her. Then Jess helped her into a bedroom to lie down."

Another throat clearing and another silence.

Even though we know this sort of thing happens all too frequently to girls and women, we don't like to think it happens at our institutions or is done by people we know. Yet it happens enough that probably in many groups of adults, there are men in the room who did it themselves but would never consider themselves rapists.

"Go on," I nudged again. I knew I didn't have much time before Mason would need my attention.

"Ma'Kayla says she must have fallen asleep because she felt someone tugging at her clothes, and that woke her. When she opened her eyes, there were three boys in the room, and they had taken off her pants and her underwear and were trying to take off her top. She said one of the boys was tugging on her top and the other two were taking pictures. She says at that point she screamed and Jess and Sadie came running in and chased the boys out. Jess says she grabbed Aaron's phone but they couldn't get Devon's."

"Who has that phone now?" I asked, hoping he would say it was the police and worried that it might have been given back to the boy.

"Campus security," he said.

From his tone, I pictured him ducking his head because he knew that the phone should be with their local police.

"Jess and Sadie got Ma'Kayla dressed, then helped her downstairs, and waited with her until her mother arrived. They told Mrs. Watson what had happened and who was involved, and then they left the party themselves. Well, I should back up. Before Ma'Kayla left, Jess stayed with her while Sadie tried to find Randy's parents, but she couldn't. Then they left. Ma'Kayla's mother gave them a ride back to campus. Each of them got phone calls later that evening their caller IDs indicated were from Randy, then from Randy's father, and then from Devon's parents and Aaron's. They didn't answer those calls. Jess says they agreed in advance that they wouldn't talk with anyone until they'd spoken with their parents and with me, so I got the calls from them that night."

"From Sadie's parents and from Jess's or from the girls themselves?"

"Their parents. I told them not to speak with the boys or their parents." He hesitated, "Or any attorney representing the boys or their families."

Good advice. But I still hadn't heard the word "police" in any of this. If this had happened on campus, I could understand his hesitation about calling in the police. But it was a sexual assault and the police needed to be involved. Since it happened off campus, it should have already been reported. Maybe the girl's parents had? But I had another question first, a question stemming from my role as an advisor protecting the school.

"What about from Ma'Kayla's parents?"

"Um... I got a call from their attorney."

"And?"

"He said he would be filing a complaint on Ma'Kayla's behalf with the local police and would be seeking a restraining order, preventing any of the boys or their families from having any contact with her, or with Jess or Sadie. Which, never mind the situation itself, is going to be a nightmare. We're a small campus. We don't have a lot of choice about which classes to place students in."

He sounded like just describing the event exhausted him. It definitely was a headmaster's nightmare, even though it had happened off campus. While the girls were boarding on campus, the school acted *in loco parentis*. And he felt he'd let them down, even if he

DEATH SENDS A MESSAGE

hadn't known about the party. And of course, two of the boys lived on campus as well. Keeping them apart would be extremely difficult.

To see if he *had*, I asked, "You reported the incident to the police as well?"

Silence. I knew it meant he hadn't. Probably figured he didn't need to because Ma'Kayla's parents already had. Technically, he might be right. Practically, he needed to be doing everything possible both to protect his students and his school's reputation. It might sound heartless, but school officials had those dual loyalties. Far too often, I've learned, instead of being proactive, putting their heads in the sand was the school's way of dealing. But there was no ducking this. Social media would see to that.

"Have you spoken with the girls?"

"With Jess and with Sadie. Ma'Kayla's parents don't want her talking with me. Even though it was her parents who let her go to the party." He sighed. "Ms. Kozak, it didn't happen on our campus or during the school year, but obviously we're involved. I just don't know what to do. That is, there are so many things to do. How do I prioritize?" He sighed again. "How do I do it right?"

Like you can't please all of the people all of the time, you can't get it all right in a situation like this. My job was to make sure the school created a record of responding in a way that best reflected on it, in conformance with the school's rules, and in a manner that demonstrated best practices in the private school world of handling sexual assault allegations. "You've called your attorney and he or she is in the loop?" I asked.

"Yes."

"Did your attorney tell you not to contact the police?"

Another silence. I thought that meant he had been advised to contact them, despite it not happening on campus. Because generally, when adults in a position of responsibility have a duty to report and don't, it looks bad. Like it or lump it, appearances are important. Those reactions become part of a school's reputation—was it a place that protected its students, in particular its female students, or

75

one that protected its football team? Getting out in front can show caring and concern.

"You need to talk to the police. They can help you craft a strategy for protecting the girls while this is investigated, especially if the department has a victim's advocate." Which made me think of something else. "Jess and Sadie are both living on campus, right?"

He said they were.

"So you should make a school counselor available to them, as well as to Ma'Kayla if she chooses. It is traumatic to find your friend unconscious and undressed and three boys taking pictures of her."

As though I had to tell him that?

I had another question before I dove into strategies for managing the situation. "As far as you know, was Ma'Kayla raped?"

He sighed again. "I don't think it got that far before her friends intervened."

"But you don't know. Did her parents take her to the doctor? Was she examined, either at the request of her parents, their attorney, or the police?"

He didn't know.

I had a lot more questions, but I could tell that Mason was about to need my attention, and he had first call on it. I quickly zipped through my initial list of advice, hoping he was taking notes, said I had to go but I would call him later, and did he want to give my name to the trustees in case they had questions?

He seemed very glad to hand their questions off to me.

I got off the phone just as Mason's fussing gave way to a wail. Still, I took a minute to pack away my feelings. An upset mother wasn't good for her baby, and that these things—these things meaning boys getting girls drunk or drugged and taking advantage of them—kept happening definitely upset me. If I weren't already too busy, and married and a mother, I could see becoming a vigilante on behalf of these girls. All the girls. Thea the Fierce and Terrible.

It was time for EDGE to draft and promote a detailed and thorough consent curriculum, starting far before students reached their teens. Luckily, our newest hire was just the woman for the job.

As Mason's cries rose to a crescendo, amazing me that such a small person could make so much noise, I picked him up. "You're going to be one of the good guys, like your daddy," I said.

ELEVEN

After Mason had been changed and fed and had dozed off, I decided to chance a shower. I didn't want Rosie and Dom to arrive and find me looking like something the cat had dragged in. A very big cat. A whole lot of dragging. The mirror said I was a fright, even though Mason stared at me with loving eyes. Or were those just curious eyes? He didn't seem to mind that I looked more like Medusa than a professional consultant. That's the problem with lots and lots of long curly hair. So much to misbehave.

I'm sure many new mothers would relate to the pleasure of an undisturbed hot shower. Quiet. Comfort. The delicious scents of body wash and shampoo. My body might still look like it belonged to someone else, but at least I could look down and see my feet, even if I did have to lean forward a little to do so. I toweled off, put on clean, soft sweats, and felt almost human.

Mason was still asleep, so I checked out the guest room—clean and ready—and tossed in another load of laundry. What did women who didn't have washing machines do? Drag all that stuff and their newborns to the laundromat?

Then, because I was learning to use every minute of sleeping baby time, I ducked into my office and made some notes for

Stonegate Academy and sent a quick message to a friend who lived near the school, asking what the local buzz was.

That done, I called Suzanne back. "Do you really have a lead on a nanny?" I asked, nearly choking on the word "nanny." I wanted to stay with Mason forever. Follow him to school, to college, to his first apartment. But I had to be realistic. We needed my income and EDGE's clients needed my expertise.

Suzanne was back at me in a flash with a name, a phone number, and a brief description of the potential nanny. The woman was late forties, a widow whose children were grown. She lived locally so she wasn't looking for a live-in position. Loved kids. Had raised six of her own. She didn't really need to work but she was restless.

She sounded pretty ideal, more like a granny than a young kid. I reached for the phone, then hesitated. Why rush? Right now, I was on leave and planned to be for the next month or two. Never mind that Stonegate Academy had gotten to me in week two. But with the current childcare nightmare that I'd been reading about, hesitation might mean I'd lose her to the dozens, if not hundreds of other new mothers or struggling parents who needed to get back to work. I reached for the phone again.

I got an answering machine and left a message, telling her who I was, how I'd heard about her, and asking if she could call me back.

At that point, the baby monitor informed me that Mason was awake and needed my attention. Still, I felt very accomplished. The laundry and I were clean and I'd gone for a couple of hours without once thinking about Addison Shirley, her missing baby, or the Faradays. Maybe there was hope for me yet.

Mason taken care of and settled in his baby wrap, I cleaned up the kitchen and made myself a cup of tea. I sipped it as I stared out the window. Wasn't it time for Dom and Rosie to arrive?

I checked the refrigerator, shifting things around to prepare for the expected onslaught of food, and went to the window again. There was a car in my driveway but it wasn't Dom's.

"No," I said aloud, walking into the hall where I couldn't be seen by someone at the door. "No. I am not accepting any visits from strangers today." Maybe never again. The car didn't belong to any of my neighbors. You live in a small town, you quickly get to know the local cars. The state police—read Andre—were handling the Faraday situation. I didn't need encyclopedias or religion or anything else some stranger might be peddling.

The doorbell rang.

I ignored it.

It rang again, a persistent buzzing like a mosquito in the bedroom in the dark.

I ignored it.

The ringing stopped and I peeked out to see who it might have been. A stocky, middle-aged woman was trudging back to her car.

Wait. What if it was Libby Frenier, my potential nanny? What if she'd decided to answer my message in person? I hurried to the door and stepped out, calling, "Sorry. I was tied up with the baby."

The woman turned and smiled, coming back toward me. "I sure know how that can be. I'm sorry if I disturbed you," she said. She had a soft, pleasing voice and a more pleasing smile. "I'm Libby, and you must be Thea."

Never mind Mason, there was something so comforting in her manner that I wanted her to take care of me. "Yes," I said, holding out a hand. "Please come in."

"You're sure this is a good time?" she said. "I don't want to disturb you. I was nearby when your partner texted me, so I thought I'd just stop in. But I know how it is in those early days. So exhausting."

"It is," I agreed. "But you're here, and Mason is quiet, so this is a good time."

"Mason?" she said. "Such a nice, strong name. Mason Kozak?"

"Lemieux, actually. His dad's last name."

We were in the kitchen now, and I invited her to sit and offered tea or coffee.

"Tea, dear, please. After noon, I try not to drink coffee. I find life stimulating enough."

There was a phrase I'd have to adopt.

"Has your friend told you about me?" She smiled. "Not that

there's much to tell. I've led a pretty quiet life. I meant about my experience with children."

I nodded. "She has."

"I know it's pretty early times yet, but do you have an idea what you'll be looking for?"

I didn't. I hadn't planned to look for a nanny quite so soon. But as Suzanne reminded me, parents were desperate for daycare. I thought about my work schedule, and Andre's. Both pretty crazy. I should jump if I had the chance at someone good.

"It's... uh... I haven't really given it much thought. I mean, Mason's only a week old. But the truth is, our schedules, both my husband's and mine, are somewhat irregular. Until Mason, we both worked far too much. We're trying to fix that, but it's hard. He's... uh... maybe Suzanne told you? He's a detective with the Maine state police and I'm a consultant to private schools. I work with Suzanne. We're partners at Edge Consulting."

I stopped, because I really didn't seem to be answering her question. "I guess the short answer is that we'll need someone who can be a bit flexible rather than a straight nine-to-five."

Libby Frenier smiled. "I don't see that as a problem, dear. I'm a widow and my children are grown, so I'm as free as a bird. Not..." She smiled again. "Not that I mean to suggest I'm flighty."

We both laughed at that and in response, Mason began to make his little noises. I popped him out of his wrap and put him on my shoulder. When he'd calmed, she held out her hands.

"May I?" she asked.

Feeling the trepidation I always felt when someone wanted to hold him—greater, perhaps, because of Addison Shirley's stolen child—I handed him over. This would be a test for all three of us. For me, to see if I could let go, for Mason, to see if he found her a calming presence, and for Libby, to see if she truly was comfortable with him.

I kept breathing. Mason calmed. And Libby lit up as she held him.

Just what I wanted. A calming presence prepared to adore my son.

There were probably a zillion questions I should be asking her and I, a skilled interviewer, couldn't think of a single one.

My electric kettle—an essential for someone who gets lost in work—turned itself off and I fixed tea, set out the mugs and a plate of cookies, and sat back down. I'd finally thought of a question.

"Where do you live?" I asked. If we weren't to have a live-in nanny, we'd need someone who could get here even in the winter.

"Near Freeport," she said. She named a town I hadn't heard of, but then, I'm a relative newcomer to Maine. "But if you're worrying about winter, don't. I've got all-wheel drive and been driving these roads for more than forty years."

"Freeport?" Before I could stop myself, I asked whether she'd heard about the disappearance of Addison Shirley's baby. I'm not a blurter. Maybe my lack of sleep was dulling my natural caution?

"Terrible," she said. "Poor Addison. Growing up in that family can't have been easy, and since then she's made some very bad choices."

Maybe I *was* a blurter, since my next question was, "What bad choices?" I couldn't help thinking she might know something useful about the situation. Useful to Andre and to finding a missing baby, information that, given people's wariness, might not come easily to the police. "You mean having a relationship with James Faraday?"

She shook her head. "Relationship? From all I hear, despite his first wife, Rebecca, who was a lovely person, and Lucia, who's so fierce people thought she'd finally put him on the straight and narrow, Faraday doesn't so much have relationships as serial addictions. He's the same with women as he is with everything else in his life—cars, real estate, business deals—he's attracted to something and he has to have it, won't let anything get in his way, then too often loses interest."

She took a sip of her tea and I thought she was done, but there was more. "People do like to gossip about the wealthy. But he gives them plenty of reasons. He's left such a trail of destruction in his wake. Broken promises. Unfinished projects. Unpaid vendors. He's so charming, see. The man can pretty much talk someone into believing him despite all the evidence that he's a liar and a cheat.

Seems like both men and women are susceptible to his charms. And the people who run the town seem to be, too, when they should know better."

Wow. A virtual flood of information. Now I was torn. I wanted her to keep talking, because her information was useful. On the other hand, I didn't want a nanny in our house who would gossip freely. Not with Andre's job, or with mine. Nor was I entirely comfortable with how freely she was sharing with me. Was it simply friendly gossip or did she have another agenda?

As if she'd read my mind, she said, "I'm sorry. You're going to think I'm a terrible gossip and really, I'm not. But you know your name was in the paper in connection with that awful business about Addison's baby, so I thought you might be interested. Are you and Addison friends?"

There was a question in her expression, as though she couldn't believe that we would be, but wanted to check.

I was focused not on her question about Addison Shirley but on what she'd just said. Why would my name be in the paper when I was so tangentially involved? Only a few minutes while I responded to the girl's hysteria and found her someone to help. There was only one way that could have happened—that blabbermouth Jeremy Bartlett.

Instead of asking a follow-up question like a good detective, I said, "I didn't know my name was in the paper. It shouldn't have been. I only saw Addison Shirley for a few brief minutes. She was screaming. I flagged down the police to help her. I didn't even know her name."

She looked relieved, as though my knowing Addison Shirley would have been a negative character reference. "I'm sure that's true, dear, but Jeremy Bartlett, he's one of the Freeport cops, has a big mouth. He went to school with my third son. Always a suck up and a talker. I'm a bit surprised they let him on the police, although I understand departments are pretty desperate these days."

Switching gears, she said, "I hope reporters haven't been bothering you?"

"Thankfully, they have not."

We were too new at this address for there to be much on the internet, and neither EDGE nor the state police would give out information about us. It was concerning, though, that Jeremy Bartlett knew our address and didn't know how to keep his mouth shut. Who knew who he'd been talking to and how freely he'd spoken. Or might speak.

Libby Frenier shook her head. "So you and Addison are not friends? Because the paper made it sound like her friend, Thea Kozak, called the police for her. Like the two of you were together on an outing with your babies."

Since I'd already told her I didn't know the girl, I wondered why she was pursuing this. Maybe just curiosity? Maybe because despite what I'd said, she thought the fact that my name was linked in the paper to Addison's was significant and I wasn't telling the truth? I sighed, trying not to sound too irritable as I said, "We are not friends. I've never really met her. I don't know anything about her. I was just passing by. There was only that moment when I came out of a store where I'd been buying a hat for Mason and found her there screaming that her baby had been kidnapped. I stopped to see if I could help, realized the situation was beyond me, and handed her over to the police. It was nothing that should have gotten me mentioned."

I hesitated. I should have stopped this conversation right there. But one of my flaws is my need to know. If this woman knew Addison or some of the other players, if she knew something useful, I wanted to hear it. No matter how much I claimed I was not involved, the situation had already come to my doorstep when Andre was called out. Or before that, when that idiot Bartlett knocked on the door. Probably Andre would learn anything he needed to know from the Freeport police, but I was curious and she was right here.

"It was a very brief conversation," I reiterated. "But that girl is in an awful situation. Does Addison have any family to turn to? Or close friends, if you know?"

She shook her head. "Dad's gone. Mom's a drunk. She's got a brother, but he's up in Warren at the prison. And a sister, much older, about the same age as my oldest son. Where Addison is flighty, though, her sister April is quiet and domestic. As for girl-friends? I doubt it. You know how some girls are, all their focus on boys? No time for other girls? Addison's like that."

"Under the circumstances, wouldn't she go to her sister's?"

"April and Addison have never gotten along. Too many years apart, I'm afraid, and of such different temperaments." She shook her head again, solemnly, like she was delivering sad news to someone who cared. "Even though April stayed in town."

The idea that such a young woman, new mother, and probably battered as well had no one to go to was sad. I wondered if there were others who might look after her. Co-workers, for example, or a caring supervisor. I've spent too much of my working life asking questions, I guess, because instead of shutting this down, I persisted. "Do you know if she was working somewhere? If she might have friends there or someone she could turn to?"

"I heard she was waitressing at one of those restaurants in Freeport, but I don't recall which one. I could find out if you'd like?"

But I didn't want to ask her to dig further, because I was trying to distance myself from the matter. I didn't "like" knowing anything about Addison Shirley and I'd shown too much interest already Yet I found myself asking, "Do you know Addison well?"

She shook her head. "Not really. Only that she's from my town, you see, and you know how small towns are about gossip."

I didn't, really, though I was definitely learning. But this woman had no way of knowing I'd grown up in a large suburban town outside Boston, too big for people to mind other people's business outside of neighborhoods or groups and anyway, growing up around all those professional parents, everyone had been working so hard there hadn't been much room for gossip. Unless it had all been there and I'd just missed it. When you're a kid and a teen, your world doesn't extend much beyond your peer group, and I'd been gone from there for a long time.

Before I left the subject, though, I asked, "After she said that her baby had been taken, she said that 'he' was going to kill her now that she'd lost his baby. And she was visibly bruised. But I have no idea who the 'he' she referred to is. Unless it was Faraday."

Libby shook her head. "Oh, that was probably Benjy Goodman. They were living together. At least, that's what I heard. And Benjy is one of those awful men who believe that women exist to be their punching bags. Property and punching bags. It's so ugly. Faraday might be selfish and verbally abusive, what I guess I'd call casually cruel? He's just an indulgent, self-involved type, thinks he's the center of the universe and other people don't matter. But Benjy? He's different. He's a monster. I should know. The Goodmans lived next door to us for a few years, and even back when he was teenager, Benjy was a brute. I really had to work hard to keep my oldest son, Josh, from hanging out with him. Because you know—girls were attracted to Benjy so guys who hung around with him figured they'd get the..." She hesitated. "The rejects? An ugly thing to say, but teenage boys can be ugly."

She gave a sad shake of her head. "I don't know why young girls are attracted to boys and men like him. I practically had to lock my daughter Charlotte in her room when Benjy had his eye on her, until she saw what happened to her friend Sally, who did go out with him. Charlotte's my oldest, and she is level headed. After she saw her friend Sally all beat up, her self-esteem and trust in men shot to hell, Charlotte understood why I was against her dating Benjy. Thing is, Benjy is too good-looking, with the kind of bad boy looks that young girls can't resist. He's got those lazy Elvis eyes and a mop of curly hair. It never worked on me when I was young, but it seems like some girls can't resist outlaws."

Libby was right about that, about good girls attracted to bad boys. I'd had a run-in with an outlaw once. My sister Carrie's ex-boyfriend. He'd gone from teenage thug to violent monster and used that violence against me. It must have showed on my face because she patted my arm. "I know. They're scary, aren't they, men like that? We all thought we were done with Benjy when he moved away, but he's been back maybe a year and a half now. I don't know anything for certain, but I've heard whispers that he was abusive to Addison. Also that drugs might be involved. That he was selling them, maybe making her sell them for him? I guess he figured if the cops stopped Addison, she'd just bat those big blue eyes and they'd let her go."

I thought about the girl I'd seen. So young and pretty and fragile. Being mean to her would be like mistreating a kitten. And yet someone definitely had been.

She paused. "I don't know how long you've lived here. Maybe you're even a native. But you do know that Maine has a dark side, right? It's not all lobster rolls, crashing surf, and pointed firs."

That kind of annoyed me, and I didn't want to be annoyed with her. I said, "I've lived here a few years, and Andre is a native. And a state police detective, as I mentioned." Which ought to make it very clear that I knew plenty about Maine's dark side without going into my own adventures with some of Maine's violence-prone denizens. I don't like to talk about it. It brings up too many bad memories.

"Did people know that Addison was pregnant?"

She nodded. "Everyone assumed it was Benjy's. Do you think the police are considering Benjy as a suspect? Because they should. If Benjy thinks that baby is his, well, anything that he thinks belongs to him, he's going to have it and nothing stops him."

If I'd been worried about how I might help with the missing baby and Lucia Faraday's death despite the constraints of new motherhood, I shouldn't have. It seemed that I could just sit here in my kitchen and strangers, like retrievers, would bring me information. The more critical question was did I want it? Wasn't I supposed to have sworn off sticking my nose in dangerous business? Didn't Mason deserve a careful mother and a crime-free home? Ha! To provide that, I'd have to lock Andre in the barn.

Except for being separated from us, though, it wouldn't be much of a punishment. He'd built a wonderful workshop out there that was almost as tempting as I. As for me, I'd vowed to reform, and yet the mere act of going out to buy a baby hat had landed me in the midst of a bad situation. Was it possible that I was a trouble magnet and it would be drawn to me no matter what I did?

My question was out before I even thought about it. "Do you

really think he would have taken Addison's baby? Just snatched it off a public street?"

So much for moving away from the subject.

"If he thought it was his and she was keeping it from him?" Libby Frenier said. "Certainly, though he has no more idea of how to care for a baby than a tomcat would. But being Benjy, he's probably already got another girlfriend and he'll expect her to do it. He did have a girlfriend, a few years back, who had his baby. But then that baby disappeared. I don't know whether he made her put it up for adoption or what. Funny..." She shook her head. "When I say Benjy would want what's his, maybe a better way to put it is that Benjy gets to decide."

She put a hand to her mouth. "Oh, dear. Now I've upset you, haven't I? I only thought that since you were involved, even if, as you say, it was only in such a brief manner, that you should know some background. Especially as your name was linked to hers in the paper as a friend. Because if Benjy doesn't have the baby, he might think you do. Of course, the Freeport police ought to know all this. Should have already checked Benjy out, I'd think. I mean we're practically right next door and I'd imagine the local police departments would talk to each other."

She cocked her head and looked at me. "Right?" Then, as if noticing where we were for the first time, she glanced out the window. "You're pretty isolated here, aren't you?"

I think my heart stopped when she said that. It was a creepy thing to say. Was she trying to scare me or just someone without a filter? Was it only moments ago that I thought she was reassuring?

Refusing to be wound up, I said, "Not really. I've got good neighbors on both sides, you just don't see their houses."

There was an empty house across the street. A shabby rental at the best of times, recently it had been the site of two homicides. That does put a damper on a place's attraction. I didn't mention that, though. She didn't seem like the type to scare easily, but I didn't want to chance it. Never mind that I didn't want to discuss it. As part of creating a peaceful environment for Mason, I'm trying to avoid thinking about the crimes I've been involved with.

I said, "Plus this is a small town, and you know how they are. People mind each other's business." Like they seemed to do in her town.

"Ah. That's comforting then," she said. "Good neighbors are so important."

Switching gears, she said, "Did you have other questions for me? Obviously, I have plenty of experience with infants, and I'm very flexible about how they are raised. That is, I am happy to abide by your rules and your schedules. I should warn you though, that I might sometimes disagree."

She looked down at her lap like she was embarrassed. "I... uh... Let me explain. I tried it out with another woman recently. But she was so rigid about schedules and rules. The baby must do this at exactly this hour and must eat only this and that." She sighed. "I felt so sorry for that poor baby. No space to play or explore, if that wasn't on the schedule. The baby had to nap when the schedule said nap. And if the poor child hated what she'd decided I had to feed it? Well, too bad. Her, I mean. The baby was a little girl. Clara. A sweet, old-fashion name. Mother was determined that the child learn discipline early."

She looked at me, her eyebrows raised. "Clara was only seven months old. I've raised six of my own, and I know how different they can be. Sure, you have to have rules, but you also need to be flexible about meeting the child where they are. I have to tell you, I wanted to stay and protect the little sweetheart but I got too depressed."

She shook her head, looking to me to share her disbelief. "I'm not a quitter but that job? If I was a minute late doing anything, the mother, who worked at home, would yell at me. Yell at the person she'd trusted to care for her child? In front of the child? Can you believe it? How could that possibly be a good thing?"

She nuzzled Mason's soft head with her chin. "Babies don't do well around yelling, and neither do I. So I quit. Almost broke my heart, though, leaving that poor little child behind. No one who isn't desperate will stay in a situation like that, and a constant stream of different caregivers isn't good for a child. Knowing that mother, though, she'll never see it's her fault. She'll blame them for not sticking to the job."

Her gossipy style had had me worried, but this story was a comfort. She might be a bit chatty, but she knew kids. Loved kids. And understood that it was important to learn how they were, not just to impose adult will upon them. "I'd like you to start in three weeks," I said, feeling my heart jump and tears start as I said it. "Slowly at first, as you ease into life with Mason and I ease back into a part-time work schedule. Would that work for you?"

"That would be fine," she said, nodding. "And you know. If you just need a few hours here and there, I can do that, too, while you adjust. Ease you into it? Maybe we should start with that? A morning next week. Maybe twice the week after that? You don't even need to leave home. You could take a long bath or go for a walk, run errands, or sort baby things. Whatever needs doing without interruption."

She was still holding Mason. Now she patted his back. "And don't you worry, Thea. However well this little fellow and I get along, you'll always come first. Babies know. Trust me."

That brought full-blown tears. Those damned hormones again. Why did I always have to get my mothering from friends and strangers? Which made me think of Addison Shirley, who might have no one to mother her. No available family in the picture and an abusive boyfriend? She'd probably needed that ice cream cone badly. True, the girl had been snappish when I offered to help, but people under stress are often not their best selves. She was young. Abused. Coping with the demands of an infant and possibly two different men.

Dammit! I did *not* want that girl in my head like this.

Libby handed me Mason and then a tissue. Just what I needed.

"I'll be off then," she said. "You've got my number, so call me any time if you need me. Or if you need to talk to an experienced mother. Not..." She held up a hand. "Not that I want to step on any toes. I expect your mother is there for you. But just in case. It can be so overwhelming at first."

She bustled away before I could say that my mother hadn't even been to see him yet. However much it hurt, that was between me and her.

I settled Mason in his little chair and turned on the flying airplanes. By the time I'd mopped my eyes and reviewed what I had to remember to tell Andre, Dom and Rosie had turned into the driveway.

TWELVE

I t was like a food Christmas as they headed toward the house, her arms laden with tinfoil trays, and Dom lugging a cooler that looked almost as big as he was. Since Andre and I love to eat, gifts of food are always the best. Back when we'd first met, when Andre was investigating my sister Carrie's death, we had hated each other at first sight. Our animosity slowly faded as he insisted on cooking a meal for me as I was trying to clean out her apartment, overcome with memories and guilt that I hadn't been there for Carrie, and under pressure from a mean and miserable landlady.

Andre had backed that old witch down with only a few words and his tough cop's look, and over steak and hot bread, we'd reached a détente and then a slow-burning attraction. We'd fought plenty during the years since. Probably would in the years ahead. But food always seemed to help bring us together. I pressed down another stab of regret that my mother—an excellent cook—couldn't be bothered to visit or feed me. I needed to appreciate my good luck in having Dom and Rosie instead.

They took a moment to park their burdens and then smothered me in a dual embrace. Rosie broke off first, going straight to the little chair and gathering Mason into her arms. "Oh, baby!" she cooed. "My first godchild. Come and tell your Rosie all about your-self." She and Mason disappeared into the living room.

"I drove as fast as I could," Dom said, releasing me. "But I have never seen her so impatient." He gave me his laser-eyed cop's scru-tiny. "You doin' okay?" Followed by, "Where's Andre? Called back already? I thought he was taking some leave."

I hardly needed to speak. He already knew, or could guess, most of what I could tell him. Except about Addison Shirley and how her situation was disrupting mine. He'd know that soon enough. I've never been able to keep anything from him. It was something he'd instinctively known when he recruited me to help him sort out the mess when my college roommate Eve Paris's mother Helene was killed. Like Andre, Dom could read people. Seemed to be able to sense good or bad without a word. It was scary, even though some-times I thought a little of it was rubbing off on me.

You can't live with cops without being changed.

"Your mother seen him yet?" he asked. I was sure he already knew the answer. He's my biggest champion when it comes to my family. He didn't ask about my father, because my father, when he isn't being a dynamic and successful lawyer, does what my mother wants. Close as we once were, he wouldn't think to visit on his own.

I shook my head.

He shrugged. "Her loss."

I nodded. "But I feel it."

"Good thing you've got Rosie."

From the living room, we could hear her crooning to the baby. I imagined Mason's wise dark eyes staring up at her.

"They're bonding," Dom said. "Let's leave them to it. You gonna offer a tired old cop some coffee?"

"Sorry. Of course. I don't seem to have much focus these days." As I headed toward the coffee pot, I added, "You may be tired, but you definitely aren't old."

"What does Indiana Jones say? It's not the years, it's the mileage?"

I laughed at him. He still played pickup basketball twice a week and went running on the other days.

"Tell you what," he said, looking around the cooler and the bags of food. "I'll make the coffee, and you can find someplace to put all this food Rosie brought. I told her it was too much, but when it comes to food and my wife, too much is never going to be enough. She worries that you'll starve up here in the Maine wilderness."

Our "wilderness" was about twenty minutes from Portland, with ready access to Trader Joe's and Whole Foods and great restaurants. True, we lived in a small town, and the house came with a couple of acres, but it was hardly wilderness.

When the food was stowed and the rich scent of fresh coffee filled the room, we sat at the table to catch up. "So what's up?" he said. "You managed to get yourself entangled in anything despite being home with the baby?"

Against my will, I thought. Reluctantly, I nodded.

"You are such a trouble magnet."

What I'd thought about myself. "I don't see how I can avoid it unless I never try to help anyone again."

He put his big, warm hand over mine. "Tell me about it."

If Libby Frenier had left me worrying that bad boy Benjy Goodman might show up here looking for his baby, having my second favorite cop around helped send those worries packing.

He was ready for anything I wanted to tell him, but I was torn between just letting him think I was basking in new motherhood or telling him about Addison Shirley and her missing baby. The murdered Lucia Faraday and her missing husband. Or I could tell him about Ma'Kayla Watson and get his take on what the local police might do. As a diversion, I could ask him what he'd been up to, except he'd know what I was trying to do.

Why did I have to spend my life with cops instead of people I could actually lie to or deflect?

Deciding to start with Ma'Kayla, maybe because that was farthest away geographically and emotionally, I told him about my client school and the issues. While the event had taken place off campus, and charges were a matter for the local police, most of those involved were juveniles living on campus and participating in school-run athletic programs. I described the headmaster, who was either a bit clueless or too overwhelmed by what he had to deal with to think clearly. After I gave a quick outline, I started with my questions.

"Will the local cops need a warrant for that phone? The one that Jess took?" I asked. "Or will they have to give it back to the owner?"

Before he could answer, I backed up. "Why would those boys do something like that? Am I ridiculously naïve to be shocked?"

"You naïve?" He laughed. "I doubt that. But yes, it is shocking, and yet the statistics on how many girls and women are assaulted every year—that's what's shocking. Ma'Kayla was lucky in one respect: she had good friends there who acted fast to protect her. Too often, the friends have disappeared when a girl needs help. Grabbing that phone was pretty brilliant. If she hadn't, in a matter of moments, once the boys knew they'd been caught, whatever was on it might have been erased. Still could be erased remotely, if someone knew how. Or shared with their friends. Knowing there were witnesses might deter that."

I wondered if Ma'Kayla's friends had been able to send the photos to themselves to preserve them as evidence? They'd been quick enough to grab the phone, so maybe they had. Teens today are so much more tech-savvy than I will ever be.

He considered my question, rubbing his chin as he thought. "How the local police will handle it will depend on how good they are. How well trained. On their culture and how seriously they take it. Whether they're a department that still hangs on to an outdated 'boys will be boys' philosophy despite all the training we now get."

He hesitated, then said, "Also, how much influence the boy's family might have, and yes, Thea, however much we wish it weren't true, we both know that still makes a difference."

He sipped his coffee, staring thoughtfully into space until, turning to me, he said, "You don't need this right now. There must be someone else at EDGE who can handle this."

"Slave of duty," I said weakly. "It's part of my job." Then, because he was still giving me his paternal look, I said, "I am trying to hand it off to Suzanne. Honest, I am."

He smiled. Dom has a great smile. He can look pretty fierce when he wants to, but when he wants to be reassuring, no one is better. Not even Andre. "We're going to practice something," he said. "Now, repeat after me. No."

"No." I tried not to laugh as I said it.

"No. Sorry. I'm not available right now."

"No. Sorry. I'm not available right now," I repeated.

"I wish I could help, but I'm afraid you're going to have to find someone else."

"I wish I could help." I was laughing so hard I almost couldn't get the words out. "But I'm afraid you're going to have to find someone else."

"I'm happy to help you with that," he said.

I got as far as "I'm happy..." and cracked up.

From the doorway, Rosie said, "Dom, you think it will work this time?"

He shook his head and held out his big hands for the baby.

Reluctantly, Rosie gave him up to his godfather and headed for the coffee pot. "Where's Andre?" she asked. "Isn't he on paternity leave?"

"He made it through six whole days," I said, trying not to sound whiny. "No. Seven."

As if summoning spirits from the vasty deep, there was the crunch of tires on the driveway, and Andre's car flew up and rocked to a stop. He really likes to do that, to zoom up the driveway. It's the kid in him. Unless it's the cop. I'm half surprised he doesn't do lights and sirens. Well, not sirens. Not now that we have Mason.

"Making up for lost time?" Dom said.

"He's trying. Maybe you should try your 'saying no' exercise with him."

Dom grinned but stayed silent. There's his loyalty to me, and then there's his loyalty to the cop brotherhood.

The door opened and Andre came in, immediately engulfing Rosie in a hug. With two big men there, my pretty kitchen, with its tall, glass-fronted cabinets, suddenly seemed small.

"Do I smell coffee?" he asked over Rosie's head.

Soon, all four of us were at the table, drinking coffee and eating a delicious almond cake Rosie had brought. Mason was now in the crook of Andre's arm, looking content. Maybe one of me wasn't enough. Maybe the kid needed a retinue. Bread and circuses. An ensemble of doting people to wait on him. If so, he was in for a lifetime of disappointment. I've been longing for domestic staff for years.

Since I needed to share what I'd learned from Libby Frenier with Andre, in case the local police hadn't, I brought Dom and Rosie up to speed about Addison Shirley and her missing baby. I got a lot of clucking disapproval and shaking heads.

"All I did was try to buy Mason a hat," I protested. I was not having the people closest to me joining the chorus of disapproval and disbelief.

"So, this Libby Frenier," Andre said. "You met her how?"

"Suzanne sent her. She's a prospective nanny."

"Sounds awfully gossipy," he said. "Last thing we need around here is someone with a big mouth."

True, but he had no idea how hard childcare was to find. "She's raised six children," I said. "She's great with Mason." It was also true that I had some niggling doubts of my own. "It's just a trial. A half day here or there so I can get some work done."

"You're on maternity leave," he said.

I graciously refrained from comment, instead, sharing what Libby had told me about Addison Shirley's relationship with a thug named Benjy Goodman, and how, in Libby's opinion, he'd be very likely to steal the baby or commit violence to get the baby if he thought the baby was his.

"He's been mentioned," Andre said. "Kinda like Faraday, he's being very difficult to find."

"Did the search around Lucia Faraday's car turn up anything new?" I asked.

He shook his head. "Nothing at the scene. We've towed her car to the lab to go over it."

"Something else Libby Frenier said. Something that really concerns me," I said.

Andre and Dom leaned forward, so much in sync, it was almost comical, though nothing about a murdered woman and a missing baby should be comical.

"She said that my name was in the news stories about the missing baby. That the story referred to me as Addison's friend and suggested we were meeting when the incident occurred."

Even as I said it, I wondered if Andre already knew and hadn't mentioned it because he knew it would upset me.

"That idiot Bartlett again," he said. "Gets in the spotlight and shoots off his mouth even though he doesn't know anything. They've come down on him hard now, but not before he shared way too much with the wrong people. If he was one of mine, he'd be back on the turnpike on the late shift."

He shook his head angrily. "I was hoping you wouldn't hear about that."

"Well, I have, and now I'm wondering whether some thug, like this guy Benjy Goodman, is going to show up on my doorstep looking for his kid—assuming he doesn't already have it—because I'm linked with Addison Shirley. I'm worried that Mason might be at risk."

I could see Andre's hands reflexively tighten around the baby. He forced himself to relax.

The thing was, I had had enough of bad guys showing up on my doorstep. Bad guys. Lost girls. Intrusive relatives. Intrusive cops. Some people might want to build a wall along the Mexican border. I was seriously considering building a wall around my property. A wall. Or a moat. And getting a couple of big, mean dogs. Dogs that would be Mason's best friends, and always ready to get between him and strangers. A boy should have a dog, right?

I asked Andre, "Do you think we should get a dog?"

The guys exchanged glances. Maybe part of cop bonding was a sense of the ironic when it came to the "little women."

Rosie put a hand on Dom's arm. "She just wants to be safe," she said.

"Do you want a dog?" he asked Rosie. "Did you?"

"Never needed one. But we didn't live way out in the country like this." She tipped her head and said, in a teasing voice, "Maybe now I'd like a dog. They're good company."

"This is delicious cake, by the way," I said, trying to change the subject. "You'll have to give me the recipe."

Never mind what I was trying to do, Mason had decided that all the attention should be on him. He began his fussy little "wanna eat" cry, the one that would escalate to a loud and shrill if it was ignored. I took him from Andre. "You guys go ahead and bond. Rosie and I are going upstairs to feed and change this mite."

Dom grinned, and Rosie popped up, following me up the stairs with a huge smile.

"He's so adorable," she said. "I'd forgotten how tiny they are in the beginning."

"Not much bigger than a roasting chicken, Andre says."

"That's not very nice."

"He's gobsmacked, Rosie. Over the moon. I don't care what silly things he says. All I have to do is see him looking at Mason."

"Dom was like that. Before the kids he was... well, you know. Pretty good at playing the tough guy, and believing it. Isabella arrives and wham! It really changed him. Then Angelo finished the job."

I settled in the rocker and she perched on the edge of the daybed. "So, this woman, Libby Frenier, who might make a good nanny. You have doubts, don't you?"

"Wouldn't anyone?"

"Of course, but I'm sensing something specific. Is it because, as Andre observed, she's too gossipy?"

"I don't know."

Which was true. It was always hard to describe a sense, an intuition. "It's just. You know. At first, I liked her so much that I wanted her to come and take care of me. Which I don't need, since I have you. And Dom. And then she seemed so easy to talk to. But then it was, I don't know... I got this almost eerie sense that she could read me too easily. That's part of it. But I can't really describe it. It may just be that I'm not ready for anything... anyone... who might come between me and Mason. I guess I never... before he was born, I always thought that I'd be a decent mother. That I'd love him, of course. But the intensity of it. It's just amazing."

I thought about it. "You know, it's funny I should say that, that I should feel so protective, so possessive about him, at the same time that I'm really upset that my mother won't trouble herself to come and visit. How can she not want to see him?"

"You know that your feelings don't have to be logical, don't you?" Rosie said. "This is a very emotional time. After all the struggles you've had with your mother, when you think you've reached a point where you've gotten over some of that and drawn closer, of course it's painful when she won't do important maternal things like visiting you and your first child. You shouldn't have to tell her that you need her. She should know."

Having Rosie on my side made everything better. I burped Mason and settled him to nursing again. From downstairs, I could hear Andre's raised voice. He was on the phone with someone, and if I were a betting sort, which I am not, I'd bet it had something to do with that idiot Jeremy Bartlett giving my name to the paper. I'd spoken to her for only a few moments, then flagged down a cop to help her. How did that make me part of the story? Maybe that's why no one else stopped to help, why people didn't want to get involved. Because there was too much hassle involved.

But who could have expected a blabbermouth like Bartlett?

Now I was thinking about something else. Wondering whether the man I'd seen in the car watching Addison Shirley might have been Benjy Goodman. That had me wondering whether I could find a photo of him somewhere. My ponderings were interrupted by Rosie.

"Thea! You should see the look on your face."

"What look?"

"The 'I'm gonna track that guy down and read him the riot act' look. Aren't you supposed to stay calm and tranquil for Mason?"

I definitely did not have a poker player's face.

"Sorry. I was thinking about Andre's case, and the man I told him about, the one that Libby Frenier mentioned."

"Well, put him out of your mind," she ordered.

"Yes, ma'am," I said.

She smiled and put a hand on my arm. "I don't mean to be critical. You know that. But these last few years... I think you've had enough. I think it's time to just be happy and domestic and enjoy these early days with your baby. You'll be back at work and in the thick of things soon enough."

Rosie was right. For now, I'd try to take her advice. But I knew that sooner or later, I'd find a quiet moment and do an internet search for Goodman.

THIRTEEN

We left Mason, fed, changed, and asleep, the baby monitor set to alert us to his every sound, and went back downstairs. Andre was on his phone, and Dom was bent over the screen of his, both obviously deep into something. Since they didn't need us, I took a basket, and Rosie and I went out to the garden to see what late summer produce we could find for a salad.

This was the first summer Andre and I planted a garden, just as this was our first house, and we found ourselves becoming awfully domestic. Unless it was agricultural. I had gotten a slew of advice from the old guys down at Agway. I was there so often they'd become like a couple of doting old uncles, full of advice about my garden, including where to get a truckload of manure. Over the years, I've gotten many truckloads of manure from my clients, but that was verbal. This was the real thing.

While I was dropping a fortune at Agway, Andre's dad and cousin had built me a series of raised beds for my vegetables and flowers. Then they'd had to build a fence to protect said veggies and flowers, since a doting mama deer and her adorable fawn had decided I was gardening just for them. Once we'd gotten that sorted, I'd had pretty good luck for a beginner.

Rosie and I harvested cucumbers, tomatoes of all sizes and colors, a few summer squash, and some lettuce. I'd replanted spinach and it seemed to be coming along well. Until this adventure, I hadn't known there were crops that liked cold weather and those that liked it hot. I also hadn't known about the myriad types of insects that wanted to eat my garden before I did. I was trying to stay organic, but there had been days when tomato hornworms, potato bugs, and something small and black that was making lace out of my broccoli and cauliflower leaves made me want to hit them with a ton of toxic chemicals. I'd had to remind myself that the ultimate goal was to grow food, and we didn't want to consume poison with every bite.

"I always wanted a garden like this," Rosie said. "But our lot is dark and the soil isn't good, and it seems like every critter in the world showed up whenever I tried. I've settled for flowers, and only a few of those." She surveyed my garden. "How do you find time for this?"

"A bit here and a bit there. It's very therapeutic. You know that Mason was... is... an acrobat. He used to kick me a lot, but he always calmed down when we were gardening. So, therapy for both of us."

"You think the guys are done with their project?" she wondered.

"Let's go see."

"I used to try and make Dom check his work at the door." She sighed. "But you know, they aren't like that, and the work doesn't lend itself to be left behind. When the kids were little, he tried hard, but he used to spend so much time whispering in the little half bath under the stairs that the kids wanted to know what daddy was up to. In the end, we had to be pretty open with them about what his work was and why he didn't talk about it in front of them."

"Something else to look forward to." If my kid was like me, he wouldn't miss much.

In the kitchen, we put our baskets by the sink and washed the produce. The guys must have gone somewhere else, because the room was empty. It must have been recent, since Dom's phone was on the table and when I bent to look at the screen, I saw a photo of a man. Being me—too curious for my own good—I picked it up and studied the picture.

"This is him!" I said. "This is the man who was sitting in the car, watching Addison Shirley."

Rosie gave me a "what are you talking about?" look, but I must have been loud, because Andre and Dom reappeared like a genie had conjured them up.

Andre looked at me, then at Dom's phone. "What did you just say?"

I held out the phone to him. "I said that this man in the picture on Dom's phone is the one I saw sitting in a parked car in Freeport the other day, watching Addison Shirley. Who is he?"

Andre shook his head, managing to look both pleased and sad. "You want to think you're not involved, and I certainly don't like your name in the paper, but..." He hesitated, then said, "This is Benjy Goodman. And..." Another hesitation, then, "You're the only person who can connect him with Addison Shirley at the time and place where her baby disappeared."

"Dammit!" I said, because I'm so articulate. Because I was at home with my dear friends and my new baby and I didn't want the outside world, especially the world of crime, intruding. It seemed to me that trouble came in just as easily as the vegetables from my garden.

Don took his phone and studied the picture. Then he enlarged it and held it out to me. "You're sure this is the man you saw?"

I thought back to the man in the car, a large, good-looking man with overlong curly dark hair. The khaki shirt that looked like a uniform. Firm jaw. Full mouth. Cultivated beard stubble. His gaze fixed on the bruised blonde girl in the summery blue dress. Sunglasses had covered his eyes, but his posture was that of a predator watching its prey. "I'm sure."

My phone rang, and the ID said it was Barron Thompson. "Have to take this," I said, and went into my office alcove to answer.

"You were going to call me," he said, without bothering with "Hello."

Sorry, but trying to guilt me wasn't going to work. "How did things go with your trustees?" I countered.

"Okay. For now. They're discussing it among themselves and will be getting back to me with their questions."

"You told them they were welcome to call me?"

Instead of answering, he said, "We really need you here at the school, Ms. Kozak. With the students coming back, we'll need your expertise to help us keep things calm on campus."

Well, that wasn't happening. "When do classes start?"

"Next week."

"You're not in the board meeting?" I asked. "Why is that?"

"They wanted to meet on their own." He didn't try to hide the resentment in his voice.

A red flag fell on the field. One important aspect of handling a sexual harassment or assault issue involving students was that the Board chair and the Head of School needed to be in sync about how the situation was to be handled. There were numerous important issues that arose from such a situation and a lot of critical decisions to be made. Among them: Deciding whether a sexual misconduct investigation was necessary under the school's rules. Deciding how the school would handle communications and managing the concerns of the student and parent community. Deciding how the victim or victims would be supported. Deciding how they would work with legal counsel and, if one was brought in, with a professional sexual misconduct investigator. Deciding whether steps needed to be taken to ensure that the victim and alleged perpetrators weren't in contact.

Depending on the school's rules and honor code, one immediate consideration was whether an accused perpetrator should be suspended. Following that, depending on what their investigator learned or the course the police investigation took, there was the very serious and difficult question of whether one or all of the perpetrators—alleged perpetrators—should be expelled.

It was a lot, and all of it needed the trustees and the head of school to be on the same page and to work together. Far too often,

I'd seen board members get lobbied or swayed by donor parents, often donor parents whose sons or daughters were involved.

"You need to stay in the loop," I told him. "It's critical that they don't make decisions without your input, just as you don't make major decisions without theirs." I didn't know anything about his relationship with his board, so I asked him straight out. "Do you and the Board chair get along?"

He sighed. "The Board chair is new, and my impression, based on our interactions so far, is that he believes he's the decision-maker and I'm his flunky. He's on the young side, an alum, of course, and ridiculously rich, one of those tech millionaires, which he appears to believe gives him insight into how to manage things. He's... uh... I guess the best way to put it is a bro, if you know what I mean."

I thought I did and I thought that did not bode well for the school.

He cleared his throat. "It's a new situation for me. I've always had a 'we're a team' relationship with the board. I'm at a loss about how to handle it."

I repressed a sigh. These situations were hard enough when everyone was cooperating. "What about the rest of the board? Do you have allies there? You've worked well with them?"

"I do. Most of the board, in fact. No one has said anything, but I get the sense that the rest of the board is annoyed by him. He charmed them into electing him and now he's systematically pissing them all off."

A pause. "I know that's not very helpful when we have a situation like this to manage."

Well, that was something. But he was right. I really needed to be there, and I couldn't. Until Lindsay joined us in a few months, we only had three full-time employees, and only two with the experience to handle a situation like this. This was a case where Suzanne should step in for me. I wondered if she would. I could brief her on what to do and she was awfully charming. Probably better with a tech bro than I would be. I have a tendency to want to whack arrogant people upside the head.

I said, "I'm at home with a newborn. I'm not sure if I told you that earlier? We can do a lot by phone, and if you need someone there, I'll see if my partner, Suzanne, can step in. She's brilliant with difficult boards."

I moved on to some of the items on my list. "In the past, has the school done some education about consent and boundaries? If so, if you've got any written materials, please send them to me. It's always a better defense if you've been proactive."

He sighed. "This didn't happen on the campus," he said.

Meaning it shouldn't be his problem? But like it or not, it was. "No. But it involved boarding students who were under your care, right? Both the victim's friends, who are secondary victims, and two of the alleged perpetrators?"

I wondered if I should have said alleged victim, as well? Certainly there had been instances where the victim wasn't being truthful. As for where it happened and what that meant for the school's responsibility? Ma'Kayla lived off campus, but her two friends, who were victims as well, given what they'd seen, did live on campus. I also wondered if he understood that they were victims? If he could imagine the impact on young girls of finding their friend unconscious and half naked, with a bunch of laughing guys taking pictures? Guys they knew. Guys who, depending on how things played out, would still be in their classes. Dining rooms. Clubs and gatherings. Guys they might meet daily in the course of their regular activities.

Any minute I was going to be interrupted, so I tried to move the conversation along. I hoped he was writing all this down. I didn't want to sound like somebody's mother and ask, though I certainly have done that at times. I walked a fine line here, since I couldn't show up and give them the help they needed.

"Do you have someone in your communications office monitoring the sites students are most likely to visit? Snapchat, Instagram, Twitter, TikTok, places like that, to see if the incident is being discussed?"

"I'll get someone on it," he said.

In other words, no. Not yet. He's putting pressure on us because this is critical and time sensitive but he'd not doing other obvious things? "Have you seen any video or photographs of the incident? Or heard of anyone seeing them?"

"I haven't."

"Have you given the police the phone Jess seized?"

"I called them after we spoke. Someone's coming to pick it up from campus security."

"Do you know whether Jess managed to send the photos to her phone, or to another phone in case they got erased from the phone she grabbed?" I'd read that people could erase things from their phones remotely, and that it had become a concern for the police when they were delayed by the need to get a warrant.

He didn't.

"That would be useful information to have." I suppressed my urge to say, "Well, what are you doing?" However annoyed I was, it wouldn't be helpful.

I thought about the risk that the boy whose phone wasn't seized would disseminate the pictures, not realizing they constituted pornography and that sharing those photos wasn't just a mean and nasty thing to do but a crime. "Do the boys involved understand that sharing those pictures is the distribution of child pornography? That they're committing a federal crime, as well as potentially breaking state laws?"

His silence told me that he hadn't been aware of that. Or at least, that if he'd known it in theory, as he should in his job, he hadn't connected that with his school, his students, and this incident. He was immersed in preparing for a new school year; I was immersed in damage control and reputation protection.

While he was pondering this new bit of bad news, I was thinking that EDGE ought to be offering our client schools some advice, or even a seminar, about sharing photos and the issue of distributing pornography. I realized I had just the person to do it, a retired cop I'd met at an independent schools conference last year. Just as quickly, I wondered why I was already thinking about making more work for myself, when there was plenty of work already.

Because, despite the spit stains on my shoulder and the way my body responded to Mason's slightest cry, I'd become a business woman and business was always about getting more business or finding new ways to serve existing clients.

Oops. My existing client was speaking again. "Really," he said. "We need you here. You're good at thinking proactively about protecting the school, while I am going in a hundred directions."

At least he had some self-awareness. More than many clients I dealt with, especially in emergencies. "I'll call Suzanne and see when she can come. She'll be fine, and she and I can consult if there are questions."

"But Randy Martinelli's parents want to sit down with me. With their lawyer. I don't know what to do about that."

"I don't think that's wise, but you need to ask your lawyer about that. And if your lawyer says you should do it, you need to make sure he or she is present at the meeting. Also, you should check your honor code to see what procedures you've included involving students facing criminal charges as well as instances of sexual harassment or assault."

I should know. I helped them write the code. But every school had their own individual tweaks that reflected the mores of the community and the particular student population. Right now, school hadn't started and he hadn't said that Martinelli or the other boys had been charged with a crime. If Martinelli had been charged, that might change things. In general, honor codes require the students to take a pledge to uphold them and acknowledge that the standards apply to both on and off-campus activities and to behavior that reflects on the school as well as the student.

He was starting to protest that only I would do when Mason's wail reminded me that there was a more immediate situation in which only I would do. It was too soon for the kid to be hungry. Maybe he was feeling left out.

"I'll have to call you back," I said, and pressed the red button to end the call.

FOURTEEN

I'd just put down the phone when Andre appeared holding Mason. Our baby was red-faced and fussing and Andre looked perplexed. "I can't seem to get him to calm down," he said. "He can't be hungry already."

"He can be anything he wants," I said. "He's still learning how to navigate this new world. Put him on your shoulder, rub his back, and talk to him. He'll find the vibrations of your voice soothing."

Andre tried it, and when our little fellow calmed, he beamed.

We went back into the living room to join Dom and Rosie. It was a warm, bright afternoon, and operating on the theory that it was wise to get out and enjoy the days while we could, we decided to take a walk in the town forest. I packed a bag with enough gear for a week-long trek, and they followed us in their car. I even remembered to bring Mason's hat, although I would never be able to look at the thing fondly. Today the tipsy yellow duck looked even more drunk.

The weather was perfect. The air smelled of drying grasses and plants, and a soft wind blew through the crisp end-of-summer leaves. It wasn't until we were deep into the woods, chatting away about this and that, when I realized that I had proposed a walk with no concern for Rosie's difficulty walking. The fact was that she was doing fine. You'd never know a few years ago she'd been stuck in a wheelchair. But I had to ask.

"Rosie. I'm so sorry I didn't ask sooner. Are you okay with this?" Pretty dumb this far into the walk.

She smiled but Dom answered. "Rosie's been walking at least three miles a day, rain or shine, for the past year." His face, looking at her, was so proud.

Andre and I both wanted a marriage like theirs, and it was a good role model because Dom was a cop with a demanding job, like Andre, and she was an independent woman who had maintained a career of her own. After the accident, she'd gone back part-time, but she'd found that she liked being a homebody. In Rosie's case, being a homebody meant getting out her hammer and saws and taking down a wall or two. She was amazing.

Walking seemed to lull Mason into a quiet state, and we got a good hour of walking and catching up done before he decided it was his turn to get some attention. Rosie wanted to know about the delivery and how I was doing. Of course she wanted to know if I was eating enough and getting any sleep. Andre and Dom were a little ahead of us, their heads together, no doubt swapping cop stories. I figured Andre was catching him up on the Addison Shirley situation and about his latest homicide.

From time to time, I heard Dom's low voice ask a question, though I couldn't catch the words.

"It's so nice that they get along," Rosie said.

I heard Dom say, "He did what?"

That was clear enough, and my guess was that the "he" in question was that idiot Jeremy Bartlett. He'd done enough harm, I thought. I didn't even want his name intruding on our pleasant walk, never mind thoughts of what future harm his big mouth might cause.

We were almost back to the car when Mason started fussing for real, so I sat in the passenger seat and fed him, then tucked him into his car seat and we all headed home for some of Rosie's great food. There's nothing like fresh air and exercise to tweak the appetite, though Andre was always hungry and right now, I felt like I wasn't eating for two, I was eating for an army.

Still, I was reluctant to go home. I love our house, even if it is a work in progress. I don't love being ensnared in a business like that involving Addison Shirley. I don't like strangers on my doorstep or learning my name has been in the paper when the matter involves a thug like Benjy Goodman. While I wanted to believe Andre's assurances that we were hard to find, my antennae were up, just waiting for him to appear.

That wasn't all. There was the Stonegate situation. I don't like clients who embroil me in their affairs when I'm supposed to be left alone. Their problems take up head space I begrudge them. I don't like having my attention divided when I want to be wholly immersed in my new career as Mason's mom.

Dammit! I needed to do a better job of banishing my anxiety. Mason was too sensitive to it.

I wondered how other mothers did it. Were they able to leave work behind? Stifle their fears? I knew Andre had learned how to compartmentalize, to put things from work away so he could be truly present when he was home. It wasn't part of my skill set, though I was trying. He was driving and smiling. Mason, in his car seat, was quiet. I, on the other hand, was dreading what we might find when we got back to the house. Bad guys on the doorstep? More emergency phone calls for me or for Andre? At least I'd had the sense to leave my phone at home. It could buzz and vibrate all it wanted but I wasn't there to be disturbed.

By the time we got home it would be five o'clock, and I was allowed to have a glass of wine. Glass? Heck. I'd like to dive in and swim in a glass of wine. But I make some effort to be ladylike. Plus, I needed to stay coherent. It was part of my new job as a mom. Not that being coherent wasn't also part of my job as a consultant.

I wasn't ladylike at all when we parked in the driveway and found that someone had broken down the door, which was now standing open, the frame splintered. Those jagged pieces of wood perfectly echoed how I felt. I'd dreaded coming home, fearing something might have happened, but I'd never truly expected this. I felt like someone had punched me in the chest.

There were no strange cars in the driveway, but our intruder might have parked somewhere else and approached the house on foot. He—and I was pretty sure it was a man—might still be inside.

I got Mason out of his car seat and held him against me, hoping he couldn't sense my pounding heart and wouldn't cry. I put the car between me and whatever might be happening inside.

Rosie put an arm around me.

"Stay here," Andre and Dom said together, and they headed for the house.

Andre had headed into danger a zillion times, I knew. But I wasn't usually there to witness it. Nor had he been a father.

Through the gap between the house and the barn, I could see into the backyard, a stretch of tamed and untamed land that led back to woods at the edge of the property. A figure in a black hoodie was just disappearing into the woods. I grabbed a breath, preparing to run, when I felt Rosie's hand gripping my arm.

"No, Thea. You can't. You've got the baby."

So she saw the figure, too.

Her firm grip reminded me of my situation. However foolhardy I might have been before, risking danger to solve or stop a crime or protect someone vulnerable, my life had changed. I wasn't going to go chasing after a bad guy with poor Mason bouncing in a sling. He *was* someone vulnerable.

It was already too late to summon Andre or Dom from the house. The figure had disappeared.

I stood in my driveway, Rosie's arm around me, fear of what might be inside clenching my heart like a huge hand was squeezing it.

FIFTEEN

"I know it must be frustrating," Rosie said. "But things have changed. Your life isn't your own anymore."

I couldn't argue because she was right. It didn't make it easier to accept that I couldn't chase down someone who had violated my house. I was a fast runner, with long legs. There was a good chance I might have caught him. I stared through the gap at the distant woods. It was as though the person who'd broken in had thrown down a challenge—catch me if you can—and I couldn't take it up.

Like she was reading my mind, Rosie said, "And what would you have done if you'd caught the person?"

Which was a damned good question, one I didn't want to ask myself. I thought I'd have more time to get used to this motherhood business. This having to always think for two, if not three. A pretty radical cure for my natural impulsivity and my need to fix things.

I sighed. "I know you're right. It's just—"

"Just that your life has changed," she said. "And it is hard to get used to. And no, you can't go after him. If it was a him. What if he was armed? Are you willing to put Mason at risk to prove you're still a tough guy?"

She tugged me toward the house. "Let's go inside, see what

Dom and Andre have learned, and start making dinner. Fresh air stimulates the appetite, and our guys are already always hungry."

No way I could argue with that. What I could have said, though, was that this wasn't about proving I was a tough guy, at least not entirely. It was about not taking the violation of my home lying down. It was about being the fixer, the one who always took care of things for others. Now I felt like I had to wear someone else's clothes and walk in someone else's shoes. Rosie probably already knew this.

Our always hungry guys hadn't reappeared to give us the all clear, so I said, "Are we sure it's safe? There might have been more than one of them. The intruders, I mean. Something might still be happening inside."

She shook her head, and said with a smile, "My bet is they've cleared the house and helped themselves to a couple convivial beers, forgetting all about the little women huddling in the driveway waiting to be assured that the house is secure."

The image of us huddling in the driveway waiting for our men to come for us was too funny. "We will never be little women," I said. "I'm too tall and you're too tough."

She patted her hair and raised an eyebrow, making me wonder if she didn't like being called tough.

"That's mostly true," she said. "But I have my moments when I like to hand things over to Dom and pretend to be the little woman. Honestly, sometimes it's because I don't want to deal with whatever it is, and sometimes it's just fun to watch a person who has been condescending to me or jerking me around have to deal with those cold cop's eyes. It was worse when I was in a wheelchair, then I was the crippled little woman." Her smile was triumphant. "Guess I showed them."

I had to admit to playing the helpless little woman myself. As recently as my dealings with the idiotic Jeremy Bartlett. 'Playing' being the operative word.

"Dinner," I agreed, and we started for the door.

I winced as I passed the broken doorframe. Andre and I were in love with this house. We'd searched for ages before we found it. Well, he found it while I was off dealing with chaos at a client school. Found it and made an offer before he even consulted me, certain that I would agree with his decision. That was only a few months ago. We were still very much in the honeymoon phase, if unfinished rooms with bare plaster walls were part of a honeymoon. Seeing it violated like this actually hurt.

No sign of the guys in the kitchen, so we tried the living room. Not there either. It seemed odd that they'd both be upstairs, but they couldn't have gone to the barn without our seeing them. Before we climbed the stairs, I checked out the porch. I found two men, sitting in dark green wicker chairs, both holding amber bottles of beer.

I opened the door, leaned out, and said, "I guess you guys forget about us?"

Two heads bent toward two pairs of shoes. And silence.

"I saw someone running out beyond the back yard, back toward the trees. In a black hoodie and black pants. The person disappeared into the woods. Might have been our intruder, but I couldn't give chase because I was holding the baby."

Give chase was such an old fashion phrase. I couldn't help using it. I was also deliberately guilting them. "You guys finding anything inside? Any clue what our intruder was up to? Looking for?"

Oh, babies and their ability to sense emotions. Mason didn't like the tension in my voice. Likely also the tension in my body, and he let us all know it with a wail. I popped him out of his sling and gave him to his father with a grin. "He might be a little bit damp."

Which was an understatement. My child did not feel like he'd done his duty unless he produced at least one load of laundry a day.

Andre carried the baby inside while Rosie and I stared at Dom, waiting for a report. But Dom, being a cop, started to interrogate us instead.

Yes, I do know the difference between an interview and an interrogation. So okay. Interview. A quick barrage of questions about what we'd seen. Trouble was, all we'd seen was a black figure disappearing into the woods. Too far away for us to provide any useful details, and since both of us were trained by cops, if we'd had any, we would have offered them up. I hated to disappoint, though, so I closed my eyes and focused back on those brief moments. Had I seen anything, anything at all that might be useful?

Rosie must have been trained in the same school, because pretty much simultaneously, we said, "The person was holding something shiny."

Something shiny like my laptop, maybe? Seized with a sudden panic, I was out of the door and in my office in a flash, my heart starting to beat again when I saw that it was still open on my desk, waiting to cause trouble for me. My work life pretty much lives in that thing. I back it up online, of course, but perhaps not as often as I should, especially now that I was distracted by the baby.

What then? I turned to Rosie, who'd followed me. "Any idea what it was?"

She shook her head. Then, as I had done, she closed her eyes. After a moment, she said, "I hate to say this, Thea, but I think it might have been a gun. Could have been a cell phone, though."

I was awfully glad I hadn't gone after the person. I didn't even know that the figure we saw was our intruder, but who else would be slinking through our backyard? It wasn't hunting season. There were no trails nearby. Absolutely no reason for someone to be there unless they'd been the person who broke into our house.

Libby Frenier's words came back to me: *You're awfully isolated here, aren't you?*

I hadn't felt isolated until now, at least not most of the time. I was thinking about what Rosie said. About guns. We had guns in the house. Well-secured in a cabinet in our closet. Andre kept his key with him. Mine was in the freezer in a package of frozen peas. Not the most likely place for a thief to look, nor, in an emergency, the most useful. But I don't do well with guns.

What if they'd found a way to break the lock on our gun safe? Andre had assured me when it was installed that it was burglar-proof. Burglar and childproof. But I'd never felt sure.

I headed for the stairs, climbed them as quietly as one can climb old, creaky stairs, and went into our bedroom. The closet door was open. Open because Andre had already checked the closet or open because our intruder had been in there?

Crossing the room, again carefully because it's an old house with very creaky floors, I pulled the door fully open and looked in. The clothes on the rack that hide our gun safe looked undisturbed. Then I saw that that wasn't true. My clothes were mashed together and Andre's shirts were snugged up against them. Not how we left them.

Even as I reached out to move them aside, I was thinking, *Oh dear. If someone gets a gun from a state police detective's house, that would be very bad.*

We have good light in our closet since both of us are too often dressing in the dark or with our eyes half open, trying not to disturb a sleeping spouse. I bent forward until I was close enough to see the lock. A lot of scratches and dents but when I wrapped my hand in the sleeve of Andre's shirt and tugged on the handle, it stayed shut. Locked. I sagged with relief. I don't like guns. They're a necessary part of Andre's world, and recently became a very handy part of mine. Well, if I told the truth, I'd used a gun on a fellow human once, but only when Andre's life had been at stake, and the person in question didn't feel much like a fellow human. More like the scum of the earth. A mud person. Someone without morals or a conscience.

Did the attempt to open our safe put a different face on things? Had someone broken in to get at our guns—assuming a cop would have guns in the house—and this didn't have anything to do with Addison Shirley or Lucia Faraday's murder? Thinking that might be true, I felt a peculiar combination of relief and renewed anxiety. I was like a human mood ring these days.

"Are you okay?" Andre, from the doorway.

Why pretend? He could tell if I wasn't being truthful. At least most of the time. "Not really. I hate it that someone's been in our house. Broken into our house. But why? And who? Did you and Dom find anything out of place? Any signs of what our intruder was looking for?" I stepped aside so he could see the safe. "Besides this?"

He sighed. He hadn't wanted me to see this. "I told you the safe is secure, Thea. So other than helping him or herself to a slice of cake, nothing seems to be missing."

"You're kidding about the cake, right?"

He shook his head. "Whoever it was, they searched the house but didn't take anything... I think the attempt on the safe was opportunistic. They saw the safe and..." He trailed off, leaving me to fill in the gap.

"But that's not what they were here for? Because they were looking for a baby?"

He shrugged. "Could be. Or looking for us."

By us, he meant me. And Rosie thought the person had a gun. I shivered. "What if it was just an opportunist looking for guns?"

"I've got our crime scene people on the way, just in case this is related to our homicide or the disappearance of Addison Shirley or her baby," he said. "Or someone looking for guns. We won't tolerate a person invading a police officer's home for any reason."

The possibility of why our intruder was here socked into me then. I was brave and Andre was tough but Mason was helpless. "I'm worried about the intruder coming back. Is Mason safe?"

"I think so. But I also thought no one knew where we lived and that's wrong. I think..."

His body language said he was already gone, so I wasn't surprised when he said, "If you can spare us for an hour or so, Dom and I need to pay a visit to the Freeport police."

"And to Jeremy Bartlett?"

He nodded. "Find out who's been talking, and to whom."

I waited for more, but that was all he was saying. Andre, when he's mad, usually goes cold and quiet. Right now, he was both.

But it was a rotten time for him to decide to go on a mission. "It's almost dinner time, Andre. And we have company."

"Right. And we've had intruders and someone on that police force has a big mouth."

"It could wait until tomorrow."

I had to say it even though I knew it wouldn't sway my husband. When he's got a mission in mind, nothing sways him. He's like a scent dog with its nose to the ground. It was a characteristic we had in common.

"Crime scene team will be here any minute."

That was supposed to comfort me or make his departure okay? He should know me better than that. I suppose it was some comfort. They could watch out for bad guys while Rosie and I caught up.

Well, the big tough cops could go and see if they could muscle some information out of the locals. Rosie and I could put something delicious in the oven and then sit in the living room and enjoy some wine. And just in case someone decided to make a return visit, I got the key to the gun safe from the freezer and put it in my pocket.

I had a bottle of Prosecco chilling and Rosie had settled into the living room and chilled along with it. Mason, bless his sweet little heart, slept in Rosie's lap. And no one came calling. Until the crime scene team arrived.

SIXTEEN

It seemed like they weren't used to arriving at a scene to find two women calmly enjoying some wine and cheese, nor to a house that wasn't in some state of chaos. The woman in charge kept looking around for Andre to give her direction, even though we'd both told her he wasn't around. I figured it wasn't worth my time to keep explaining. He'd called them; he could deal with them. I dialed his number and got the promised immediate response.

"Your crime scene people are here and they need direction," I said, making no effort to keep exasperation from my voice. "Here. You talk to her." I handed the phone to the woman in charge.

Predictably, the clatter and noise woke Mason, and any chance of more peaceful time with Rosie and our Prosecco was lost. I think I'd managed two sips. I vowed as soon as I had the chance, I was going to leave Andre alone with the baby, then arrange for various service people to show up. I guess I have a mean streak. But example always works better than explanation.

Meanwhile, we retreated to the kitchen, turned down the oven so Rosie's stuffed shells wouldn't overcook, and sat at the island with our cheese. I'd put out a very special Mt. Tam cheese from a company in California that I'd been saving for the right moment. It was so delicious it almost made up for the chaos.

Almost.

Andre must have given them clear marching orders because they went to work without bothering us, except for removing the cake and cake knife from the counter and checking it for prints and evidence. The knife, I mean. I don't know if you can get fingerprints off a cake. Trying to imagine it almost made me laugh. Must have been the effect of Rosie's company. Otherwise I probably would have stayed cranky and mad at Andre.

The tech who was working on the knife kept looking at the cake so hungrily I asked if she would like piece. Maybe all of them would like cake? She said maybe when they were done but I thought she visibly perked up at the offer. It might have been because of Mason, though, who was watching her with his bright brown eyes.

"How old is he?" she asked.

"A week."

"Oh my gosh. He looks older. He's so alert."

Something I wouldn't have known. Before Mason, I hadn't spent much time around babies except for my partner Suzanne's two and we were always so busy I adored them but didn't get that much one-on-one time. There had been moments, though, when I'd been baptized with baby spit or thrown cereal. I said, "You have kids?"

She laughed. "I wish. I'm still looking for a husband."

"I've found they appear when you least expect it," I said. "I met mine when he was investigating my sister's murder."

She grinned at that. "Not ready to give up a family member yet. Though with my brother, if things get desperate, it's tempting." A pause. "Forget I said that. I'm sorry for your loss." She bent over her work again.

"Shall we make a salad?" Rosie suggested. She was an astute reader of my moods and sensed that I was getting anxious. Crime techs in the house and Andre off doing manly things? Unless it was coppish things, if there was such a word. Why wouldn't I be? "You've got all these great fresh vegetables here, and the season is almost over."

I held out my glass. "More wine first. Then salad."

"Salad first, then wine."

She meant we should drink our wine in peace, when we could enjoy it. I deferred to her wise judgment.

We made a delicious salad, so pretty with all the late summer vegies and a scattering of nasturtium flowers, I was tempted to take its picture. I was grateful to have Rosie here. Her warm and comforting presence reminded me that however much I might wish my mother would visit, that visit would be filled with tension. She's never liked me the way I am and I can't stop trying to please her. I used to think I was a slow learner but over time I've realized that my relationship with my mother is like having malaria. I get over trying to please her. I have a flare. I get better. It flares again.

The techs finished their work and happily ate cake. The woman who'd been working on the knife said, "It's not often we get offered cake at a crime scene."

I said, "I guess I don't know the rules. It's not often we have a crime scene."

We all laughed at that, but there was an underlayer of seriousness we all felt. Smashing in the door of someone's house is a violent act. Doing that to a state police detective raises all sorts of questions. It could be tied to the current homicide, or a previous case he'd worked, or simply a criminal who'd found the house empty. I didn't for a second believe it was the last. I wasn't even sure it was about Andre. No. I don't think I'm the center of the universe but I think the business with Addison Shirley and Lucia Faraday was the most likely reason for the intrusion. I just wasn't sure why or what they were looking for.

"Did you find anything?" I asked.

The tech who was looking for a husband gave me a sympathetic look. "We're just collecting evidence at this point. We won't know anything until we process it."

Which I was sure wasn't entirely true, but I nodded. "You find fingerprints? Footprints? Something to help identify our intruder?"

She nodded but she didn't elaborate. I was just the little woman, after all. Little women offer cake. Big, tough detectives solve crimes.

I needed to be whacked upside the head to make me drop this self-pity.

Then they all left, carrying away whatever they'd found. The house seemed unusually quiet after they were gone. Their presence had provided an additional level of security. Bad guys don't usually return when a clearly labeled crime scene van is parked in the driveway.

I looked over at Mason, snuggled into his little seat, and thought about another baby who was missing. Allegedly missing. It made me wish I'd never gone looking for a hat. Seemed like I did a lot of wishing these days.

Another virtual head slap was needed to end this pity party.

Outside, the bright day was drawing to a close, the early darkness coming way too soon. The weather and the seasons seem out of sync these days. Even as the August days are their warmest and sunniest and we want them as long as possible, they grow shorter. By September, the days end well before we're ready. The earlier darkness is an unwanted reminder of the cold and dark to come. I'm more attuned to that now that we're living in the country. Right now, I was also living in the country with an unlockable door.

It was past time for Andre and Dom to be back. Rosie looked at the clock before she popped some bread in the oven. "They'd better be here by the time this is done," she muttered.

Like Andre, Dom gets a pass pretty often because he does important work. Rosie and I are a long-suffering pair, but we have our limits.

We set a timer so the bread wouldn't burn, then went into the living room. I carried the bottle and glasses, she brought Mason. I could already see that he was going to be very close to his godmother. Lucky boy. It's important to have some wise adult to talk to besides one's parents.

My phone rang and I answered without checking the number, assuming it would be Andre with an update. A voice I didn't recognize said, "We know you've got him. We'll be back." It sent chills down my spine.

SEVENTEEN

"What?" Rosie said. "Thea. Who was on the phone? You look like you've just received a death threat."

Most people would say "seen a ghost," but most people aren't married to cops. I set the phone down on the table, holding it between two fingers like it was hot or contaminated. "Not quite a death threat, but close," I said. "It was a male voice, one I didn't recognize, and he said, 'We know you've got him. We'll be back.'"

"Dear God!" she said. "I'm calling Dom. They shouldn't be out there playing cops and bad guys when they are needed here at home."

I was shaken enough to let her. I picked up Mason and held him close, wondering what I would have done if I'd been at home by myself and someone had tried to take him away. I was already thinking that I needed to get my gun from the safe and keep it near me. There might be lots of sensible rules about guns when there are children in the house, but there was no way that Mason was going to get his hands on it anytime soon.

When I poured some Prosecco into my glass, my hand was shaking. I poured some for Rosie, too.

The timer told us that the bread was ready. While Rosie spoke with Dom, I put Mason in his seat, went to the kitchen, took the bread out, and turned the oven off. It would be a crime to cook Rosie's great food into a dry and tasteless lump.

I went to lock the kitchen door, pausing to look out the windows to see if anyone was out there. I didn't see anyone. I felt foolish when I got closer to the door and realized that I couldn't lock it—the lock was busted along with the splintered doorframe. At least I could lock my other door. I went to the front of the house and locked the door to the porch. I should have done it earlier, but darkness and a threatening phone call had made the situation seem far scarier. Too bad it was so late in the day, or I would have called an alarm company and set up an appointment. It went right to the top of Monday's to-do list.

Who thought I would need such things? I was just a new mother in her lovely old farmhouse, a woman who was supposed to have her tough and protective husband by her side. It was bad enough that the state of Maine didn't understand paternity leave. It appeared that my own husband didn't either. If asked, he'd say he was doing something necessary to protect his family, but right now, after that threatening voice on the phone, I wasn't feeling protected.

Back in the living room, Rosie was holding Mason and singing him a song. He seemed to like it. She looked up when I came in.

"Dom says they're on their way back. I'm afraid I told him what I thought about their taking off like that. Maybe during an ordinary visit, I wouldn't mind as long as I got to spend time with you and my godson, but with so much mystery surrounding you right now? Not a good time to leave you alone."

"I've got you," I said. "Imagine if Andre took off like that and I was here alone?" Changing the subject, I said, "I am giving them fifteen minutes, and then we're going to eat without them."

"Sounds right to me."

My phone rang. I stared at it warily. I certainly wasn't answering. If it was a real someone who didn't want to deliver a malevolent message, they could use voicemail. I suppose someone could leave a malevolent voicemail, but what would be the point?

It appeared someone had left a voicemail, my phone told me.

Still wary, I picked up the phone and looked at the message. It was from Barron Thompson at Stonegate, and he was clearly very agitated. Damn! I had to listen. When he was done, I wished I hadn't.

Apparently, when they picked up the phone from campus security that Jess had taken from one of Ma'Kayla's attackers, the police had also paid him a visit and it hadn't been pleasant. He said they'd acted like he was holding out on them. I wouldn't tell him, but I thought that was probably a good thing. It meant the cops were taking things seriously and not in someone's pocket, covering things up.

Or were they? It was possible they wanted the phone so things wouldn't get out, which brought me back to an earlier question— had Jess sent the photos to her own phone? I'd have to ask. Damn but this stuff was hard to do at a distance. No faces or body language to read. So difficult to gauge the situation and ask follow-up questions.

He wasn't done. He said Ma'Kayla's parents' lawyer had phoned to be sure that none of the boys involved would be in any of her classes or have any contact with her, which would be impossible in a small school. What was he supposed to do?

Well, that was a hard question. A lot would depend on the contract the students all signed about conduct and the honor code. These guys were the school's star athletes, and it was always difficult to deal with athletes and misconduct. Suspensions and expulsions, however well-deserved and required under the school's rules, riled up the community, especially when there was a strong sports tradition. But if we've learned anything from the Me Too movement, it's that women's issues need to be taken seriously and handled promptly. Stonegate, I shouldn't need to remind him, had a population that was 50% female.

Then there was another problem he needed help with. The wider world of parents and students had learned about the event, and his email and phone were going crazy. The school needed to communicate with their parent and alumni community about the incident. He needed me, in person, and he needed me now.

Well, sorry, but he couldn't have me. I sighed and called Suzanne. "The situation at Stonegate is an exploding mess," I told her, giving her a quick summary of his message. "Someone needs to be there to guide them and hold their hands, and it can't be me."

"It's the start of the school year," she said, as though that was news to me. "I'm already crazy busy."

She was right, but our business depended on our being available when our clients needed us. I'd certainly picked up plenty of slack when she had her babies, and done it without complaint. "It has to be done, Suzanne, and you're the only one who can do it."

There was a silence so long it made me nervous. Then she said something that made me far more nervous.

"I'm just not sure I can do it, Thea. I've been wondering if we've stretched ourselves too thin. If maybe we should cut back on the emergency stuff and concentrate on what we do best."

Her words were a punch in the gut. The emergency stuff was a critical service we offered to schools, and one that had become my specialty. It was the stuff that I did best. Now, because once I ask her to step in, she thinks we should drop it?

I took a breath, ready to argue. "Suzanne, that doesn't make sense, we—"

She cut me off. "Look. Sorry. I have to go. Got an emergency of my own right here, right now. Talk later, okay?" And my partner of several years hung up on me.

I sat there, stunned, staring at the phone in my hand. What had just happened? Had I really heard what I thought I heard?

Then there was Rosie's hand on my shoulder. "Thea? What's wrong now? What happened? Another threatening phone call?"

"It's... my partner... there's a work issue. A client with a problem. I asked her to fill in for me, and she... she blew me off. Said she didn't think she could do it and then hung up on me. I really..." I felt like I couldn't catch my breath. "I really don't know how to process this. She's never—"

I quit trying to explain something I didn't understand myself. All of a sudden, I felt confused and dizzy. I dropped into my chair, set the phone on the table, and buried my head in my hands. "I can't do this. Any of it."

Meaning work, including my partner's peculiar behavior, and the ridiculous situation with Addison Shirley, but Mason, my little emotion-sensing acrobat, decided to add his voice to the chaos and began to wail. At least feeding him and changing him were things I didn't need to think about. They didn't need a carefully thought out response. They just needed an immediate one. I picked him up and started to feed him. But babies, dammit, they're such brilliant sensors. He wouldn't be comforted, or nurse, until I calmed down.

I handed him to Rosie and started to cry. Of course, the bold and brave defenders of public safety chose that moment to return and burst through the broken kitchen door.

EIGHTEEN

I love my husband, but there are times, like this one, when I don't like him very much. Andre and Dom spilled into the kitchen in a noisy confusion of apologies and information. I didn't care about the former and couldn't absorb the latter, so I left them there, with Rosie putting food on the table, and carried Mason upstairs.

In the relative quiet of his room, a room designed to be soothing, we both calmed down. He got changed, ate, and fell into a peaceful baby slumber. I set the monitor and went downstairs. The others were at the table, already digging into Rosie's food.

I took my chair and said, "So, fill me in. What have you guys been up to?"

They'd been up to a futile attempt to find Jeremy Bartlett, who appeared to be on some sort of leave; an acrimonious conversation with the Freeport chief who was too defensive about what had been leaked to the papers; and chasing down a possible sighting of Faraday that was unsuccessful. Not a whole lot of progress.

I decided I'd eat before I told them about my phone call and wasn't sure I'd share the situation with my client school and my uncooperative partner. Except at my most extreme moments, I can always eat, though

I sometimes forget to. I'm reforming, though, and eating delicious food in the presence of good friends, even if I was annoyed with some of the people present, put a brief buffer between me and my trying day.

We'd had cake earlier—us, Dom and Rosie, the crime scene techs, and our intruder—so I figured there was no dessert on the menu, but I should never underestimate Rosie. She makes the best tiramisu in the world, and there was a big dish of it waiting on the counter.

"So what have you two been up to?" Andre asked after his third helping of stuffed shells.

"We changed the baby and made a salad," I said brightly. But that threatening call was too important to ignore, however much I wanted to. I needed them on the case. "And I had a disturbing phone call," I said. "Actually, two disturbing phone calls, but only one that relates to..."

I had to stop and think about how I would describe it. Andre's case? My encounter with Addison Shirley? The missing baby? Finally, I said, "To Addison Shirley's missing baby. I think."

Now Andre was leaning forward, his eyes fixed on me as though a stare could pull out the information my hesitation was holding back. I've often thought about how fierce he could be with bad guys. Now it felt like I was coming in for some of that ferocity and I didn't like it much. Didn't he understand how fragile I was? He should know I wasn't stalling. I was just trying to recall the threat clearly, to get the words right.

While I was doing that, Rosie, who was more experienced with cop husbands than I was, put a hand on Andre's arm. She didn't say anything, just kept her hand there, but the laser cop stare disappeared and my husband was back, brown eyes and rigid posture softening.

"It was a man's voice. One I didn't recognize. There was no greeting, just a few growled words. He said, 'We know you've got him. We'll be back.'"

The mere recitation of the words pulled Andre right out of his chair, furious. He was used to living in a world where a cop's family was untouchable, so this was a complete outrage, especially on top of someone breaking into our house.

"That's all he said? That's everything?"

I nodded.

"Give me your phone."

I gave him my phone and he scrolled through. "Blocked number, dammit!" he said. "We can trace it, but it takes time." He fiddled with my phone for a while, seemingly oblivious to the fact that we had company. Company who had just provided a delicious dinner. Who were, in fact, still eating that delicious dinner.

I looked around and realized the only one still eating was me, because I'd been late to the table. I started eating again, trying not to gobble. It wasn't like anyone was going to take my plate away before I finished, and I wasn't raised in a boarding house.

The minute I set my fork down, though, Rosie was on her feet, gathering up plates.

"Who wants tiramisu?" Rosie asked.

"Everyone," Dom said, rising to help her.

Only a fool passes up anything Rosie has cooked.

Andre left the room with my phone, perhaps to write down a number. He was back almost immediately and handed me my phone.

"That's all?" he asked again, as though he thought I was holding something back.

I nodded. "That's all."

"You said there was a second disturbing phone call." Like I *was* holding out on him.

"Oh. That was work. The school with the assault on the soccer player I told you about. The headmaster is in a tizzy and wants me there immediately. So I called—"

"You can't go," he said. 'You're on maternity leave. Mason needs you here."

I could have said the same for him, but I saved my breath. "It wasn't his call that upset me," I said. "Well, not just his call. Mostly not his call."

Damn, I was becoming inarticulate. Had childbirth done something to my brain? "It was when I called Suzanne to say that the school badly needed someone there in person and she blew me off."

I was still shaken by that, and Andre, seeing it, was outraged on my behalf.

"You covered for her twice, with both of her kids. Worked overtime and weekends for months so that she could bond with her babies. Now she does this? Something must be up because it doesn't sound like her at all, does it? But I understand why you're so upset."

"I'm ready to bury my phone in the compost pile and get my gun from the safe."

"Not a bad idea. Getting your gun, I mean. You might need your phone."

"Only to call you, sweetheart, except you're supposed to already be here."

He momentarily ignored my comment and said, "Mason might need something, and you'd want to be able to make a call." Then he added, "Go ahead. Rub it in. I deserve it."

This was why we were still together, despite some epic fights. Because we were both willing to admit we were wrong and apologize. Also, because deep down, we were really madly in love.

"Go tell Rosie what a delicious dinner it was," I suggested. As he was getting up, I added, "Monday I'm going to call an alarm company. We can't be having strangers in the house now that we have Mason. It's just not safe."

I swear the boy already recognized his name, even though he was too far away to hear. There were little baby sounds coming from the monitor.

Andre started for the stairs as I added, "And your father will fix the door, right? Fix it soon?"

He paused. "Tomorrow. Dad's coming tomorrow."

"Give him a minute," I said. "Mason, I mean. Not your father. Maybe he'll settle. It's too soon for him to be fed, and he's got to learn to sleep more than an hour or two at a time."

"But I've missed him."

Politely refraining from reminding him that he was the one who'd left for a couple hours, I said, "He'll be awake soon enough, and you can change him and hold the little beast and comfort him with your deep, manly voice."

He laughed and went to the kitchen, returning almost immediately with an immense serving of tiramisu, which he placed, with ceremony, in front of me. "Rosie says you have to eat it all."

I was already pretty full, but just looking at that dish of lusciousness, I knew I couldn't resist. "That won't be a problem."

Someday I was going to learn to make it myself.

I waited impatiently for the others to return. Everyone had a generous serving, and Rosie was beaming. She did love to feed people. Her own kids weren't close and were still in that phase of life where they were separating from their parents and needed to be left alone except when they called for help.

I was one spoonful into the delicious dessert when we heard the sound of a car coming up the driveway. I dropped my spoon with a clatter.

Dom put a hand on my arm and said, "Relax. We got this."

No polite way to tell him that I didn't want anything happening here that required two cops to handle. He already knew that anyway.

Andre went to the window and peered out. He called over his shoulder, a not entirely reassuring, "It's okay. It's Roland."

Roland Proffit wasn't a bad guy, but Roland arriving meant he was bringing business that would distract Andre from the rest of dinner and the company of our friends. To forestall the end of a pleasant meal, I said, "See if he wants something to eat."

A clever ploy since I'd never known a time when Roland didn't want something to eat. This time was no exception. I fixed him a plate while Andre set another place at the table, and we resumed eating dessert while he dug into Rosie's stuffed shells. Roland has been a bachelor for a long time, and he radiated happiness as he ate.

"Thank Rosie," I said. "She's the cook."

"Will you marry me, Rosie?" he said.

"I don't think Dom would like that," she said, "and I think one husband is enough."

Despite the speed with which he'd come up the driveway, which suggested some urgency, Roland politely refrained from sharing the purpose of his visit until he'd eaten. Then he said, "Sorry, Thea, but this can't wait any longer. We searched one of Faraday's rentals this afternoon, acting on a tip. We didn't find him or anyone else, but we did find an awful lot of blood and signs of a struggle. Blood's being tested so at least we'll know if whoever bled was male or female."

Andre was on the cusp of saying, "And you didn't call me?" when he caught my look. I didn't even have to say, "There are other capable detectives in Maine," because we are good at reading each other's minds.

In my turn, I refrained from asking whether the amount of blood suggested wound or death. It's just not very nice table conversation, even with a table full of cops.

He did say, "Where? When? Fill me in."

So I said, "Why don't you guys have coffee in the kitchen. Or a beer or wine or whatever, and Rosie and I will go in the living room at talk about less gory things." In truth, I was conflicted. I wanted to know the details, too, but a visit with Dom and Rosie was too rare to spend it talking about a crime I already felt too involved in.

On the other hand, listening to the details of Roland's story would distract me from thinking about Stonegate Academy and what on earth was going on with Suzanne. We'd always had each other's backs. Andre was right that this wasn't like her.

Tomorrow was another day. Maybe it would bring some clarity somewhere.

Andre and Roland had moved to the kitchen, and I realized that Dom was standing in the dining room doorway, looking at me and Rosie as if he needed permission to go with the guys or a command to come with us.

Laughing, Rosie walked over to him and wrapped her arms around him. "If you want to go with the guys, go. It's okay. Thea and I can talk about girly things like childbirth and stretch marks."

He made a face and headed for the kitchen. He didn't mean it, though. This was the guy who'd washed out my bra when I was in a nasty accident so I'd have something to wear. I've worn his pants and his shirt and even his shoes. He was a guy who wasn't squea-mish about women's things. But he might be valuable in the kitchen, where he might have something useful to add to the conversation.

He smiled. Waved. Said, "Have fun, ladies," and disappeared.

As soon as Rosie and I were seated, me in my favorite chair, her on the couch, I turned off my phone. If someone wanted to threaten me further, he'd have to do it via voicemail.

NINETEEN

Miraculously, Mason went back to sleep and was quiet for another hour. It gave us plenty of time to talk. Since my mother hadn't deigned to visit, I had a million questions for Rosie about what was normal. She was the perfect person to ask, too. She understood the wide range of normal as well as new mother anxiety. I've heard that women of my generation don't like to ask their mothers for advice. They get it from their friends or from "experts." Childrearing via Instagram or Tik Tok? No way. I was happy to be an outlier. It was much more reassuring to get information from someone who'd successfully raised some kids than from a talking head or an influencer.

When I told her that, Rosie laughed. "Not sure I can claim to have been successful, unless the fact that they're still alive counts. For the children of such normal parents as me and Dom, ours sure are quirky."

Not so quirky. Just quirky by conservative cop standards. Angelo, a college senior, wanted to be an artist, though his kind of art was digital and hard for his parents to understand. Isabella, their daughter, was an environmental engineer studying ways for humans and wildlife to interact safely. They were lovely people, both of them, although Angelo was going through a period of being estranged, and Isabella was so busy with her work that Rosie feared she'd never find a boyfriend. Perfectly normal kids, in other words, though Dom and Rosie found the distance difficult.

It was wicked of me, I knew, but nice to have Rosie confide in me for a change.

Soothed by wine and sugar, and in such excellent company, I was able to let the things that were troubling me slip away. I've been driven and responsible for so long that relaxing almost isn't in my vocabulary. Andre and I don't take vacations. We may plan them, but something always comes up at his work or mine. Today's adventures reminded me of our vow to reform. Was it possible, with Rosie's help, that I could?

Not without Suzanne's help too, a little voice in my head whispered. I hoped that when I turned my phone back on, there would be a message from her apologizing and affirming that she would step up. For now, I didn't want to check because I didn't want to be disappointed. I liked being happy and at ease.

At ease, that is, with three cops strategizing in the kitchen about a pool of blood and what it might signify.

As at ease as someone might be whose house had been broken into, especially if that someone was a fixer. It had taken a lot of will power not to race through the backyard and head into the woods to see if our intruder had left any signs that might lead to his or her identity.

Eventually, Mason woke and Rosie and I went upstairs to tend to him. Rosie claimed the task of getting him out of his wet little clothes and dried and dressed again. She did it with such joy that I hoped her kids would eventually make her a grandmother. Some people are such natural caretakers. She didn't seem terrified that she'd drop him or do something wrong. I couldn't help comparing her to how my mother would be. Uneasy and uncomfortable right along with critical of how I was doing things. I often wonder how she managed to raise the three of us.

"I'm so glad you're here," I said. "I think I've been in need of some mothering."

"And I guess I've been in need of doing some mothering," she said. "I'm looking forward to being a grandmother but it will be years before Angelo or Isabella—" She stopped. "I know they need to live their lives."

She was so wise. I couldn't imagine ever being so wise, but then, I couldn't imagine Mason as a young adult.

Eventually we carried Mason back downstairs to see if the guys were done with their confab. It looked like they were. Andre was loading the dishwasher. Dom was having a beer. So was Roland.

"Looks like I'll have to work tomorrow," Andre said. "DNA results aren't back yet, but the blood is female. We needed to canvass the neighbors, look for surveillance video, and check the neighbor-hood. It's very wooded, so—"

He stopped, staring at Mason in my arms. As though the little lad, perceptive as he was, understood what his daddy was talking about.

Part of me wanted to wave my arms around and yell, "What part of paternity leave don't you understand?" but another part of me was fearing that the blood belonged to Addison Shirley, and what that meant for her chances of still being alive and for her baby's chances of having a mother. If the baby was still alive. Who could have imagined an expedition to buy a baby hat would have so much fallout? Briefly, I wanted everyone gone so I could be alone and think things through. How did anyone make intelligent plans when they were sleep deprived and overwhelmed?

I said, "Dammit!" which was shorthand for all of that.

"I know," he said. "I know. I'm sorry." He loaded a few more dishes. Said, "At least you'll have Dom and Rosie."

Did he not get that they'd come to visit *us*? They weren't here to babysit new mother me while he went off to save the world.

Of course he got it. He was just as wedded to his job as he was to me. Someone had been killed. He had to catch the person who'd done it.

Our son was only nine days old, and already I was tired of this conversation. I popped Mason out of his sling and handed him to Andre. "It's not just about me, or us, anymore."

I didn't want to have a fight. Not in general and not in particular in front of our guests. So to distract myself, I did something stupid. I got out my phone and turned it on. Then, while Andre held his son and Dom and Rosie tried to fade into the background, I checked my messages and voicemail.

Three messages. Two voicemails.

I started listening to the first voicemail, then stopped when I realized that everyone needed to hear it, so I put the phone on speaker and started the message again.

The voice was female and very faint, like the speaker lacked the energy to speak any louder. I turned up the sound.

"I hope this is Thea Kozak. This is Addison Shirley... the girl... woman you tried to help? When my baby was taken? I'm afraid... that is... I need your help again. Badly. I... uh... there was a fight, and I got hurt, I'm afraid I'm going to die and I don't have anyone to call... I'm afraid to call the police. They'll blab everything to him. I... I don't even know where I am. An... uh... basement, maybe? It's dark and damp and cold and the walls are stone."

The voice faded out even as all five of the people in the kitchen yelled some version of, "Don't call us. Call 911." There might have been some expletives involved. Never mind that we were yelling at a voicemail.

Andre handed me the baby, then took my phone and wrote down the number she'd called from.

He turned to Roland. "Faraday's place where you found the blood. Is it a cottage? A stone cottage?"

Roland shook his head. "Gray shingle."

"Describe it."

Roland did. It didn't have a basement.

"What about Faraday's other properties? Did you search them all? Was there anything like a stone cottage?"

"She might not even know whether it's a stone cottage," I suggested. "She could be in a basement with a stone foundation. She wasn't very coherent."

But Andre's attention was still on Roland. "The properties?" he repeated.

"What the man owns or has an interest in is a complete tangle," Roland said. "Property he owns personally. Property his companies own. I can't be sure we've checked them all. We're still sorting that out."

"We've got to find her," Andre said. He looked around at the rest of us like we might be hiding some secret map that would guide his search. His eyes finally rested on me.

I shook my head. "This is all I've got." But there had been a second voicemail. Quickly, I checked it. Suzanne. Much as I hoped it was an apology and an invitation to start working on Stonegate's problem, now was not the time for that. It could wait until the cavalry had mounted up and ridden away.

"Blabbermouths or not, we're going to have to work with the locals," Roland said. He said it like the words left an unpleasant taste in his mouth. I understood why.

"Right." Andre scrolled through his phone, then looked at Roland. "You call this guy. He's a captain in the department and he's a straight shooter. Tell him what we know and see what he suggests." He gave Roland the number.

Then he turned to the rest of us. "I'm sorry, but I've got to go."

We understood, though some of us were less easy with his need to go than others. At least, as Andre had pointed out, I would have Dom and Rosie with me. Since there was someone out there who had articulated plans to snatch Mason, believing he was Addison Shirley's baby, that felt awfully important right now.

He looked guiltily toward the broken door. "I... uh... hate to leave you with that. But you know Dad. He'll be here first thing tomorrow to fix the door."

Like cowboys jumping on their horses and riding rapidly away, Andre and Roland were gone in a flash. Two powerful engines, tires on gravel, and they were off.

Without those two big men in my kitchen, the place felt almost empty once the door had shut behind them. I put a chair against it to hold it shut. Not much of a safety measure, but if a bad guy did come in, the crash of a falling chair would be some warning.

Mason, who was such a brilliant sensor of tension, began to cry.

"It's okay, pumpkin," I said, putting him on my shoulder and rubbing his back. "Daddy will be back."

I hoped that I was right. There had been a few times in my past when it looked like Daddy wouldn't come home. I pushed those memories away.

TWENTY

R osie yawned and stretched. "This is too much excitement for an old lady like me. If you don't mind, Thea, I think I'll head up to bed."

"You are not an old lady," Dom and I said together.

He added, "I think I'll join you, unless Thea needs me down here guarding the door with a shotgun?"

"No shotgun," I said, feeling a small twinge that we couldn't lock the broken door. "I think we're all ready for bed. Rosie's food is delicious but absolutely coma-inducing."

She smiled benignly. "You know, when I'm cooking, I'm always thinking of the pleasure people will have, eating what I've made. The phrase "food coma" never crosses my mind."

"Oh, it's a good coma," Dom told her and I agreed.

He turned to me. "You sure you don't want to me sit up until Andre comes home?"

I shook my head. "Waiting for Andre to come home can take a very long time. You can understand that. You and Rosie might as well get some sleep. We should all get some sleep."

Actually, I knew Mason wasn't in the mood for sleep right now.

He was in the mood to lie in my lap and study the world he'd recently entered. Those curious brown eyes seemed to see everything and be fascinated by it. Fine with me. But we would be doing our observing upstairs in the bedroom. There was plenty to see up there. Lamps and paintings and a colorful quilt on the bed. He was too young for it, but Andre had started telling him stories anyway.

"Yes, Mason," I told the warm creature on my shoulder, "Yes, mommy will tell you a story."

Mommy? I hadn't settled on what I wanted to be called. Mama? Mom? Mummy? I'd known a few kids whose parents insisted on being called by their first names. But in my wildest dreams, I couldn't imagine saying, "Oh, honey, tell Thea what's the matter." Nor did I want my kid's first word to be Teea, which is what my little sister Carrie had called me.

I was beyond exhausted but knew I wouldn't sleep. Not with that weak and desperate voice from my phone stuck in my head. If I couldn't sleep, I could at least rest, so I lay down with Mason on the bed beside me. He seemed to like it there, curled next to the warmth of my body while he studied the world around him.

Eyes closed, I was doing the relaxation exercise where you concentrate on each body part as you slowly move up from your toes, when I remembered that there had been a message on my phone from Suzanne. My phone was on the bedside table. Given my work, and Andre's, never mind our current situation, it was never far away.

Moving slowly, trying not to disturb Mason, I turned and reached for it, finding Suzanne's voicemail and pressing play.

"Darn it, Thea! I am so sorry for being such an ass when we spoke earlier. Paul had just called and said we were having unexpected guests. I was trying to police the house while Paul Junior was having a meltdown and my daughter was proudly showing off the results of a raid on my cosmetics. You can't imagine what that looked like, never mind the counter where I keep my stuff. At that moment, the idea of taking on one more thing was too overwhelming."

There was a silence, and I thought she was done, but then she went on. "Of course I can pick up the slack with Stonegate. After all you've done for me, how could I possibly say no? Hope you are enjoying your time bonding with Mason, and that Andre is actually taking paternity leave. It's hard to imagine that he'll last at home for long, but look at us, right? The work never ends and we know we're the best people to do it. Anyway, I've got to go shove some of the kid's stuff into closets and drawers and sweep up a layer of crumbs, then conjure dinner out of thin air. Talk tomorrow?"

I felt like tender hands had lifted me up and showered me with magic dust. My relief was really that big.

Mason was staring at me, as though he wanted an update, so I said, "Buddy, we're off the hook for a road trip." I almost thought I read disappointment on his face. He did like riding in the car.

"Sleepy time," I said, curling back next to him and closing my eyes.

In some sort of minor miracle, we both went to sleep.

It was newborn sleep, so it didn't last long, but I was still grateful for the rest when he began his little fretful cries. Before I could get up, big hands picked him up and carried him away. Andre was back. He'd come in so quietly I hadn't heard him, and hadn't curled up next to me because Mason was there.

"Did you find her?" I murmured.

"We did. Unconscious, so we couldn't ask her any questions. That will have to wait for morning."

"But she was alive?"

"Yes."

"You think she'll make it?"

He didn't answer.

"Was she in one of Faraday's properties?"

"No."

"Then how did you find her?"

"We didn't. She was in a little stone... uh, I guess it was a root cellar... behind someone's house."

He named the town where Libby Frenier lived, which I guess

was probably Addison's hometown as well. Did that mean we were looking at Benjy Goodman for this? And what did I mean by "we" anyway?

"Lucky for her," he said, "the homeowner went out to get some beer they'd stored there to keep it cold. They found her and called 911." He murmured something to Mason, then said, "We've got a crime scene team there now."

"This is such an odd case," I said.

"We'll see. Misdirection is pretty common among our smarter perpetrators. If this was done by Faraday, there's no question that he's smart."

He handed me the baby.

"But Addison's baby is still missing?"

"Still missing."

We shared a silence in our dark bedroom, me curled around Mason and Andre right beside us, thinking about another baby with a mother in the hospital and an unknown father. Where could the baby be and was he being taken care of? What would it be like to be snatched from his mother and given to a stranger? Could a baby that young tell the differ-ence? Would it miss its mother's familiar heartbeat and the sound of her voice?

I didn't want to go there—to think about this—but with Mason in my life, our lives, I couldn't help myself. I pictured him hungry, wet, crying, cared for by someone who did it from duty and not from love. There were worse things to picture but I definitely wasn't going there. I felt like I was bracing myself firmly against the door of dire possibilities.

"We got DNA off the car seat in Lucia Faraday's car," he said. "She'd only bought the car seat that morning. We can match it to Addison Shirley's, now that she's been found." Silence. Then he said, "It doesn't help us find the baby, but it will confirm some facts, so that's something."

"Won't Benjy Goodman's DNA be in the system, given his history? So couldn't you match it to that, too, to see if he is the baby's father?"

"We don't collect DNA for the kinds of crimes Benjy's committed."

"Not for serious assaults? For sexual assaults?" I said, trying to remember what Libby Frenier had told me about Benjy's criminal past. Not enough, probably because I hadn't wanted to know. In wanting to avoid tainting a potential childcare relationship, had I missed a chance to gather vital information?

My new mantra was supposed to be: This isn't my problem.

It wasn't working very well.

"When will the crime scene techs know something about our break-in?"

We had a strange kind of pillow talk, my husband and I.

"We have to be patient, Thea. They're very busy. Normally, they wouldn't even be called out for a case like this. They only came because it's me. It's us. More concerning now that there's been the threat on the phone."

"How worried should I be?"

He started to answer but I held up a hand. I had to stop this. There were questions that needed answers but Mason didn't like it when he lacked my full attention. Plus, he was very sensitive to my anxiety and talking about missing babies, women left for dead, and break-ins in my home were all sources of anxiety.

"Mason," I said, shorthand for all of that.

"Sorry," Andre said. "Sensitive little bugger, isn't he?"

"Maybe they all are. I don't know much about babies. Do you?"

"I'm an uncle," he said. "A whole lot of times."

Andre's sister Aimee had five children. "But have you ever cared for an infant on your own?"

"At a crime scene."

"Doesn't count."

"Does, too."

I was not having this argument. I was gonna feed the kid and go back to sleep. If Mason wanted some face time, he could stare into Andre's nice brown eyes. My eyelids were drooping.

I burped him and handed him to Andre. My husband probably needed sleep as much as I did, but he liked to play the tough guy, so he could tough this out. I fell back asleep with questions about my conversation with Libby Frenier floating through my head. If I'd had the energy, I would have gotten up and done an internet search or two. Instead, I had to hope I'd remember what I was wondering—something about addresses in her town—when I woke up.

TWENTY-ONE

O f course I didn't remember. Between having guests and Mason's demands, I didn't think about Libby Frenier and my questions again until noon the next day.

Before that, we all decided that we'd go out for breakfast. Maybe it was silly, when our house was stuffed with Rosie's excellent food, but the visit was a getaway for her and Dom, and they were both huge breakfast fans. We took them to a local diner, the place where everyone congregated on a Sunday morning. It was the kind of place where the home fries were delicious, the bacon unusually crisp, and the lemon-ricotta blueberry pancakes absolutely world class.

I was surprised to discover that between us, Andre and I knew quite a few of the people present. We greeted the librarian and her husband, my two old garden consultants from Agway, our nextdoor neighbors, and of course a few members of the local constabulary. I could tell everyone was eager to ask for updates on Andre's latest homicide since it had been plastered on the front page of the local newspaper, but they politely refrained.

Mason was an angel. He took in all the stares from people who wanted to admire him, and then settled onto the seat beside me and watched sunlight streaming through a piece of stained glass hung in the window. Just when I'd begun to think I'd never eat an undisturbed meal again, it was a miracle. Of course, the meal *was* disturbed, not by the newest Lemieux, but by his father, who excused himself twice to make phone calls.

"He's trying," Dom said.

"He can be very trying," I agreed. I was, after all, ignoring the vibrating phone in my own pocket, which I suspected was an ever more agitated headmaster at Stonegate Academy. I hoped the frequency of his calls didn't mean that further bad things had happened, but I was not going to spoil our lovely breakfast to find out. If they'd already happened, there wasn't much I could do anyway, and I'd already given him my best advice about averting catastrophe.

Eventually, full of delicious food, we headed back out to our cars and drove home.

Rosie said she was going to sit on the porch and work on the sweater she was knitting for Mason. Andre and Dom disappeared to the barn, either to admire Andre's workshop, discuss a project, or talk about Andre's strange intertwined cases away from the delicate ears of the ladies.

I excused myself to carry a now somewhat fretful baby upstairs for attention only his mom could provide, and once he was settled and watching his mobile turn, I checked my phone.

I'd been right that my caller was Barron Thompson, if possible more agitated than he'd been in our person-to-person calls. He was under pressure from Ma'Kayla's attorney to assure her that none of the boys involved would be in her classes, and they couldn't accept that it was simply impossible to do. He needed our help, he needed it right now, and if I couldn't be there, he'd have to find someone else to advise the school.

"Go right ahead," I told my phone. "If you can find such a person." Nobody else was Thea the Great and Terrible who could bring wayward boards to heel with a snap of her fingers.

Still, damage control was my business, and so I forwarded his voice message to Suzanne and then called her.

She sounded better today. I got a warm, "Hey there, Partner, how are things going with the new one?" When I felt my body relax, I realized how much I'd been dreading a different response.

"I sent you my latest from Barron Thomson at Stonegate," I said. "It's a voicemail. I think, as our friends across the pond might say, he's losing the plot."

"You want me to listen and call you back?"

I wanted her to listen and call *him* back, but it would be good to bring her up to speed first. "That would be great."

Carrying my phone and the baby monitor, I joined Rosie out on the porch. It was another perfect day, warm breezes ruffling the healthy green grass on our lawn and cooling us where we sat in the shade. A day I couldn't truly let myself enjoy. I try to be a sensible grownup, but sometimes it is too infuriating when life simply won't leave me alone.

To put it back in perspective, I reminded myself that Addison Shirley was in the hospital, having nearly bled to death, and her baby was missing. Compared to that, an annoying headmaster and a troubled school were not such big deals. I hoped things would stay that way and there would be no escalation at Stonegate. I've seen some pretty bad things happen on boarding school campuses, and I didn't have enough information to get a read on whether there might be more serious problems brewing there.

As though what had happened to Ma'Kayla wasn't serious. But if the situation was badly managed, it could get so much worse for the school, and my specialty was crisis management.

So much depended on leadership. Thompson had been so upset during our conversations I hadn't had the chance to do any threat assessment and predict whether any of this might blow up into something worse. That was something I needed to encourage Suzanne to do. That and damage control.

Damage control including coaching them on the importance of following their own rules, including their honor code and any hearing process they'd devised to deal with student infractions. Following their own rules was one of the best defenses if the erring students' parents wanted to challenge the school's actions. Damage control was also about listening to their attorney and about getting their board and headmaster on the same page—I'd done that, or tried to, but Suzanne might have to do some arm twisting with the new board chair.

What I hadn't done was a deeper dive into the parties involved and what that might mean for managing the situation and reassuring the school community, or following up on the information that one of the boy's parents was connected. I didn't know enough about any of the parents. It was the kind of thing I'd normally do when I got there. Now it was something that Suzanne was going to have to do.

She was tough enough. She started this business and has dealt with schools for a long time. She just wasn't Thea the Great and Terrible. I had to hope that her diplomacy and experience would give the school what it needed without me there to bully the board and headmaster into cooperating and scaring them into seeing the light.

This all came so naturally to me that it was hard to imagine handing it off, even though I know I'm not the only competent person in our shop. I'd done enough crisis management by now I could almost do it in my sleep. Come into my bedroom at four a.m. with a problem and I'd have a list of actions for you to follow before I'd even finished opening my eyes.

Couldn't do that now for Stonegate. I was embarked on my own situation—mothering—which was taking up all my energy. Unlike those situations where I knew what to do, with respect to mothering Mason, I was really at sea.

I looked over at Rosie, happily bent over her knitting.

"How did you know what to do when Isabella arrived?"

She set down her needles. "I had my mom practically next door, which turned out to be lifesaving, since Dom was often gone, and I was so worried about him. Plus my sister was a few years ahead of me. She already had two, and we were close, so I could always call her and ask if something was normal."

She picked up her needles again, then put them down. "It's sad that your mother isn't stepping up. But even if she won't visit, can't you call her and ask your questions?"

Could I? I considered how that conversation would go, then shook my head. "She lives to find fault, at least with me. And for being right. That's the last thing I need right now."

"I agree. So you call me instead. That way I can keep up with my godson's development. You can even Zoom. I have learned how to Zoom. So he can see my face and won't run and hide the next time we visit."

"I hope you'll be visiting again before he starts to walk."

"Of course. Of course. Crawl and hide. Though I expect he's going to be very precocious."

I thought about the challenges of babyproofing the house. "Fine with me if he's a late bloomer."

She shook her head. "He won't be. You'll see."

She bent back over the rainbow sweater she was knitting. I could already see it was going to be the kind of treasured garment we would put on him with joy and then save for his children. Mason having children? It was a gobsmacking thought.

Speaking of gobsmacking, that was the moment when the questions from last night that I hoped I'd remember came back to me.

The town where they'd found Addison Shirley was the town where Libby told me she lived, and she'd given me her address along with her phone number. She'd also told me that Benjy Goodman lived in her town. I wondered if he lived nearby? Then I decided I was being silly. Andre knew where Goodman lived, I was sure, and would be able to make any connection between Goodman's address and where they'd found Addison Shirley. It was silly of me, and unnecessarily suspicious, to wonder whether where they'd found her was also close to where Libby Frenier lived.

Neither Andre nor Roland had mentioned the location of the property where they had found what proved to be Addison Shirley's blood, only that it belonged to Faraday. But wasn't Benjy Goodman a better suspect than Faraday? Surely Faraday was smart enough to avoid harming someone in one of his own properties? Except there was the arrogance factor. Sometimes bad guys thought they were so smart no one would suspect them. But if Faraday was so smart, why had he disappeared when being unavailable focused suspicion on him?

Then there was the question of why Lucia Faraday had an infant seat in her car when she didn't have an infant. Had she taken the baby only to have someone take it from her?

These were not my questions to answer, but I had no way of keeping them out of my head. That damned accidental encounter with Addison Shirley had dragged me into this mess against my will, and now I couldn't stop puzzling about it. It's my nature to try and find answers. My nature and my job.

I had definitely lived with cops too long. Cops and crimes and criminals.

Still, I couldn't let it go. Somewhere out there, hopefully alive and cared for, was a small, innocent baby. Had the police searched Goodman's residence? If not before, had my identification of Goodman as the person who was watching Shirley around the time her baby disappeared given them cause for a search? Did they even know where Goodman's residence was?

I had to stop thinking about this. I was working on calm and happy thoughts when my phone rang. Suzanne.

"He's definitely losing it," she said.

I had to refocus from Benjy Goodman to Barron Thompson and Stonegate Academy. "You're going to have to go there and hold his hand," I said. "He's being squeezed by the students' families on one side and by an arrogant, thinks he knows it all, board chair on the other. It's a rotten position to be in."

"It is," she agreed. "Though not that uncommon. I'll call him today and plan to go down there tomorrow. It would be a huge help if you could give me an outline of the various issues and your advice on handling them."

She hesitated. She'd been a new mother. She knew how fractured time could be and how foggy the maternal brain was. "If you can."

I could. It might take a few interrupted sessions, but I could. I'd already run the list in my mind and told her part of it. If I could just dictate, it would be easy, but she wanted me to organize it. So now I had to get it down in an email, in a coherent fashion.

"I will. Too bad Sarah isn't here," I said. "I could really use her for this."

Sarah was my wonderfully competent and understanding secretary. I could tell Sarah to find me the crisis management plan and the honor code we'd written for Stonegate, and she'd have it on my desk in minutes. I really needed both documents to put together a good strategy outline for Suzanne. But it was Sunday and Sarah was home with her kids.

For a moment, I was overwhelmed. I wanted to tell Suzanne I couldn't do it. She could just figure it out for herself. But that wasn't how we worked. We were partners. We shared expertise. We didn't break down and cry because things felt hard. There would always be things that felt hard and we had to suck it up and go on. She had figured that out when her babies were small. Now I needed to remember it, too.

"It may take me a while."

She made an affirmative sound.

"How are things on your end? You handle the unexpected guests okay?"

"Thanks to the miracle of Trader Joe's," she said. "I can give you a list of the best things to keep in your freezer."

"Ah," I said, looking over at Rosie, "but I have Rosie Florio, the world's best cook, stocking my freezer."

She sighed with envy. "I'll let you go," she said, "and I'll call Barron Thompson. See if I can calm him down a bit."

"You're very good at that. Good luck, and thanks," I said. I was already wondering if I could find the time to make a quick trip to the office, even though I'd been sharp with Andre when work called him away. Work and family relationships were complicated.

Rosie and I had a few more peaceful minutes chatting, before 'he who must be obeyed' or at least changed, started up.

"May I?" she said.

"Be my guest. I'll be up in a few minutes."

Live in help, I thought. Live in help in the form of Rosie Florio.

That was what I needed. But as the song tells us, we can't always get what we want. Dom had first call on Rosie. I needed to be grateful they'd come at all. Come and brought calm and help and love and enough food to last us for weeks. It was a lot and I needed to be more grateful.

Through the monitor, I could hear Rosie crooning to Mason. She sounded so happy, and it reminded me that whatever else was going on in my world or Andre's, we needed to remember that our son deserved a happy and peaceful atmosphere. He deserved warmth and love, no matter how stressed we found ourselves. For some reason, thinking that made me feel calmer. Clients were clients, work was work. Mason was a miracle. The thought of leaving him, even for an hour to dash to my office, seemed overwhelming.

He had a father, I reminded myself. Andre was comfortable taking off and leaving me in charge. I could steal a little time away to go to the office and pick up the documents I needed, especially if it meant that I could then offload my worries about Stonegate onto Suzanne's competent shoulders.

I checked my watch. It was three-thirty. Once Mason was fed, I could hand him off, and I was sure that Rosie and Dom wouldn't mind if they had only Mason and Andre to entertain them for a while.

A look at what I was wearing—decent enough to go out to breakfast—said I couldn't wear it out of the house again. There was milky baby drool on my shoulder. I might have grown more casual, hanging out around the house or trying to stay comfortable while pregnant, but not this casual. I went upstairs to deal with Mason and then change.

At the top of the stairs, I paused. I couldn't help looking out the window for strangers who might be lurking.

TWENTY-TWO

Once fed, Mason was happy to hang out in Rosie's lap, looking at his new world. Rosie was very happy with the program, too, so I headed out to the barn to tell Andre where I was going. His hesitation made me nervous, but I figured it was just because he wasn't sure about handling Mason on his own.

"You've got Rosie," I said. "You'll be fine."

I watched him decide not to worry me by sharing whatever other concerns he had. Maybe the same concerns that had caused me to look out the window for strange cars. But I wasn't bringing Mason with me, and if there were bad guys lurking, Mason was their target, not me.

Ugh! What a horrible thought, that little Mason might be someone's target when his only fault was that he'd been born to me and Andre, a pair of professional trouble magnets. Too bad there was no way we could tell the source of our mysterious threat that we did not have Addison Shirley's baby.

Before I could have second thoughts, I grabbed my purse and briefcase and got in my Jeep. It felt odd to be leaving my baby behind, but I pushed that thought away and focused instead on what I'd need from our files to best prepare Suzanne for the job.

The office was twelve minutes away. If I drove fast, and I should be in and out in less than ten.

Of course, I got behind the world's slowest driver, the insecure sort who brakes for every curve and slows down going uphill as though there were monsters lurking just over the crest. And of course, because I was feeling anxious, it seemed like once I passed that idiot—Andre and I call them "meanderthals"—another car loomed up in my rearview and hung there much too closely, even though I was well over the speed limit. My heart rate didn't settle until the jerk passed me in a no-passing zone and almost hit an oncoming truck head-on.

This drive was doing nothing for my anxiety. No one tells you that when the stork brings that baby, it also brings a lifetime of worry. If we truly knew what we were getting into, would any of us have kids? I thought of Mason's big brown eyes and knew I would do it again in a heartbeat.

After fifteen tense minutes, I was at the office. I parked on the curb by the door—it was a Sunday and no one was going to be policing my parking—and ran inside, scurrying up the stairs like someone was chasing me.

I dropped my briefcase on my desk and headed to the files, quickly finding the file for Stonegate. I pulled out the two reports I needed, plus two memos I'd written for them explaining how to use the plans we'd devised, and headed for the copy machine. Since it was Sunday, I had to wait for the beast to warm up. At least it was working. In the past, we had a copier that required a full-time technician to keep it running. I'd always considered it a sign that I was becoming a grownup when one day, I got tired of nursing it along, said to hell with the expense, and ordered a new one.

While I waited for it to be ready, I pulled a copy of Stonegate's student handbook from the files. These, plus the form all students had to sign to acknowledge having read it and the form agreeing to be bound by the honor code, would provide the guidelines for the headmaster in handling the situation.

Eventually—probably a matter of minutes that felt like hours— the machine was ready and spat out the copies. I returned everything I'd copied to the file and the file to the cabinet. I stood a moment gazing at the quiet, empty office. The familiar clutter on my desk. The posters on the walls. I'd only been away a little over two weeks, and already I missed it. The work might be challenging if not overwhelming, but at least here I knew what I was doing.

I'd be back soon enough, I reminded myself. Then I'd be missing Mason. I shoved the papers into my briefcase and hurried downstairs.

There was a truck parked at the curb right behind my car.

My heart rate jumped. I tucked myself into a corner where I could see out but anyone outside couldn't see in, and studied the truck. Beyond that it was big and black and dusty, I couldn't tell much. The windows were dark. The license plate was obscured by my car. It looked like there was a man sitting behind the wheel but I couldn't tell.

Go away, I thought. *I'm in a hurry. I need to get home.*

I vacillated between thinking it was just someone like me from another office who, like me, had stopped by to pick something up and that it was a bad guy who was waiting for me to emerge. My finger was poised over the screen on my phone, about to call Andre and ask what to do, when a man in a shirt and tie came hurrying out of one of the first floor offices, rushed past without noticing me, and headed for the truck.

My sigh of relief must have been heard all over the state of Maine.

When the truck was gone, I let myself out, made sure the door was locked, and started home.

The return journey went more smoothly than my drive to the office. No car in front of me that was ambling through the pleasant afternoon and no jerk hugging my rear bumper like he wanted to run me down. It was only when I turned onto the road that led into town and to our house that a truck, which had been idling by the side of the road, abruptly pulled out behind me and did hug my bumper. By hug, I mean that if I'd braked suddenly, he would have been in my backseat.

I've had my run-ins with guys in trucks, so my anxiety level rose.

I reminded myself that half the vehicles on the road in Maine were trucks, and plenty of them were driven by macho jerks who got a kick out of pushing people out of their way. Still, when I sped up, going a little too fast for the road, the truck stuck to me like a remora.

Luckily, our driveway was just around the next curve. I flipped on my turn signal, slowed as little as possible while still being able to make the turn, and whipped into the driveway, roaring up in true Andre Lemieux fashion and parking beside Dom's car.

Behind me, the truck slowed almost to a stop. The driver peered up at me and then sped away.

Too creepy.

The driver could have just been a jerk, but my intuition said I'd been followed.

I grabbed my briefcase and purse and headed inside.

Andre's father was down on his knees, measuring something to repair the broken door frame. He can't stand it if he isn't busy, which is great for us. After my encounter with the truck, I was even more grateful that we wouldn't go any longer without a door we could lock. I ignored the smarmy little voice in my head reminding me that if someone wanted to get in, they could just break down the door again. The alarm company I'd broken down and called didn't work on Sunday except for emergencies. Tomorrow I was calling them again.

As I passed Mr. Lemieux, I bent and kissed him on his cheek. He's a shy man who doesn't like praise but he likes to be noticed. "You're a lifesaver," I said. "Can you stay for dinner?"

He shook his head. "Aimee's coming over with the kids, and it's more than my wife can handle. They're a wild bunch. Hope yours will be a bit quieter. Andre was. He was always watching, but he didn't say much."

It was more than he usually said. Andre's sister Aimee had five kids and couldn't control any of them.

Andre was in the kitchen, Mason on his shoulder, and he and Dom were eating cake. Rosie was watching them with a benevolent expression, like an indulgent mama watching her boys.

"It's almost dinner time. You'll ruin your appetites," I said, channeling my mother. Then added, "Some guy in a truck followed me on my way home."

Both my favorite cops were instantly alert, and like a pair of mismatched twins, said, in tandem, "What can you tell us about the truck?"

What could I tell them about the truck? I'd been concentrating pretty hard on not getting run into, but I am trained in the Lemieux school of observation.

"It was a white Chevy Silverado. Double cab. Maine plate, but it was too close to read, and smeared with mud. There was a dent on the right front bumper, a Trump sticker, and something, maybe a credential on a lanyard, hanging from the mirror."

"She's good," Dom told Andre.

"Oughta be. I trained her myself."

I considered clapping my flippers together and barking "Arf. Arf," like a trained seal.

Dom, sensing this, asked, in a jovial voice, "What are we having for dinner, anyway?"

"Chicken Marbella," Rosie said. "We can't always be eating pasta."

"I could," Dom said.

"And you'd get slow and fat."

"I'm in the prime of life," he said.

"Prime as in aged, like beef?"

Their banter was fun to watch and helped create a space for me to calm down. "I'm just going upstairs to get my gun," I said, opening the freezer and taking out the peas. Then I remembered I'd put the key in my pocket yesterday. Not a smart move. If the gun was going to be available to keep me safe, I needed to be religious about where I stored the key. In the peas or on my person. Either was fine. Consistency was the key. With the key.

Ignoring the way they were staring, I put the peas away and went upstairs. I found the key, got my gun, and brought them both back downstairs. I put the key back in the peas and tucked the gun in the drawer where I kept my potholders and dishtowels.

"Think of it as a security blanket," I said, feeling defensive. Instead of offering some further explanation, I added, "Rosie, when do we need to start dinner?"

"Soon," she said. "Want to see if we can find more ingredients for a salad?"

Leaving the guys behind, I picked up my trug, and we went out to the garden.

"Are you okay?" she asked as I picked lettuce, and she pulled mini carrots and searched for a cucumber.

"Sort of. I guess I feel angry and victimized, things I don't need right now."

I stared out toward the woods, where I'd seen the person I suspected was our intruder disappearing. This whole business didn't make sense. If Lucia Faraday had taken the baby, and Goodman had been watching her and killed her to get his baby back, where was the baby? Why had Addison Shirley disappeared? Was she hiding from Goodman? If he'd found her and attacked her, why would it have happened in one of Faraday's properties? Why had she ended up in someone's root cellar? If Benjy Goodman was the guilty party, where did Faraday come in? Why was he also being hard to find?

It seemed like things were too convoluted to sort out, at least for me, who was probably unaware of many other facts.

I tried to answer Rosie's question. "I'm okay. I'd be more okay if life and work would leave me alone. It's bad enough when trouble arises as part of my work... or my love for Andre. But this whole mess just from going out to buy my baby a hat? Never mind my clients, who have problems that really need my attention. It's enough to turn me into a hermit. Or a misanthrope."

"That's a thousand dollar word," she said. "So, if you could go back and do it over, would you not have stopped to help?"

As I considered her question, I moved to the tomato plants, looking for a ripe one. The trouble with gardening, I was learning, is that it is very much feast or famine. Right now, we were having a tomato feast. If I were more domestic, I'd put up some spaghetti sauce for winter. But canning and freezing were not in my skill set.

Not yet, at least. I wasn't about to take up anything that couldn't be abruptly interrupted by Mister Mason's demands. Would it be kinder to say needs? Yes. His needs.

"That's a difficult question," I said as I piled tomatoes into the trug. Dom and Rosie were definitely going home with some of these. "I'm afraid I'm hardwired to stop and help. But if I'd known it would bring so much misery?" I shrugged. "I don't know. All I do know is that I did not and do not need any more reasons to watch my back or lose sleep. This is supposed to be a happy time. Family time. Time for me and Andre to settle into being parents, into a new phase of our lives. We promised each other we'd work hard at not being workaholics and on bringing better balance into our lives."

I spread my hands in a gesture of frustration. "Here we are, little more than a week after Mason's birth, and Andre's back at work, our house has been violated, and I'm enmeshed in someone else's troubles and being dragged into a campus mess by an anxious headmaster."

We walked to two of the Adirondack chairs on the deck and sat down. "I'm sorry, Rosie. I don't mean to be wallowing or complaining. I don't know how to do this better."

"Give yourself some time," she said. "You can't change your ways overnight, and neither can Andre."

"Did you and Dom—"

"Have an adjustment period? You bet. It was awful. I was young and scared with this little baby on my hands, and I didn't really know anyone in the neighborhood, and Dom was always gone. He often worked double shifts to help pay for the mortgage. Like you, I'd always worked and I didn't know how to adjust to a life that was mostly meals and housework and baby care and laundry. I didn't have anyone to talk to. Well. That's not entirely true. I did have my sister and my mother, who were both great. My problem was that I thought I was supposed to be able to do it on my own, so I was trying not to ask them for help. I didn't realize until later that they were dying to help and trying not to be a bother."

"At least you weren't chased by bad guys in trucks and threatened over the phone."

"True," she agreed.

We sat a while in silence. Once again, I was being comforted by her presence, but what was she getting out of this relationship? It seemed like I was always the needy one. Because I'm me, the blurter out of truths, I said, "What's in this for you?"

"This?" she said. "You mean Dom's and my relationship with you and Andre?"

I nodded.

"Friendship. Connection. Some people to love who really appreciate it. Dom gets Andre, a colleague he can talk to without interoffice politics. I get you, a daughter I can talk to without stepping on a hornet's nest. And now, of course, there's Mason. We're a lot like you and Andre, you know. We're caretakers. It's too soon for our kids to need us, well, to need us as fellow adults, so we've fixed on you, and if you don't like it, that's just too bad. Dom loves you like a daughter and you know it."

I did know it.

"I should put dinner in the oven," Rosie said. "But it's so peaceful out here I think I'll sit a while. I've never been good at sitting, even when I was forced to. Now that I've left that miserable wheelchair behind, I'm learning to let myself sit and just be." She smiled. "Like a lot of things we do, it's a challenge."

Changing the subject, she said, "I wonder if we could get one of those guys inside to bring us a bit of refreshing white wine while we sit and contemplate the universe?"

As though she'd conjured him up, Dom stuck his head out the door and said, "Could I get either of you ladies a glass of wine?" Before we could answer, he added, "And I've put the chicken in the oven."

We both said yes and he disappeared.

"It's the little things," Rosie said.

At that moment, Andre appeared with another little thing, a rather unhappy one. "I changed him. But it seems that only you will do."

The squinched up red face and flailing fists said he was right. I held out my arms for our squalling son as my husband added, "After

164

dinner, I'm heading over to the hospital to question Addison Shirley."

Defensively, like he expected me to object. Objecting was a waste of time, though. He had a case, he had to work it. Besides, in my own small way, I'd gone to work for a while, too, and tonight I'd have to spend a few hours putting materials together for Suzanne.

Clearly, when it came to leaving our work behind, we were hopeless. At least we'd managed to spend much of a nice weekend with Dom and Rosie. They were leaving in the morning and I knew I'd feel bereft.

A minute later, I heard a phone ring, and then Andre's head poked out. "Sorry. Gotta go," he said. "That damned girl has disappeared again."

TWENTY-THREE

I was beginning to dislike Addison Shirley immensely, even though I didn't know her. She was a pea under my mattress, a burr under the saddle. Despite her evident travails—being left for dead was definitely a travail—she seemed determined to make more trouble for herself. Lying about me to the police. Disappearing so they couldn't help her. Then disappearing again when she had been rescued. I had to wonder what was going through her head. Her information was critical to finding her baby, and probably to finding Lucia Faraday's killer as well. Yet she had disappeared again rather than cooperate. Clearly there was someone she feared more than the police.

I wondered if they'd put an officer on her room. If so, and she still managed to disappear, that someone was in trouble. Perhaps after Andre's visit to the hospital, I might learn something about the circumstances. For now, though, all I had was an empty chair at the table, and a mystery that kept compounding without resolution.

I sighed and shrugged. I was trying to disengage from this mess. Hard when it kept coming right into my house.

"Three for dinner, I guess," I told Rosie. "I think that calls for a bit more wine."

I don't drink that much, no matter how it sounds. But after nine months without any alcohol, I was finding my evening glass, or sometimes two, a real treat.

Rosie snapped her fingers in the direction of the door, like a rude patron calling for a waiter, then grinned at me. "Like I was actually expecting him to appear?" she said.

"He offered wine before. And put dinner in the oven."

"But it's so pleasant sitting here. He should come out and join us. We might even let him hold the baby."

She went inside, returning moments later with a bottle of wine, a tray of snacks, and Dom Florio. She moved a small table closer and set down the snacks while he held out his hands for the baby.

"I hope you're not too upset with Andre," he said. Cops, of course, like to have each other's backs.

I shook my head. "Not as long as he isn't gone long. And as long as Addison Shirley doesn't show up here, looking for her baby."

I was joking, but given all that had happened, it wasn't impossible that that might happen. Addison Shirley or someone else. That threat on the phone lingered like a bad scent in the air.

Time passed. Dinner time arrived. Andre didn't. We ate Rosie's delicious food and pretended nothing was wrong.

My irritation grew like a slowly spreading itch that I couldn't scratch.

We had coffee in the living room and Dom and Rosie described their plans to redo a part of their house. "It's been thirty years," Rosie said, "and everything is getting tired. If we take down a few trees outside, knock down the wall between the kitchen and the living room, and put in some bigger windows, we can have a great room with a fireplace and sun."

"Rosie says that as we get older, we need more light," Dom said. He spread his hands. "And I don't argue with Rosie." He looked at his wife. "It's a great plan. We can grow old together, sitting by the fire and knitting."

The image of Dom knitting made me laugh, and then our peaceful evening was shattered when someone banged on our newly repaired kitchen door.

"I'll go," Dom said.

I thought of my gun in the kitchen drawer. Of that threat on the phone. Someone thinking that I had Addison Shirley's baby.

It could just be a neighbor dropping off some goodies to welcome Mason. Or even Suzanne, come to get the materials I hadn't had a minute to work on yet.

The pleasant room that only a minute ago had seemed so companionable and domestic felt suffused with danger, like a poisonous gas in the air.

"No. I'll go," I said, "You watch Mason." Dom handed the baby to Rosie and rose, standing guard. I see him as benevolent, because of the ways he's been there for me, but he is a big, tough man with fierce cop's eyes.

I crossed the kitchen like I was walking on a rope bridge over a chasm and reached the door just as whoever was there pounded again.

"Hold on. I'm coming," I called, thinking we should have had Andre's father install a peephole, like in a hotel room. We'd only had the house about four months, but they'd been a pretty eventful four.

"Friends not foes," called a woman's voice, and I opened it to find Norah Kavanaugh and Tommy Munro on the doorstep.

She was carrying a foil-wrapped dish while he was carrying a bundle wrapped in a shiny blue paper. "Sorry to barge in without calling but it's been so crazy lately that when we had a moment, we figured we'd better just drop in."

She held out the dish. "Lobster mac and cheese. I hope you like lobster."

"Love it," I said, "and Andre does, too. Plus he loves mac and cheese, so it's a double win."

Seeing that he wasn't needed to protect me, Dom had retreated to the living room.

I hugged Norah, then hugged Tommy Munro. "Aren't you guys supposed to be on a honeymoon?"

They laughed, and Tommy said, "If only people would stop making trouble, maybe we could." They exchanged looks, and then he said, "We got a few days before we were called back in. Speaking of called back in, is Andre around?"

"What do you think? It's that problem with people making trouble. He's got a homicide, plus a beating victim who's a possible witness to that homicide who just disappeared from the hospital. He got the call, and whammo! He was gone. So much for paternity leave. The way things are these days, it's kind of a miracle we even got to paternity, never mind leave."

It was then that I noticed how Norah's belly was straining the buttons on her uniform shirt. "Speaking of paternity, how you'd guys do that so fast? Didn't you just get married like two weeks ago?"

I knew exactly when it was, since I'd gone into labor at the reception and had to leave before the cake. As a slightly panicked Andre was dragging me toward the door, I remember asking them to save me a piece.

Norah shrugged. "All I can say is that I'm glad I didn't pop until just now or my dress would never have fit."

"You looked beautiful," I said. "You both did."

I stepped back. "Come on in. We've got some company up from Massachusetts and I know they'd love to meet you. And of course, Mason loves company."

"Can't wait to meet him," Norah said. "And I have so many questions for you."

As we headed for the living room, Tommy said, "You having some work done on your barn?" Casually, but it was the kind of casual that had a warning in it. I practically live on the phone with my school clients. I'm a pretty good reader of voices.

Wondering what was up, I said, "Andre's dad's been fixing up the workshop, but he's not working today. I mean, he's come and gone." It was after dinner on a Sunday, a time when almost no one would be working on a barn unless it was their own.

He nodded, like that was the response he'd expected, and said, "So what's that truck doing parked out there? Seemed kinda odd, someone parked out behind your barn like that." He paused. "I got a plate. You want me to run it?"

I wanted him to run the person off in a way that would guarantee they never returned, but running the plate was a smart first step. Could it be the truck that had followed me? Had someone actually had the audacity to park right by our house? The soft evening air suddenly felt chillier.

"That would be great," I said.

Figuring it would be useful for them to know, I added, "I was followed by some guy in a truck earlier today, coming back from picking something up at my office. They were way too close and threatening, but they sped off when I turned into the driveway. Given Andre's current case, and our recent break-in... plus Mason, everything makes me nervous."

I was saying 'they' but had I seen two people in the truck? I thought so but couldn't be sure. I hesitated. "You did hear about the break-in?"

He nodded.

"So you'll check out the truck?"

"No problem," he said, handing me the package and ducking out the door.

Norah shook her head. "You must wonder whether things are ever going to calm down in your life."

"I do. I'm getting kind of tired of emergencies and bad guys on my doorstep. When we were house-hunting, we never considered a castle, but now I'm thinking a wall and moat are great amenities."

I switched the conversation to her. "So, you never told me you were pregnant."

She shrugged. "Being a woman in what's still mostly a man's world, I try not to give anyone any reason to judge me or keep me from doing my job. I know you would have kept our secret, but we decided not to tell anyone, not even our families, until little Lulu here forced our hand."

"Lulu?"

"It's a joke. Kinda like you guys calling your kid MOC, for Mason, Oliver, or Claudine."

"But you know it's a girl?"

"Tommy couldn't stand the suspense."

We went into the living room and I introduced Norah to Dom and Rosie. Mason was on Dom's thighs doing his starfish number, arms and legs going, tiny fists opening and closing. Tuning up to take on the world. Rosie was knitting, that little sweater almost finished. Something like that would take me a year, and that would be without constant interruptions. It looked so cozy and domestic. I briefly entertained the thought that if it had been my parents here, things wouldn't have seemed so pleasant. My mother's constitutionally unable to stop finding fault and that makes me totally unable to relax.

My father might be holding the baby, though. His absence made me sad.

Hot on the heels of that was a wish that Dom and Rosie never leave, or at least buy a house nearby so they could be closer.

Dom tucked Mason in the crook of his arm and stood up. Always such a polite guy. He extended the hand that wasn't holding the baby.

"Pleased to meet you. Looks like pretty soon Mason's going to have a playmate," he said.

"Dom!" Rosie chided, setting down her knitting and standing to shake hands. "That's not polite."

Norah Kavanaugh laughed.

That was when Tommy returned, holding a small notebook. After I'd made introductions, he said, "Truck's registered to a Joshua Frenier." He named a town. "That ring any bells?"

Unfortunately, it did. Joshua Frenier was Libby Frenier's oldest son. The one she said she'd had to fight hard to keep from falling under Benjy Goodman's influence. At least, Libby Frenier lived in that town and had a son she'd called Josh. Had she failed, in the end, to steer her son away from Benjy's bad influence? And was I now about to kiss my potential nanny goodbye? Unless that small town was overrun with Freniers, and more than one of them was named Joshua, this was bad news for her and for me.

"Was there anyone in the truck?" I asked, not eager to know the answer. I figured if Tommy had found someone lurking in a truck on our property, he would have snagged him.

Tommy Munro shook his head.

Which meant somewhere around here, someone might still be lurking. Frenier or maybe Goodman. Or maybe both of them. Damn that tinted glass. Between that and trying not to get rear-ended, I hadn't gotten a good visual.

"Does Frenier have a record?" I asked, another question I didn't want to know the answer to.

Tommy nodded his head sadly. "Afraid he does, Thea. He's a pretty bad guy."

TWENTY-FOUR

Before I could say anything, he had his phone out. "I'm calling Andre," he said. "Whatever's going on where he is, someone else can handle it. He needs to be here."

I couldn't agree more, and that was despite the fact that I already had three cops in the room. Andre could have sent Roland, but he had the same problem I have: he thought he needed to be there because he knew he was good at what he did. He thought he needed to be there because of his commitment to justice, doing good, taking care of victims. Another reminder of the challenge for both of us. We seemed to be getting an awful lot of those.

As Tommy stepped out of the room to make his call, Mason decided he needed some maternal attention, and Dom handed him to me.

Knowing how sensitive Mason was to maternal anxiety, I took several deep, slow breaths as I held him against my shoulder and rubbed my chin over his warm, soft head. "I'd better feed this fellow," I said, and headed for the stairs.

"Mind if I tag along?" Norah asked.

"Feel free."

She followed me up the stairs and into Mason's room, settling herself on the daybed while I changed him and then settled into the soft upholstered rocker to feed him.

"Can't believe I'm going to be doing this myself in about four months," she said. "How's it going?"

"I love it but it's challenging," I said. "I was already sleep-deprived from his acrobatics before he was born. Now he demands my attention every two to three hours and only I will do. It's worth it, of course, but I hope his sleep cycle stretches out soon. I also hope your maternity leave will go better than Andre's paternity leave. I suppose it has to, right? They're not going to keep calling *you* in to work."

I sighed. "I don't know if Andre could do better. They're always so short-handed. I mean you are. The state police. Maybe Tommy will have better luck."

I didn't like being the bearer of bad news, but Norah needed my honest assessment. "You'd better brace yourself for doing much of it alone."

"We'll be fine. We're lucky. I've got a mom who's been waiting for this almost since I was born, and she lives just a couple miles away. I expect I'll be fighting her for who gets to hold the baby, and my dad will be almost as bad. They've retired early with too much time on their hands, and a grandkid is the perfect use for that time. I won't even have to look for childcare."

I wondered if I really turned green with envy or just felt like I had.

She nodded toward the stairs. "So what's up with Dom and Rosie? Your aunt and uncle?"

"Related only by affection," I said. "Dom is kind of my knight in shining armor. I met him when he was investigating my college roommate's mother's murder. He latched on to me as his best informant about the family. And Rosie is my surrogate mom. My parents are... uh... well, kind of the opposite of yours, I guess. My mother is the sort of diva who expects me to bring the baby to her to be admired without getting her hands dirty or spit up on, and I am not signing up for a long drive with a newborn just because she can't be bothered to come here."

She nodded. "That'll be Tommy's family. For some reason, they always think they are owed, and it's our duty to figure out what they need, what their latest resentment is, and then give it to them or apologize. It's a ridiculous mind game and I get very tired of playing it. It's a wonder Tommy turned out so well under the circumstances."

I put a sated Mason on my shoulder and rubbed his back. "That truck really bothers me."

"Don't blame you. You haven't exactly had a smooth ride here in your dream house. But Tommy looked around and he didn't find anyone."

"That's not entirely reassuring, though, is it? The truck is here for a reason."

Not that I had any idea what the reason was. A message? A warning? A threat? Who uses their truck for those things, though? For most Maine people, a truck is an essential piece of equipment, not something you can casually park at someone else's house and then leave it there. Whatever the reason, I wanted it gone. It loomed too large on my mental horizon.

Stay calm and relaxed, I reminded myself. Don't upset the baby. This poor kid was going to have a very hard time in the years to come if he stayed so sensitive to parental stress. Reform, I reminded myself. Andre and I had taken a vow to reform. We were both discovering that reform was more easily said than done.

"I'm going down," Norah said.

"Great. I'll put him down and then join you."

The little guy on my shoulder, who'd nuzzled into my neck just like I did with Andre, was totally zonked. I put him in his crib, turned on the baby monitor, and went downstairs.

We'd waited on dessert until Andre got back, but evidently Rosie had decided that everyone needed dessert now. Probably a smart decision. Like me and Andre, Tommy and Norah love to eat. They'd had some of Rosie's food before, when she and Dom came to check up on our preparations for the baby and assert their right to be godparents. No one who's ever had Rosie's cooking says no a second time. I found them all in the kitchen, gathered around another giant pan of tiramisu. Great inroads had been made and all four of them looked happy.

Not that Norah and Tommy hadn't already looked happy. A wedding and a baby? What could be better?

Maybe a nanny. Peace of mind. Jobs that didn't try to steal our lives?

Reminder: We bring this on ourselves.

There was a knock on the door. Andre. I'd forgotten that I'd locked it.

He came in with so much momentum, he was almost through the kitchen before he took in the scene. This was Andre the anxious father and husband, not Andre the detective, who would have entered slowly, taking time to observe the situation.

"Dessert?" Rosie asked, like this was her kitchen and he was a guest. "Or maybe some dinner? It's still warm in the oven."

"Dinner soon," he agreed with a brusque nod, his eyes on Tommy. "The truck? Fill me in," he said.

Tommy filled him in, and I added that I suspected Josh Frenier was the son of Libby Frenier, the woman I'd interviewed about being our nanny. That she lived in the same town where they'd found Addison Shirley, that the missing Benjy Goodman had also lived there, and Goodman and her son had been pals in high school.

When people remark that Maine is just like a big small town, they are often right. I don't know if it's more of a small town when it comes to crime or not.

"The truck's still there," Andre said. "I came in the back way. Parked behind it." He hesitated, looked at me, then focused on Tommy again. "You searched? There's no one here?"

Tommy Munro nodded.

Only then did my husband focus on Norah. More specifically, on the way Norah's trim uniform shirt no longer fit.

"Wow!" he said. "Congrats you two. How'd you keep that a secret so long."

"Oh, we tall gals," Norah said. "More space to expand. That makes it easier to hide."

Andre smiled. "I didn't know Thea was pregnant until your

wedding reception. Couldn't figure out why she wanted me to take her to the hospital when we were having such a good time."

Everyone laughed.

Andre got his dinner from the oven and sat at the table to eat, while the rest of us stood around the counter and tried not to have second helpings of tiramisu. It was such a pleasant scene that I wished I wasn't feeling anxious about that truck while simultaneously wanting everyone to go away so I could go to my home office and start putting together materials for Suzanne. With Mason wanting to eat every two to three hours, my windows of opportunity for work were small. I vaguely remembered a movie I'd seen once where a distracted baseball pitcher would tell himself "clear the mechanism" so he could focus on his pitch. I badly wanted to clear the mechanism.

Andre had just finished eating when we heard the roar of a truck outside. I looked out and saw a tow truck.

"You're towing that truck away?" I said.

"Private property," Andre said. "The owner has no right to leave it here and I expect we'll all feel easier when it's gone."

"Where will they take it?"

"Towing company's got a yard."

"So not to Augusta for crime scene techs to check?"

"Far as we know, the only crime is trespassing."

"What about threatening?" I said. "I think it's parked there to threaten us. It's a visual 'hey guys, we know where you live, so watch your backs.' Something like that." As Andre carried his empty plate to the sink and got a smaller plate for dessert, I added, "I don't suppose we can get your father to dig us a moat?"

"He'd probably love to. But it would spoil the lawn."

"A moat," I said, "with alligators. And maybe some fierce dogs loyal only to us and our friends."

"We have enough to do without taking care of dogs," Andre said. "Though someday I'd like a dog. Mason should have a dog."

The image of tiny Mason and a great big dog was both amusing and scary. I looked at Rosie, who was watching Andre demolish what was left of enough dessert to feed a dozen. Where I might be thinking that this crowd was rather excessive in their consumption, she was smiling. I could use an infusion of her temperament.

"So what now?" I said to the room full of cops. "The truck gets towed away and that's the end of it?"

"Not very likely," Andre said. "Someone is going to come looking for it."

"And you guys are sure there isn't someone lurking in the barn or a body out beyond the vegetable patch?"

Someone else, some ordinary civilian, might have considered my question absurd or a flight of fancy, but this was not that crowd. "I checked," Tommy said.

He was not inclined to be careless, I knew. But four people good at reading the room, along with Rosie, who'd lived with a cop for decades, knew I wasn't comforted.

"We'll go look again. Soon as I finish this." Andre held up his half-finished plate. "Rosie's food deserves my full attention."

I couldn't argue with that.

After the last bite was gone—and I could tell if we didn't have company, he would have licked the plate—the four cops set out to do one last check of the property. Rosie said my friends were very nice, and she was happy to see Mason would have a little playmate.

"I'm going back to my knitting. Want to get this sweater done before we leave, and Mister Impatience will want to leave early in the morning. You know how he is."

I nodded. I was Ms. Impatience right now, and trying to hide it took a lot of energy. I was heading for my office when I realized that I needed to look at that truck myself. It felt safe now, with four cops around.

"Just going to take a look at that truck before they haul it away. See if it is the one that was following me."

Rosie nodded. "Good idea," she agreed.

She went off to knit and I went outside. Andre had moved his car, and a large tow truck was backed up in front of our unwanted automotive visitor, the driver getting ready to hook it up. I stepped close enough to check the front, and yes, there was the dented bumper and the Trump sticker, the lanyard with what looked like credentials still hanging from the rearview mirror.

It was the kind of truck that had a large tool box installed in the back. Shiny quilted silver. Well, once shiny and now a bit weathered, like the truck. A box big enough to hold a body. I assumed that Tommy would have checked it, since he was a careful cop. But I was also careful and had learned from experience that making a list and checking it twice wasn't just for Santa. It worked pretty well for consultants, too.

I held up a hand to stop the driver. "Just want to check that toolbox before you take it away," I said.

He shrugged and said, "Whatever." An easy-going whatever, not a snotty one.

I went around to the rear and climbed into the truck bed, approaching the box warily as I stepped over scattered tools. Bad guys lurk in closets, under beds and cars, and come suddenly out of the darkness. I'd never found one in a box before, but there was always a first time. Heart in my throat—a trite expression but one that fit the moment—I was reaching for it when Andre's voice from behind me said, "Thea, hold on. What are you doing?"

"Checking the box," I said. "In case Tommy didn't. This is definitely the truck that was following me."

"Let me do that," he said.

He didn't exactly elbow me aside, he wouldn't, but he somehow managed to get between me and the box. He's bigger. Wider. And even more certain than I am. One of our regular fights is about who is being protective and who is being pigheaded. But I was learning to embrace knights in shining armor when visions of Jack in the Box boogiemen danced in my head. I stepped back and let him check the box.

I was glad I had, though I was still close enough to see what was inside. A man I didn't know, curled up on his side, a lot of blood on his head and face.

I thought, *what if this is Libby Frenier's son and he was just helping out a terrible friend?* But Tommy had said he was a bad actor. Then I jumped down from the truck and ran inside.

TWENTY-FIVE

I closed the door on Andre's voice calling the others, knowing soon our yard would be swarming with public safety personnel, and went upstairs to check on Mason. Maternal instinct and all that. I needed to see that he was all right before I could begin to process what was happening out there.

He was sleeping like a baby, looking so small, sweet and vulnerable I wondered if he wouldn't be safer with a different mother, one who wasn't a trouble magnet like I was. Too late for that. I bucked myself up and went back downstairs.

"Your phone's been ringing," Rosie said. "I figured if it was important they would leave a message." She held up the little sweater. "It's almost done." Then she set down her knitting and studied my face. "Something's happened, Thea. What's wrong? Is Mason okay?"

"He's fine. Happily sleeping. It's what's happening out there." I gestured toward the driveway. "Looks like we've got ourselves a body. Or a victim, at least. I don't know whether he's alive or dead. He was in the toolbox in the truck."

"Darn it," she said. "That is just so wrong!"

We exchanged the looks of women whose significant others

dealt with "so wrong" all the time, the looks of women who don't want that in our lives yet it kept finding its way in.

"Maybe a moat isn't such a bad idea," she said.

"Would make it hard to do my work, though. I can't always work from home. And once he's crawling, Mason's bound to fall in. I understand that Andre was an intrepid explorer from a very early age, and I've been called headstrong by some people myself."

"Headstrong in a good way. So now what? We sit here in safety while the menfolk deal with the situation?"

I had to smile at her use of the word "menfolk."

"Norah's out there, too," I said.

"Being one of the guys. It's going to be interesting to see how her husband deals with a pregnant wife who is also a cop," she said. "That protect versus respect thing can be a real challenge."

"I know, right. Andre was like a yo-yo about the pregnancy. I'll bet Dom was, too. Never mind about the perils of my work life. It's hard for them to check 'serve and protect' at the door. Or develop a more nuanced version of it."

Rosie nodded. Switching subjects, she said, "So you think you may know the victim's mother?"

"Victim? Oh, you mean the man in the box? We don't know who our victim is yet," I reminded her. "Whether it's the owner of that truck or someone else. Or whether he's dead or only injured." I paused. "I guess either way he's still a victim, isn't he? But yes, I did recently meet a woman named Libby Frenier. I interviewed her about being Mason's nanny. During the course of our conversation, we were talking about the woman, Addison Shirley, whose baby's disappearance had gotten connected to me. Ms. Frenier, Libby, knew Addison Shirley and some of her history. In the course of talking about Addison Shirley, and the man Shirley was involved with, she mentioned a son named Josh who had been friends with Addison Shirley's boyfriend, a bad guy named Benjy Goodman, when they were younger."

I stopped. I was cramming far too much information into this, probably making it totally incoherent. "Sorry. I'm babbling. Finding bodies does that to me."

I took a breath and tried to calm down. "Anyway, Tommy said the truck was registered to a Joshua Frenier. For all I know, there might be a dozen Joshua Freniers around here. But in the same town? And showing up here, when Andre and I are involved in a case that Frenier's former friend is involved with?"

"So you think he might be this woman's son?"

I nodded, thinking about how awful it would be for Libby if this were her child, even if he was a known bad actor. "It would be a pretty big coincidence if this isn't the Josh Frenier who was friends with Benjy Goodman back in the day, when Goodman is one of the prime suspects in a recent homicide my name has been connected with."

Connected with. Like I had had something to do with these people. Once again, I silently damned that blabbermouth Jeremy Bartlett. When this mess was sorted out, I would make it my job to try and get him fired for the way he'd put us at risk. I'm not vindictive. I just have strong opinions about who belongs in the public safety professions. People whose loose tongues cause trouble for innocent people do not.

Andre and Dom came inside to update us. Dom moved protectively to Rosie's side, while Andre stayed in the doorway. His expression was an odd mixture of pride and concern. "It was good thinking, looking in that box, even if Tommy is out there beating up on himself for missing it."

I asked the question I didn't want to ask. "The man in the box... Is he?"

"Deceased?"

I nodded.

Andre shook his head. "Injured. He may not make it. The injuries are bad. But he has a chance. Because he isn't sitting in a tow yard."

"Better put a guard on his door," I suggested. He gave me his patented "put a cork in it, Thea" look. A look I did, and didn't, deserve.

"This doesn't make any sense," I said. "What's the point of leaving the truck here?"

"Might not have been planned," Dom suggested.

The phone rang and I went into my office to take the call. Suzanne. Her first words were, "I am so, so sorry."

I should have hung up right then but I didn't. She couldn't know about the body in the truck, so I asked, "So sorry about what?"

"About tripping over a plastic firetruck and spraining my right ankle."

Definitely should have hung up. Or not answered in the first place. If it was her left ankle, she might have been able to drive down to Massachusetts tomorrow to deal with our client school's trouble. With her right, that option was off the table.

I was silently running through all my best curses when she added, "I tried to find someone who could drive me. I've been on the phone ever since we got back from the emergency room. No luck so far."

Though I waited for her to offer an alternate suggestion, I knew none would be forthcoming. We had a small staff, they were already crazy busy, and this was a situation that called for one of us.

Obviously, we could put the school off until Suzanne was back on her feet—literally—but the school year was starting and Stonegate had too many issues to be dealt with that were serious and immediate.

I wanted to press my head between my hands and scream, but that would only hurt Suzanne's ears and bring the crew from the living room on the run. There was only one solution, one I wasn't ready to offer up. At least, if she was bowing out, she should have to make it.

"I know it's a big ask, Thea, with Mason so young. But could you?"

Tomorrow was too soon. Dom and Rosie were leaving and I needed some time to prep, both for the school and any lengthy outing with my small baby. This was crazy. I should have just said no but I was already pretty deep into things. Deep enough to care about seeing that the school handled things well. Besides, these days it felt like my former avatar, Thea the Great and Terrible, or even Thea the Competent, has been replaced by an emotional wreck, so making a big decision like this was hard. My default, in the interest of our clients and our business, was always to say yes.

Did I have the stamina and presence of mind to handle such a fraught situation? I wasn't sure. At least I could set some boundaries.

"You call them," I said. "Explain the situation and tell them I can be there on Tuesday if they can find someone to watch Mason while I have my meetings. Stress that I must be able to meet with the board, relevant school staff, and with the school's attorney and it has to be on Tuesday. If Barron Thompson gets abusive or starts offering up excuses, remind him that he is welcome to find someone else who can help him. He told me that he could. I would love to see him try."

"I'm sorry," she repeated, sounding genuinely wretched. "I know you covered for me brilliantly and here I am failing my very first test."

"Not a test," I said, because truly we were not in competition, "a partnership. We aren't keeping score here."

"You are too good. Too understanding."

I didn't feel like either of those things.

"Let's just hope he listens to you and does what needs to be done," I said. "And that there are no unhinged people with guns or poisons or agendas. I am so done with all that."

Just saying it made me wonder if I was crazy to consider a trip to Stonegate. The answer was yes. But something besides my loyalty to EDGE Consulting was driving my decision. Something irrational, perhaps, but powerful. After tomorrow morning, Dom and Rosie would be gone, and I expected that Andre would be off pursuing this latest wrinkle in his case. That meant Mason and I would be home alone here, with the specter of strangers in the woods and bodies in trucks joining all the other things that had happened here. I'd be jumping at every creak of the house and every gust of wind.

While I had no idea what I'd do in the long run about reaching a rapprochement with my new house and its accumulating baggage, right now I knew I did not want to be at home alone with little Mason and a gun in my kitchen drawer.

TWENTY-SIX

W hen I came into the living room, Rosie was holding up the tiny sweater she'd been knitting, frowning with concentration as she turned it this way and that. It was shades of blue yarn, from dark to light, like the sky and sea on a summer's day. I paused in the doorway to watch her, thinking that this wasn't just a sweater, it was an act of love and a way for Rosie to wrap Mason in that love.

We were so lucky to have these people in our lives. It helped to have them to balance all the bad stuff that has happened, and Andre and I desperately needed balance. We had a house now, a home, and the baby we'd longed for, but despite our resolution to reform, Mason's arrival hadn't brought the change we'd promised each other. I wondered if it was even possible.

Maybe I was just expecting too much too soon. I reminded myself that change was a process, not a new shirt you could put on and life would be different. It had taken us some years of struggle to get to marriage, then to a home, and now a family. Why should we expect our natures and habits to change overnight?

Rosie looked up from the sweater and studied my face. "More bad news?" she said.

I nodded. "My partner Suzanne was supposed to visit a client school that's in chaos tomorrow and sort them out. She called to say she's sprained her ankle and can't drive, so she can't go. It's a serious situation and one we, well I, can definitely help with, and with the school year starting and complex student management issues involved, they need that help right now."

Sighing, I sat in my favorite chair. "A young girl was assaulted by three football players and the headmaster is waffling about what to do. I think I have to go."

Andre would say I'm crazy. To just tell them no. But Andre was also the one who'd answered the call from *his* work. Maybe I was being unreasonable thinking that my work was important, when his was life and death, but if we started down that road, I didn't like the view.

"Where is this school?" Rosie asked. "Is it far from here? Can you drive? Do you need to fly? Because while I try not to be opinionated, I do not want my godson on an airplane. He's too young."

As Dom would be quick to tell me, you don't argue with Rosie when she's this certain.

There are probably people who would resent someone coming into their house—into their lives—and being so directive, but that was not me. Well, not me in this case. I am definitely of the pigheaded ilk. Ask my mother.

"Just northwest of Boston."

"And you want to go on Tuesday?"

I nodded. "More like need to, if I'm to do any good."

"Then there's no problem," she said. "It's a short drive for me. I can meet you there and watch Mason while you do what you have to do. We wouldn't want to trust our baby to strangers. Not this soon. I have a therapy appointment on Tuesday, but I can move it."

"It's a wonderful offer, but I can't ask you to do that."

"You didn't ask."

There was a definite "don't argue with me" tone in her voice, so I only nodded. "You are a lifesaver."

"Another day with Mason? I consider myself lucky. Although..." She gave me a searching look. "Are you sure you're up for this? It's asking a lot so soon after giving birth, and you know you're exhausted and sleep deprived."

"I am," I agreed. "But I expect I'll be those things for years. Work won't wait for Mason to grow up, I'm afraid, and we've got bills to pay."

"Work could wait a while, Thea."

Interesting that it was Rosie and not Suzanne trying to talk me out of this. Suzanne knew what I was getting into and had fairly recently had a baby herself.

"It's... I don't know. Not just work," I said.

Rosie nodded, her face full of sympathy. "Right. It's threatening phone calls and someone breaking into your house. It's ominous trucks in your yard and a husband who's out chasing bad guys, isn't it? You don't want to be home alone here with the baby."

I wasn't sure how I felt about being read so easily. "Am I really so transparent?"

"You're not transparent. I've been here. I've seen these things myself so I understand. Despite their being good men and good husbands, I'm not sure that Dom or Andre would understand as well. They're used to dealing with danger and shrugging it off and going on. But while you've had your share, you're not trained for it. You're not able to shrug it off. And it's a fact that having a child changes everything, especially for a mother."

She reached out and put her hand over mine, her warmth so comforting. "It's a basic instinct. You're the mother bear now and anything that threatens your cub is going to bring an oversized response. Hopefully, things will settle down soon. This case... or these cases... will be solved, and you and Andre can start working on how to live your new lives. But right now, he's clicked back into his cop world while the changes in yours are radical and go in a different direction. When we had Isabella, it took Dom a while to recognize that our lives—not just mine, but ours—had changed."

She pulled a packet of tissues from her pocket and handed me one. I hadn't realized I was crying.

"You can't go home, Rosie. I can't do this without you." Who cared if I sounded pathetic.

"Yes. You can. You're strong and you're tough and you're resilient. You just have to remember that you're doing something you love, however hard it seems. You know if you get stuck or things get too hard, you can call us. But I know you can do this."

She looked at her watch and yawned. "I am not waiting up for Dom. I'm going to go pack and then get some sleep. You should do the same."

I debated. I had work to do, and according to the rule of "while the baby sleeps" I should be doing it now. But there was also "sleep when the baby sleeps," which seemed like good advice right now. Tomorrow I would have to dig in and get ready for Stonegate. Tonight I'd be digging into how to tell Andre that my decision to go wasn't a question. It was a done deal.

I picked up the baby monitor and waved an airy hand toward the stairs. "After you," I said. I hadn't made it to the stairs before a noisy commotion of all four cops who'd been outside spilled through the door. As Andre offered them beer or wine or juice for Norah, I detoured to find out what they could tell me.

It wasn't much. The guy from the truck box, presumably Josh Frenier, had made it to the hospital alive. They'd found a bloody hammer in the weeds that was the probable weapon used. There were multiple sets of fingerprints in the truck. There was no sign of Benjy Goodman.

"Have you told his mother what happened?" I asked.

"Whose mother?" Andre asked.

"Frenier. Or does he have a wife? A family? What do we... uh, do you, know about him?"

"We have an address, and we're in touch with the sheriff's department. And the Freeport police. His town doesn't have a police department." Andre looked annoyed. "Waiting for someone to call us back."

It looked like they were going to talk shop. It wasn't my shop, so I went upstairs to bed. There was a light under Rosie's door, so I figured she was reading while she waited for Dom.

I looked in on Mason, who was, surprisingly, still asleep. I figured that by the time I got to sleep, he'd be waking up, so I slipped down to my office and brought up my briefcase. Washed and brushed and in my nightgown, I crawled into bed and started reading the student handbook, making notes and attaching yellow stickies on pages I wanted to refer back to. Then it was on to the honor code. I should know it. I wrote it. But we tweaked them to fit individual school's culture and mission, so it made sense to read it again.

Of course just as I was digging into it, again with a flurry of yellow stickies covered with my notes, the phone rang. I could let it ring, I knew, but instinct said it was Suzanne, calling to report on her phone call with Barron Thompson.

I was not wrong.

She plunged in without a hello. "Dammit, Thea! I don't know how you put up with these people or how their emergencies make them insufferably rude."

"It didn't go well?"

Using language she rarely uses, she said, most succinctly, "Thea, it's a shit show."

"Do go on."

There was silence. A deep breath. And my normally unflappable partner said, "He couldn't understand why I couldn't come tomorrow. Then he couldn't understand why you couldn't come tomorrow. He said everything is going to hell and he needs our help and he needs it now."

She sighed. "Took me a while to calm him down enough to give him his marching orders, but I think I have successfully done that. He should be ready for you on Tuesday, and while he seemed dubious about assembling his board, I think he'll do that, too. Plus call in his lawyer. I also asked him to scan and email any relevant documents that we'll... that you'll need to be up to speed on the situation. Or emails from the parents or their lawyers."

"Sounds like you did a good job," I said. "Headmasters can be very difficult when they're faced with any crisis, and a crisis involving minors and sex abuse and cell phone photos and potential issues of pornography are very difficult. Add in race and football stars and it's a huge mess."

"I'm sorry," she said. "I truly am. I ran the situation by Paul and he says the three boys should already have been suspended, if not expelled."

Her husband Paul was headmaster of a private school himself. His reaction pretty much echoed mine, but that decision had to be made by the headmaster and the board, and in accordance with the student handbook, which required a determination of the immediacy of the situation, followed by a fair hearing.

"Well. Looks like I'm going to have a fun day on Tuesday. One piece of good luck is that Rosie Florio has volunteered to meet me there so she can look after Mason."

I thought for a minute, hesitant to mention any criminal matters, but I decided to. "So that woman, Libby Frenier, the one you referred to me as a potential nanny?"

"Uh. Yes?"

"Well, today a truck was following me when I came back from the office. Later we found it parked behind the barn, and inside the tool box in the back was her son. At least, I think it's her son. Someone tried to kill him."

"I don't believe this! She was... seemed like... such a sweet woman. How could her son get mixed up in... Never mind, Thea. I think I don't want to know."

"I'm right there with you," I said.

Further conversation was interrupted by Mason, who woke with a few whimpers that quickly accelerated to a lusty cry.

"Gotta go," I said.

"I guess you do. Good luck."

She went to nurse her wounded foot. I went to nurse my child.

TWENTY-SEVEN

G etting ready for a trip to a client school always felt a little like embarking on a military campaign. I had to be on top of my game, geared up to handle people who were often in the throes of emotional chaos. I had to be the one who stayed calm and directive, giving the necessary orders and advice to people who were used to giving orders themselves. I sometimes had to get down to almost kindergarten-level communication to make people understand their situation, its risks, and their responsibilities.

I would have to have the school's own documents and regulations ready to quote, along with explanations of how they needed to proceed to conform with them. In Stonegate's case, I anticipated I would have a pigheaded chairman of the board to deal with along with a frazzled and frantic headmaster. All of that, by itself, would be enough of a challenge.

This time, though, I had to conduct the entire campaign loaded down with baby gear. As a baby gift, Suzanne had given me a wonderful backpack that held everything I needed, in a chic shade of black, with a fold out changing mat and a separate pocket to hold a day's worth of soiled baby clothes. I also faced a new version of a dilemma I often faced: what to wear.

At a full-chested 5' 11", finding clothes that fit and look professional has always been a challenge. Before she had children, Suzanne used to take care of my wardrobe. Despite being petite herself, she always managed to find clothes that worked for me. Shopping bags would appear on my desk when she went shopping for herself and everything was perfect. She no longer had time for that, leaving me, a woman who really doesn't care about fashion, on my own. Maternity clothes had been a nightmare. Now I had to find things that fit my postpartum body, while hiding the inevitable baby spit and still looking professional. Suiting my sense that I was going to war, camo would have been perfect, but it wasn't right for a boardroom.

A bit of digging in my closet turned up a black, white, and gray animal print cardigan and a matching tank. I didn't remember buying it but it was perfect. Animals were smart about camouflage. Add black pants and my comfy wedge loafers and I was ready to rock and roll. Or was that lock and load?

When I packed Mason's things, I added a simple black tee shirt for myself in case I still needed a change. In terms of both baby and wardrobe, I was heading into unfamiliar territory.

Then I settled him into his carrier, what I'd taken to calling his "baby bucket."

"We are going for a nice long ride in the car, kiddo," I told him.

He made a face.

"I am sorry. I'd leave you home with your daddy, but your daddy is nowhere to be found and you're too little to become a latch-key infant."

His eyes—Andre's eyes—stared at me as though he was contemplating his reply. Probably I was reading too much into them, but it seemed like he was already wise. Wise and skeptical, as if he was wondering what he'd gotten himself into. This was day ten of his new life and each day brought so many changes.

His daddy had left early to follow up some lead or other after once again expressing his disapproval about my plans. His own conduct might not have given him standing to complain, but he managed to get a whole lot of criticism into his glares, his body language, and the thud of his feet. Not even my reassurance that Rosie would be there helped. He thought it was too soon for Mason to be out among people.

Not that our home hadn't been kind of a circus, with Andre's family, then Dom and Rosie, and a regular parade of Andre's colleagues.

He didn't have to say, "Look how that last outing with the baby went," because we were both still dealing with the consequences of that. Although I would note that Lucia Faraday's death had not conclusively been connected to Addison Shirley.

After I settled Mason in his car seat—rear-facing for safety so I couldn't even look back at his face—I set off, so unnerved I wasn't sure I remembered how to drive. I settled down pretty quickly and forced my thoughts away from whether every other vehicle on the road presented a danger to me and my son. Of course they did. Instead, when I should have been thinking ahead to my work at Stonegate, I was thinking about yesterday afternoon.

I'd been at my desk prepping for today's meetings while Mason lay in a baby seat and watched bits of sunlight reflecting through a piece of stained glass that were dancing on the wall. Occasionally his moving fist would catch his attention and he'd stare at that instead. It was hard not to be distracted by how amazing he was, but I had work to do. I was making extensive notes about the student handbook and the honor code when someone knocked on the door.

No one else was home. I could ignore it but the last time I'd tried that I'd almost missed a visit from Libby Frenier. "Be right back," I told the kid. To be on the safe side, I slipped my gun into my pocket. My other pocket had pepper spray. Andre likes me to be prepared. Before I opened the door, I peeked out the window.

It *was* Libby Frenier again, but a far different woman today from the sweetly comforting and composed woman who'd visited me before. This woman had uncombed hair. She wore a red and orange flowered blouse with a pair of blue and green plaid pants. An outfit not even the most experimental influencer would choose. Her blouse was on inside out. It would have been comical if it hadn't been for her face, which was devastated.

"I'm sorry to bother you, dear," she said, sliding past me into the kitchen. "But I need to know... everything. I need to know what happened to Josh and no one will tell me anything. What was he doing here? What happened? Who did this to him?"

When she paused for breath, I offered her a seat and some tea. I put the kettle on and got out a tin of Rosie's cookies.

"Let me get Mason and we can talk. You should understand, though, that I don't know much more than you do."

"Anything would be a help. I know nothing." It came out as a sigh. "You know how the police are."

She swiped some loose strands of hair away from her face and secured them with a bobby pin from her pants pocket. "Well. Maybe you don't, being married to one. I expect he talks to you. But me? I'm just the mother, when there's my boy in the ICU and no one's offering much hope that he'll wake up, never mind be okay and not brain damaged."

She knew more than I did. I knew nothing about Josh Frenier's condition. I might be married to a cop, but he could still be very close-mouthed. That was the nature of the job. Besides, while he was home we'd been arguing about my work and that had precluded my getting an update.

I went and got Mason, putting his seat on the counter between us.

Babies have a kind of magic, I think, because as soon as he turned his brown-eyed gaze on her, she softened. "Oh. He's such a little angel." She reached for him, then hesitated. "May I?"

"Of course."

I said of course but I was still uneasy about letting anyone besides me and Andre hold Mason. Dom and Rosie being the exceptions. I'd done it the last time she was here, though, so it would seem odd to refuse her now. Especially when she seemed so fragile.

She settled him in the crook of her arm.

"What happened here?" she said. "What was Josh doing here and why was he attacked? Who attacked him?"

I shared the little I knew. That Josh's truck had followed me back from my office and how menacing it had been. How I'd thought it had driven away, and then a couple of state troopers who'd come to visit the baby had spotted it behind the barn but when they searched, they found no one around, just the truck.

"They were about to tow it away to some storage lot when I decided I'd look in the tool box. It was... well, I guess it was just a hunch. There were tools scattered around the truck bed, which seemed odd, when there was that box there to store them. So I... we... checked and found your son."

"Oh my God!" she moaned, shaking her head. "You mean the truck might have been towed away and Josh might not have been found and he might have..." She couldn't go on.

"I'm sorry," I said. "Do *you* have any idea what he might have been doing here? When we spoke before, you told me that back when your son was a teenager, he was friends with Benjy Goodman and you had to work hard to get him away from Goodman's influence. Do I remember that right?"

She nodded, looking like she might break down in tears at any moment.

As I moved a box of tissues closer, Mason, with his exquisite ability to sense emotions, made a small sound. She looked down, ran a gentle hand over his soft head, and whispered, "Sorry."

"Do you know whether the two of them have reconnected?" There was no good way to finesse it. It was a blunt question and one important to Andre's investigation.

I could tell the answer was yes and she didn't want to admit it. Didn't want to admit a maternal failure, as though she was responsible for an adult son's behavior.

She was silent for a while, distracting herself by letting Mason wrap his fingers around one of hers. It must have been a hard-wired survival instinct that babies had, wrapping their tiny hands around adult fingers. It was a gesture so amazing that it ensured the adult would want to care for them.

"He... uh... long story short? Yes. I've tried to stop it. Tried so hard to make him see what Benjy is like, but..."

She shifted in her chair, staring at my kitchen cupboards but clearly seeing something else. "Josh was always a soft boy. Gentle. A follower. Easily influenced. We did our best, my husband and I, to help him understand his own character, his weaknesses, and to be watchful about bad influences. We did our best, but Josh became a soft man. Then he married a harsh woman who nearly broke him. When that marriage ended, he was devastated. Lost. Unable to get his feet back under him. Lately, I thought he was coming out of it. He seemed more decisive, more willing to take charge of his life, only then we, well I, my husband being gone now, found out that he was getting his direction from Benjy."

She bent over Mason again. "You'll learn, as he grows up, there's only so much you can do as a parent. The anxiety... the worry... it never ends. I thought that he'd broken off with Benjy. This time, I mean. That's what he told me. I probably should have known better. Josh was always telling us what we wanted to hear instead of the truth. He was afraid of confrontation."

"Was he working with, or for, Benjy or just hanging out with him?"

"Josh is a carpenter. A handyman. He can pretty much fix anything. So that's his job and because he's good and comes when he says he will and doesn't charge outrageous prices, he's got plenty of work. Benjy's work is selling drugs, drinking, and scamming people. So as for working with, or for, or just hanging out? With Benjy, it's all pretty much the same thing. You spend time with him, you get dragged into his world. He's been trying to... uh..."

She broke off. "This is so painful. Josh is a good man. An honest man. But Benjy Goodman has been trying to get Josh to give him information about the people, and the places, where he works, so that Benjy can then break in and steal their stuff. So far... I think... Josh has resisted. But Benjy has a way about him, a way of getting people to do what he wants."

I could feel my day slipping away and I had so much more to do. On the other hand, she had information that would be useful not only to me, in helping me understand about that menacing truck, and the who and why of those threats on the phone, but to the police.

"Could Benjy have persuaded your son to follow me?"

She shook her head, the bobby pin coming loose and dropping to the floor. "I don't know. What you describe sounds more like terrorizing than following. I can't see Josh doing that."

She considered how to say this next. "What I can see, from knowing him, is Benjy planning the thing, and then insisting that he be driving—doing what he wants no matter how dangerous—and Josh a passenger in his own truck, protesting but not knowing how to stop him."

Her voice got softer, so low I could barely hear her. "Which might have been what nearly got him killed. Benjy doesn't have much patience with anything that gets in his way or doesn't let him have his way. As I said before, he's a monster. He's always about what he wants and what he needs, or thinks he needs. So if Josh tried to stop Benjy from doing something, even if they were in Josh's truck, I can see... I can see Benjy attacking him like that, just because. He's like the spoiled kid no one has ever said "no" to. He won't hear it."

Sitting there in her awful mismatched outfit, her shoulders slumped, Libby Frenier looked utterly defeated. I was sure it was a lesson I would be learning soon enough—that once you have kids, you always have kids, and will always worry about them.

"I'm sorry about your son. I hope he'll be okay. It can be so frustrating when the doctors won't tell you anything, but they're always so cautious about making promises. Head injuries are tricky. They do require some patience, even the doctors have to wait and see how things turn out."

Switching subjects, I asked, "If Benjy got your son into this, if he's the one who hurt your Josh, you must want him caught. Right?"

She nodded.

"Do you know where Benjy is living right now? Because the police have been trying to find him."

She nodded again. "I do. I... uh... I've been hesitant to say because unless he's arrested and stays in jail, I'm taking a big risk, telling you. Telling anyone. I know the police always promise people they'll keep them safe, but restraining orders and threats don't work with someone like Benjy. He believes the rules don't apply to him."

Libby Frenier might have come here for information but I was the one who was getting it.

"They will try," I said. "Getting him off the street is so important. Important to me in terms of keeping Mason safe. There have been threats. A man called and left a scary message suggesting I have Addison Shirley's baby, and he, or they, I think he said they, were coming to get it."

She shifted her gaze from the cupboards to me, suddenly very focused. "Do you still have that message?"

I nodded. "On my phone."

"May I hear it?"

I couldn't see why not, so I got out my phone and played it for her.

She listened attentively, her head cocked to one side. When the brief message finished, she said, "Again, please?"

I played it again, watching her as she listened. She nodded. "I'm pretty sure that's Benjy."

What I, what we, had suspected, but none of us were familiar with his voice, while she was.

Relief warred with worry. Knowing who made the call was helpful but having the caller still at large meant the threat hung there like a big black cloud. It meant something else, too. That Benjy Goodman was still looking for Addison Shirley's baby and thought I had him. I didn't, so who did have the baby?

It seemed like the only possible choice was James Faraday, but why would he kill his own wife to get the baby? That level of desperation didn't fit with the mercurial, self-indulgent man who had been described to me. But people can change, and maybe, after all those wives and girlfriends, Faraday was looking for a son to be his posterity. He was in his late forties or fifties and wasn't that when people began to realize they were entering the second halves of their lives?

Nor did I have any idea why Lucia Faraday had had the baby in the first place. I could believe that she'd taken him—I'd seen her on the street with that basket right as he disappeared. But then what had happened? Going farther back in time, how had she known about the baby? Would her husband have told her? And who, other than Faraday, would have known she had the baby? It felt like there had to be some other players here we didn't know about.

I wondered if Andre did.

This was not supposed to be my problem, was it?

After a long silence, Libby Frenier drank her tea, ate a few cookies, and told me where Benjy Goodman had been staying. Because of my sometimes scattered postpartum brain, I wrote it down.

Then, with a sigh, she surrendered Mason and stood up.

"I should get back to the hospital," she said.

"You might want to change first." I had to say it. Hospital personnel can be very judgmental. She needed good information from them and right now she looked like a bag lady.

She looked at her blouse. Her pants. Grimaced as she ran a hand through her unkempt hair. "Oh my goodness. I've never in my life left home looking like this. What you must think of me."

"I think your only concern was for your son."

"You're too kind."

Which I was not. I'm kind enough, I suppose, but not someone who would be considered generally kind. Too busy. Too stressed. Too businesslike and impatient.

She stood with her head bent like a penitent. "Now that you know this... about me... about my son, do you still think you'll want me caring for your little one? I would understand if..."

"I haven't changed my mind." I added a silent "yet."

She blinked away some tears. "Thank you. Now you're right. I'd better go. Only. I hate to ask you this, but I was planning to head straight to the hospital from here and I don't have any spare clothes in the car. Could you..." She fingered her blouse. "Would you maybe have a top I could borrow?"

A top I could do. Good thing she hadn't asked for pants. Those she'd have to roll up. "Sure."

I tucked Mason into his seat and headed for the stairs. At the bottom I hesitated. I thought I believed her. She seemed genuine. Sincerely distressed. But I still felt uneasy leaving her with Mason while I was upstairs. Yes, I planned to leave her with Mason once she was working for me, but by then, hopefully the issues with Goodman and Faraday would be resolved, the missing baby found, and I wouldn't be so anxious. Right now, if my instincts were wrong and she was here to learn what I knew, or assess the situation on behalf of someone else, I shouldn't trust her.

I popped back into the kitchen and picked Mason up. "Just going to check and see if he needs changing. Be right back with that top."

At the top of the stairs, I hesitated, my legs so wobbly I needed a minute to get myself calm.

"Pretty soon, there will be no one I can trust," I told Mason as I put him in his bassinet. I stood there another minute, thinking about Libby Frenier. How her outfit was awfully odd for the woman I'd met before to have hastily thrown together. How she couldn't have buttoned that blouse when it was inside out without noticing. How she'd already been to the hospital, which is why she knew about her son's condition. So why had she come here? To share Benjy Goodman's whereabouts? To pump me for information? Or something else? Was Benjy somehow involved? Still a threat to her son? Or was she just genuinely distraught?

I didn't know.

I figured I'd better bring down a top so she wouldn't know about my suspicions.

As I was digging through my drawer for a suitable top, I heard the door close and then a car engine. When I got to the window, Libby Frenier was driving away, leaving me with no idea why she'd come.

———

The blast of a car horn shot me away from thinking about yesterday and back to the present. I was in my car, driving on a highway with a small baby in the back, and I'd let my mind drift. The surprise of it left me trembling.

TWENTY-EIGHT

I t was a good thing that the Stonegate School was easy to find. In my shaken state, I might otherwise have been unable to navigate despite help from my phone. I drove through tall stone pillars—thus the name, I supposed—and along a curving drive to a landscaped circle at the back of which stood an imposing white building. A house once, I assumed, that had grown wings as it needed to accommodate a growing school population.

Every school has its own personality and every school has things in common. Today, as I parked my car, slung the pack over my shoulder along with my purse and briefcase, and unfastened Mason's baby bucket from its frame, I could tell that school hadn't started yet. Private schools often started later, and there wasn't the buzz of energy that went with an active campus. Soon, students would be outside, playing frisbee or riding on scooters or gathering in groups on the grass. This place had an expectant air, everything freshly mown, painted, and put in order in preparation for the onslaught of parents and students that would begin in two days.

We were cutting it awfully close.

I felt like a beast of burden as I walked to the door, shifting Mason's carrier to my left hand to open it. I stepped into a wide hall with a staircase on the right, and rooms opening off to the left and right before the stairs. The room on the right had a plaque beside the door that identified it as the headmaster's office.

"Thea Kozak," I told the woman at the desk. "Here to see Mr. Thompson."

She popped to her feet with a smile. "We've been expecting you. Your mother is already here, I've put her across the hall in the sitting room. If you'll follow me. Oh, and I'm Maddie, if you need anything."

Without waiting for a comment from me, she came out from behind the desk and headed into the hall. It took me a minute to understand that my mother was not here—thank goodness—and it was Rosie waiting in the sitting room.

"Great," I told her bustling back. "We'll just get the baby settled, and I'll be ready to work."

Rosie was sitting on a comfortable-looking green velvet sofa, reading. She stood up and smiled when my bustling guide led us in.

We were greeted with a flurry of questions. "Thea, dear. How was the drive? Did Mason cry? Does he need to be fed? Changed?"

I set the baby carrier on the coffee table and hugged her. "He's probably ready for a change and something to eat."

As though he understood those words, Mason began to whimper. I picked him up and settled in a chair across from Rosie and fed him.

"The drive was easier than I expected. I think he likes riding in the car."

"A lot of babies do. I used to settle Isabella, when I picked her up after work, by driving around the block a few times. Worked like a charm. She'd nap while I made dinner and then be awake when Dom came home, which he appreciated. Otherwise, she might not have known she had a father. At least not until she was older."

We chatted quietly until Mason was done, then Rosie held out her hands. "I can burp him and change him. You've got work to do."

"Thank you. You know I couldn't be doing this without you."

"The pleasure is all mine," she said. And she meant it.

202

I had just put myself back together when a man rushed through the door with such a flurry of words I had to make a time-out gesture to slow him down.

I held out my hand. "Mr. Thompson?"

"I've been waiting almost fifteen minutes since Maddie said you'd arrived."

It was all I could do not to roll my eyes. I said, "Yes. I believe I told you, when we made this plan, that I had to bring my small baby with me?"

I waited for him to nod, which he did with all the grace of a sullen teen, and added, "Small babies need care, Mr. Thompson. I assume you know that?"

Another, very reluctant nod. I could already see this was going to be tough sledding. But when you've faced down an armed militia, one huffy headmaster isn't so daunting.

"I'm ready now, so if you are, we can go to your office and talk."

He walked out of the room, obviously assuming I would follow like a good baby duckling.

I am nobody's duckling.

Still, he was anxious, and calming him would work better than calling him on Thompson's behavior, so I picked up my purse and briefcase and turned toward the door. "If you need me," I told Rosie, "ask Maddie in the other room."

"We'll be fine, won't we, Mason?"

I thought they would be fine. I just hoped I would be.

Thompson was behind his desk, his expression the adult male version of a pouty three-year-old, hands on hips, declaring, "You aren't the boss of me."

He looked young for the job, which might be part of his uncertainty. I knew he hadn't been headmaster very long. This was only his second year. Long enough to have redone what must have been a very traditional office in the style of the house in an aggressively modern way. Blond wood desk, mid-century modern chairs upholstered in bright fabrics. A bright floral carpet on the floor.

I set down my bags, pulled a pale raspberry and lime green

chair closer, and said, "Bring me up to speed. What is the situation with the three boys, Ma'Kayla, and the other girls?"

He sighed. Instead of answering, he said, "You kept me waiting."

Time to nip this is the bud. I understood he was stressed and looking for someone to off-load some of that stress on, but it wasn't going to be me. I already had enough stress in my life and we didn't have time for anything but the nitty gritty.

"Before we go any farther, let's be clear. I am a professional with expertise in your areas of concern. I am also on maternity leave with a newborn, but I stepped back in to help you out with what is obviously a difficult situation. I appreciate your putting your trust in EDGE and our expertise. However, if you can't respect or appreciate the sacrifice I'm making to be here, and work with me in a cooperative way, then I'm leaving."

I gave him a beat to absorb that, and said, "Understood?"

He waved his hands like he was trying to dissipate the stink of his bad behavior. "Sorry. Sorry. I didn't mean... look. Right. Understood. Let's get down to it."

The first thing we got down to was me having him sign a contract confirming that he was hiring EDGE's services. I've found it's better to get that signed right away before the client realizes I will be a straight shooter with my advice and won't rubber stamp whatever the client has planned.

That done, I put the contract away and took a legal pad and pen from my briefcase and waited. When he didn't get down to anything, I said, "Let's get today's schedule squared away. When are we meeting with your attorney and when are we meeting with your board?"

I felt like there was a giant hourglass in the room and sand was running through very fast. At last, he checked his watch and said, "Our attorney should be here in about twenty minutes. The board? Uh... our board chair said he was tied up today and couldn't meet. He wants you to come back tomorrow. Or maybe Thursday? He wasn't sure. He said he had to check his calendar."

Note to self: When your instinct tells you something is going to be a nightmare and you should avoid it, trust that instinct.

"What about the rest of the board? Are they available? Are they on our schedule? We were very clear that it had to be today."

"I didn't... I...uh..." He looked at his watch, as if that might have an answer, then at his desktop. "Well, they are still coming in... because I forgot to cancel them when Kristoff said he couldn't make it."

Not bad news. In the absence of the chair, the assistant chair could step in and might be a more reasonable person to deal with anyway.

How had this man gotten to be head of a prestigious school like Stonegate when he was this indecisive or careless about details? Unless this was all a ploy. We'd certainly seen that before at EDGE, schools where they called us in as window dressing, to give themselves cover that they'd taken the right steps when they planned to ignore our advice and go in their own direction anyway.

He was reaching for the phone, to cancel them, I feared, so I quickly said, "Let's keep that meeting. We need them on up to speed and clear about what steps need to be taken."

Trying not to sound as pissed off as I felt, I said, "You did speak with Suzanne yesterday, right? And she stressed the importance of having your board involved in making crucial decisions in this case? I'm sure they can act in his absence."

He seemed to deflate in his chair. "He certainly doesn't think so. The man is impossible. Thinks he's the only one who matters. Thinks all the decisions are his to make. Doesn't have a clue about how to play well with others. The rest of the board are as frustrated with him as I am, particularly since he won't take this matter seriously. He's as much as said 'boys will be boys' and girls should know that."

I paused, realizing that I didn't know the guy's name, so I asked.

"Kristoff. Kristoff Fitz."

"And the rest of your board?"

"Deeply concerned about the reputation of the school and

about handling this matter with discretion... and according to their bylaws and the school's rules."

It was looking like this was a classic case of "It's better to ask forgiveness than permission," and that the majority of the board would back Thompson if he did that. No sense in wasting any more of our precious time on this.

"And after your attorney, we have your dean of students and your communications director?"

He looked down at a legal pad on his desk, frowning like he was having trouble reading what was written there, then back at me. "Yes."

It was an awfully hesitant "yes," but I hoped it meant things were in place despite his slipshod manner. I moved on. "What's the situation with the parents? Are they speaking through their attorneys?"

"Martinelli's parents have said they will sue if the school takes any action against their son. Ma'Kayla's parents will sue if action isn't taken and she's forced to attend school with her attackers. Ma'Kayla's parents are also putting a lot of pressure on the police to charge Martinelli and the others. And of course, Martinelli's parents are pushing back because there's also the matter of their hosting a party with teenage drinking. I believe the other boys' parents are waiting to see how things go and letting the Martinellis take the lead. So far, that's pretty much where it stands. What I need you for is to help me sort through what we must, and can, do under our own rules, and the best way to handle the fallout within the larger school community."

"Right."

"What about the girls and the boys? Have you had any contact with them?"

He shrugged. "Not really. You know that this didn't happen on campus, right?"

I bit down on a comment about making sure the girls were in a supportive situation and asking whether counseling had been offered. We would get to that. I took out the honor code, student handbook, and my notes.

"Your honor code, which all students have to sign, confirming they will abide by it, provides that conduct both on and off the campus is subject to the rules. So despite the fact that this happened off campus, you're still going to have to conduct an investigation. If you're unsure whether your staff are up to the task, or want to put some neutral distance between your administration and the investigation, I've got an ideal consultant we can call in to help."

I knew what he would say before he said it. "But we've called *you* in to help."

"And I am helping. But I'm crisis management—how to handle the various issues arising from the event, communicate with parents and the media, and protect the school's reputation. With regard to an investigation of the alleged assault on Ma'Kayla, we're talking about a hands-on, multi-day project. It helps to have someone who has done this before, and it helps to have someone who is deeply sensitive to the feelings of a student who has been assaulted, as well as those bystanders who could be considered secondary victims."

I paused. "I know that Ma'Kayla's friends weren't simply bystanders in the traditional sense. I'm talking about those bystanders who were there and intervened."

"So you think..."

"Yes. I think getting in an expert will be good for the school's reputation and an enhancement to the communications you'll be sending to the community."

He liked the sound of that. What I was about to say, he was going to like a lot less. "In the meantime, you, or you and your board, have to decide what you are going to do about the boys' presence on the campus. School is about to start, so there's no time to be lost. My recommendation, based on your handbook and the honor code they all signed, would be to suspend all three of them pending an investigation and a hearing."

I was looking down at my notes as I said it. When I looked up, he was staring at me like I'd just said something blasphemous. I realized that both Suzanne and I had made the mistake of assuming he understood this would be the least he needed to do. Evidently an unfounded assumption.

He could barely get out the words, "Suspend them? But our football team... our reputation as a strong sports school. The alumni..." before shaking his head vigorously. "I thought our challenge would be how to arrange classes so that Ma'Kayla wouldn't have to be in class with them."

All three of them. Ma'Kayla, Jess, and Sadie.

What did he think this was, some naughty kids drinking under the bleachers? This was three older boys getting a freshman girl drunk and then stripping off her clothes and taking intimate photos of her. If Jess and Sadie hadn't intervened, who knew what else might have happened, but this was enough to make the three of them and every other girl on campus feel unsafe and disrespected if nothing more was done than a slap on the wrist.

It wasn't just about current students, either. The way they handled this would have a huge impact on the school's reputation and its ability, going forward, to attract future students. Potential female applicants, and equally important, their families, needed to know the school would be a safe place. The situation needed sensitive handling, and it needed to be handled according to the rules. The handbook and the honor code were there to protect the students. They were also there to protect the school.

Still, I felt like I was climbing onto my feminist soapbox when I said, "You're concerned about the boys being in class with Ma'Kayla but not in class with Jess and Sadie? Who saw it all? Who had to rescue their very young teammate from what those three boys were doing?"

The thought of what they'd seen in that bedroom made me shiver.

His assistant, the woman he'd called Maddie, knocked, then stuck her head in. "Attorney's here. Shall I send her in?"

Sexist of me, maybe, but I was glad the school's lawyer was a woman. Not just a woman but a fierce and tough-looking black woman taller than I am. Of course, appearances could be deceiving. She could be a big football fan ready to rubber stamp whatever the guys wanted. She could be a "let's not make waves, here's how to sweep it under the rug" type.

I stood and held out my hand, "Thea Kozak. From EDGE Consulting, I'm working with Stonegate on crisis management."

"Alana Jackson." Her grip was strong. "Working on helping this place save its ass."

Turning on Thompson, Jackson said, "You took your sweet time calling me. You do know that the whole town is watching. Gossiping. Waiting to see what happens. Hard to get out in front of something when you're already playing catch-up."

I couldn't have said it better myself.

TWENTY-NINE

S he sat down next to me. "You know you should have called me in sooner," she told Thompson. "Too late now. We'll work with what we've got." No pleasantries. No chitchat.

That was fine with me. I did have to keep surprise off my face that Thompson hadn't been in touch with her sooner. I'd told him to talk to his lawyer. So had Suzanne. Obviously he or his assistant had called Jackson's office. But it sounded like he and his lawyer hadn't spoken. With threats of lawsuits being thrown around, and Martinelli's attorney and his parents asking to meet, why hadn't he? Was it because Kristoff didn't want him to? Something odd was going on here. A risk-averse headmaster would have been leaning on his lawyer from the beginning. So would a cautious one.

If I'd been a fly on the wall, this meeting would have been an interesting sight. There was Thompson, with his gelled hair, fashionably untucked plaid shirt, a slender 5' 9" in his lime green bucket of a chair, facing two tall women with briefcases and game plans. He looked a bit like he was afraid of being eaten.

"I was just telling Mr. Thompson..." I began.

"Dr. Thompson," he said, making me wonder why he hadn't corrected me before.

"Dr. Thompson," I amended, "that I believe, according to the school's handbook and honor code, that the three males involved, Randall Martinelli, Aaron Short, and Devon James, should be suspended until the matter can be thoroughly investigated and a hearing held."

She nodded. A slow, solemn nod, all the while watching Thompson to gauge his reaction. "I concur."

"But that will be a nightmare," Thompson said. "They're some of our star athletes. The alumni will be up in arms. The parents. You both must understand that our reputation as a powerhouse sports school is so important to our ability to recruit—"

The way we responded, Alana Jackson and I might have been twins.

"As opposed to your reputation as a school that condones gangs of male students, male athletes, sexually assaulting a very young girl?" I said.

She said a version of the same thing, adding, "And as a school that ignores its own rules and honor code when athletes are involved?"

He backed up a little farther in his chair.

"But their rights?" he said. "What about their rights?"

I knew he fancied himself very modern and progressive, so where was this BS coming from? Too many times, when EDGE came in to help in these situations, it felt like we were doing a remedial class in Consent 101. Too often, the school's reaction was about protecting the boys from the consequences of what they'd done. I was sick of it.

"What about their rights?" she asked. "Did they sign the honor code, which means they confirmed that they read and agreed to it?"

He nodded.

"Let me be more clear," she said. "Have you actually checked their files and confirmed that they, and their parents, signed the honor code and the affirmation that they'd read the student handbook and agreed to be bound by those rules, which I understand is a condition of attending this school? Or are you just assuming that they have?"

A question I was going to ask. It had been one of the things Suzanne was supposed to remind him to do.

He looked down at the piles of papers on his desk. Then looked up with a little shrug. A much too casual shrug. "I haven't gotten around to that. It has been so busy around here, getting ready for the new school year, I planned to—"

She cut him off. "Can you have someone do that right now, please."

I thought it. She said it. High fiving would have been out of place, but I felt like it. Sadly, there wasn't much to celebrate here. It appeared, despite his anxiety and the sense of emergency he'd expressed rudely and loudly in his calls, that he'd put off doing the most basic things, the essential things Suzanne and I had both advised him to do. It seemed he'd been waiting for someone to show up and force him to do what was necessary, when he'd needed to be proactive and get ahead of the mess that was coming at him.

I was ever more grateful that Kristoff Fitz was unavailable. I thought I could see the hands of an arrogant bro behind Thompson's decision-making. That or something else. There had to be an explanation for why a man competent and experienced enough to be put in charge of this school, and sensible enough to call for our expertise to help manage the situation, was shirking like this.

He used the intercom to ask Maddie to check on whether the school had signed copies of the honor code for Martinelli, Short, and James. There was something in the way he said, "As we discussed," that sent up a red flag for me.

He'd barely gotten the receiver down when Jackson jumped again. "What about an investigation and a hearing?" she asked. "What are your plans for that? Is there an investigation underway and who is handling it?"

"Ms. Kozak has some thoughts about that," he said, as though dumping it into my lap let him off the hook. As though saying it needed to be done was the same as doing it. As though thoughts were the same as actions.

I told her about the consultant we'd used with other schools, who was skilled at helping them through the process in a fair and sensitive way.

"Of course you are going to hire this person," she told him.

"Uh... I want to take that question to the board," he said.

"When?" she asked.

I might be brusque sometimes but she was a steamroller.

"Uh. They're meeting this morning," he said.

"Have you been threatened with legal action?" she asked.

He nodded.

"By whom?"

I was sure she already knew.

"Randall Martinelli's father says he'll sue if the school takes any action against his son, and I expect Short's and James's parents will join in. Of course, Ma'Kayla's parents say they'll take action if the boys aren't expelled, and even if we can weather that, they'll make a huge fuss if any of the three boys involved are in any of her classes."

He ran his hands through his hair, the crisp gelled strands parting for his fingers like sod turned by a plow. "I... we... just can't win. It's going to be so difficult to keep Ma'Kayla separate from those boys."

This wasn't about winning, and protecting victims from their abusers wasn't "making a fuss." I couldn't help myself. I said, "And Jess and Sadie, of course."

"But they—"

"All three of the victims, of course," his lawyer said.

I was seeing the return of that pouty look. Clearly he thought he was being picked on and didn't think it was fair. I thought what wasn't fair was a young female athlete being tricked into consuming liquor or some date rape drug at a party hosted by a football player's parents and then subjected to outrageous indignities. Criminal indignities. If I were Ma'Kayla's parents, I'd be looking for another school for her, one that wasn't as wishy-washy as Stonegate seemed to be.

I reminded myself that Stonegate was my client. "Has there been any communication with your parent community about this matter yet?" I asked. "By the school, I mean?"

He shook his head. "We've been waiting for you."

"When we're done here, and I've met with the board, I'll be sitting down with your dean of students and your communications person to start working on that."

"You could do that now," he said.

"At the meeting you've scheduled," I corrected, trying to keep the edge from my voice. "And once we've confirmed you have those signatures from the individuals involved. We don't want to go public with messaging that's not correct."

He looked about to protest, so I said, "It's a lot harder to shape the message that you are handling this matter in conformance with the school's own rules if you've been slipshod about enforcing compliance."

I waved off whatever he was about to say next. "We'll work with whatever we have, of course. But communications are delicate. Facts matter. And tone is everything."

As though he hadn't been listening, he said, "I've had communications from some of our most generous alumni donors. They're concerned about the football season. Those games are a big draw, and of course Martinelli is our quarterback. College recruitable, his coaches think."

As though Martinelli's character and his conduct didn't matter at all. As though this was all about Martinelli, and the fact that two other male students were also involved wasn't an issue. To test him, I asked, "So would it be okay if Martinelli wasn't suspended but Short and James were?"

The way he shifted uneasily in his chair made me think he'd actually considered it.

He said, "Well, we couldn't do that, could we."

Time to switch subjects before I lost my currently very fragile cool. "Has the school arranged for counseling for the girls?"

"School hasn't started yet," he said.

"But they are already on campus, doing preseason training. They are under the school's purview. They, except for Ma'Kayla, are living on campus, aren't they?" It was something I'd already talked with him about. I guess I was just getting it on the record by saying it in front of the attorney, for whatever that was worth.

Inwardly, I sighed. I'd done crisis interventions on campuses dozens of times, so why did it feel so difficult today? I knew the answer. I'd never had my attention so divided before, never had to make the effort to stay present in the room while Mason was somewhere else. I reminded myself that he was safe with Rosie. But even though his behavior wasn't uncommon, having my attention divided made me less patient with a client who'd ignored all my advice.

After waiting for another answer that wasn't forthcoming, I asked, "What about your relationship with the local police? Are you in contact? Do you know the status of their investigation?" I was trying to keep moving forward even if his passive-aggressive behavior made me want to shake him.

It was common for schools to have a close relationship with their local police departments, since they were bringing a significant number of adolescents to the community and kids would be kids. Working together could prevent charges and complications neither the school nor the cops wanted.

When he didn't respond, I looked at the lawyer. "Are you in contact with them?"

"Just called in, remember?" she said. "But yes, of course I've been in touch with them. They've got the phones from all three of the boys involved and they're going through them. As the lieutenant in charge of the investigation told me, 'If they did it this time, who knows whether they did it before?' Investigation's taking time because they had to get warrants before they could search those phones. They've interviewed the boys, all of whom lawyered up, as you'd expect, and Ma'Kayla but not yet Jess or Sadie. Their dorm mother wasn't letting them be interviewed without herself and myself present. That's supposed to happen this afternoon."

Hooray for dorm mothers. At least someone was being protective on the girls' behalf. I think we were both surprised when Thompson said, "She shouldn't be doing that without consulting me first."

As though what? He wouldn't let her sit in on an interview with one of the students she was supposed to be supervising? Besides, if he was doing his job, staying in touch and checking on how the girls were doing, he'd know all this. "She meaning their dorm mother?" I asked.

I was about to add, "But of course you'd want the girls to have an adult with them," when there was a gentle tap on the door. His assistant, Maddie, stepped in. "Excuse me, Ms. Kozak, your mother needs you."

Not great timing. Never mind how the idea that I'd come here with my mother seriously diminished my authority, we were just getting rolling. I thought I understood what was going on with Thompson. A few more questions and one of us—me or Alana— would have reached the "aha!" moment when he admitted his goal was to sweep the whole business under the carpet, despite having called on us for help. Was one of us supposed to wield the broom while the other lifted the rug?

Alana Jackson gave me a quizzical look.

"Not my mother. A friend. She's taking care of my baby," I explained. "He's a newborn. Can't be left for long. But this situation was serious enough to drag me away from maternity leave. I won't be long."

"We'll wait," she said. "It will give Dr. Thompson time to find those forms."

It was too soon for Mason to need to eat, so I was anxious as I headed into the room where I'd left Rosie.

She was standing in the middle of the room, arms spread wide, looking distraught. The woman named Maddie was right beside her, looking more confused than upset, her head swiveling around the room like she was looking for something.

There was no sign of Mason.

THIRTY

Rosie and Maddie's words crossed as they both offered their defenses.

"I only left him for a minute to go to the rest room," Rosie said, tears in her voice. "She said she'd watch him for me."

"I just left the room for a moment," Maddie said with a shrug that suggested to her a missing baby was no different from a missing ream of paper. Things went missing. She had a lot on her plate. Don't expect her to keep track of it all. "He was right there on the couch across from my desk. I went to grab something from the copier and when I came back, he was gone." Another shrug. "The kids around here are always taking things."

"Things?" I probably yelled it. "We're talking about a baby."

All that stuff about hearts breaking and hearts leaping and hearts stopping? It's all true. Mine went through a series of dramatic behaviors before I could settle it enough to go on. Settle down and quell my urge to grab her by the throat and shake her. Instead, I became directive.

"Maddie, you call campus security and get them over here, then check the building in case he's still here somewhere." When she hesitated, I added, "Top to bottom. Look everywhere. Rosie and I will look around outside."

"I was only gone a minute," she said.

I waved my hands at her. "Go on. Go! Call security. Check the building."

As Maddie hurried out and down the hall, her phone to her ear, Rosie and I headed outside. It was a lovely day, the kind that should have been spent taking Mason for a walk somewhere shady and pleasant instead of trying to nudge a reluctant headmaster to do the right thing. I was an idiot to think I could bring my baby to a client school and somehow make it work. The situation was much too complicated to have my concentration divided. Thompson was ignoring my advice, and hiding something. His assistant couldn't keep track of anything. And good as I was, I was not a miracle worker.

Rosie was in tears and couldn't stop apologizing. I needed to get her calmed so I didn't lose it myself. The combination of anxiety and terror was choking me.

"Calm down, Rosie. Please. It's not your fault that woman couldn't do the simple job of looking after him for a few minutes. It's not. Truly. I never should have considered doing this. Please don't cry, because if you cry, then I'll cry, and then I won't be able to work, and we'll just have to sit here on the steps, a pair of sobbing wretches."

That made her laugh through her tears. "We'll find him," she said.

"Yes. We will. We'll start by circling the building," I said. "You go to the right, I'll go left, and we'll meet in the back."

As she headed off, I scanned the drive and the grove of trees and the parking area. I was sure that I hadn't been followed this morning and there was no way that some bad guy involved in that whole mess back in Maine could have found me here unless I was followed. No one on our office staff would give information about my schedule to a stranger, and I don't exactly post my comings and goings on social media.

I don't post anything on social media. I use social media to track people and trends and sometimes it has been helpful in solving mysteries or understanding students' view on what was happening on their campus. But share my personal life? No way.

I began my slow walk around the building, looking right, looking left, looking high, looking low, all the while wanting to run and scream. As I came around the side of the building's left wing, I could hear the chatter of girls' voices somewhere off to my left. In the shade of a big oak tree was a picnic table. Four girls were sitting at the table, and in the middle was Mason in his baby bucket.

I did start running then, stopping just short of the table, breathless and furious. I snatched up his carrier and clutched it to my chest, my heart pounding so hard I was surprised it didn't send baby and carrier rocking.

"What on earth were you thinking?" I yelled, when I could catch my breath. "You think stealing someone's baby is funny?"

"We didn't steal him," the tallest girl said. "We just borrowed him."

"Rescued him," the Asian girl said.

"Because it wouldn't be safe to leave him with Maddie Monson," the third, a very pretty redhead said. "Because she is a total airhead."

"It was kind of a joke," the tallest girl said. "We wondered if Maddie would even notice he was gone."

The fourth girl, an athletic-looking Black girl, was silent.

"Well, I'm his mother and I noticed he was gone, and my good friend Rosie, who is taking care of him for me, noticed he was gone. It wasn't a joke on me or on her. It was terrifying and heart stopping and you four all owe me and Rosie an apology."

I included Rosie because I could see her coming toward us, walking fast, her face set and furious.

She arrived before the girls could respond and opened up on them with a furious burst of anger. She ended with, "Do you have any idea what it might be like for a mother to discover her baby has been taken? Any idea at all?"

She glared at them. "And do you know that kidnapping is a serious crime?"

Four embarrassed faces looked down at four laps. They were lovely and young and fit and careless, because in their immortality, they hadn't been thinking about how they might be inflicting harm.

"Oh man. We made an awful mistake and we are so sorry." From the tall one who seemed to be their leader. The others nodded and murmured agreement.

In that moment, seeing them together, obviously close, and on campus before school had begun, I knew who three of them were. "Jess, Sadie, and Ma'Kayla, right?"

The three of them nodded.

I shouldn't have said it. Usually I'm good at keeping my mouth shut, but the threat to Mason must have unhinged me. "So suppose that the other night, when those three boys got Ma'Kayla drunk and assaulted her, they'd just said they were only joking, no big deal. Nothing to get upset about? Would it make that okay?"

There was a long, stunned silence around the table. I didn't mean that the two events were comparable, but these girls needed to think about their behavior and its impact. I said as much and they visibly relaxed.

"Who are you?" Jess said.

"I'm a consultant here to help the school handle..." I thought about how to put it. "To handle Ma'Kayla's situation with respect to the boys who assaulted her. With respect to the school community. The parents. The community of independent schools."

"What's the school got to handle?" Jess asked. "We've been told it's a matter for the police since it happened off campus." She was clearly the leader of this group. "That's not true, but it's what we've been told."

I wanted to know who'd told them that. Decided I'd get a little more information first. I nodded toward the fourth girl. "I know who three of you are. Who's this?"

"I'm Courtney," the girl said. "Courtney Laukka. I'm a forward, like Jess."

"Wait," Jess said. "Maybe you can explain. You're here because the school needs help to handle what Randy, Carson, and Devon did? I mean, I don't get that. It's obvious what they did. There's no he said/she said about it. Headmaster's got the video, plus what we saw and told him. Doesn't take a rocket scientist to know what's supposed to be done. We all read the rules. We all signed the honor code. They did, too. But we're waiting and nothing gets done and when I asked Dr. Thompson what was happening, he said the police were handling it because it was off campus. Which is just wrong!"

It *was* just wrong. I wanted to explain my role to them, but my duty was to the school, and ultimately, it would be up to Thompson and the board to decide what approach they would take and how they would apply their own rules. I could advise, and my sense was that Alana Jackson's advice would be much the same. But the final decision about how to enforce the rules and what would be appropriate steps to take with respect to the three boys was up to the school

Still, I said, "I agree with you that the handbook and honor code are clear. My role here is as a consultant. They make the final decisions."

"Oh. Well, that's reassuring," Sadie said. "Because you may not know it, but we all know that Randy's father is connected." She looked at the other three. "Right?"

Two of them nodded. Ma'Kayla said, "I'm new here, remember?"

Feeling kind of dumb, I said, "Connected?" I was thinking political or country club or best friends with the police chief or the DA.

"Not what you're thinking," Jess said. "Sadie means mafia... if it's still called that. Whatever, his father has friends who make sure the Martinellis get their own way. That's what my dad says."

Not what you're thinking. That's what she'd said. It made me wonder if I'd become transparent to the whole world. If everyone could tell what I was thinking. Was it something that had happened during childbirth, maybe? An alien invasion? Here I thought I'd developed a pretty good cop's face, and now a bunch of teenage girls could read my mind?

"Not everyone knows," Sadie said. "We do 'cuz Randy... he...

uh—" She stopped, looking at Ma'Kayla. "Do we tell her what Randy said?"

Ma'Kayla considered. "Yeah. We tell her. We gotta tell someone. I told my dad and he said that shouldn't matter, that it's a different world now and the cops won't back down just 'cuz someone threatens 'em."

Oh, I knew all about cops being threatened. Cops. Their families. Their friends. But could this happen in a progressive Massachusetts town in the twenty-first century? Who was I kidding. Of course it could still be problem, whether it was a criminal organization, as Sadie suggested, or just a very bad actor with some very bad friends.

"You should tell me what Randy said."

They hesitated.

Courtney said, "Coach says maybe we should let it go. That it will be harder on us than on the boys and we might not get the result we want."

Well, that was damned supportive, wasn't it? Whenever we think the culture of valuing athletics over honor, rules, and decent behavior is behind us, there's another example.

Then Jess, their spokeswoman, said, "Randy said nothing's going to happen to him, or to them, because his dad has the headmaster and the cops in his pocket. We don't know if it's true, but something like what happened to Ma'Kayla happened last year to another girl, and nothing was ever done about it. That's why I grabbed that phone. Because this time there's no way they can say that they don't have enough evidence, or that it's just he said/she said. Because it's wrong. It's just wrong if they get away with what they did. Again."

"Same group of boys?" I asked.

Four nods.

"And the Stonegate community knows about this?"

Four nods.

This was so not okay. But if he was in someone's pocket, why had Thompson been so insistent on getting our help? Window dressing? Or something he'd put in motion before he got the threat?

There was something else at play here, something they weren't telling me. I looked at the four faces and realized I need to probe a little further. "In the incident last year, did the victim report it? Was she willing to go forward with a complaint?"

Three nods. Ma'Kayla shrugged. She must be wondering what she was getting herself into at this school. Her freshman year had not yet started and already she was up to her ears in school politics, when the school should have been bending over backward to care for an assault victim.

"She told the police and she told the administration. Then..." Jess shrugged. "Then one day she just said she was dropping the whole thing. It was too much trouble."

"You think someone threatened her? That she was coerced into backing off?"

"Yes. That's what we think," Sadie said. "Actually, we pretty much know that."

"Know that how?"

"What she told us. She said there was a guy... he came up to her when she was off campus doing some errands... he said she should forget all about it or something a lot worse than some dirty pictures would happen to her." Sadie shook her head. "She was terrified. Actually, we're terrified. But it can't be allowed to keep happening."

"What's her name?" I asked.

They told me.

"Do you think she'd be willing to talk to me?"

Three shrugs.

"She told the headmaster or the police about the threat?"

"We don't know," Jess said. "But Ma'Kayla... you should tell her..."

She broke off, looking at Ma'Kayla. Giving her the opportunity to tell her story.

I waited.

Ma'Kayla looked down at her lap. At her knotted hands. "I think..." she said slowly. "I told my dad, but I think I want to talk to my family's lawyer first. Before I decide."

Jess nodded. "Up to you, of course." A pause. "But we can't

keep letting this happen. We can't let them get away with this again, Ma'Kayla. And this woman is here to help."

Ma'Kayla shrugged. "Let me think about it."

They couldn't tell me whether last year's victim had told anyone other than them about the threat. From Ma'Kayla's behavior, it sounded to me like there had already been another threat, a recent threat, and she was still deciding what to do about it.

This was a whole lot of bad news dropping on me in the middle of such a lovely day. I wondered if Alana Jackson knew about any of this? It seemed like she and I needed to have a talk, if her ethics would let her talk to me without Thompson, her client, in the room. I had to get back in there with a whole new batch of questions.

First, though, Master Mason needed some attention.

I handed out my cards to the girls and got their contact information.

"We need to talk about this some more. Right now, though, the baby comes first."

I picked up the baby bucket and Rosie and I headed back inside.

"It sounds like something from a novel," she said. "A bad novel."

"Yes. And it sounds perfectly plausible. Maybe not the mafia, if it's even called that anymore. But a bad actor? A known bad actor who seems to escape consequences? Someone like that can be very scary."

"I'm just here to babysit," she said. "The rest of this? I feel like I should have brought Dom."

"We still might need his advice, depending on what I learn."

"I think we will."

Almost at the door, she said, "I'm still upset with myself about what happened. I should have just taken him to the ladies room with me, but I didn't like the idea of a baby in a bathroom. Guess I'm still new at this, too. It has been a couple decades."

We were just through the door, no campus security having ever arrived, when Alana Jackson appeared.

"There you are," she said. "I thought you'd been kidnapped."

"Just the baby," I said.

She looked at Mason, then back at me.

"We got him back."

"Well. Glad you and he are back, because we need to talk about Thompson and what the hell is going on here."

THIRTY-ONE

Suzanne says these things never happen to her and doesn't let me forget she considers me a trouble magnet. I wondered what she would have done if she were here instead of me? Probably she wouldn't have met those girls and heard their story, but would she have picked up on the strange vibes in the room with Thompson, the ones that I, and evidently the school's attorney, had picked up?

No way to know. Perhaps whatever hand of fate that determines how things happen had known Suzanne wouldn't sense it, and sent me instead. I wasn't grateful.

"I've got to feed the baby," I said. "He and I, well, he and I and Rosie, have had a bit of a scare."

I introduced Rosie.

"In the middle of discussing this mess, Thompson went off somewhere without a word of explanation," Jackson said. "So if you don't mind, I'll sit with you," she said. "Can you talk while you…" She trailed off. I was learning that people don't know how to refer to nursing, as though for all those centuries before the invention of the bottle, babies somehow miraculously were fed and survived without maternal intervention.

As we went into the lounge, Thompson's assistant bustled by

carrying a manila envelope. There was something surreptitious about her demeanor that stopped all three of us. We lingered in the doorway as Mason began to fuss. I put him on my shoulder and rubbed his back. That usually worked for a few minutes and I needed to see what was up with that envelope.

Ordinarily, such a thing wouldn't catch any of our attention but her furtive manner did.

She disappeared into the bathroom, only to appear a moment later—too short a time even to have washed her hands—without the envelope.

"I'm on it," Jackson said.

I settled down in an armchair to feed Mason. Rosie sat across from me. As soon as Maddie Monson disappeared back into her office, Alana Jackson headed down the hall. She was back in a moment carrying the envelope.

"Found it in the bathroom trash," she said. "Shall I open it?"

She didn't wait for our agreement. She tore open the flap and pulled out a stack of papers. Even before she looked at them, I knew what they would be. They'd be the consent forms that the three boys involved in the assault had signed. Perhaps Thompson thought this would be a clever way to duck his responsibility to hold them accountable. If they hadn't agreed in writing the school's rules, he could argue, the rules couldn't be enforced against them. It was a feeble argument—there was a presumption each student accepted the rules by enrolling even if there was no signed form—but he could try to make it.

It's depressing, and discouraging, that he would even consider it.

"Not just this year," she said, after going through the stack. "Their forms for prior years as well." She sighed. "Looks like my client is more in need of my advice than I realized."

"Were you aware that there was a similar incident last year, involving the same three perpetrators?" I asked.

"What?"

"You didn't represent the school last year?"

"The firm did, but not me."

"Well, you should ask about it. Seems someone put pressure on the victim and she backed down. Now it looks like that same pressure may be coming back into play. The three girls involved in this year's assault tell me that Randall Martinelli's family is connected. I don't know exactly what that means, but someone got to that girl, last year's victim, and I'm concerned that the same thing may happen again. Ma'Kayla was reluctant to talk about it. She wants to confer with her lawyer first, but it looks like someone has tried to pressure her to back down."

As Alana shook her head, maybe in disbelief, maybe in frustration, I continued. "We need... or you need... I'm not sure which of us the school will listen to... to make sure the girls are protected. Given whatever support services they need. And to keep anyone who might apply pressure in person off campus while monitoring other modes of communication."

She was making some notes as I spoke. Now she looked up. "Sounds like you've been here before."

"Situations like this aren't uncommon in the independent school world. The assault, I mean. Pressure from outside thugs not so much. Nor is it uncommon for the administration to try and duck responsibility." I pointed to the envelope she was holding. "But this goes beyond ducking. This is blatant dishonesty."

Mason mumbled his disapproval of my conversing while he was dining, so I shut up.

"He's awfully cute," Jackson said.

"Got his daddy's brown eyes. And his daddy's way of expressing disapproval when he doesn't get the attention he thinks he deserves."

"What does his daddy do?"

"Maine state police detective."

"Ah. So you're attuned to the criminal issues here, aren't you?"

I nodded toward Mason and she understood. She put the forms back in the envelope. "Guess we've got our work cut out for us, don't we? When my supervising partner gave me this assignment, he told me to expect a challenge. Guess I didn't grasp what he meant. I thought he was referring to helping the school handle its own issues while also helping to liaise with the local PD. I wasn't expecting to have to explain to the school that they have to follow their own rules. I mean, I thought they'd understand their rules and my job would be to help implement them."

She grinned. "Understanding their rules? Guess maybe that's your job, huh?"

"I helped write them. Some of them. But I think it's going to be both of our jobs."

I put Mason on my shoulder and patted his back. I was already weary and there was much more of the day ahead. I could foresee hours of trying to persuade people to do their jobs.

Reluctantly I handed him back to Rosie.

"We're going to get clean and dry and then go for a walk," she said. "No sense in wasting this lovely day sitting around inside."

She was right. "I use a baby sling, and it's in the pack," I said. "If you'd rather use the stroller, his baby bucket fits into the one in my car."

She held out her hand. "Keys?"

I gave her my keys. I've had some tense moments at client schools when having my car available for an escape was handy, but I wasn't expecting I'd need to make a fast getaway anytime soon. Still, given the incident with the clumsily discarded forms, I might be wrong.

Maddie Monson appeared in the doorway. "Ladies, Dr. Thompson is waiting for you."

The same Dr. Thompson who'd disappeared on some errand without saying where he was going or when he'd be back?

I checked my watch. Twenty minutes before I had to meet with the deans and the communications director, then with the board. And Jackson and I had a lot to cover in those twenty minutes.

"It's puzzling, and concerning," he began before we'd even sat down, "but Maddie has searched the files and cannot find the signed forms for any of the boys involved. I'm not sure what that means, going forward. I mean, if they didn't agree, can we—"

"To allay your concerns, Dr. Thompson," Jackson interrupted, skewering him with an expression that had him pushing his chair back and wearing that 'about to be eaten' look again. "The forms aren't missing. It seems they were just misfiled. In the wastebasket in the staff bathroom."

She held up the manila envelope. "You can relax. They're all right here. Four years for Martinelli, three for the other boys. So, no issues there with enforcing your student regulations or your honor code."

Thompson was about to say something, something we were curious to hear, but we were short of time. Jackson was revved up and eager to take the lead, so I let her.

"Tell me about the incident with these same boys and another girl last year," she said. "It looks like you've got a serious, and ongoing, problem here."

"Oh, that," he began. "The girl retracted her allegations."

Had he really said, "Oh, that?"

I looked at her. She looked at me. And we jumped on him with all four feet.

THIRTY-TWO

U sually I had to do this by myself. It was nice to have someone else there who was on my wave-length. In a fast twenty minutes, we got the story of the previous year's events, explained to him how bad it would look for the school to sweep a second incident involving the same three athletes under the rug, and had him understanding what he needed to do.

I hoped he understood. I wasn't getting a very positive vibe. Before I left for my meeting—Jackson was staying behind to cover some further details—I asked him about campus security. "Will they be attuned to the issue of strangers on campus? Of people trying to get at Ma'Kayla or the other girls to dissuade them from pressing charges against the boys?"

"We have an excellent security team," he said.

Not an answer to my question. "I meant will you be giving them a heads up about what happened before, and making them aware that these girls will need protection?"

I tried to keep anger or frustration from my voice but it was probably creeping in. I'd been in this place before with other students who needed protection and seen how it could fail.

"We really can't do much about strangers on campus, at least for the next day or two, as our students are moving in."

A perfect time for someone to come on campus and approach Ma'Kayla, Jess, and Sadie. "So you'll confer with their dorm parents, right?"

I waited for his nod. "And campus security will be alerted to pay attention after that?"

He shrugged.

Shrugged? Seriously?

Climbing onto my soapbox, I said, "I can't stress enough the importance of protecting your students when they've been victims of a sexual assault. The word will get out and how you, how Stonegate handles things with respect to those victims, indeed, with respect to all of your female students and campus security, will matter a great deal. If the female students feel vulnerable, and if their parents don't feel that this is a safe place, you'll lose students to transfer, and it will also have an impact on your incoming classes, possibly for years to come. This isn't a trivial matter and it can't be brushed under the carpet. You need to be proactive."

I was late for my next meeting so I left it at that and headed upstairs to the conference room where Dr. Thompson had said the meeting would be held. No one was there. I waited five minutes, then went back downstairs to ask Maddie Monson what was up.

"Meeting?" she said brightly. "Oh. Right. I'm sorry. Dr. Thompson asked me to arrange something and I totally forgot."

Parents were trusting their children to an institution that allowed this airhead to hold an important administrative job?

Trying to hold onto my temper, I said, "Can you call them please and see if they're available? Now?" As she reached for the phone, I said, "Before you make that call, did you, or did Dr. Thompson set up my meeting with the trustees? It's supposed to be in an hour?"

Another bright smile. "Oh. Right. Well, I did set that one up. They are waiting for you in the board room."

As I entertained homicidal thoughts, I said, "Which is where?"

It was upstairs, too, next to the one I'd just found empty. As I pounded up the stairs again, I figured the universe wanted me to get my exercise today. I also wondered whether Dr. Thompson knew about this meeting, since he'd given me a different time. Had that been deliberate? And there was another problem: It would be difficult to work at getting the board and the headmaster on the same page if the headmaster didn't attend the meeting.

Before I entered the room, I paused and pondered. Did I start without him? Call him and remind him? Since he'd thus far been pretty useless, I decided I'd start without him and when his presence became essential, I could make that call.

Yup. In my work I dealt with a lot of weasels, and over the years, I've become a bit of a weasel myself. In the interest of my client schools, of course.

They all turned toward me as I came through the door, nine heads swiveling in my direction. Unlike the décor mess he'd made of the headmaster's office, this room retained the dignity that befitted a boardroom. Creamy walls, deep blue drapes, a shiny, dark wood table, and swivel leather armchairs for the board.

I introduced myself, explained my role, and said, "I apologize for being late. I was given an incorrect meeting time by Dr. Thompson."

Since there was an empty chair at the head of the table—perhaps belonging to the missing Kristoff Fitz?—I took it. I spread out my papers and my notepad and said, "Shall we begin?"

There was a murmur of agreement. They introduced themselves and a woman named Margot Inglebright identified herself as the assistant board chair. Her name was familiar, as I'd worked with her on the team updating the student handbook and crafting the honor code. I hoped that meant she'd be on the same page as I was.

I quickly ran through my understanding of the incident and the status of the investigation, and tried to clarify the school's role. "It is important to distinguish Stonegate's role from the role that the police will play in investigating this incident. Their purview is determining the facts and the applicable law. Stonegate has a different role to play. The school's job is to protect the integrity of the community and the school's reputation, protect and support the victims, and conduct their own investigation and deal with alleged perpetrators in accordance with the rules set forth in the student handbook and the school's honor code."

The woman on my immediate right said, "May I interrupt you for a moment?"

"Of course."

"Since Kristoff isn't here, to be on the safe side, should we designate Margot as acting chair, so there will be no procedural issues with any decisions we make today?"

There was a murmur of agreement and the board took a confirming vote.

Following procedure made sense. Our purpose in being here was to follow procedures set up to protect the school and the students. Still, I could feel time slipping away. It was a struggle to stay focused. I was exhausted. There was only so much I could ask of Rosie. And I was missing Mason terribly. Coming here had been a bad idea. Now I had to efficiently make use of the time we had and get the heck out.

Luckily, they were with me on that—a group of people with busy lives who just wanted to get down to business. Once I confirmed that the school records showed all of the boys involved had signed the honor code, we quickly reached agreement on how the rules applied to the three students who had perpetrated the attack. A suspension pending a hearing. Hiring the investigator I suggested. Ensuring that the girls involved were offered counseling and protection, and a carefully crafted set of communications to parents and students about the incident.

Smart. Efficient. Done.

I decided not to share with them the information that Thompson's assistant had tried to dispose of those signed consent forms.

I wanted to fold my tent and steal away, but I still had concerns. I asked whether the board was aware of a similar incident the year before, involving the same three boys where the girl involved had decided to withdraw her complaint. They were not. Were shocked. Were concerned that they hadn't been informed. I shared a second concern—that Dr. Thompson had never appeared at the meeting when one of its purposes was to get the board and the headmaster on the same page with respect to the school's response.

"I'll talk to him," Margot Inglebright offered. "We have a good working relationship."

I stifled a hallelujah. Plenty of times I have to fight with my clients to get them to do the things they've hired me to help them do.

It looked like we were done here. I thanked them and rose to go, hoping the incompetent Maddie Monson had scheduled my forgotten meeting. Communication was everything in a case like this. I was almost out the door when Dr. Thompson appeared. He held up a hand to stop me.

"Sorry I'm late," he said. "Got tied up with our attorney. I'd like to start by saying that I think that with sports season about to begin, suspending three of our most valuable athletes is a bad decision."

Visions of homicide danced in my head.

THIRTY-THREE

I was wondering whether I had pepper spray in my bag and whether I had the courage to give him a little squirt when Margot Inglebright stepped in. "Sorry you missed the meeting, Barry," she said. "You told us it was important. Critical. Time-sensitive. Which is why we all gave up a portion of our busy days to be here."

I loved her for saying that.

She waved a hand at the chair I'd just vacated. "Plunk yourself down and we'll bring you up to speed. I believe Ms. Kozak has another critical meeting to attend?"

"Yes, but..."

"I'm sure we can handle this. We've had a very productive meeting and made some critical decisions about how to go forward." She motioned for me to leave and I didn't argue.

Back downstairs, I found Maddie Monson humming happily at her desk. "My next meeting?" I prompted. "Have you set it up?"

"Oh. Sorry. They were busy and then I got busy and it completely slipped my mind."

Something else I should have raised with the board: how quickly they could find a replacement for this woman. That, at least, I could

DEATH SENDS A MESSAGE

do that by email or a phone call. I did wonder, though, how much of her behavior was character and how much was an act, possibly an act developed with Barron Thompson to protect him from people who wanted him to do his job when he had another agenda. He hadn't seemed this wishy-washy when we were working on the honor code, which suggested something else was going on.

But then why bring me in? Why all the urgent calls, all the pressure? His urgency had felt genuine. I'd heard it in his voice. Had someone gotten to him after I'd agreed to come? Maybe the same person who'd gotten to that girl last year? Or the person I suspected was trying to contact Jess, Sadie, and Ma'Kayla? How did he think that was going to work? Shining a bright light on threats and shady attempts to hide wrongdoing makes it harder to carry out.

The sand had almost slipped through the giant hourglass in the corner. Sand in the hourglass and more sand where it appeared Thompson was burying his head. I no longer had the time or the energy to dig him out.

I looked at my watch. By the time she could assemble the people I needed to speak with, it would be too late. I wanted to be on the road before rush hour. I'd budgeted for an efficient day and given them the information they needed to make that happen. They'd chosen to play a game of inefficiency with their own dollars. I'd still be billing them for a day.

"That's unfortunate," I said. "Can you please give me a list of names and contact information for these people?" I told her who I needed to see. It would have to be facetime or zoom at this point, but I was growing used to that.

"Oh. Of course. I'm pretty busy right now but if you could come back in, say, an hour?"

I leaned over her desk, using my full 5' 11", or 5' 12" in shoes, to dominate her space, and put on my best cat about to eat a mouse face. "I set aside this day to help Stonegate with its sexual assault issues because Dr. Thompson said it was urgent. I gave up a day of my maternity leave and drove for hours to get here, with my vulnerable newborn. You've wasted enough of my time. I need it now. Right now. Before I leave."

Her own urgent business seemed to involve a cup of tea and a scone that was scattering crumbs all over the papers on her desk. She gave a little flutter with her hands. "Well, really. If you must... I suppose I could..."

"Don't suppose. Just do it," I said.

I could hear Suzanne's voice urging me to be sweeter, nicer, more patient. Saying something about flies and honey and vinegar. But I had no sweetness to spare for this bullcrap. Maternity leave was finite and I'd missed most of a whole day with Mason.

While she was consulting a list and typing up the information for me, the door opened, and Rosie and Mason came in.

Rosie looked frazzled. "Oh good. You're here. I think our little one has had about enough of Aunt Rosie today." She gave me a rueful smile. "Guess I'm not as good at this as I thought. He's rather out of sorts."

He wasn't the only one who was out of sorts.

"We'll be in the lounge," I told Maddie. "Please bring it to me as soon as you're done."

I wouldn't put it past her to stop typing the minute my glaring eyes were around the corner.

As Rosie took Mason out of his carrier and handed him to me, I said, "It's not you. This is too much for him. He gets upset easily and doesn't have a routine yet."

He burrowed into my shoulder, making little baby noises.

"I couldn't have done this without you." I hesitated. "Whatever this is. They're not the most cooperative of clients."

"I was getting that impression. I'm sure you did your best. So, I put the stroller back in your car, and here are the keys."

I took them with my free hand and stuffed them in my pocket.

She gathered her things and gave me a hug. Kissed Mason on his warm head. "When will we see you again?" she asked.

"Any time you want to drive to Maine. Seriously. Mason needs to know you both and you don't want to miss his milestones. Think of us as your country house."

"You're right. We don't want to miss his milestones." She tucked some stray hairs behind her ear. "And I love the idea of having a country house. Are you done here?"

"I am so finished here. Couldn't do some of my jobs because they didn't bother to prepare the schedule I asked for. I've done my best, but there's no value in lingering, hoping I might do more."

"Aren't you getting wise," she said.

Given what had happened here today, I said, "Think I'm a pretty slow learner."

With my free hand I gathered up my things and put them together.

Maddie Monson appeared in the doorway, clutching a sheet of paper. "Hope this is what you wanted." She held it out between two fingers like it—or I—might bite her.

Rather than stick it right in my bag, I took the time to check. She'd done the minimum I asked. I could probably get anything else from the school's website.

"Thank you. This is very helpful."

She nodded and left.

"That's the public face of the school?" Rosie said.

I nodded.

We gathered our things and walked out to our cars. Mason would need feeding soon, but I could stop somewhere on the road. Right now I needed to see this place in my rearview mirror.

As I was fastening Mason's seat into its holder, I sensed someone standing behind me. As I often remind others and myself, I am not a cop. I am not a detective. But I've spent enough time around bad guys to have a heightened awareness of my surroundings.

It was not Rosie. She does not douse herself in men's aftershave or cologne.

I closed the door quickly, putting it between Mason and whoever was lurking too close behind me, pushed back abruptly, and turned. My hand automatically went to my pocket, where my pepper spray usually lived.

A man was standing there. Tall and broad, with longish dark hair slicked back with so much product it gleamed in the sun like it had been oiled and didn't look like a hurricane could dislodge it. He had unfriendly dark eyes and a scar on his lip that gave his mouth a perpetual sneer. Or maybe he just always sneered. No one I'd ever seen before and not someone who looked like they belonged on this campus. Not with the aura of sliminess he gave off. The denizens of the independent school world might be slimy but usually it was hidden beneath a veneer of civility.

This guy wasn't civilized. He didn't step back when I closed the door but stayed too close, invading my personal space in an infuriating way. Have I mentioned how much I dislike having people— usually of the male persuasion—invading my space?

If I were a betting person, which I am not, I would have bet this was the person who'd threatened Jess and Sadie, maybe unable to get at Ma'Kayla. They hadn't told me there had been a threat. Not in words. But I'd seen it on their faces.

"Excuse me," I said, slipping past him and going around the car to my driver's door.

He followed without a word, staying too close and positioning himself so I couldn't open my door. Evidently a graduate of some course in "Menacing 101."

I was supposed to be scared but instead I was angry. It was how I got when people threatened me, and that went doubly if someone's threats also threatened Mason. Mama Bear mode really is a thing.

I steadied my breathing. Assessed how much room I had to move. "Excuse me," I said again. Calm voice. Not betraying my anger. "You're in my way."

"Got a message for you," he said. "Stay out of the business with the football players and those girls, you get me? The school should leave it alone."

His voice, a low growl, was as slimy as his appearance. It might work with a bunch of high school girls. But not me.

I'm not very good at being pushed around and I can draw my pepper spray as fast as a cowboy in an old Western can draw his gun, so I did. I gave him a heavy dose right in his sneering face and when he bent down, his head between his hands, I gave him a knee in the chin as a follow up. Still not certain that he was sufficiently disabled, I added kicks to both his kneecaps. That probably hurt me as much as it did him. It's hard to find steel-toed women's business shoes.

I heard the crunch of tires. Rosie had stopped beside my car.

"Are you okay?" she asked. "Who's that?"

"You wouldn't happen to have any handcuffs, would you?"

"Sorry. Those would be in Dom's car. Will zip ties work?"

I have the coolest friends and anyway, when your husband's a cop, you get some training and are given some devices the other girls don't get.

She brought zip ties, and for good measure, her cane, which was seriously sturdy. We secured him and then searched his pockets, ignoring his language, which was not suitable for our ladylike ears and his face, which was streaming with snot and tears.

We both took photos of his driver's license, and his face, although with the red, watery eyes and snarl he didn't look much like his picture. Assuming the car parked beside mine was his, I also took a photo of his license plate.

"We done?" Rosie asked. "You need to get on the road."

We left the man with the alliterative name Matteo Martinelli cursing and pawing at his stinging face with his bound hands, and headed home. Maybe campus security would come to his rescue, even if they hadn't come to mine.

THIRTY-FOUR

During the drive, I called Andre and told him about the slimeball who'd threatened me, as well as a recap of my day. I figured it would be good to give him some time to process it. He's very protective, and there was Mason. If I was Mama Bear, then he was Papa Bear on steroids. It was a good thing that guy had only tangled with me. Andre would have killed him.

No. He wouldn't. He's too good a man for that, but the creep would certainly have felt the weight of his wrath.

Oh, even just running it through my tired brain, I liked the sound of that. Might be a good book title. **The Weight of His Wrath.** Readers would probably assume it was a religious book, though, whereas my wrath, and Andre's, was only righteous.

There were a million things to think about after the events—the debacle?—at Stonegate and I decided to postpone all of them. Not for long, though, since the appearance of that thug had raised serious concerns in my mind about campus security and their responsiveness. No one had shown up when Maddie Monson called security when Mason disappeared. If she'd even bothered to make that call. Her incompetence—real or pretend—was shocking. Such carelessness could put students at risk.

I made a mental note to call Margot Inglebright and get her read. Then I deliberately put my questions about the day out of my mind.

It didn't stay empty, though. The space was filled with questions about the other big mystery in my life: Addison Shirley's missing baby. With so much of my life centered around Mason, the idea of that baby being somehow at risk, and the impact on his mother, felt personal. It wasn't supposed to be my problem and yet it wouldn't leave me alone.

Miraculously, Mason slept or dozed in his seat almost all the way home. When he did wake and start to fuss, we'd almost reached a picnic area beside a scenic lake not far from home. I didn't mind at all sitting on a picnic bench feeling the sun and watching the water while he nursed, so glad to be back in Maine and back in the country again. I burped him. Changed him. Settled him back in his seat.

"We'll be home in fifteen minutes, Kiddo," I told him, "and your daddy can't wait to see you."

I was projecting, of course—I couldn't wait to see his daddy, too—but I thought he made an approving sound as we started to drive. He was the most brilliant child in the history of the world, after all.

Andre was in the yard supervising some guys on ladders who were installing what I assumed were motion-activated lights. There was also a security camera by the kitchen door. I wondered if there were cameras on the other two doors as well. It was all bringing us closer to Fortress Lemieux even if no one was digging that moat yet.

He opened my car door and kissed me. "You go inside and put your feet up. I'll bring the kiddo."

"He's been missing you," I said.

I didn't know if that was true, but long before Mason was born, Andre had talked to him and read to him and generally made his presence and his voice known.

As I headed for the door, he called after me, "Did you and Rosie really zip tie the guy?"

"I'm afraid we did. I've got pictures if you'd like to see. That plus his face, driver's license, make of his vehicle, and the license plate. In my opinion, people shouldn't mess with us. We can be fierce where Mason is concerned."

I could be fierce where anyone I loved was concerned.

I headed inside. Rosie had brought us some sandwiches but we'd never gotten to eat them and I was starved. I was also in need of a bio break, a tall drink of water, and to kick off my shoes.

Andre came in with the baby bucket in one hand and the other on Mason, who was perched on his shoulder. The baby looked so teeny next to his tall, broad-shouldered dad.

I got out a pitcher of iced tea and poured some for each of us. "So how was your day, Honey?"

Before he could answer, the weight of the day and the fact that I really had been scared of that thug hit me. Being awash with new mother hormones, of course I began to cry. That made me angry because I hate to be weepy, and of course made me cry harder.

Andre, who, like many good cops, always had one at the ready, handed me his handkerchief. "It's okay. You're okay. Mason's okay. Really."

"I am so pathetic. Everywhere I go, there's a big black cloud. My clients were jerks. The situation is so critical and they won't—"

I stopped. He really didn't need to hear this. He knew what my clients could be like.

"You are not pathetic. You are strong and capable, and it is not your fault if your clients behave like jerks. You and I, we like to win, but none of us can always make the jerks cooperate. No one knows that better than I do."

He got up and opened the refrigerator. "You hungry?"

"All the time. Your son is a ravenous beast."

"Takes after his old man," Andre said as he got out some containers and then got a plate from the cupboard. "Leftover lasagna okay?"

Much better than a sandwich, even if it was a sandwich Rosie had made. "It's perfect."

It was almost dinner time but neither of us cared. I was grateful for being taken care of and Andre was happy he got to do it. I was thrilled that he was home when I needed him. That was so important. Maybe my absence had reminded him that our time with Mason, who changed so much every day, was very important.

He put the plate in the microwave, punched some buttons, and came back to the table. I showed him the pictures while we waited.

"I spoke with Dom and Rosie about that guy," he said. "Dom's going to check his driver's license and run the plates, see what we can learn about him. In the meantime, I am very glad you are back here."

"With the moat and the dragons and motion-activated lights." I brandished my fancy container of pepper spray, designed to look like a lipstick or perfume. "And this. One of the best presents you ever gave me."

He wasn't much of a one for gift giving, so this was pretty special. He smiled. "With all of that. You would be very hard to replace."

My phone rang. Suzanne, wanting to know how things had gone. "Not well," I said. "But I'll have to call you back with the details. Right now, Mason needs my attention."

Actually, it was Andre, but she'd be more likely to respect the needs of a newborn. "Catch you later then," she said. "But you will call, right?"

"I will call."

After I'd gobbled my food, and Andre, made hungry by watching, had devoured some, too, we made ourselves some tall summer drinks—mojitos with mint from our garden—and took them out to the porch overlooking the road. I curled up on the porch swing. Andre, with Mason on his shoulder, took the rocker.

It was peaceful, looking down over our rolling green lawn to the street. Very little traffic. A gentle breeze shifting the leaves on the trees. The faint sound of a lawnmower in the distance and the sweet scent of new mown grass.

Across the street, two vehicles were parked in the driveway of the shabby house, half hidden by a hemlock hedge. Maybe someone would buy it and fix it up. Cut that scraggly hedge and paint it something other than that depressing shade of mildewed gray. The

Maine real estate market was so hot right now it was crazy. I wondered if the realtor would tell a prospective buyer about the bodies that had been found there. Did they have an obligation to do so?

There's a Dr. Seuss book called **Oh The Places You'll Go.** The places my mind went when it was supposed to be relaxing were pretty scary. Especially on a beautiful early September afternoon. I chased those thoughts away and looked up at the cloudless blue sky.

We sat as though there were no troubles in our world until I disturbed our peace and calm by asking, "What's happening with your investigation?"

"You really want to know?"

I nodded.

He took a long drink. Shifted Mason to the crook of his arm. Said, "Addison Shirley tried to do another disappearing act. This time, there was a cop on her door so she didn't get far. Wish she'd tell us what, or who, she's so afraid of."

"No luck finding Faraday?"

"None. His business associates are getting concerned. He's never disappeared like this before."

"Or Goodman?"

He shook his head. "We've been looking. Man's awfully good at being one step ahead. We get a tip, check it out, and it's always, 'well, he was here, but he left and didn't say where he was going.' We figure some of them know where he is but he scares people."

"What about Josh Frenier? How's he doing?"

"Still touch and go."

Was there no good news? "What about Addison Shirley's baby?"

He shook his head again. He looked sad. Detectives had to deal with a lot of sadness, but having this happen when he had a small baby of his own made it hit much harder.

He rocked. I swung. Mason watched the trees. It was perfect. So perfect that I squelched the next thought that came to me about the case. It could wait a few minutes. Moments like this were too rare to spoil.

We rocked and swung and drank our drinks and watched our

son. As we did, I could feel the tension of the day draining away. When I'm immersed, as I had been at Stonegate, I don't pay much attention to how I'm feeling, beyond sometimes tired or hungry. It's all about the clients. All about advising them in ways that will produce the right results and protect the school's reputation. It was only now that I was safely home that I could look back and see what a frustrating horror show it had been. Not only the incompetence of the headmaster and his assistant, but those girls who felt free to kidnap Mason, and that thug who felt free to accost me, believing that no one would notice or stop him. Parents expect boarding school campuses to be safe places for their children. This one was not.

Was it the school's culture? The type of students it attracted? Just a fluke that sexual assaults were left unaddressed and students had no respect for the headmaster's office? That thugs were allowed onto campus to threaten and intimidate? There was a whole lot more that needed to be done there. Not only helping the school deal with the sexual assault, but helping the school provide a safe—and reliably competent and responsive—atmosphere for all their students. I wasn't sure anymore that it was a task EDGE wanted to take on. The slipshod way they'd handled today didn't bode well for making improvements. It felt more like one of those cases where we were window dressing.

Even as I thought about it, I could feel my hands begin to curl into fists. Not now, I told them, forcing them to relax. Something else I *do* notice when I'm at a client school: when they make me lose my temper. What my mother used to call my famous little temper. I've gotten good at tamping it down until I'm done, but the anger lurks there. I've been told by wise therapists that hanging onto anger is bad for me. I whispered to myself, "Let it go."

Easier said than done.

I thought back to my first conversation with Libby Frenier. "I wonder..." Then I stopped. Did I really want to disturb our peaceful family time with speculations?

But now he was curious. "You wonder what?"

I fortified myself with a little of my delicious mojito and considered. "When I first spoke with Libby Frenier, when she came to talk about possibly being Mason's nanny, she told me a few things about Benjy Goodman. She said that he'd had a girlfriend in the past who had his baby, and then that baby was gone. Just gone. Disappeared with no explanation. Maybe, if you could find her, and find out what happened to her baby, it might lead you to Addison's?"

I shrugged. "Just a thought." Libby had told me that Benjy Goodman was possessive. That if something was his, he was going to have it. But that didn't square with his baby disappearing, did it? What if he'd made that baby disappear? What if his sleazy, grifter ways extended to selling a baby?

The thought made me shiver. Hot on its heels came the thought that someone out there thought I had Addison's baby. Could it be someone who wanted to sell that baby, not simply possess it?

"What if Benjy Goodman sold that baby?" I said. "What if he wants Addison's baby for the same reason? What if he's not possessive because the child is his but possessive because it's a possession he wants to turn a profit on?"

The thought was absolutely horrifying.

"We'll look into it. I think I should talk to Ms. Frenier myself. But not right now. Right now, this is perfect. I don't want to spoil it."

We watched Mason, who seemed to be staring at the way the wind was moving the leaves.

"Don't you wonder what he's seeing?" Andre asked.

"He's learning to be a detective by practicing his observation skills."

"When will he learn to talk?"

"Smart as he is? Probably any day now. You know his first word will be dada, right?"

"The Lemieux family genes. They're powerful."

We both laughed.

Andre offered his finger for Mason's hand to curl around. "Kid's got a nice, strong grip."

"He was very good today, but I wasn't comfortable having him there. He's not ready to be exposed to a lot of people. Right now, I don't think I am, either."

But I was still thinking about Addison Shirley. "Addison has a sister, Sarah. Older sister. They aren't close but do you think it's possible that she might have the baby? Libby Frenier says she still lives in their same town, so she wouldn't be hard to find."

Then I thought that if the police could find Addison's sister, so could Benjy Goodman. I didn't want to think about any of this, but when I looked at Mason, safe and cared for in his father's arms, I couldn't help worrying about another baby who wasn't so lucky.

"Why would someone kill Lucia Faraday to get at Addison Shirley's baby? It seems so extreme."

"We don't know that she was killed to get at the baby," Andre said. "She was a tough woman. She and Faraday were both ambitious. And ruthless. She was harsh with people who worked for her. She made some enemies."

Something else to consider but I was still thinking about the missing baby. "There was an infant seat in the car but the Faradays don't have any children. You found the baby's DNA in the car, didn't you?"

I suddenly couldn't remember what he'd told me about that. Maybe that they were testing for it? "Did you? Or am I misremembering?"

"We did find the baby's DNA in the car. Well, we found DNA in the car. Addison Shirley got away before we could get hers. But we have it now. And yes, her baby was in that car."

I agreed with Andre that this special time should be preserved. My mind is a willful thing, though. While I was in the process of trying to relax, a thought I'd been repressing almost popped out. A thought about Faraday. Something Libby had mentioned. I decided it could wait until another time. Andre had enough to deal with right now with my questions about Benjy Goodman possibly being in the business of selling his babies.

It must have been influence of my drink, because then it did pop out. "Libby Frenier said the thing that probably broke up Faraday's marriage to his first wife, Rebecca, was their inability to have a child. What if—"

I forced myself to stop. I wasn't going to talk about this. It was

just gossip and anyway, his contacts in the Freeport police department had probably already shared this. I wanted my sleuthing days,
even if that sleuthing was only speculating from the safety of my
front porch, to be over. But you can't utter half a thought in front of
a seasoned detective, and then say, "Oh, never mind." They don't
work like that, even when the detective in question is your husband.
Even if that husband also wants to preserve a peaceful afternoon.

"What if what?" he said.

"Libby said that despite his womanizing, people thought
Rebecca was the love of his life. What if Rebecca Faraday has the
child and he is with her? Is that a totally far-fetched possibility?"

"I really need to talk with Libby Frenier," he repeated.

Thea, the reader of voices, thought he was moving toward
needing to talk with her soon. I didn't want him going anywhere,
but I agreed.

"Yes, I think you do. She stopped by on Monday. Dressed oddly
and acting odd. She wanted to know about her son Josh. Whether I
knew if he'd be all right. Then she said she was going to the hospital
and asked if she could borrow a top. When I went upstairs to get
one, she left without waiting for it. I wondered if she was here to
find out what I knew about the relationship between Josh and Benjy.
It was such an odd encounter. Then things got so busy I forgot to
tell you about it. Or to tell you that she gave me a location where
Goodman might be staying. I was afraid I'd forget, so I wrote it in
my phone. Which is inside."

"Really need to speak with her," he repeated. "And I need that
address." He handed me the baby, pulled out his phone, and went
inside. He popped out a second later with my phone. "That
address?" he repeated.

I found it for him, he put it in his own phone, then disappeared
back inside.

THIRTY-FIVE

Dammit! Why hadn't I kept my mouth shut? Evidently, Mason agreed with me, because he decided if I could disturb a peaceful afternoon so could he. I established that he wasn't wet and he wasn't hungry. He was just unhappy. Very unhappy. An unhappy that wouldn't be consoled with a pacifier or having his back rubbed. I ended up putting him in his baby sling and walking around until he finally calmed down. It looked like even though he'd appeared to view the world through calm and curious eyes, the day's stresses had gotten to him, too.

A lesson for his mama. Just like I absorbed the stresses of the day and needed to learn to relax and let them go, so did Mason. It took a lot of walking to settle him down and by the time he did, he was red-faced and sweaty.

I had so much to learn about babies. So much to learn about being a family and the challenges that came with that.

So much to learn, as well, about keeping my mouth shut when I wanted peace and quiet. In our own ways, Andre and I had been solving crimes and problems for so long it was our default mode. Now our default mode had to be to also consider what was best for our family, especially for Mason, who was totally dependent on us.

As soon as I'd gotten him settled and snoozing on my shoulder, my phone rang. I checked the number—Thompson at Stonegate—and didn't answer. He'd had enough of my day and hadn't used it, or me, well.

He could leave a message and I'd call him back when I was ready. Right now, that felt like never. More important was to call Margot Inglebright and get her read on the situation, and call Suzanne to report on what a debacle the day had been. Those calls could wait, too. Right now, Mason was quiet and I was reclining on the swing with him in my lap, slowly pushing us back and forth with one foot. The magic of the swing worked on both of us. When Andre finally came back from making his calls, we were both asleep.

I woke to find him sitting in the rocker, watching us, a contented smile on his face.

"I never thought I'd want this," he said. "Never thought I'd have it. Watching you two is just amazing." He held out his phone. "Look. I took your picture."

This to a woman who hates having her picture taken. I was asleep, probably crease-faced and drooling. Reluctantly, I took the phone and looked. My hair had come loose, falling in wild curls around my face, and Mason was snuggled up against me, his face so peaceful in sleep. We *were* beautiful.

"Nice." I handed it back. "Have you restored order to the world?"

When he didn't reply, I said, "Please don't tell me you're just waiting for the right moment to tell me you have to leave."

"I have to leave." He said it in a soft voice. Reluctantly. "Roland and I are going to talk with Libby Frenier, and if we can find her, with Addison Shirley's sister Sarah. As for Rebecca Faraday? No one seems to know where she is. It's like she disappeared from the face of the earth. We've got people looking."

"Maybe Libby can tell you more about Benjy Goodman's ex-girlfriend. The one with the baby?"

Why would I make that suggestion? I didn't want him gone even longer, did I? But I was caught up in this, too. I wondered if Libby

Frenier was at home or at the hospital, waiting to see what her son's outcome would be.

"Wish you wouldn't go. I have an uneasy feeling right now that something's going to happen."

I wasn't just saying it because I'd had a hard day and wanted him home. The feeling was genuine, another thing I'd been trying to keep at bay along with the Stonegate mess. Sensible people learn to trust feelings like that, the sense that something bad is lurking on the horizon. Particularly sensible people who've dealt with bad guys and bad situations.

He studied my face and nodded. Female intuition or cop gut—they were pretty much the same. "Want me to send Norah over?"

"What? To watch over the little woman while her man is out chasing bad guys?"

Right. I can go from beautiful to edgy in a heartbeat. I liked Norah. We'd met under terrible circumstances, when Andre was in grave danger, and she'd definitely come to my rescue before. But I wasn't ready for our sweet afternoon and evening to come to an end. Plus, if there were bad guys lurking, I wanted Andre here. If I couldn't have him, if he didn't understand what was important here, then I had my trusty gun in the kitchen. Along with some sadness and disappointment to cope with. Another cop, even one who was my friend, wasn't an adequate replacement.

As for my trusty gun? I very much hoped it wouldn't come to that. The trouble with something as vague as an uneasy feeling is it's just that—a feeling. There's no way to assess the amount of danger. Danger can range from someone poking around outside or things that go bump in the night to bad guys breaking down the door looking for a baby who wasn't here. I've had a bad guy with a gun in my kitchen. It wasn't an experience I was eager to repeat.

"But if you're feeling uneasy..." he began.

I cut him off. I wanted him to stay because he knew he should, not because I was some fearful woman who couldn't be left alone. "You're supposed to be on paternity leave. Here with me and Mason while we all adjust to this new life. But that's not what is happening. If you are going to be gone, if this is how it's going to be, I need to learn to live with that. Getting Norah here to babysit me is a one-time thing, but our life is an on-going thing. Do you understand what I'm saying?"

We don't fight. Almost never. This was a crappy way to end a crappy day that had temporarily segued into a wonderful late afternoon. It was all too much for me.

Evidently, it was too much for Mason as well, since he woke from his beautiful, peaceful sleep with another bout of red-faced crying.

"He doesn't like when we get upset," I told Andre. "He may have been a crazed acrobat before he was born, but now it seems he's a sensitive soul."

I passed a wet, unhappy Mason to Andre. "Before you go, see if you can make him clean and dry and happy again."

"I think only you have what it takes to make him happy," Andre said.

"Give it a try."

We don't fight much, but each of us has something of a talent for sulking. Andre exhibited his now as he carried Mason inside. I heard his heavy feet on the stairs. Dammit! He really had no idea what it was like to try and work with a baby in tow. Maybe if I could send him off to do good works with Mason and a nanny along for the ride? I wouldn't send Mason alone. When Andre goes down a rabbit hole, his focus is total. Anyone who can focus in the chaos of a crime scene could certainly screen out the cries of one small infant.

When they'd disappeared up the stairs, I looked at my phone. I could call Suzanne. I could listen to that message from Thompson, but that would only make me more cranky. Instead, I did a bit of soul searching. Or instinct searching. What, besides the nagging questions raised by Addison Shirley's case and my frustration with the Stonegate situation, had led to my feeling of unease? I hadn't been followed. There had been no menacing vehicles on my journey today. There had been that thug but he hadn't followed me home. Indeed, he and whomever he was working with, or for, should have been glad to have me gone.

What was it then? Just general uneasiness knowing Benjy was still out there? Benjy or whoever our intruder was. I reviewed the journey home. Nothing on the highway. Nothing on my trip through town. Wait. There had been something. There had been a car—a Subaru—idling on the side of the road just as I passed the Agway. Nothing so unusual about that except for the way the driver had his ballcap pulled down over his face and seemed to be trying to slouch down behind the wheel. Was it the way his head had popped up right after I drove by? No. It was the color. It was the same color as the Subaru that Benjy Goodman had been sitting in that day in Freeport when this all started.

Subarus in Maine were ubiquitous, though. So had there been something else? Whatever it was, it had triggered a reaction, though it had taken a while for that reaction to set in. Had I seen the car again while we were lounging on the porch? I couldn't know for certain, but I thought there had been a car that color in the driveway across the street.

That was why I was feeling uneasy.

It could be nothing, but I wasn't going to discount it.

Before Andre announced he was leaving, before I'd foolishly shared my suggestions about his investigation, I'd entertained visions of a hot bath after Mason went to sleep. It looked like that was only a vision now. Luxuriating in the bath with my gun waiting on the toilet seat just didn't work as a concept.

Closing my eyes, I savored my last minutes of peace and quiet. I listened to the birds doing their evening settling. A rising wind in the trees. The sound of tires out on the street. Until they stopped and I heard the slamming of a heavy car door.

Had Andre called Norah after all? No. It was too soon, and anyway, she would have sped up the drive just like he did, sending gravel flying.

I didn't wait for the sound of footsteps coming up the drive, but slipped off the porch swing and went inside, locking the door behind me. Quietly, I opened the kitchen drawer where I kept my gun. Even as I readied it for action, I wondered how any bad guy could be dumb enough to come to a police detective's house in broad daylight?

Andre said that the majority of criminals they dealt with *were* stupid.

But this stupid?

I locked the kitchen door, then went into the living room to look out the windows, choosing an angle where I could see out but someone outside couldn't see me.

A man I'd never seen before was standing in the driveway studying the house. But wait. I *had* seen him before. He'd been sitting in a car in Freeport, watching Addison Shirley and her baby. Standing on the street while she was screaming.

Our unwanted visitor was the elusive Benjy Goodman.

I guess Andre was right. Criminals *can* be stupid.

I headed up the stairs to where I could hear Andre singing to our baby.

He looked up when I came in, his laser gaze going from my face to my gun before I could get out a word.

"Benjy Goodman," I said. "Outside. In the driveway. Armed."

He handed Mason to me. "Into the bathroom. The guest bath. In the bathtub. Now."

THIRTY-SIX

As Mason and I headed for the bathroom, Andre was going into our closet, where we kept the guns, his phone clenched between his chin and his shoulder.

Feeling like a fool, I pulled back the shower curtain and curled up in the tub with the baby. I might be brave as can be—ready to march forth and face down bad guys—but Mason needed to be protected. Our bathroom was at the front of the house, this one was at the back. Andre must have figured we'd be safer here.

Not that long ago, I'd been involved in another situation involving a baby and a bathtub while a gunfight raged outside. I hoped this wasn't becoming a habit.

That hadn't been here. I was thinking that if there was a gun fight here at our home, we would have to sell it and find somewhere else to live. The last time I'd found our dream house, I'd also found a dying woman in the living room. That had nixed the place from consideration. We'd searched and searched until Andre found this house, buying it before I'd even seen it. We loved the place, but love might not conquer all when all included bad guys breaking in, a nearly dead person behind our barn, and now this.

Were our newly installed cameras up and running yet? Would

there be video of what was about to happen downstairs while Mason and I huddled in the tub?

A zillion jumbled thoughts tangled up in my head as I waited. I needed to calm down. Mason was too susceptible to my anxiety. I was working on some calming breaths when my phone rang. Suzanne. Impatient to know what had happened at Stonegate. Like that really mattered now? But if I didn't answer, she'd keep calling.

"I've got a few minutes before all hell breaks out around here," she said. "Tell me what happened today?"

"Can't talk right now. Mason and I are huddled in the bathtub while Andre is outside dealing with an armed intruder," I said.

All hell had already broken out here.

She laughed. "No, really, Thea, I know you're busy, but you need to catch me up."

There was gunfire from outside.

"What the heck! Thea, was that a gun?"

"Like I said, armed intruder outside. Why don't I call you back?"

Saying something that normal almost made me laugh, except that my husband was out there.

I set my phone to vibrate. Mason didn't seem to like the ring and he didn't need any more upsets.

I wanted to leave Mason in the safety of the tub and go see what was happening. What if Andre was in danger? What if he needed my help? Who knew if Goodman was alone? It took willpower to stay put, but no, I couldn't risk leaving Mason with no parents.

How many gunshots had I heard? Three? After that, a silence that was more frightening than the shots themselves. Waiting has never been my strong suit and every minute seemed to crawl by at a snail's pace. It was as though those minutes were heavy and visceral, and I could feel them passing.

Eventually, I heard the sound of sirens and a while after that, Andre's voice from downstairs. "It's safe. You can come out now."

Awkwardly, I got out of the tub, one hand on Mason, the other on my gun, just as Mason let me know that he was hungry and he needed to eat right now.

Not a subtle child. Babies aren't. As I was discovering, this baby was anything but easygoing, at least not in the situations his parents were subjecting him to. We went into his room. I sat in the wonderful gray-green chair, set my gun down beside me, and let the little lad have his way. We'd just settled into our routine when Andre burst in, needing to know we were okay. Words were already spilling out as he started to give me an update.

I put a finger to my lips, stopping the flow of words, as I assessed him with a laser gaze of my own. I didn't see any blood or bruises. If he was okay, the news could wait.

He nodded, mouthed, "I'll be back," and left.

By the time Mason was done, I was done. Fried. Weary beyond words. Having a gunfight at your house, even if you don't participate, will do that. I settled him in his bassinet, picked up my gun and the baby monitor, and went downstairs to get my report.

No one was there.

I searched the whole house and the front porch and back deck. No one was there!

The kitchen door was unlocked.

Andre's car was gone. His whispered, "I'll be back," hadn't meant he'd be back upstairs after going downstairs. It had meant he was leaving.

Mason and I were alone in an unlocked house and no one had thought to leave a note.

THIRTY-SEVEN

My sense of betrayal was overwhelming. Nothing I could do about that now so I segued into my default mode: work. As long as Mason slept and I could keep busy, I could keep that dark cloud of disappointment and concern at bay.

I took my phone, my gun, and the baby monitor into my office and found a phone number for Margot Inglebright. She sounded cheerful when she answered and I had a moment of regret that I was about to dampen that cheer.

"It's Thea Kozak," I said. "Do you have a few minutes?"

"Oh, Ms. Kozak, I am so glad you called. Today has been such a disaster. And after you drove all this way and with your baby and everything. I believe we owe you an apology."

I heard genuine regret. I started to say something but she rushed on. "We sat with Dr. Thompson, of course, after you left, and his resistance to our questions and to our plans for handling the situation was, frankly, shocking. When we pressed him, he confessed..." She hesitated, then said, "Yes, I believe confessed is the right word, that he'd been pressured to sweep the whole matter of those three athletes under the rug. As though we could."

As he already had once before.

There was what I thought was the tinkle of ice in a glass. It seemed she'd needed to fortify herself after today's revelations. Unless that was comfort? I was tempted to fortify myself but with Andre gone and the situation unclear, I needed my wits about me.

"We've got him back on track now," she said, "and I've already been in touch with the person you recommended to help us handle the investigation and hearings. She sounds fabulous. We're lucky she's available."

I felt a twinge of pride. We were getting good at developing a stable of experts to help our clients.

"We also met with the school's attorney, Ms. Jackson, and crafted the suspension notice. She was very helpful."

Unsure I should raise this, yet feeling she should know, I said, "Did she tell you about the issue regarding the consent forms?" It's always a complicated question who the attorney represents and answers to, but Dr. Thompson's assistant's behavior—and character—was something I felt had to be discussed.

"She did." There was anger in the voice now. Anger and frustration. "I don't know how we got so far down this road without anyone noticing how much damage his obliviousness, or intimidation, whatever you'd call it, plus an utterly incompetent assistant, has caused. How can we claim we're keeping our students safe when behavior like this is overlooked?"

"The whole board is aware of this?"

"Yes."

I felt about twenty pounds lighter.

"There's more," I said.

"Why am I not surprised? What else should we be concerned about?"

I told her about my concerns that campus security wasn't taking the necessary steps to ensure that the campus was secure and the students were safe. In particular, that the three girls who'd already been subjected to a terrible experience were vulnerable to outsiders trying to pressure them to change their stories and might have already been approached.

"The school's job is to protect them, and that requires a campus-wide awareness and effort. How well the school handles that will have repercussions for the rest of the student body, the school's reputation, and success in attracting future classes. I was supposed to meet with the dean of students and the communications staff today but somehow Maddie Monson got busy and forgot to schedule it. How could she forget when Dr. Thompson has been describing the situation as an emergency, which is why we were called in? I gave him very specific instructions about what we needed to accomplish today. It's as though EDGE was invited to the campus as window dressing and not to do our job."

"You're angry," she said.

Oh, she didn't know the half of it. "Yes. I am. I've been doing this a long time, Ms. Inglebright. Over the years I've tangled with plenty of headmasters who didn't get it and a few whose agendas really did involve using EDGE as window dressing. This is different. There's a deliberateness in Thompson's indifference that's reflected in his behavior and his assistant's. If he's doing this because of an outside threat from one of the boy's families, that's a problem beyond my area of expertise. It should be a police matter."

What else could I say? I could dive in with detailed plans and advice but they would only work if the headmaster cooperated and implemented them. "I don't know where to go from here. I asked that a Zoom meeting be scheduled for tomorrow to work on communications strategies with the parents. But at this point, I'm wondering whether I should plan to continue working with Stonegate."

"We need you."

I had to raise the issue of the man who'd accosted me today. Sitting alone in my house with no information about what my husband was up to or whether I was safe, it was hard to talk about that encounter. But if that thug could get to me so easily, he could certainly get to three vulnerable girls. Maybe only two, since Ma'Kayla lived at home? No. She'd still be on campus much of the time.

I shivered as I stared out into my dark yard, then said, "Excuse me a moment." I put down the phone and closed the blinds. As though if someone out there couldn't see me, I was safe? I'd never felt less safe and I've had some very scary moments.

"Here's why I'm so concerned about security." I struggled to find my voice. My throat felt tight just thinking about it. "Today as I was getting ready to leave Stonegate, as I was putting my baby in the car, a man appeared and blocked me from opening my driver's door. He refused to move when I asked him to. He said he had a message."

I had to stop for a moment, the memory of that menace was so fresh. He'd been close enough I felt his body heat. I'd smelled him. I could describe the spot he'd missed while shaving. The trouble with being trained in Detective Lemieux's school of observation was that I observed. And remembered. He said, "Stay out of the business with the football players and those girls, you get me? The school should leave it alone."

I swallowed. "I think he's already delivered a message to Jess and Sadie, trying to scare them into backing off. Not from anything they told me but from reading their body language."

"This is what happens when the board gets complacent," she said with a heavy sigh. "Or when we've backed off because working with Kristoff is so difficult."

"But Dr. Thompson is in line now?"

Another heavy sigh. "I hope so. He and I and the police chief are meeting tomorrow to strategize about how to handle outside pressure as the school deals with the assault. It really helps to know about this."

Difficult to know how that would go but it gave me hope. "Take your lawyer, too," I said. "She's good and she understands the situation."

She was quiet. Then, "I should be sure the dean of students speaks with their dorm mother so she knows to be watchful." More silence. "This should be Barry's job but I'm not waiting for him."

So many times the work that needed to be done was stymied by people whose mantra was "not my job." By contrast, Margot Inglebright was a treasure.

We made a plan. Tomorrow, I'd have that virtual meeting with the dean and the head of communications. I asked her to add the head of security to that meeting and to be sure that the meeting actually got scheduled. Something else that was not her job but she was willing to make happen.

It was optimistic to plan anything when I wasn't sure who might watch Mason but I was in this too deeply to quit now. At least as long as I had the board behind me. If things around here stayed chaotic, Suzanne could take the meeting. She wouldn't be frazzled from the after-effects of hiding in a bathtub while guns went off on the same day as being threatened by a menacing thug. Being badly scared screws up the adrenaline system. Something about cortisol? I was feeling the effects of that now. Feeling deeply, overwhelmingly tired.

But another question nagged at me. "What about Kristoff Fitz? Is he going to be a problem?"

There was touch of humor in her voice as she said, "He won't. Kristoff has decided he's really too busy to sit on something as insignificant as the Stonegate board. Sad, isn't it? He has so much to offer." She added, "I'm hoping he makes a generous donation on his way out the door."

When the call was over, even though I was tired, I felt better. I decided to call Suzanne with an update.

That was when I found myself listening to the voice mail Barron Thompson had left. His message? I was informed that the services of EDGE Consulting were no longer needed by Stonegate Academy. So much for moving forward and making plans. It looked like I was going to have to call Margot Inglebright back.

I called Suzanne and went to *her* voicemail. It was hard, sometimes, to see voicemail and texting as an improvement over the way life had been back when people spoke to each other in person or on the phone. I texted her: gunfire done. Lots to report re: Stonegate Call me.

Either she would or she wouldn't but now the ball was back in her court. I was doing this for her, after all. I was on maternity leave.

Ha ha ha. At least I was better at it than my husband was at paternity leave, although I expected his defense would be he was doing what was necessary to protect his family.

I was tired but I didn't dare go to sleep, not with the chance bad guys might show up again, so I turned back to my computer and began searching for Faraday's ex-wife Rebecca. Earlier, I'd seen pictures of her with Faraday during their marriage and liked the way she looked. I thought I'd seen them growing apart, literally, physically, in the pictures I could find. Now I wanted to go farther back, back before they were a couple.

With a little digging, I found her maiden name: Rebecca Stein. Rebecca Alexis Stein, an artist who signed her pictures R. A. Stein. I found notices of various art shows, with photographs of some of her paintings. They were spare and Wyeth-like, not a lot of color but a profound sense of place, somehow both peaceful and intense. Several were of what looked like a small cottage by the ocean. There was something in the way that cottage was painted that suggested she cared deeply for the place. It wasn't one of the grand houses I'd found when I looked up Faraday. It was simple. Humble. But as she'd painted it, it conveyed a sense of security. Solidity. Sanctuary. She'd painted a place she loved.

When I thought the word "sanctuary" I was sure that whatever grander places Faraday might have provided during their marriage, this place, if it was one that she owned, was one she would never give up. Could it be a place she and Faraday might retreat to now, with Addison Shirley's baby? Was that so far-fetched an idea?

Could I possibly find an address? A town, at least? Some mention somewhere about the location of a place she'd frequently painted? I dug in, reading interviews and articles. Looking at old websites where her art was still displayed. I was discouraged to find the cottage didn't appear in her more recent work. Did that mean she'd sold it or just that she'd moved on, as artists did, to something new as the creative spirit moved them? The more recent works were much bolder and more colorful, some of them verging on abstract. I preferred the earlier ones. They were more peaceful. Thoughtful. They were the kind of paintings I would enjoy having around.

I'd been at this too long. My eyes were burning and I was getting a headache. "Just one more article," I said, as though the computer was listening. That one more article was a bingo. It was an interview in one of those slick new Maine magazines. The ones that don't display towers of lobster traps or the scenic yard decorated with a doorless refrigerator, an ancient metal box spring, or an abandoned car repurposed as a planter. The ones that don't suggest the ways old hubcaps can be reused for décor and old tires for swings. This magazine featured architech-designed homes and gorgeous, expensive landscaping.

The photos took readers on a tour of a spare, modern home—lots of blond wood and white rugs—where the walls were covered with R.A. Stein paintings. Most of them were the newer, more colorful ones, but in a serene white bedroom—the kind no real human ever lives in, the kind without even a book or a box of tissues—there was an earlier one on the wall. It was that cottage with its weathered gray shingles and white trim and a deck with two white rocking chairs.

The caption was: Stein has frequently painted her retreat, a Bristol cottage that's been in her family for generations.

Bingo!

THIRTY-EIGHT

I could share that information with Andre in the morning. If he was home by morning. I've grown used to having a husband who disappears with no set return time. Something we would need to work on. Right now, I had other concerns. The baby monitor said that Mason was stirring. After his eventful day, he'd slept more than four hours. Kind of a miracle.

Baby monitor in one pocket, my phone in the other, and gun in my hand, I climbed the stairs and went to his bassinet. I set the gun down nearby and picked him up. He stopped fussing and looked at me with his wise baby eyes, as though all he'd wanted was a conversation. A little company after a pleasant rest.

"What's up, little guy? Did you miss me?" I asked as I put him on his changing table. His eyes left my face and went to the mobile above my head. I touched it and rainbows and clouds and unicorns danced in the dim light. Probably punchy from lack of sleep, I thought that a cop's kid's mobile should have guns and pepper spray, badges and handcuffs. Not enough color to catch a baby's eye, though. What would my mobile look like? Even duller? A laptop, stacks of paper, maybe my Jeep since I spent so much time of the road. It made me wonder if I needed a more colorful career.

Downstairs, I heard a car door thump.

Andre?

A bad guy?

Sorry, world, but right now, we were dealing with wet pants, and as the expression goes, the only person who likes change is a wet baby.

Clearly, my brain was on the fritz.

With only the nightlight for illumination, I wrestled him out of his damp clothes, put on one of those absurdly tiny diapers that look like no human, however small, could wear them, then a onesie and a soft yellow sleeper. He was beginning to fuss, so we adjourned to the rocking chair.

Each time we moved, the gun moved with us.

He ate. We rocked. I listened for whoever had shut that car door. If it was Andre, why hadn't he come inside? Perhaps checking the moat and reminding the dragons of their duties? Or was he off tilting at windmills while the bad guy was here?

Definitely on the fritz.

I was so tired. Should have slept while Mason slept, except who could possibly sleep after the day I'd had? Who could sleep after gunfire and a missing husband? When the demands of work dragged me out of my leave to deal with a client whose behavior was beyond frustrating? When I needed to do all I could to bring calm and order back into my life?

Now that he was dry and fed, Mason wanted to watch the world for a while. I set him in his little baby seat and went across the hall to look out the windows. The only car in the driveway was mine.

I went back in his room and set Mason on the floor, away from windows and doors, then circled the rest of the upstairs, looking out all the windows for signs of movement.

The night was absolutely still and quiet. I went to the upstairs front window and looked across the street at the only house that was close to ours, the house where I'd earlier spotted a car like the Subaru I'd seen Benjy Goodman driving.

Too dark to tell but there might have been a car parked there.

I called Andre, swearing to myself that if I went straight to voicemail I'd pack up Mason and go to Suzanne's.

He answered with a brusque "Can't talk right now. On surveillance."

He would have hung up but I said, "At our house?" before he could.

His "yes" was almost a whisper.

"Because I heard a car door and it looks like there's a car parked across the street."

"Stay away from the windows," he said. "Don't turn on any lights. Maybe you should—"

"Mason and I are not going back in the bathtub, if that's what you were about to suggest." I had to clench my teeth together to hold back all that I wanted to say about where he should be right now. In here with us, not out there, no matter what his training and experience said.

As thought he'd read my mind, he whispered, "I'm right outside."

"Alone?" I asked, since he could only cover a part of the house.

"With Norah and Tommy."

Norah, who was pregnant and still doing her job. My tired brain wanted to know whether they made bullet-proof vests to fit pregnant women. I hoped so.

"This should be over soon," he whispered. "I love you." And he was gone.

What did soon mean in a patient cop's lexicon? Minutes? Hours? Days?

I lay down on the daybed in Mason's room, Mason beside me, and closed my eyes. I would have said that it was impossible to sleep under these circumstances, but I drifted off just as gunfire came from outside.

Jumping up, I grabbed Mason's baby seat, rushed into the bathroom, and put him in the tub. I'd just pulled the shower curtain when the window beside me exploded and I was either hit by flying glass, or a bullet, or stung by a very large bee.

The fate of a stubborn woman who wouldn't take her husband's advice.

THIRTY-NINE

I gnoring the blood oozing down my arm, I checked to be sure
Mason was okay. It appeared that the curtain had protected
him. The noise had scared him, though, and he looked at me with
those big, worried eyes, scrunched up his face, and began to cry.

I wrapped a hand towel around my arm, then snatched him up
and ran into our bedroom. I carried him into the closet, far away
from any windows, and pulled the door shut. In the quiet darkness, I
took him from his seat and put him on my uninjured side, resting
my chin on his downy soft head. Closing my eyes and trying to
ignore my bleeding arm, I rubbed his back and took slow, calming
breaths. Calm mother, calm baby. He didn't need to know that I was
in pain and utterly furious with his father. If they wanted to have a
gunfight here, they should have evacuated me and Mason first. This
was not how our child should be spending his first precious weeks.

I knew, and didn't care, that they hadn't chosen to have a
gunfight here.

As soon as I knew there were no bad guys out there, as soon as
Andre came to tell me it was all right and we were safe, I was
packing a bag and Mason and I were leaving. This was not a safe
place for small baby. I didn't yet know where I'd go, whether to a

270

hotel or the longer drive to Rosie and Dom's. Certainly not to my parents' house. Refuge was supposed to feel safe, not cold and critical. Right now, the last thing I needed to hear was how I'd made a mistake marrying a detective. Living in Maine. Choosing to work for EDGE. Probably I had also failed by not having a girl. My parents already had a grandson, after all.

True, it was my actions that had probably set this in motion. My experience was a warning to would-be good Samaritans everywhere. Don't stop to help, the risk it will turn your life upside down is simply too great. If I hadn't stopped to ask Addison Shirley what was wrong, eventually someone else would have and this whole mess might be their problem.

Thinking like this was not who I am. I'm a rescuer by nature and often by profession as well. But those two idiots Addison Shirley, whether lovely, helpless girl or liar and manipulator, and Jeremy Bartlett, shamefully loose-lipped policeman, had turned a moment of kindness into a nightmare by putting my name out there. The next time I saw someone in distress, I was crossing the street, driving away, turning my back. I had had enough.

Mason gave a little gasp, preparing to cry. "Sorry, baby. Sorry. It's okay. You're safe." I rubbed his back and felt him relax against me.

My phone vibrated in my pocket.

I ignored it. There was no one I could think of that I wanted to talk to right now. Not even Andre. Especially Andre. I might be being unreasonable and I didn't care. He'd deserted us and left us feeling vulnerable.

Time passed. The world outside was silent. No more gunfire. But Andre didn't appear.

The world stayed silent.

Under my slow-moving hand, I felt Mason relax. He was asleep. "Poor little guy," I whispered, rubbing my chin against his warm head, "I hope we haven't traumatized you for life."

More time passed. I dozed with my sleeping baby on my shoulder.

Feet pounded on the stairs and I heard doors opening and closing, Andre's voice calling my name. If I answered, I'd wake the baby. If I didn't answer, he'd probably wake the baby.

Slowly, I stood up and opened the closet door just as he burst into the bedroom and snapped on the light. As I'd done before he disappeared, I put my finger to my lips so he wouldn't wake Mason.

He looked like he'd just been through a war. Sweat-soaked, his face dirt-streaked, his shirt torn, his pants and shoes muddy.

He took in the bloody towel, my furious face, and his sleeping child in one frantic glance, then held out his hands for the baby. "The blood? Mason? Is he okay?"

I considered refusing to hand Mason over, but my quarrel was with Andre. Mason and Andre had no quarrel. Well, maybe they did. It could be argued that his father had put the baby at risk. I didn't know the whole story yet. But I did need to do something about my arm. It hurt like the dickens.

"What happened?" he asked.

Shouldn't that have been my question to him?

"Bullet came through the window as I was putting Mason in the tub."

I left him with the baby and went to our bathroom, which wasn't covered in broken glass and my blood. He was starting to say something, maybe asking where Mason's infant seat was? I didn't linger to find out.

In the bathroom, I unwrapped the bloody towel and used the mirror to inspect my arm, hoping despite how it had bled that it was something I could slap a bandage on. I'm allergic to Emergency Rooms and stitches. I am not entirely joking when I say I've had more stitches than a baseball. It was a nasty gouge. I'm not an expert on wounds, but I thought I could handle it without stitches.

I opened the storage cupboard to see if we had any large bandages but sorting through the boxes in there was all of a sudden too much, so I got myself a clean towel, sat on the toilet, and cried into it, ignoring the blood that dripped down my arm.

All too much.

I wanted to be a happy new mom enjoying a peaceful bonding experience with my baby. What I was getting was so very far from that. Normally, I can cope. I'm the one who stays calm when everyone else is losing it. Tonight, my coping skills had deserted me.

My phone buzzed in my pocket, reminding me that I'd never gotten around to calling Margot Inglebright about Thompson's odd message. Never spoken with Suzanne. That I had important information to share with Andre, if I was ever speaking with him again. Reminding me that it was all too much. All too much.

I pressed the towel against my face, leaked blood, and cried.

FORTY

ndre wisely left me alone for a while. He is a professional reader of people, after all. I could hear him moving around the bedroom, probably changing out of his dirty clothes, talking to Mason as he did so. I knew he was talking to Mason, and not on the phone to the state police, because of his tone. It was the voice he'd used to talk to Mason before he was born.

Mason was quiet. No baby noises, no fussing. Either he was mesmerized by his father's voice or stunned into silence by the chaotic events of the evening. I was projecting. He was only a baby. Watching one of his parents was part of his day's work.

When I got bored with mopping up blood, and cold from the aftermath of an adrenaline rush and sitting around without my shirt, I summoned the energy to root through the cabinet and find a large bandage. I slapped it on the wound, washed blood off my arm and my hand, and went to the bedroom to find a warm sweatshirt.

Andre, dressed in soft gray sweats, was lying on the bed beside Mason. They were both asleep.

I couldn't choose between being madder that he hadn't made sure I was okay, or mad that he hadn't given me a report, or just furious that he could go to sleep while I, an exhausted new mother, was brooding and bleeding in the bathroom. Men could be such simple creatures. Exhausted from two gunfights, he'd stretched out on the bed and fallen asleep.

The two of them looked very sweet together. Too sweet to disturb. Never wake a sleeping baby. Maybe there was a corollary: never wake a sleeping husband after a gunfight. Probably not too many people needed to know that one.

Quietly, I gathered up my own soft gray sweats and tiptoed into the guest room. I changed and crawled into bed. Despite the throbbing in my arm, I almost immediately fell asleep myself.

I woke, as mothers will, just before Mason woke up hungry and started fussing. Good thing I had mother's instincts, because Andre was still deeply asleep. I carried Mason away, even his small weight pulling on my wounded arm, and we sat in the rocking chair in his room while he ate, then I put clean, dry clothes on him and took him downstairs. I left him in the kitchen while I went back up for his laundry. He made a lot of it and if I let it pile up, it seemed to accuse me of getting nothing done, which depressed me. I grabbed Andre's muddy clothes as well, going through the motions of normal when the world felt anything but.

It was very early morning. Too early to be up. Way too early to make any phone calls. I knew I wouldn't be able to go back to sleep, and anyway, I was starving. That lasagna I'd eaten after I got home from Stonegate was a long time ago.

I put two slices of bread in the toaster and some eggs in the microwave to poach. I started a wash. Made a pot of coffee. I took Mason to the window to watch some birds at the feeder. The toast popped and the microwave beeped, their noises seeming awfully loud in the quiet house, the quiet morning.

After I'd eaten, I carried Mason into my office. He could watch sunlight while I checked my mail and printed off that page from the article about R.A. Stein for Andre. I resisted going outside to see if our house was damaged by bullets beyond that upstairs window. The guy who'd been in the gunfight could do that.

Once my computer was fired up, I decided I'd communicate with Margot Inglebright via email so I could put in writing what we'd discussed and agreed on, along with the news about my phone call from Dr. Thompson terminating EDGE's services. I needed to know whether I should plan on a meeting later today or whether we were done and I could hand off any final details to Suzanne and go back to being on maternity leave. Because I was copying Suzanne, I included a reiteration of my encounter with the man who'd threatened me and told me to back off the sexual assault issue.

It appeared that neither of Mason's parents were any good at taking leave, but today was a new day.

Since Andre had fallen asleep without telling me what had happened, I decided I should look at the news. Maybe some annoying reporter could update me even if my husband couldn't. Before I did that, though, I realized what had been missing when Mason and I were looking out at the birds. Beyond the feeder was the driveway. My car was there but Andre's was not. Yet Andre was upstairs asleep.

I went back to look at the news and wished I hadn't.

The long silence after the gunfire was because Andre wasn't there. Andre's car wasn't here because it had been shot to hell in a gun battle between state police and a man identified as Benjamin Goodman in a hospital parking lot. I knew it was the hospital where Josh Frenier was a patient. Goodman had died in the fight.

No wonder Andre had collapsed after something as intense as that. Not surprising that, close as we were, he hadn't wanted to talk about it. He was tough and resilient but sometimes the job got to him. I'd seen this once before when his best friend was killed.

I'd been thinking about myself and my sense of vulnerability and abandonment, but this news brought back all the worry and fear that came with being married to a cop. How every time the phone rang when he wasn't home, it might be bad news. How my mind would fill those spaces when he didn't answer his phone with the direst imaginings. How even though we had both wanted this baby, our Mason, so much, there was always the possibility that Mason would grow up without a daddy.

Sure, everyone faced the possibility of accident or a bad actor, but Andre and his colleagues went out looking for danger and trouble every day. Last night, in the midst of that fight with Goodman, he must have realized the risk that he might never see Mason again.

That made me cry. Again. I was like a leaky old bucket these days.

I dabbed at my eyes as I watched Mason, so innocent in the midst of his family's chaos. He was studying his fist as it moved through the air. Then his gaze shifted to the patches of colored sunlight on the wall. So new to the scary world we'd brought him into.

I practiced my relaxing breathing and joined Mason in watching the light dancing. That's what we were doing when Andre stumbled in, unwashed and unshaven.

"It must have been awful," I said. "Are you really all right? And Tommy? And Norah?"

He shook his head. Too many questions. "Is there coffee?" It took effort for him to ask even that.

I understood that words could wait. Had to wait. I nodded. "Yes, there's coffee." Though he might not be ready for me and my questions, I thought Andre could use a dose of Mason. Watching our baby watching his fist was very Zen. It had helped calm me. It might be therapeutic for Andre. "Why don't you take Mason while I fix you some. Do you want food?"

I gathered the pages of the story I'd printed about Faraday's first wife, Rebecca, and the beloved family cottage that frequently appeared in her paintings and left them on the kitchen counter. I'd share them when Andre was ready. There was still the matter of Lucia Faraday's murder and the missing baby to be resolved.

I set Mason's seat on the table beside Andre, and fixed him a bagel even though he hadn't responded to my question about food. Best to take things slowly.

He watched Mason. Drank his coffee. Ate the bagel without seeming to notice he was eating.

I gave him more coffee and threw a second bagel in the toaster. The only sound in the kitchen was Mason's baby noises.

The day seemed to be on slo-mo.

277

I put the laundry in the dryer and made a fresh pot of coffee, then went upstairs to wash my face, comb my hair, and brush my teeth. My wounded arm felt like it was on fire. I should have peeled off the bandage and drenched it with peroxide or something. Taken myself to Urgent Care for stitches. But I wasn't leaving Andre or Mason. Not right now. I was remembering our time in San Francisco, right after Ray Dolan was killed. Andre had been like this then. Despairing. Unreachable. I'd forced him to talk. We'd gotten through it.

We would get through this.

Mason had his hand wrapped around Andre's finger again and I wondered, as I studied my husband's face, whether this time it would be Mason who got him through this.

"He looks so wise," Andre said. "Like he's studying everything and thinking about what he sees."

"Takes after his father. Look at those eyes. Your eyes. I've never been able to resist them and I probably will be a sucker for him, too. I'll be trying to say, 'Mason, you can't...' and I'll look at those eyes and just melt."

Andre said, "We made this kid. It's amazing."

It was amazing.

I poured myself a cup of fresh coffee. It tasted almost as good as it smelled. We liked our coffee strong and dark. Andre's black. Mine with cream and sugar. In my pre-domestic days, I used to forget to eat a lot, and it was that cream and sugar that kept me going. Pregnancy made me more sensible. Now I carry protein bars and almonds. Water.

The slow day kept its slow pace. The outside world didn't intrude. We must have spent forty minutes in our silent kitchen before my phone rang. Suzanne, looking for an explanation of the email I'd copied her on.

I carried my phone into the office and updated her. "I know you worry about our bottom line," I said, "but I think we've got to start firing clients when they behave like Thompson. We don't do our reputation any good if we're associated with a school that insists on sweeping sexual assaults by its male students on its female students under the rug. Or any assaults. Or that refuses to follow or enforce its own rules and honor code."

"You're right. I am sorry I dumped this mess into your lap." She did sound contrite. "Do you want me pick up the ball from here? Get back to Margot Inglebright and figure out how to go forward? Whether we go forward?"

In the background, I could hear her son, Paul Jr. patiently explaining something to his toddler sister. "You're at home?" I said.

"Nanny is sick. Paul's tied up in meetings. And the idea of taking both kids to the office is just crazy. Not that work from home isn't also crazy, especially when young children are involved." She sighed. "Remember when we used to think we should be able to do it all?"

"I'm just getting started on that. Mason seems to reluctant to do things for himself."

She laughed. "Right. The way those infants feign helplessness. Otherwise, how are things?" She hesitated. "I read about the... uh... about the situation with Andre."

Ah, this was so us. Both Suzanne and I, taking care of business before discussing a gunfight.

"How are things? Not good." Really, there wasn't more to be said about that. I was still trying to understand it myself. "He's not talking about it yet."

"Oh." Silence. "Right. So I'll let you go, but call me or text if you need anything, and I'll keep you in the loop about Stonegate."

I didn't need a huge apology, even though she'd let me down. We both knew how life could get in the way. Besides, her taking on the Stonegate matter from here was a huge weight off my shoulders, even though I am not very good at letting things go. Probably this would come back at me in some form, as further questions or even just Suzanne needing to vent. There was not going to be a message replying to Dr. Barron Thompson. Anyone who fires their consultant by text after days of frantic and demanding phone calls doesn't deserve the courtesy of a response. Any further communication could be with Margot Inglebright and the board.

I still didn't know if I—or Suzanne—was supposed to be having a distanced meeting later but the ball was in someone else's court.

I tucked my phone into my pocket and went back to the kitchen.

Andre was standing at the counter, reading the pages I'd printed out. "What's this?"

"R.A. Stein is Rebecca Faraday. Faraday's first wife. When I looked her up online, I saw that she'd painted the same cottage many times. Then I found that article which said... well, you've read it... that it was a beloved family place that had always been her inspiration. I think that if she and Faraday and a baby he believes is his are missing, that's where they'll be."

FORTY-ONE

Andre slapped his pocket for a phone that wasn't there, then looked down, seeming surprised to find he was wearing sweats without pockets. He was never without his phone. "Just getting my phone," he said, heading for the stairs.

I looked at Mason, who seemed to be wondering where his daddy was. "He went upstairs, kiddo. He'll be right back."

He wasn't right back. I heard him on the phone, then footsteps and the shower running.

By the time he emerged, clean and shaved and in his regular "I'm a detective who might be called in at any time" clothes, there was the sound of a car in the driveway and then Norah and Tommy were knocking on the door.

From silence to bustle with still no word to me about what had happened or was happening.

I am not good at being a mushroom.

The two people I let into my kitchen didn't look any better than Andre. They all had a depleted, haunted look.

I hugged them and offered coffee, which was accepted. Then the three of them huddled up while I dug around in the freezer for a coffee cake and quickly thawed it in the microwave.

By the time I got it, and some plates on the table, Norah was holding Mason, rubbing her chin across his head. Not that I can read minds or anything, but I knew she was thinking about last night and how, given their jobs, she and Tommy might never have this moment.

Tommy was reading through the papers Andre had given him, the results of my research into Rebecca Faraday. When he finished, he looked at me.

"This is great. You should have been a detective, Thea."

He didn't mean to be condescending, did he?

Still, I couldn't quite keep the edge from my voice as I said, "Am a detective. I detect trouble and fix it. I detect lies and call people on them. I go into emergencies and handle them. I write the rules and enforce them. I make the world safer with my expertise. Just in a different sphere and without a badge or a gun."

They all laughed. I made another pot of coffee as they demolished the cake. Sure, it looked like I was wearing my "little woman" hat today, but it was okay. Right now they needed caring for. Maybe some of Rosie's need to feed people was rubbing off on me. I rescue. She feeds. Maybe what today was showing was that feeding can be a form of rescue.

Andre made some calls. Tommy made a call. Norah held Mason and looked like she was about to cry.

When he began to fuss, I took him from her. "Someone wants food and dry pants," I said. "Wanna watch?"

Because I knew she did.

We went upstairs, leaving the two haunted guys to their planning.

When we were settled, Norah said, "Did he tell you about it?"

I shook my head. "Not a word. He was practically catatonic, almost immediately fell asleep."

So she told me about it. How Goodman had led them on a chase from here to the hospital parking lot, how he'd parked right outside the ER entrance so they couldn't fire without risking people inside. How he'd brought an arsenal. How Andre had gone through the hospital and come out behind him. How Goodman had grabbed a nurse who was trying to run by and used her as a shield.

"It was crazy, Thea. We're trained. We're prepared. Careful. But when someone is determined that if he's going down he's going to take others with him, you've got to slow it way down." She sighed. An exhausted sigh just from remembering. "It felt like it went on forever. All of us trying to get a clear shot. That nurse's terrified face. Goodman like a madman, which I suppose he was."

"Why the hospital? Was he trying to get at Josh Frenier?"

"I don't know. Maybe? Probably."

I had a million questions. I tried to keep it simple and get answers to the most pressing. "What was he doing here? Did you learn that?"

"He was after the baby. After your baby, which he was certain was his. Only here's the ugliest thing. It wasn't because he cared about getting custody of his child. After he was shot—" She stopped, uncertain how much she should tell me, then decided I had a right to know.

"After he was shot, while he was dying, he said... and this is so horrible... he said that his baby was worth fifty thousand dollars and he had a buyer just like the last time."

FORTY-TWO

It was horrifying in every possible way. I thought about him trying to steal Mason, thinking the baby was his. What if he'd succeeded and Mason had disappeared forever? "What a monster," I said. Maybe the understatement of the year.

"Absolutely."

There was still so much I didn't understand about the sequence of events. Thinking Norah might know some of it, I said, "This is such a mixed-up mess. Who took Addison Shirley's baby? Who killed Lucia Faraday? Who attacked Addison Shirley? Do you know? Do Andre and Tommy?"

She shook her head. "We know that at some point, the baby was in Lucia Faraday's car. The rest we're still working on."

"You don't know who beat Addison Shirley and then dumped her in that cold cellar? The beating was in Faraday's property, but that cold storage place was in Benjy Goodman's town."

Norah shook her head sadly. "Despite what was done to her, she's been absolutely uncooperative, Thea. Fear of Benjy Goodman? Fear of losing her baby?"

"Any speculation? Such as Faraday might have done it to cast suspicion on Goodman? Or the other way around?" I suggested. I really didn't want to think about any of this, but the mess had intruded into my life and I wanted it solved. Wrapped up. Gone.

She just shrugged, leaving me without knowing whether it was information they didn't have or information they were keeping to themselves. Cops are like that. It can be pretty much a one-way street. The trouble was that I lived on that street. It was at my house that too much of this had played out.

"No idea whether the baby is Faraday's or Goodman's?"

She shook her head again. "We've got DNA from Lucia Faraday's car. Now we'll have DNA from Goodman. And of course, we have it from Addison Shirley. But all of that takes time. It's not like on TV."

As if I didn't know that?

"Sorry," she said, reading my face like the good cop she was.

"Now you need Faraday's DNA?"

"Yes. We need to find him for a number of reasons."

"Well, maybe you will find that cottage and you'll get lucky and Faraday will be there. They will all be there. First wife, Rebecca, Faraday, and the missing baby."

I realized that while Tommy had read the material I printed out, I didn't know if she had. "Did you read that stuff I found on the internet?"

"Not yet. What did you find?"

I put a finger to my lips. "Let me get Mason settled and then we can talk."

He took his time. It was fascinating how his personality was developing. Sometimes he was so hungry he couldn't drink fast enough. Other times, it was more like he wanted to be close and snuggle, and eating was secondary. That was how he was today. At last he was finished. I put him on my shoulder and rubbed his warm back, then changed him and handed him to Norah.

I sat on the daybed and she rocked slowly in the chair and Mason stared up at a mobile, in no hurry to go to sleep but not fussy, either. I described what Libby Frenier had told me about Faraday's first wife, Rebecca, and how sad she'd been about not being able to have children. About what I'd seen looking at photographs of them, a close and happy couple growing sad and distant.

"It's pure speculation on my part, of course. I could be reading too much into what I saw in some pictures, but I wondered if she might be the missing piece in this puzzle. I kept on looking online to see what I could learn about her. I found that she was an artist using her maiden name, R.A. Stein, and that she'd often painted a simple cottage, paintings that to me appeared to show powerful feelings of attachment to the place."

I check to be sure Norah wasn't bored with all this. She was paying close attention. But I was getting bored with myself. I'd been excited when I found this last night, thinking I might be able to make a useful contribution to the investigation and hopefully get the business of the missing baby, the attack on Addison Shirley, and Lucia Faraday's murder over and done with so that Andre and I could get back to our job of learning how to care for our child. Telling it to Norah made me feel more like Nancy Drew, girl detective, emphasis on "girl." I hurried to finish.

"Her painting style had evolved. She'd moved on from those stark and simple pictures to more vibrant and colorful ones. More abstract. Then I found an article with a picture of that cottage, and the caption was something about a family place she often painted and was deeply attached to. I figured that if she cared so much about the place, she'd never sell it. I know as part of your effort to locate him, you've tracked down and searched many of Faraday's properties, without success. The thought that followed was what if she had property, and that this might be where she and Faraday were hiding out—with the baby."

"I should get back to the guys," she said, standing up and handing Mason to me. "It sounds like you're onto something here."

Right, Nancy Drew, hand over your intel and the grownups will take it from there.

I was feeling a lot like I needed a disposition transplant. These first weeks of Mason's life had been anything but the peaceful bonding time I'd imagined.

Mason looked like he sympathized.

My phone rang. I took from my pocket and checked to see who was calling. Not anyone I was interested in speaking with right now. I was pretty sure the number was Barron Thompson. Or Barry, as Margot Inglebright had called him. "Later, Barry," I murmured. I put the phone away.

It rang again. Was he going to persist until I answered? I checked the number. One I was very familiar with—my parents.

My father, actually. A surprise since he rarely called. Could he be calling about the gunfight? Had the news down there covered it? But no. That was wishful thinking.

He didn't waste any time with pleasantries, but dove right in to the purpose of his call. "Your mother's upset because you haven't brought the baby to see us," he said.

Even aside from the fact that his timing was awful, he should know better than to try and guilt me like this. My father and I used to be very close, and another time, when I was rested, not wounded, and didn't have a bullet hole in my bathroom window, and a house full of cops, I might have been more patient. Probably not any more. He's taken my mother's side when she was being irrational or unfair to me too many times.

"He's too young to make such a long trip," I said. "And I'm upset because the two of you can't be bothered to make the trip to come and see him. When you can find the time, Andre and I would love to see you. Your grandson is adorable. You're going to love him. And of course, you can finally see our house."

They hadn't bothered to do that, either.

I wondered how he'd respond.

I waited through a hesitation so long I considered hanging up. I figured my mother was in the room, making him make the call, and he was trying to decide what to do next.

"You're well?" he asked.

I decided not to mention the wound. They do get so judgmental when I'm injured, as though I deliberately went out and sought trouble.

"Sleep deprived, of course. Otherwise, yes."

"And the baby?"

"Mason, Dad. Your grandson's name is Mason. He's fine. He's perfect. He's gorgeous. A very curious fellow. He seems to always be studying something. I sent you some pictures. Don't you think he looks a little like you?"

Okay. I was being a bit mean. For the most part, my quarrel wasn't with him. But Mason was two weeks old and this was the first time they'd called. I'd called them from the hospital, because I thought they'd be excited. I'd been too out of it then to get much of a read, but their silence since was one kind of message.

"I hope you'll come and see him soon. They change so quickly. You haven't seen the house yet, but we have a lovely guestroom."

Andre was standing the doorway. I could tell he knew exactly who was on the other end of the call. He said, in a voice loud enough for my father to overhear, "Excuse me, Thea. The baby needs you." The baby was in my lap and didn't need anything, but my husband is a clever man.

"Sorry, I've got to go. The baby. Give my love to mom and do come and see us soon." I hesitated, then said what I really felt. "And just so you know, Dad, I'm deeply disappointed that you and Mom can't find the time to come and see our son, instead of expecting that I, a new mother, would drive for hours with a tiny, vulnerable newborn in the car."

I ended the call feeling both mean and satisfied.

"We've got local police checking out that cottage you found," he said. "If they're there, we'll need to—"

"Leave," I finished. "Of course."

"Was that your mother?"

"My father. I figure she made him call thinking he'd have better luck guilting me into visiting. I told them Mason was too young to travel and it would be better for them to come here."

He crossed the room and gathered me and Mason into a hug. "I'm sorry. Sorry about all of this. Last night... last night was... I thought, what if I..." He shook his head. "What an awful damned mess. And your arm? Is it okay? I should take a look--"

I shifted Mason so he wouldn't get squashed but didn't leave the comfort of Andre's embrace.

"It hurts. I could use a visit from Dr. Detective Lemieux. But I am not getting stitches." Before he could respond, I asked, "Is Suzanne right that I'm a trouble magnet?"

"No."

I liked the way that "no" rumbled through his chest.

"Are you going to get Jeremy Bartlett fired?" I didn't need to explain that it was Bartlett's carelessness that had caused so much trouble here at our house.

"Going to try. I promise."

"What about the moat? And the dragons?"

"How about that alarm system with security cameras and a great guard dog? I hate to dig up our nice lawn and dragons are so hard to find, never mind expensive."

"I've never had a dog. How about some real maternity and paternity leave?"

"That I think I can do."

My phone rang. Suzanne. This one I considered taking. No. I'd call her back. I wasn't ready to leave the comfort of Andre's arms.

His phone rang. As he reached for it, I said, "We should toss our phones in the moat."

He answered. Listened. Said, "You're sure they're there?" Then, "Thanks. Just keep an eye on the place. We'll be there as soon as we can."

He pocketed his phone.

"They're there. At the cottage." A pause. "You're brilliant, you know. Tommy may have said it clumsily, but you make a great detective."

Make, not would make. I liked it better coming from him. "What will you do now?"

"A lot of things, Thea. Bring them in for questioning, for starters. Search the place. If they have a baby, figure out who it belongs to. Just... a lot. I'll..." He struggled with this, I could tell. "I'll hand it off as soon as I can and come home to you."

I couldn't ask for more. Not right now, anyway. In the future? We'd have to do some renegotiating. Being slaves of duty was not going to change overnight but some change was needed.

"Mason doesn't want you to go," I said. Those intense brown eyes were fixed on Andre. "Look at him."

"You two aren't going to make it easy, are you?"

"Nope."

Tommy appeared in the doorway. "Any news?"

"They're there."

Tommy wanted to say "then what are we waiting for" so badly. But though he looks like a big lug, albeit a handsome one, he's a perceptive guy. He said, "I'll be downstairs."

Of course. They wouldn't go without Andre because he was lead detective. Andre couldn't go without them because he didn't have a car.

"You'll call me, right?" I said. "You'll call me as soon as you know what the situation is? You won't wait until everyone's been arrested and the house has been searched, and I've passed another endlessly long day being fearful and anxious?"

"I will call you."

He kissed me. He kissed Mason. He said, "I'll call you. I promise. And I'll call my dad and get him here to fix that window just as soon as our tech guys have a chance to take their photos. Be prepared, though. My mom will probably come, too. She says it's been too long since she's seen the baby."

Oh boy. Of course the crime scene techs would be coming to call again. I wished I could invite myself over to Suzanne's, but not if Andre's parents were coming. I couldn't complain, though, could I? After all, my parents didn't come at all.

Mason and I watched from the window as the three cops drove away. Then I put him in his little seat and got out my phone to listen to Suzanne's message.

FORTY-THREE

She sounded positively chipper when she said, "I spoke with Margot and got things straightened out." A pause. "I think. I mean, we're unfired, if there is such a word. There's a conference call scheduled for today at one. We should both be on it, so when you hand Stonegate off, I'll be up to speed on what advice has been given and what decisions have been made. So. Now you're in the loop. Call me. Oh. Uh...about that business last night. Andre doing any better? Are you?"

In the spirit of words like "unfired" I supposed that I was more okayish than I'd been last night. I called her back.

Her first words were, "Are you okay? And Andre?" Because I'd told her he wasn't communicating so of course she was worried.

"We're okay. Well, he's shaken up. Of course. So am I. I look at Mason and—" I stopped. She didn't need to hear it and I didn't want to say it. "It's an awful mess. I hope it will all be over soon."

"It's not over yet? That gunfight wasn't enough?"

Pretty much what I thought, too. "Not yet. There's still a homicide to solve, as well as an assault and a missing baby. Like I said, an awful mess. Makes it difficult for us to settle into our quiet, at home with the baby, routine."

"I'm sorry," she said. "I know you didn't need the Stonegate mess on top of everything else. Anything else I should know about what happened yesterday?"

She'd read my email. She already knew. This was just a "is there anything you want to add" question.

Before I could answer, she said, "When I called last night were there really people shooting outside?"

"You heard them, remember? But it's okay. Andre's dad will fix the broken window, and we're going to build a wall and a moat and get a guard dog."

She laughed. Stopped. Said, in a more sober tone, "Really, Thea. How much of that is true?"

"Maybe the dog. He says building a moat will ruin the lawn. I've never had a dog. Have you?"

"Nope. But Paul Jr. really wants one, and Paul Sr. thinks boys should have dogs. I think, not that they're interested in my opinion, that if the guys want a dog, it becomes their responsibility. We both know how that will go, don't we?"

We did.

I didn't add that someone around here had really wanted a baby, and look at how that had gone. Complaining is so unattractive. Besides, that someone hadn't been alone in wanting our baby.

"Did you speak with Dr. Thompson? We're sure he's back with the program?" I asked.

"Oh, Barry?" She laughed again, from which I gathered that she'd gotten corrected from Mr. to Dr. as I had, or perhaps called him Barron. "The two of us had a lovely chat. He even tried to call me Susie." Another laugh. "People don't often make that mistake."

As opposed to my tall and dark five eleven, Suzanne is about five three and blonde and sweet-faced and has a wonderfully gentle manner. For all that, she's no marshmallow, she just gets more of her results with charm while I get mine with a whip, a cattle prod, and a glare that freezes people in their tracks. Together, we make a good team.

"Well, Susie," I said, "any idea what Stonegate is planning to do about the thugs who are threatening the headmaster and the students who reported the assault?"

"Bringing in the local police. And beefing up security. Security was understaffed but I understand they have a brilliant candidate to fill out their ranks. Female with a lot of experience with sexual harassment and abuse. She's just what they need."

"They found this amazing candidate overnight?" I asked it even though I thought I knew the answer. They hadn't made the woman an offer earlier because someone was afraid she'd actually do her job. What a cynic I've become.

"We both know what that story is," Suzanne said.

"You get any sense of Stonegate's relationship with the local police?"

"Not really. Thompson sounded unenthused but that could be because he wanted to duck the issue not because he didn't think they'd be responsive. And Margot didn't know. But they are meeting, which is an important step."

"And the school's lawyer is on top of things and tough as nails," I added. "When she and I were first talking with Dr. Thompson, she was so fierce he looked like he thought we were going to eat him."

"And luckily, Margot Inglebright is a paragon," she added.

"Too bad it all falls on her," I said.

"Actually, I think she's enjoying this. She was passed over for board chair in favor of this Kristoff guy, the hotshot, and then he bolts at the first sign of trouble."

"Which is good, since it sounds like he didn't get the sexual assault thing at all." Switching subjects, I said, "What time are we convening our online meeting? One?"

"Mm hmm. That work for you?"

"I hope. I'm too new at this to predict when Master Mason will need my attention."

"Oh, man, do I know what that's like. Until you found me that nanny. Speaking of which, what did you think of Libby Frenier?"

I wasn't ready to deliver a report about that. Libby Frenier been all over the place, and when she showed up in that weird outfit and then fled while I was getting her a shirt? It could be just a mother being rattled by her son's condition. I also worried that having her around would be a constant reminder of the whole mess with Addison Shirley. So I was still pondering. Plus I needed Andre's input. I made a noncommittal sound. "Still on the fence. She's great with Mason, though."

"Well, don't wait too long. The childcare situation is practically a crisis."

"I've heard. So, we'll convene at one? Who is organizing the video conference? I hope it's not Thompson's secretary. She's either the world's biggest airhead or she's a devious, dishonest little sneak."

"Not that you have a strong opinion or anything," Suzanne said.

"She tried to throw the consent forms from the male students involved in the assault in the trash."

"Right. Devious. Well, we can relax about that because Margot is getting the Dean of Students to do it. We should be all set."

All set would be when the students who perpetrated the assault had been suspended and the campus was secure enough for the girls involved to be safe from thugs and threats. But the meeting should move us closer to that point.

Belatedly, we were getting the cooperation we'd asked for, but I still felt uneasy. So much can go wrong when a school's leadership waffles. It's too easy for young girls to cave to threats or be convinced not to press their cases. It had already happened at Stonegate once. Was Margot Inglebright's involvement enough to keep it from happening again?

I pushed Stonegate's issues to the back of my mind and decided to take Mason for a walk like normal mothers do.

He was in his sling and we'd gotten out the door into a lovely September morning when the crime scene techs arrived in their van.

Life kept sending me the message that I should consider becoming a hermit. Sometimes it seemed like death was sending the same message.

My new life as a hermit would have to wait. I gave the techs a brief description of what had happened and led the tech who'd enjoyed cake in my kitchen upstairs to my damaged bathroom. The others swarmed around the outside of the house, seeming disappointed that Andre wasn't there to give them clearer direction.

Once they were at work, the little woman and her small companion went for a walk. I decided to avoid the road and head out across our back yard and through the woods. Back there I could connect to a dirt road that lead down to a lake. A pleasant walk and one on which we were unlikely meet anyone. I was feeling seriously antisocial today.

As we disappeared into the tree line and found the winding path to that road, a patch of flattened weeds and brush, along with some discarded cigarette butts, soda cans, and candy wrappers told me a disturbing story: someone had been there more than once, hidden from sight yet able to spy on the house. Benjy Goodman? Had he been the mysterious figure Rosie and I had seen disappearing into the woods?

Benjy was dead now. He wasn't going to be coming back. It was still chilling to think of someone lurking here in the woods, watching us, possibly waiting for an opportunity to snatch Mason. Benjy's assistant or co-conspirator or whatever Josh Frenier's role had been, was also unable to return. I reassured myself that any plot regarding the baby should be ended without its instigators. Instead of enjoying a pleasant walk in the wood on a perfect day, though, I was spooked. The empty woods felt menacing, every rustle and scrape a potential danger. If Benjy could recruit one assistant, might he not have recruited another in his scheme to sell Addison Shirley's baby?

Was I worrying unnecessarily? Was I willing to take any chances with Mason's safety? I gave up on a walk, turned around, and headed home.

When the phone in my pocket beeped, reminding me that in an hour I had a video conference, I jumped. My anxiety didn't ease until I was back inside the house.

The wary person I had never wanted to be checked for a gun in her kitchen drawer. I settled Mason in his seat and was opening the refrigerator to see what I could eat when a voice close behind me said, "Excuse me."

I dropped the plate, and the last of Rosie's lasagna exploded like a meat and tomato crime scene all over my kitchen floor.

FORTY-FOUR

I screamed. The evidence tech who'd disturbed me jumped back with a cry. Mason, upset by the commotion, added cries of his own. One of the techs from outside burst in to see what was wrong.

Ignoring them and the mess on the floor, I grabbed Mason and hurried up the stairs to his room, closing the door behind us. The dimly lit room, with its peaceful gray-green paint, curtained windows, and thick carpet, felt like a sanctuary from the rest of the house.

We settled into the soft upholstered rocker and comforted each other until my heart stopped racing and he stopped crying. I hoped Andre would return soon to tell me that the last pieces of the mystery of Addison Shirley's missing baby and Lucia Faraday's murder had been put into the puzzle and we could move on. But what if he didn't? We couldn't go on like this, squandering our peaceful bonding time in the midst of so much anxiety and chaos.

The clock said my video conference was in fifteen minutes and I was as ready for it as if it was happening in fifteen hours. Or fifteen days. At least in fifteen years Mason would be a teenager and giving me new and scary things to worry about.

Looking down at his sweet baby face, I tried to imagine what he'd be like in fifteen years, a poor half-orphan boy being raised by his father after his mother, who'd fancied herself tough as nails, expired from terminal anxiety. He'd look a lot like Andre, I figured. Given my height, and Andre's, he'd probably tower over his father and already be subject to the testosterone-driven stubble his father sported by dinner time despite a morning shave.

"I don't want to go back to work," I told him. "Not in fifteen minutes and not in a month and maybe never, ever."

Heresy of the highest order. I was a compulsive worker. A partner in a business that depended on me. I even loved my work. Just not right now. I didn't know about the long run, but for now, I vowed that after this conference call was done, I was going back to being on maternity leave. I would devote myself to this special time with Mason and resist anything that threatened to pull me away from it.

Feeling better after this resolution, I carried Mason downstairs to my office and settled him to watch his rainbows while I got on the computer. As I passed the kitchen, I saw that some kind soul had cleaned up the spilled lasagna.

The call went well, if overriding anyone's resistance like I was driving a Russian tank could be termed "well." I ended it feeling like we'd made great strides in ensuring that Stonegate would be protecting its students and adhering to its rules. A letter to the parents had been crafted. Campus police would be on the alert for strangers. The students who'd assaulted Ma'Kayla were suspended. The expert I'd recommended to investigate the assault would be on campus tomorrow, and as part of her job, would train the dorm parents, the deans, and the campus police in handling sexual harassment.

After it was done, I made a quick follow-up call with Suzanne confirming that she'd raise my concerns about Barron Thompson's behavior, and his assistant's, with the board. There was no sense in bringing in an expert to help handle the situation if the headmaster was going to undermine whatever was done. As for the assistant? She needed to go. Maybe Thompson did, too. I hadn't spent enough time there to know whether the value he otherwise added outweighed his behavior in this situation.

When I was done, I found that the house was empty. The crime scene van was gone.

Stonegate, done. Evidence techs, done. As though I was working from a checklist of items to be dealt with before I could settle back into focusing on Mason, I called Andre for an update.

As promised, this time he answered on the first ring. "I'm on my way home," he said. "Be there in less than an hour. Want me to pick up some takeout on my way? Cornbread and barbecue?"

It was past lunch time and too early for dinner but who cared? My lunch had ended up on the floor instead of being eaten. Besides, pulled pork sounded great. "Please. So what did you find?"

"You were right. We found Faraday and his first wife at that cottage, the one she liked to paint, and the baby was with them." He hesitated. "It's a pretty sordid story. You want to hear it now or wait until I get home?"

I'm not always receptive to his desire to protect me but today I was grateful. "When you get home is fine. I might want to fortify myself with some rich, dark beer. Full of B vitamins and other benefits for the new mother."

"Do we have dark beer?"

"Oh. I don't think so. I think my husband will pick some up on his way home. It will go well with the takeout he's getting."

"You've got quite an amenable husband there," he said.

"He has his moments."

The amenable husband arrived in less than an hour, food and beer in hand. He set the food on the counter and picked up Mason.

"It might need to be warmed up," he said.

I put it in the oven, then opened two beers. We sat at the table, Mason, a week older and wiser, on Andre's lap, his curious eyes studying his father.

Andre drank some beer. I drank some beer. Guiness, which I've always thought of as kind of a beer milkshake.

"Faraday is just as selfish and narcissistic as we've heard," he began. "Saw an opportunity and took it. But for her, his ex-wife, to go along with it?" He shook his head.

"Sometimes people's desire for a baby can completely warp their judgment."

A nod. "That appears to be the case here. So... uh... we'll have to do testing to be sure, but it looks like Addison Shirley's baby is Faraday's, not Goodman's."

Another hesitation. As the father of an infant himself, he didn't like this story. "It appears... he says... Faraday says... that he was just coming out the door when his wife, Lucia, when she was shot. That she'd grabbed the infant from Addison Shirley's carriage because she knew he wanted the child. The shooting didn't happen where the car was found. It was at their house. Lucia Faraday had just opened the garage and was about to drive in. He says he ran out, took the baby from the car seat, and ran inside. Left the baby there and went back to the car. He found that his wife was dead, so he drove it farther from the house, parked, left her there in the car, and called an employee to pick him up and drive him home."

"He never called for help or tried to save her?"

Andre shook his head.

"He left the baby alone in the house while he went to dispose of his wife's body?"

Andre shrugged. "He didn't say. But he must have."

He was right. This was an ugly and upsetting story. If it was even true. I didn't believe it. "The employee didn't wonder what was going on?"

"I guess people didn't question what Faraday wanted. They just did it to avoid his temper and keep their jobs. We'll be following up."

"If Lucia Faraday was shot to get the baby, the story doesn't make sense," I said. "The gunman didn't shoot Faraday."

"Bad guys often don't make sense, Thea. You know that."

"But... I don't understand. Why would anyone shoot her, then let him grab the baby and run?"

"We still have a lot of questions. Hopefully further interviews and investigation will answer those questions. I suspect part of the answer is that there are no good actors here. Faraday wants us to think that the gunman was Benjy Goodman. We have Goodman's guns. And of course will search Faraday's house to see if he also has guns. Then we'll need to test to determine whether the bullet that killed Lucia Faraday came from Goodman's gun. Or one of Faraday's. If we can establish that he owned guns. Find the guns. If he's smart, he'll have gotten rid of them."

"My money's on Faraday," I said. "It doesn't make sense that he'd shoot Lucia Faraday and then leave without the baby. Plus, if Goodman knew Faraday had the baby, there would have been no reason for him to come here. To target us. To think that Mason was the baby he was looking for."

Andre looked down at Mason and then back at me. "You know that Benjy Goodman had a scheme to sell the baby, right? That he'd done it before? And he was expecting to get fifty thousand dollars for the baby?"

I nodded.

"We think Faraday was the buyer."

"Even though he thought it was his own child? That's crazy. And what about Addison Shirley? Where does she fit into all this? Does she want the baby? Was she part of the scheme to sell it? Was it possible she had her own plan to cut Goodman out and sell the baby herself? To his own father?"

My questions just kept spilling out. "Why would Faraday go along with that?"

But Addison trying to sell the baby didn't make sense, either. None of this did. Someone had hurt Addison Shirley badly, possibly even believed her dead. She'd been attacked in one of Faraday's properties but left to die in a root cellar in Benjy Goodman's town. So which one of them had attacked her? Would she be willing to talk now that Goodman was dead and Faraday in custody? Be honest about her own plans despite the likelihood that Faraday wasn't going to be around to pay her for the baby? Or to support her and the baby?

It was frustrating after all we'd gone through to reach this point with so few answers. At this point, though, it was a frustration I was ready to live with. I was ready to let the police handle it. I did still have some questions, though. "Do you know who attacked her? Was it Faraday or was it Goodman? What about DNA at the scenes? Can it show who attacked Addison?"

Andre nodded. "It may. Obviously, we'll have to take another run at her."

I picked up my beer and realized I'd drunk it all without noticing.

Andre shook his head. "I know you wish this was all wrapped up so you could stop thinking about it but we have a lot more investigating to do. Starting with Faraday. We've got people going back to look at that root cellar and talk to the neighbors, see if anyone noticed Faraday or his car around the time we believe she was placed in there. Goodman doesn't make sense for that while Faraday does. The blood evidence suggests the attack was in his property. He wanted that baby and she was an obstacle. And having her found near where Goodman was living looks like an obvious attempt to make him the suspect."

"Except..." I began.

But what did I know? I reminded myself that I'd figured out about Faraday and his ex-wife and the place they were keeping the baby. "Except maybe Goodman went to pick her up and bring her back to his place to further pressure her about where the baby might be, they had a fight, and when he thought she'd died or was dying, he took her home and stashed her in the first place he could think of where she wouldn't be found?"

He nodded. "There was no sign of forced entry at Faraday's place. Of course, she could have let Goodman in, especially if she was still thinking she could play one of them off against the other. If she, like Goodman, saw the baby as a moneymaking opportunity."

So many pieces in play. It made me glad I wasn't a detective. "It's all troubling," I said. "Goodman is a known bad actor. But it's worse, somehow if Faraday shot his own wife, hoping it would look like a stranger did it, so he could go off with Rebecca and the baby. Does it after his wife steals the baby because she knows he wants it."

"It is." He sighed. "As I said, it's not wrapped up yet. Yes, it looks like Faraday probably shot his wife. His story about someone else shooting her is BS. But our suspicions and theories aren't enough. We work with facts and we've got a ton of work to do now that we have this new information. We still have to search Goodman's place, and his phone, see where it places him at the times in question. Same with Faraday's phone. And we have to go through Faraday's house. Probably several of his properties. We'll need to interview people close to Faraday who might know if he has guns. We're looking for the employee who helped him after he dumped the car."

Another weary sigh. "I understand how frustrating this is for you. The world likes things tied up nice and clean, like on TV, but more often cases go like this. We go through a door thinking we're finding the answer and instead we find a major clue and a whole raft of questions opens up. That's the case here. We'll finish searching and gathering evidence so we can have proof of what happened. Then things will be tied up."

A pause. "I could have stayed and worked on them but I came home to you and Mason. Because we need to start figuring out how we're going to do things differently, going forward."

I watched him run his finger along Mason's soft cheek, not wanting to interrupt the flow now that he was talking.

"Seeing them there with that baby. Faraday and his ex-wife. The happy parents. The cozy domestic scene was actually sickening when you know he might be involved up to his ears. Sickening that that smiling guy with his baby might have gotten his wife to steal that baby and then shot her so he could deliver the baby to his ex? And the ex, Rebecca, was at least complicit. Although I think..."

He stopped to consider how to say it. "I think that despite her longing for a baby, Rebecca Faraday, or Stein, if that's the name she's using, is a good person. By that, I mean an honest one, possibly duped by her ex-husband just like he duped so many other people."

"But wouldn't she have asked where he got the baby?" I asked. "About the baby's mother? She must read the papers or watch the news and there has been plenty about the attack on Addison and the missing baby on the news. Plus, didn't she have to know that Lucia had been murdered?"

"Maybe not. They were tucked up in their love nest. Her special cottage. With the baby they'd always wanted. Who knows what stories he told her? Maybe he convinced her to ignore the world while they took the time to bond with the baby? Or if she didn't want to know? Being desperate for a baby can warp people."

I'd had the same thought myself. This time I did interrupt with a question. "Has Faraday been arrested?"

He nodded.

"What about Rebecca? Where is she now? Has she been arrested?"

"Interviewed. Tommy and Norah are still with her, and they're both skilled interviewers. I believe we'll know more soon."

Andre stared into space as he spoke, probably reliving those moments when he found Faraday with his ex-wife and baby. The ugly implications of what he'd found. "As soon as the scene was under control, I had to come home to you and *our* baby. To a place where things were decent and good. I borrowed Norah's car and came home."

I wanted to let it go and focus on us. But I wasn't quite done. Almost, but not quite. I wanted to float my theory first. "Here's what I think happened," I said. "Goodman was planning to sell Addison's baby to Faraday. Addison decided she wanted to be in charge of what happened to her baby, went off on her own and got in touch with Faraday, asking for—"

I stopped and considered. "Asking for whatever Goodman was going to get. Faraday, figuring the kid was his anyway, wasn't about to pay for it. Addison was staying at one of his houses to hide from Goodman. She and Faraday argued and she threatened to contact Goodman and give him the baby. Faraday nearly kills her and then hides her near Goodman's house to put the blame on him."

I considered again. "Meanwhile, Goodman is looking for Addison and the baby and learns that she's in the hospital. He threatens her—"

I broke off, realizing that however huge the whole mess had

loomed in our lives, I didn't want to do this. I wanted to put it behind me or push it away from me and concentrate on our lives and our baby.

"Too darned convoluted for me, I'm afraid. But I believe that Faraday killed his wife and then left her in the car. It's the only thing that makes sense."

I gave up. We could go back and forth endlessly but I was done. However much people told me I'd make a good detective, I would leave that to the professionals. I had my version of the answer. Andre would wait for the evidence to form his. I made shooing motions with my hands as though I could drive all thoughts of the sordid business out of the house.

Before I could move on, I realized that our conversation had ignored two important players. Two victims. "Where is the baby now?" I asked.

"Social services has taken him for now, until we can get a better handle on whether Addison is in the clear and a suitable caretaker for him."

Which raised another question. I guess I wasn't done yet. "Lucia Faraday is a victim, yet we barely mention her. You've only got his version of the story. What do you know about her? Was she thinking she would raise the baby? Are there friends of hers you can interview, to get a clearer picture?"

He nodded. "Of course. We've got people working on that, too. Her best friend says Lucia thought she'd tamed him. That his womanizing ways were over. They'd done the paperwork to adopt, so adopting his baby wouldn't be a stretch."

He broke off. We'd done enough talking about this. As with most criminal cases, the discovery of the perpetrator(s) was the tip of the iceberg. Thorough investigation would supply the rest.

I was done with the business of Addison Shirley and her baby just like I was done at Stonegate. There was only so much I could do. I'd set the process in motion. The rest of the work was up to them.

I moved from my chair to the couch and snuggled up next to him. We'd chosen these lives. Or they'd chosen us. Now we had some new choices to make about how we'd manage them going forward. I'd been tired. Angry. Scared. Frustrated by the way it looked like we were just going to go back to living the way we always had, with lives that didn't make much room for Mason. Now Andre was saying that it would be different and sounding like the events surrounding the disappearance of Addison Shirley's baby had brought home the necessity for change in a way talking never could.

I said, "I don't know how we'll do it."

"I don't either. But we will. We have to. Mason isn't a pawn in the game of 'who is busier this week?' He isn't a problem or an inconvenience. He's a gift and a serious new responsibility. We owe it to him to make sure he's our priority."

"But when your lieutenant calls? When there's another crime that you'd be good at solving?"

"Then we'll talk about it. We'll decide together what to do. And when a client school calls with a crisis you're the best person to handle? We'll talk about that, too."

We stayed there, me tucked under Andre's arm and Mason in his lap, watching us, until the timer I'd set announced that our food was ready.

The man who loves to eat didn't move.

"Food is ready," I said.

"I really mean it," he said.

"I do, too."

With Mason tucked in the crook of Andre's arm, we stood and went to the kitchen.

It wasn't going to be easy. We both truly believe we're the best people to do the jobs we have. There were still so many issues floating around that we'd have to deal with. Going forward, though, we would have to find a better balance. And face our biggest challenge yet, to become the best people to do the new job we had: being Mason's parents.

ABOUT THE AUTHOR

Maine native Kate Flora's fascination with people's criminal tendencies began in the Maine attorney general's office. Deadbeat dads, people who hurt their kids, and employers' discrimination aroused her curiosity about human behavior. The author of twenty-four books and many short stories, Flora's been a finalist for the Edgar, Agatha, Anthony, and Derringer awards. She won the Public Safety Writers Association award for nonfiction and twice won the Maine Literary Award for crime fiction. Her most recent Thea Kozak mystery is **Death Sends a Message**; her most recent Joe Burgess is **A World of Deceit**. Her crime story collection is **Careful What You Wish For: Stories of revenge, retribution, and the world made right**.

Flora is a founding member of the New England Crime Bake and the Maine Crime Wave and runs the blog **Maine Crime Writers** https://mainecrimewriters.com. Flora's nonfiction focuses on aspects of the public safety officers' experience. She divides her time between Massachusetts and Maine, where she gardens and cooks and watches the clouds when she's not imagining her character's dark deeds. She occasionally swims in the shark-filled sea. She's been married for decades to an excellent man. Her sons edit films and hang out in research labs.

www.kateclarkflora.com

facebook.com/katecflora

twitter.com/kateflora

www.ingramcontent.com/pod-product-compliance
Lightning Source LLC
Chambersburg PA
CBHW021953010726
47494CB00003B/717